Grace was a girl who loved stories.

She didn't mind if they were read to her or told to her or made up in her own head. She didn't care if they were from books or on TV or in films or on the video or out of Nana's long memory. Grace just loved stories.

And after she had heard them, or sometimes while they were still going on, Grace would act them out. And she always gave herself the most exciting part.

گریس ایک ایسی لڑکی تھی جسے کہانیاں بہت پسند تھیں۔

اس کو اس بات سے فرق نہیں پڑتا تھا کہ کہانیاں اسے پڑھ کر سنائی جائیں یا اسے زبانی بتائی جائیں یا خود دماغ سے بنائی جائیں۔ اسے اس بات کی پرواہ نہیں تھی کہ کہانیاں کتابوں سے ہوں یا ٹی وی سے ہوں یا فلموں میں سے ہوں یا وڈیو سے ہوں یا پھر نانی کی لمبی پٹاری سے ہوں۔ گریس کو تو بس کہانیوں سے بہت پیار تھا۔

اور کہانیاں سننے کے بعد یا کبھی کبھی جب وہ اسے سنائی جا رہی ہوتیں، تو گریس ان سے ادا کاری کرنے لگتی تھی اور وہ ہمیشہ اپنے لئے سب سے سنسنی خیز کردار رکھتی تھی۔

Grace went into battle as Joan of Arc...

گریس جان آف آرک بن کر لڑائی کے میدان میں چلی گئی

and wove a wicked web as Anansi the spiderman.

اس نے انانسی سپائیڈر مین کی طرح ایک بھیانک جال بُنا

She hid inside the wooden horse at the gates of Troy...

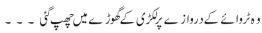

she crossed the Alps with Hannibal and a hundred elephants...

وہ ہینیبل اور سو ہاتھیوں کے ساتھ الپس کے پہاڑ کو پار کر گئی

she sailed the seven seas
with a peg-leg and a parrot.

وہ ایک ٹانگ کے ساتھ لکڑی بن کر اور ایک
طوطا لے کر سات سمندر پار کر گئی

leading cause of death. While not all accidents are preventable, many are. A significant amount of fatal accidents are related to drug abuse and lack of use of seat belts. The fourth cause of death, chronic and obstructive pulmonary disease, is largely related to tobacco use.

The most prevalent degenerative diseases in the United States are those of the cardiovascular system. As shown in Table 1.2, close to half of all deaths in this country are attributed to heart and blood vessel disease. According to the 1987 estimates by the American Heart Association, 66.89 million Americans were afflicted by diseases of the cardiovascular system, including nearly 61 million suffering from hypertension and almost 5 million affected by coronary heart disease. Many of these individuals often suffer from more than one type of cardiovascular disease. Additionally, the 1987 estimated cost of heart and blood vessel disease exceeded $94.5 billion. Heart attacks alone cost American industry approximately 132 million workdays annually, including $15 billion in lost productivity because of physical and emotional disability.

It must also be noted that more than 1.5 million people suffer heart attacks each year, with over half a million of them dying as a consequence of the attack. About 50 percent of the time, the first symptom of coronary heart disease is the heart attack itself, and 40 percent of the people who suffer a first heart attack die within the first twenty-four hours. In one out of every five cardiovascular deaths, sudden death is the initial symptom. About half of those who die are men in their most productive years — between the ages of forty and sixty-five. Furthermore, the American Heart Association estimates that over $700 million a year is spent in replacing employees suffering heart attacks. Oddly enough, most coronary heart disease risk factors are reversible and preventable and can be controlled

by the individual through appropriate lifestyle modifications (see Chapter 12).

The second leading cause of death in the United States is cancer. Unlike cardiovascular disease, the mortality rate for cancer has steadily increased over the last few decades (see Figure 1.1). Even though cancer is not the number one killer, it is certainly the number one health fear of the American people. Cancer is defined as an uncontrolled growth and spread of abnormal cells in the body. Some cells grow into a mass of tissue called a tumor, which can be either benign or malignant. A malignant tumor would be considered a "cancer." If the spread of cells is not controlled, death ensues. Approximately 23 percent of all deaths in the United States are due to cancer. Almost 510,000 people died of this disease in 1990, and an estimated 1,040,000 new cases were expected the same year. The overall medical costs for cancer were estimated to be in excess of $20 billion for 1990. Table 1.3 shows the 1990 estimated new cases and deaths for major sites of cancer, excluding nonmelanoma skin cancer and carcinoma in situ.

Testing procedures for early detection of cancer as well as treatment modalities are continuously changing and improving. In fact, *cancer is now viewed as the most curable of all chronic diseases.* Over 6 million Americans with a history of cancer are now alive, and close to 3 million of them can be considered cured. The American Cancer Society now maintains that *the biggest factor in fighting cancer today is prevention through health education programs.* Evidence indicates that *as much as 80 percent of all human cancer can be prevented through positive lifestyle behaviors.* The basic recommendations include a diet high in cabbage-family vegetables, high in fiber, high in vitamins A and C, and low in fat. Alcohol and salt-cured, smoked, and nitrite-cured foods should be used in moderation. Cigarette smoking and tobacco use in general should be eliminated, and obesity should be avoided.

BENEFITS OF PHYSICAL FITNESS AND WELLNESS PROGRAM PARTICIPATION

A most inspiring story illustrating what fitness can do for a person's health and well-being is that of George Snell from Sandy, Utah. At the age of forty-five, Snell weighed approximately 400 pounds, his blood pressure was 220/180, he was blind because of diabetes that he did not know he had, and his blood glucose level was 487. Snell had determined to do something about his physical and medical condition, so he started a walking/jogging program. After about eight months of conditioning, Snell had lost almost 200 pounds, his eyesight had returned, his glucose level was down to 67, and he

---

TABLE 1.2

Leading Causes of Death in the United States: 1987

Cause	Total Number of Deaths	Percent of Total Deaths
1. Major cardiovascular diseases	963,611	45.4
2. Cancer	476,927	22.5
3. Accidents	95,020	4.5
4. Chronic and obstructive pulmonary disease	78,380	3.7
5. All other causes	509,385	24.0

Source: Advance Report of Final Mortality Statistics, 1987. National Center for Health Statistics. U.S. Department of Health and Human Services.

———— *TABLE 1.3* ————

Estimated Deaths and New Cases for Major Sites of Cancer: 1990.

	Estimated New Cases			Estimated Deaths		
	Total	Male	Female	Total	Male	Female
Lung	157,000	102,000	55,000	142,000	92,000	50,000
Colon-Rectum	155,000	76,000	79,000	60,900	30,000	30,900
Breast*	150,900	900	150,000	44,300	300	44,000
Prostate	106,000	106,000	—	30,000	30,000	—
Pancreas	28,100	13,600	14,500	25,000	12,100	12,900
Urinary	73,000	51,000	22,000	20,000	12,600	7,400
Leukemias	27,800	15,700	12,100	18,100	9,800	8,300
Ovary	20,500	—	20,500	12,400	—	12,400
Uterus**	46,500	—	46,500	10,000	—	10,000
Oral	30,500	20,400	10,100	8,350	5,575	2,775
Skin***	27,600	14,800	12,800	8,800	5,700	3,100

*Invasive cancer only
**New cases total over 50,000 if carcinoma in situ is included
***Estimates are over 600,000 if new cases of nonmelanoma are included
Source: From 1990 *Cancer Facts and Figures.* American Cancer Society.

was taken off medication. Two months later, less than ten months after initiating his personal exercise program, he completed his first marathon, a running course of 26.2 miles.

Most people exercise because it helps improve personal appearance and it makes them feel good about themselves. While there are many benefits to be enjoyed as a result of participating in a regular fitness and wellness program, and although there are indications that active people live a longer life (Table 1.1), the greatest benefit of all is that physically fit individuals enjoy a better quality of life (Figure 1.7). These people live life to its fullest

potential, with fewer health problems than inactive individuals who may also be indulging in negative lifestyle patterns. Although it is difficult to compile an all-inclusive list of the benefits reaped through fitness and wellness program participation, the following list provides a summary of many of these benefits:

1. Improves and strengthens the cardiovascular system (improved oxygen supply to all parts of the body, including the heart, the muscles, and the brain).

2. Maintains better muscle tone, muscular strength, and endurance.

3. Improves muscular flexibility.

4. Helps maintain recommended body weight.

5. Improves posture and physical appearance.

6. Decreases risk for chronic diseases and illness (coronary heart disease, cancer, strokes, high blood pressure, etc.).

7. Decreases mortality rate from chronic diseases.

8. Decreases risk and mortality rates from accidents.

9. Helps prevent chronic back pain.

10. Relieves tension and helps in coping with stresses of life.

11. Increases levels of energy and job productivity.

12. Increases longevity and slows down the aging process.

13. Improves self-image and morale and aids in fighting depression.

———— *FIGURE 1.7* ————

Regular participation in a lifetime exercise program increases quality of life and longevity.

14. Motivates toward positive lifestyle changes (better nutrition, smoking cessation, alcohol and drug abuse control).

15. Decreases recovery time following physical exertion.

16. Speeds up recovery following injury and/or disease.

17. Eases the process of childbearing and childbirth.

18. Regulates and improves overall body functions.

19. Improves physical stamina and helps decrease chronic fatigue.

20. *Improves quality of life; makes people feel better and live a healthier and happier life.*

In addition to the many health benefits, the economical impact of sedentary living has left a strong impression on the nation's economy. As the need for physical exertion steadily decreased in the last century, the nation's health care expenditures dramatically increased. Health care costs in the United States totaled $12 billion in 1950. In 1960 this figure reached $26.9 billion, in 1970 it increased to $75 billion, in 1980 health care costs accounted for $243.4 billion, and in 1990 they soared over $600 billion (Figure 1.8). If this rate of escalation continues, health care expenditures could double every five years. The 1990 figure represents over 10 percent of the gross national product. Experts have also indicated that by the year 2000,

health care could consume 17 percent of the gross national product.

There is now strong scientific evidence linking fitness and wellness program participation not only to better health, but also to decreased medical costs and improved job productivity. Most of this research is being conducted and reported by organizations that have already implemented fitness or wellness programs. This is due to the fact that approximately 50 percent of the health care expenditures in the United States are being absorbed by American business and industry. As a result of the recent staggering rise in medical costs, many organizations are beginning to realize that it costs less to keep an employee healthy than to treat him/her once sick. Consequently, health care cost containment, through the implementation of fitness and wellness programs, has become a major issue for many organizations around the country. Let's examine the evidence:

The backache syndrome, usually the result of physical degeneration (inelastic and weak muscles), costs American industry over $1 billion annually in lost productivity and services alone. An additional $250 million is spent in workmen's compensation. The Adolph Coors Company in Golden, Colorado, which offers a wellness program for employees and their families, reported savings of more than $319,000 in 1983 alone through a preventive and rehabilitative back injury program.

The Prudential Insurance Company of Houston, Texas, released the findings of a study conducted on its 1,386 employees. Those who participated for at least one year in the company's fitness program averaged 3.5 days of disability, as compared to 8.6 days for nonparticipants. A further breakdown by level of fitness showed no disability days for those in the high fitness group, 1.6 days for the good fitness group, and 4.1 disability days for the fair fitness group.

The Mesa Petroleum Company in Amarillo, Texas, has been offering an on-site fitness program since 1979 to its 350 employees and their family members. A 1982 survey showed an average of $434 per person in medical costs for the nonparticipating group in the company, while the participating group averaged only $173 per person per year. This represented a yearly reduction of $200,000 in medical expenses. Sick leave time was also significantly less for the physically active group — twenty-seven hours per year as compared to forty-four for the inactive group.

Data analysis conducted by Tenneco Incorporated in Houston, Texas, in 1982 and 1983 showed a significant reduction in medical care costs for men and women who participated in an exercise program (see Figure 1.9). Annual medical care costs for male and female exercisers were $562 and $639 respectively. For the nonexercising group, the costs

---

FIGURE 1.8

U.S. Health Care Cost Increments since 1950.

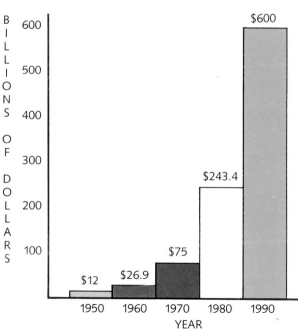

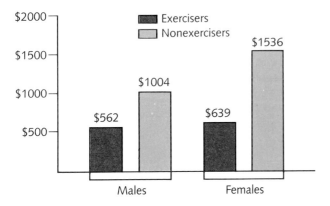

———— *FIGURE 1.9* ————

Annual Medical Care Costs for Tenneco Incorporated, Houston, Texas: 1982-83.

From *"New Fitness Data Verifies: Employees Who Exercise Are Also More Productive."* Athletic Business 8(12):24-30, 1984.

were reported at $1,004 for the men and $1,536 for the women. Sick leave was also reduced in both the men and women participants. Furthermore, a survey of the more than 3,000 employees found that job productivity is related to fitness. The company reported that individuals with high ratings of job performance also rated high in exercise participation.

Strong data is also coming in from Europe. Research in West Germany reported a 68.6 percent reduction in absenteeism by workers with cardiovascular symptoms who participated in a fitness program. The Goodyear Company in Norrkoping, Sweden, indicated a 50 percent reduction in absenteeism following the implementation of a fitness program. Studies in the Soviet Union report increased physical work capacity and motor coordination, lower incidence of disease, shorter illness duration, and fewer relapses among individuals participating in industrial fitness programs. In the Federal Republic of Germany, the law mandates that corporations employing workers with jobs sedentary in nature must provide an in-house facility for physical exercise.

Another reason why some organizations are offering wellness programs to their employees, and one that is overlooked by many because it does not seem to directly affect the bottom line, is simple concern by top management for the physical well-being of the employees. Whether the program helps decrease medical costs is not the primary issue for its implementation. The only reason that really matters to top management is the fact that wellness programs help individuals feel better about themselves and help improve quality of life. Such is the case of Mannington Mills Corporation, which invested $1.8 million in an on-site fitness center.

The return on investment is secondary to the company's interest in happier and healthier employees. The center is also open to dependents and retirees. As a result of this program, Mannington Mills feels that the participants, about 50 percent of the 1,600 people eligible, can enjoy life to its fullest potential, and the employees will most likely be more productive simply because of the company's caring attitude.

In addition to the financial and physical benefits described, many corporations are using wellness programs as an incentive to attract, hire, and retain employees. *The information presented in this book, along with a lifetime commitment to a fitness and wellness program, may prove to be extremely valuable to the reader.* Many companies are now taking a hard look at the fitness and health level of potential employees and are seriously using this information in their screening process. As a matter of fact, some organizations refuse to hire smokers and/or overweight individuals. On the other hand, many executives feel that an on-site health promotion program is the best fringe benefit they can enjoy at their corporation. Young executives are also looking for such organizations, not only for the added health benefits, but because an attitude of concern and care is being shown by the head corporate officers.

THE WELLNESS CHALLENGE FOR THE 1990s

Since a better and healthier life is something that every person needs to strive to attain individually, the biggest challenge that we face in the next few years is to teach people how to take control of their personal health habits by practicing positive lifestyle activities that will decrease the risk of illness and help achieve total well-being. With such impressive data available on the benefits of fitness and wellness programs, it is clear that improving the quality and possibly longevity of our lives is a matter of personal choice.

Researchers have indicated that *practicing simple positive lifestyle habits can significantly increase health and longevity.* These are:

1. **Participate in a lifetime exercise program.** Engage in regular exercise three to six times per week. The exercise program should consist of 20 to 30 minutes of aerobic exercise, along with some strengthening and stretching exercises.

2. **Do not smoke cigarettes.** Cigarette smoking is the largest preventable cause of illness and premature death in the United States. When considering all related deaths, smoking is responsible for over 350,000 unnecessary deaths each year.

3. **Eat right.** Eat a good breakfast and two additional well-balanced meals every day. Refrain

from snacking between meals. Avoid eating too many calories and foods which are high in sugar, fat, and sodium. Increase your daily consumption of fruits, vegetables, and whole grain products.

4. **Maintain recommended body weight.** Maintenance of proper body weight through adequate nutrition and exercise is important in the prevention of chronic diseases and in the development of a higher level of fitness.

5. **Get sufficient rest.** Sleep seven to eight hours each night and use adequate stress management techniques when necessary.

6. **Be wary of alcohol.** Drink only moderate amounts of alcohol or none at all. Alcohol abuse leads to mental, emotional, physical, and social problems. Even small amounts of alcohol can be detrimental to health and well-being.

7. **Surround yourself by "healthy" friendships.** Destructive behaviors and poor self-esteem are often the result of unhealthy friendships. Association with individuals who constantly strive to maintain good fitness and health will help preserve a positive outlook in life and encourage the practice of positive lifestyle behaviors. Constructive social interactions also enhance well-being.

8. **Be informed about the environment.** Seek for clean air and a clean environment. Be aware of pollutants and occupational hazards such as asbestos fibers, nickel dust, chromate, uranium dust, etc. Exercise caution when using pesticides and insecticides.

9. **Implement personal safety procedures.** While not all accidents are preventable, many are. Failure to take simple precautionary measures; such as using seat belts, keeping electrical appliances away from water, etc. (see Lab 16A); increases the risk of an avoidable accident.

Because of current scientific data and the fitness and wellness movement of the past two decades, most Americans now see a need to participate in such programs to improve and maintain adequate health. However, many people are still not participating because they are unaware of the basic principles for safe and effective exercise participation. Others are exercising erroneously and therefore do not reap the full benefits of their program. Although almost half of the adult population in the United States claims to participate in some sort of physical activity, a recent report by the U.S. Public Health Service indicated that only 10 to 20 percent exercised vigorously enough to develop the cardiovascular system. Since cardiovascular activities are the most popular form of exercise, perhaps even a lower percentage of the population engages and/or derives benefits from strength and flexibility

programs. In addition, it is estimated that at least half of the adults in the country have a weight problem.

Since fitness and wellness needs vary significantly from one individual to the other, all exercise and wellness prescriptions must be personalized to obtain optimal results. The information presented in the ensuing chapters and the respective laboratory experiences, contained in the second half of this book, have been written to provide the reader with all of the necessary guidelines to develop his/her own lifetime program to improve fitness and promote preventive health care and personal wellness. These laboratory experiences have been prepared on tear-out sheets so that they can be turned in to class instructors. The corresponding lab(s) for each chapter and any other information necessary to prepare for the lab(s) are given at the end of the chapters. As you study this book and complete the respective laboratory experiences you will learn to:

- Determine whether medical clearance is required for safe exercise participation.

- Conduct nutritional analyses and follow the recommendations for adequate nutrition.

- Write sound diet and weight control programs.

- Assess and improve the health-related components of fitness (cardiovascular endurance, muscular strength and endurance, muscular flexibility, and body composition).

- Assess the various skill-related components of fitness (agility, balance, coordination, power, reaction time, and speed).

- Determine potential risk for cardiovascular disease and implement a risk reduction program.

- Follow a cancer risk reduction program.

- Determine levels of tension and stress and implement stress management programs.

- Implement smoking cessation programs.

- Avoid chemical dependency and know where to find assistance if needed.

- Write objectives to improve fitness and wellness behaviors.

- Discern between myths and facts of exercise and health-related concepts.

SAFETY OF EXERCISE PARTICIPATION

In recent years, several tragic deaths occurred while some prominent national figures were participating in an exercise program. These unfortunate events raised some questions as to the safety of exercise participation. While exercise testing and/or exercise participation is relatively safe for most apparently healthy individuals under the age of forty-five, the reaction of the cardiovascular system to increased levels of physical activity cannot always be totally predicted. Consequently, there is a small but real risk of certain changes occurring during exercise testing and/or participation. Some of these changes may include abnormal blood pressure, irregular heart rhythm, fainting, and in rare instances a heart attack or cardiac arrest.

Health History Questionnaire

Before you start to engage in an exercise program or participate in any exercise testing, fill out the questionnaire given in Lab 1A. If your answer to any of the questions is positive, you should consult a physician before participating in a fitness program. Exercise testing and/or participation is contraindicated under some of the conditions listed in Lab 1A and may require a stress electrocardiogram (ECG) test (see Figure 1.10). In the event that you have any questions regarding your current health status, consult your doctor before initiating, continuing, or increasing your level of physical activity.

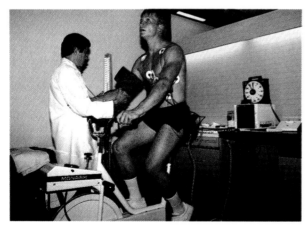

FIGURE 1.10

Exercise Electrocardiogram. An exercise tolerance test with twelve-lead electrocardiographic monitoring may be required of some individuals prior to initiating an exercise program.

Heart Rate and Blood Pressure Assessment

In addition to the health history questionnaire, in Lab 1B you will have the opportunity to determine your heart rate and blood pressure. Heart rate can be obtained by counting your pulse either on the wrist by placing two fingers over the radial artery (inside of the wrist on the side of the thumb) or over

the carotid artery in the neck just below the jaw next to the voice box (see Figures 4.5 and 4.6 in Chapter 4). You may count your pulse for thirty seconds and multiply by two or take it for a full minute. The heart rate is usually at its lowest point (resting heart rate) late in the evening after you have been sitting quietly for about thirty minutes watching a relaxing TV show or reading in bed, or early in the morning just before you get out of bed.

Unless a pathological condition exists, a lower resting heart rate is an indication of a stronger heart. The physiological adaptation of the heart to cardiovascular or aerobic exercise is an increase in the size and strength of the muscle. A bigger and stronger heart can pump a larger amount of blood with fewer strokes. Resting heart rate ratings are shown in Table 1.4. Although resting heart rate decreases with training, the degree of bradycardia (slow heart rate) is not only dependent on the amount of training, but also on genetic factors. While most highly trained athletes have resting heart rates around forty beats per minute, Jim Ryan, world record holder for the one-mile run in the 1960s, had a consistent resting heart rate in the seventies even during peak training months during his athletic career. Nevertheless, for most individuals the resting heart rate will decrease as the level of cardiovascular endurance increases.

Blood pressure is assessed with the use of a sphygmomanometer and a stethoscope. The sphygmomanometer consists of an inflatable bladder contained within a cuff and a mercury gravity manometer or an aneroid manometer from which the pressure is read (see Figures 1.11 and 1.12). The appropriate size cuff must be selected in order to get accurate readings. The size is determined by the width of the inflatable bladder, which should be about 40 percent of the circumference of the midpoint of the arm.

The measurement of blood pressure is usually done in the sitting position, with the forearm and the manometer at the same level as the heart. Initially the pressure should be recorded from each arm, with subsequent pressures recorded from the arm with the highest reading. The cuff should be

TABLE 1.4

Resting Heart Rate Ratings

(beats/minute)	Heart Rate Rating
<59	Excellent
60-69	Good
70-79	Average
80-89	Fair
90>	Poor

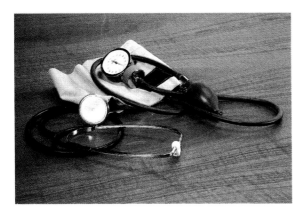

FIGURE 1.11

Aneroid Blood Pressure Gauge and Stethoscope

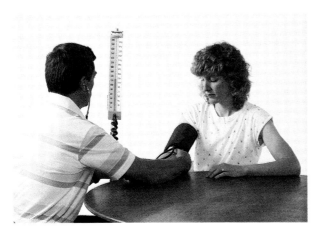

FIGURE 1.12

Blood Pressure Assessment Using a Mercury Gravity Manometer

applied approximately one inch above the antecubital space (natural crease of the elbow), with the center of the bladder applied directly over the medial (inner) surface of the arm. The stethoscope head should be applied firmly, but with little pressure, over the brachial artery in the antecubital space. The arm should be slightly flexed and placed on a flat surface. The bladder can be inflated while feeling the radial pulse to about 30 to 40 mmHg above the disappearance of the pulse.

Avoid overinflating the cuff, as such may cause blood vessel spasm, resulting in higher blood pressure readings. The pressure should be released at a rate of 2 mmHg per second. As the pressure is released, systolic blood pressure is determined at the point where the initial pulse sound is heard. The diastolic pressure is determined at the point where the sound disappears. The recordings should be made to the nearest 2 mmHg (even numbers) and expressed as systolic over diastolic pressure, i.e., 124/80. When more than one reading is taken, the bladder should be completely deflated and at

least one minute should be allowed before the next recording is made. The person measuring the pressure should also note whether the pressure was recorded from the left or the right arm. Resting blood pressure ratings are given in Table 1.5.

TABLE 1.5

Blood Pressure Ratings in mmHg*

Systolic	Diastolic	Rating
<120	<80	Very Low Risk
121-130	81-89	Low Risk
131-140	90-99	Moderate Risk
141-150	100-105	High Risk
151>	106>	Very High Risk

*Ratings expressed in terms of cardiovascular disease risk.

In some cases, the loudness of the pulse sounds decreases in intensity (point of muffling of sounds) and can still be heard at a lower pressure (50 or 40 mmHg) or even all the way down to zero. In this situation, the diastolic pressure is recorded at the point where there is a clear/definite change in the loudness of the sound (also referred to as fourth phase), and at complete disappearance of the sound (fifth phase), e.g. 120/78/60 or 120/82/0.

A final consideration when measuring resting heart rate and blood pressure is that several readings by different people or at different times of the day should be taken to establish the real values. A single reading may not be an accurate value because of the various factors that can affect blood pressure.

LABORATORY EXPERIENCES

LAB 1A: Clearance for Exercise Participation

LAB PREPARATION: None.

LAB 1B: Heart Rate and Blood Pressure Assessment

LAB PREPARATION: Wear exercise clothing, including a shirt with short or loose-fitting sleeves to allow for the placement of the blood pressure cuff around the upper arm. Do not engage in any form of exercise several hours prior to this lab.

References

1. Allsen, P. E., J. M. Harrison, and B. Vance. *Fitness for Life: An Individualized Approach*. Dubuque, IA: Wm. C. Brown, 1989.

2. American Cancer Society. *1990 Cancer Facts and Figures*. New York: The Society, 1990.

3. American College of Sports Medicine. "The Recommended Quantity and Quality of Exercise for Developing and Maintaining Cardiorespiratory and Muscular Fitness in Healthy Adults." *Medicine and Science in Sports and Exercise* 22:265-274, 1990.

4. American Heart Association. *1989 Annual Report*. Dallas, TX: The Association, 1989.

5. Blair, S., D. Jacobs, and K. Powell. "Relationships Between Exercise or Physical Activity and Other Health Behaviors." *Public Health Reports* 100:172-180, 1985.

6. Blair, S. N., H. W. Kohl III, R. S. Paffenbarger, Jr, D. G. Clark, K. H. Cooper, and L. W. Gibbons. "Physical Fitness and All-Cause Mortality: A Prospective Study of Healthy Men and Women." *Journal of the American Medical Association* 262:2395-2401, 1989.

7. Davies, N. E., and L. H. Felder. "Applying Brakes to the Runaway American Health Care System." *Journal of the American Medical Association* 263:73-76, 1990.

8. Duncan, D. F., and R. S. Gold. "Reflections: Health Promotion — What Is It?" *Health Values* 10(3):47-48, 1986.

9. Enstrom, J. E. "Health Practices and Cancer Mortality Among Active California Mormons." *Journal of the National Cancer Institute* 81:1807-1814, 1989.

10. Gettman, L. R. "Cost/Benefit Analysis of a Corporate Fitness Program." *Fitness in Business* 1(1):11-17, 1986.

11. Hatziandreu, E. L., J. P. Koplan, M. C. Weinstein, C. J. Caspersen, K. E. Warner. "A Cost-effectiveness Analysis of Exercise as a Health Promotion Activity." *American Journal of Public Health* 78:1417-1421, 1988.

12. Hoeger, W. W. K. *Lifetime Physical Fitness & Wellness: A Personalized Program*. Englewood, CO: Morton Publishing Company, 1989.

13. Hoeger, W. W. K. *The Complete Guide for the Development & Implementation of Health Promotion Programs*. Englewood, CO: Morton Publishing Company, 1987.

14. Kaufman, J. E. "State of the Art: Physical Fitness in Corporations." *Employee Services Management* 26(1):8-9, 26-27, 1983.

15. Koplan, J. P., C. J. Caspersen, and K. E. Powell. "Physical Activity, Physical Fitness, and Health: Time to Act". *Journal of the American Medical Association* 262:2437, 1989

16. Marcotte, B., and J. H. Price. "The Status of Health Promotion Programs at the Worksite, A Review." *Health Education* 4-8, July/August, 1983.

17. Paffenbarger, R. S., Jr, R. T. Hyde, A. L. Wing, and C. H. Steinmetz. "A Natural History of Athleticism and Cardiovascular Health." *Journal of the American Medical Association* 252:491-495, 1984.

18. Smith, L. K. "Cost-Effectiveness of Health Promotion Programs." *Fitness Management* 2(3):12-15, 1986.

19. Staff. "America's Fitness Binge." *U.S. News & World Report* 58-61, May 3, 1982.

20. Staff. "New Fitness Data Verifies: Employees Who Exercise Are Also More Productive." *Athletic Business* 8(12):24-30, 1984.

21. Van Camp, S. P. "The Fixx Tragedy: A Cardiologist's Perspective." *Physician and Sports Medicine* 12(9): 153-155, 1984.

22. Wilmore, J. H. "Design Issues and Alternatives in Assessing Physical Fitness Among Apparently Healthy Adults in a Health Examination Survey of the General Population." In Drury, F. (editor). *Assessing Physical Fitness and Activity in General Population Studies*. Washington, D.C.: U.S. Public Health Service. National Center for Health Statistics, 1988.

23. Wright, C. C. "Cost Containment Through Health Promotion Programs." *Journal of Occupational Medicine* 22:36-39, 1980.

Principles of Nutrition For Wellness

OBJECTIVES

- Define nutrition and describe its relationship to health and well-being.
- Describe the functions of carbohydrates in the human body and be able to differentiate simple from complex carbohydrates.
- Describe the role and health benefits of adequate fiber in the diet.
- Describe the role of fat in the human body and be able to differentiate and characterize saturated, monounsaturated and poly-unsaturated fats.
- Describe the functions of protein in the human body.
- Describe the role of vitamins and minerals in the human body.
- Identify myths and fallacies regarding vitamin and mineral supplementation.
- Learn to conduct a comprehensive nutrient analysis, be capable of recognizing areas of deficiencies, and be able to implement changes to improve overall nutrition.
- Introduce the four basic food groups and learn how to achieve a balanced diet through the proper use of these groups.

The science of *nutrition studies the relationship of foods to optimal health and performance*. While all the answers are not in yet, ample scientific evidence has long linked good nutrition to overall health and well-being. Proper nutrition signifies that a person's diet is supplying all of the essential nutrients to carry out normal tissue growth, repair, and maintenance. It also implies that the diet will provide sufficient substrates to obtain the energy necessary for work, physical activity, and relaxation.

Unfortunately, *the typical American diet is too high in calories, sugars, fats, and sodium and not high enough in fiber* — none of which are conducive to good health. Over-consumption is now a major concern for many Americans. In fact, according to a 1988 report on nutrition and health issued by the United States Surgeon General, the first ever of its kind, diseases of dietary excess and imbalance are among the leading causes of death in the country. It is estimated that of the total 2.1 million deaths

in the U.S. in 1987, an estimated 1.5 million people died of diseases associated with faulty nutrition. In this report, which is based on more than 2,000 scientific studies, the U.S. Surgeon General indicates that dietary changes "can bring a substantial measure of better health to all Americans."

Results of epidemiological studies indicate that diet and nutrition often play a crucial role in the development and progression of chronic diseases. A diet high in saturated fat and cholesterol increases the risk for atherosclerosis and coronary heart disease. High sodium intake has been linked to elevated blood pressure. Equally, some researchers feel that 30 to 50 percent of all cancer is diet related (see Chapter 12). Obesity, diabetes mellitus, and osteoporosis have also been linked to faulty nutrition. An effective wellness program must definitely incorporate current dietary recommendations to reduce the risk for chronic disease. A brief summary of guidelines for a healthful diet are provided

——— *FIGURE 2.1* ———

General Guidelines for a Healthful Diet

- Eat a variety of foods
- Avoid too much fat, saturated fat, and cholesterol
- Eat foods with adequate starch and fiber
- Avoid too much sugar and sodium
- Maintain adequate calcium intake
- Maintain recommended body weight
- If you drink alcoholic beverages, do so in moderation

in Figure 2.1. A detailed discussion of these guidelines will be provided throughout this chapter and subsequent chapters (3, 12, 13) of the book.

NUTRIENTS

The *essential nutrients required by the human body are carbohydrates, fat, protein, vitamins, minerals, and water.* The first three have been referred to as fuel nutrients because they are the only substances used to supply the energy (commonly measured in calories) necessary for work and normal body functions. Vitamins, minerals, and water have no caloric value but are still essential for normal body functions and maintenance of good health. In addition, many nutritionists like to add a seventh nutrient to this list that has received a great deal of attention recently — dietary fiber.

Carbohydrates, fat, protein, and water are called macronutrients because large amounts are needed on a daily basis. Vitamins and minerals are only necessary in very small amounts, therefore, nutritionists commonly refer to them as micronutrients.

Depending on the amount of nutrients and calories, foods can be categorized into high nutrient density and low nutrient density. *High nutrient density is used in reference to foods that contain a low or moderate amount of calories, but are packed with nutrients. Foods that are high in calories but contain few nutrients are of low nutrient density.* The latter are frequently referred to as "junk food."

The term "calorie" is used as a unit of measure to indicate the energy value of food and cost of physical activity. Technically, a kilocalorie (kcal) or large calorie is the amount of heat necessary to raise the temperature of one kilogram of water from 14.5 to 15.5 degrees Centigrade, but for the purpose of simplicity, people refer to it as a calorie rather than kcal. For example, if the caloric value

of a given food is 100 calories (kcal), the energy contained in this food could raise the temperature of 100 kilograms of water by one degree Centigrade.

Carbohydrates

Carbohydrates are the major source of calories used by the body to provide energy for work, cell maintenance, and heat. They also play a crucial role in the digestion and regulation of fat and protein metabolism. Each gram of carbohydrates provides the human body with approximately four calories. Carbohydrates are classified into **simple** and **complex carbohydrates** (Figure 2.2). The major sources of carbohydrates are breads, cereals, fruits, vegetables, and milk and other dairy products.

——— *FIGURE 2.2* ———

Major Types of Carbohydrates

SIMPLE CARBOHYDRATES
(simple sugars)

Monosaccharides

Glucose
Fructose
Galactose

Disaccharides

Sucrose
(glucose + fructose)
Lacrose
(glucose + galactose)
Maltose
(glucose + glucose)

COMPLEX CARBOHYDRATES

Polysaccharides

Starches
Dextrins

Fiber

Cellulose
Hemicellulose
Pectins
Gums

Simple carbohydrates, frequently denoted as sugars, are formed by simple or double sugar units with little nutritive value (e.g., candy, pop, cakes, etc.). Simple carbohydrates are divided into **monosaccharides** and **disaccharides** and can be easily recognized because of their -ose endings. Eating too many simple carbohydrates often takes the place of more nutritive foods in the diet.

Monosaccharides are the simplest sugars, formed by five- or six-carbon skeletons. The three most common monosaccharides are glucose, fructose, and galactose. Glucose is a natural sugar found in food, but it is also produced in the body from other simple and complex carbohydrates. Fructose or fruit sugar occurs naturally in fruits and honey. Galactose is produced from milk sugar in the mammary glands of lactating animals. Both fructose and galactose are readily converted to glucose in the body.

Disaccharides are formed when two monosaccharide units are linked together, one of which is glucose. The major disaccharides are sucrose or table sugar (glucose + fructose), lactose (glucose + galactose), and maltose (glucose + glucose).

Complex carbohydrates are formed when three or more simple sugar molecules link together, therefore, they are also referred to as **polysaccharides**. Anywhere from about ten to thousands of monosaccharide molecules can unite to form a single polysaccharide. Two examples of complex carbohydrates are starches and dextrins. Starches are commonly found in seeds, corn, nuts, grains, roots, potatoes, and legumes. Dextrins are formed from the breakdown of large starch molecules exposed to dry heat, such as when bread is baked or cold cereals are produced. Complex carbohydrates provide many valuable nutrients to the body and can be an excellent source of fiber or roughage.

Fat

Fats or lipids are also used as a source of energy in the human body. They are the most concentrated source of energy. Each gram of fat supplies nine calories to the body. *Fats are also a part of the cell structure. They are used as stored energy and as an insulator for body heat preservation. They provide shock absorption, supply essential fatty acids, and carry the fat-soluble vitamins A, D, E, and K.* Fats can be classified into three main groups: **simple, compound, and derived** (Figure 2.3). The basic sources of fat are milk and other dairy products, and meats and alternates.

Simple fats consist of a glyceride molecule linked to one, two, or three units of fatty acids. According to the number of fatty acids attached, simple fats are divided into monoglycerides (one fatty acid), **diglycerides** (two fatty acids), and **triglycerides** (three fatty acids). More than 90 percent of the weight of fat in foods and over 95 percent of the stored fat in the human body are in the form of triglycerides.

Fatty acids vary in the length of the carbon atom chain and in the degree of hydrogen saturation. Based on the degree of saturation, fatty acids are said to be **saturated** or **unsaturated**. Unsaturated fatty acids can be further classified into **monounsaturated** and **polyunsaturated**. Saturated fatty

FIGURE 2.3

Major Types of Fats (lipids)

SIMPLE FATS

Monoglyceride (glyceride + one fatty acid*)
Diglycerides (glyceride + two fatty acids)
Triglycerides (glyceride + three fatty acids)

COMPOUND FATS

Phospholipids
Glucolipids
Lipoproteins

DERIVED FATS

Sterols
(cholesterol)

*Fatty acids can be saturated or unsaturated.

acids are primarily of animal origin, while unsaturated fats are generally found in plant products.

In **saturated fatty acids** the carbon atoms are fully saturated with hydrogens, therefore only single bonds link the carbon atoms on the chain (see Figure 2.4). These saturated fatty acids are frequently referred to as saturated fats. Examples of foods high in saturated fatty acids are meats, meat fat, lard, whole milk, cream, butter, cheese, ice cream, hydrogenated oils (a process that makes oils saturated), coconut oil, and palm oils. If the carbon atoms are not completely saturated with hydrogens, double bonds are formed between the unsaturated carbons, and the fatty acid unit is said to be unsaturated (an unsaturated fat). In monounsaturated fatty acids (MUFA) only one double bond is found along the chain. Olive, canola, rapeseed, peanut, and sesame oils, and avocado are examples of monounsaturated fatty acids. Polyunsaturated fatty acids (PUFA) contain two or more double bonds between unsaturated carbon atoms along the chain. Corn, cottonseed, safflower, walnut, sunflower, and soybean oils are high in polyunsaturated fatty acids.

Saturated fats typically do not melt at room temperature, while unsaturated fats are usually liquid at room temperature. Coconut and palm oils are exceptions since they are high in saturated fats. Shorter fatty acid chains also tend to be liquid at room temperature. In general, saturated fats increase the blood cholesterol level, while polyunsaturated and monounsaturated fats tend to decrease blood cholesterol (the role of cholesterol in health and disease is discussed in detail Chapter

——— *FIGURE 2.4* ———

Chemical Structure of Saturated and Unsaturated Fats.

Saturated Fatty Acid:

Monounsaturated Fatty Acid:

Double Bond

Polyunsaturated Fatty Acid:

Double Bonds

*Glyceride component

12). Polyunsaturated fats, nonetheless, also appear to cause some lowering of the "good" (HDL) cholesterol, which may not really help improve the cholesterol level (see total cholesterol/HDL-cholesterol ratio in Chapter 12). Monounsaturated fats, on the other hand, appear to reduce only the bad (LDL) cholesterol.

Another type of polyunsaturated fatty acids that have gained considerable attention in recent years are **Omega-3 fatty acids**. These fatty acids seem to be effective in lowering blood cholesterol and triglycerides. Fish, especially fresh or frozen mackerel, herring, tuna, salmon, and lake trout have Omega-3 fatty acids. Canned fish is not recommended because the canning process destroys most of the Omega-3 oil. These fatty acids are also found to a lesser extent in canola oil, walnuts, soybeans, and wheat germ. Limited epidemiologic data suggests that consumption of one or two servings of fish decreases the risk for coronary heart disease. People with diabetes, a history of hemorrhaging or strokes, on aspirin and blood-thinning therapy, and

pre-surgical patients should refrain from consuming fish oil unless they are instructed to do so by their physicians.

Compound Fats are a combination of simple fats with other chemicals. Examples of compound fats are **phospholipids**, **glucolipids**, and **lipoproteins**. Phospholipids are similar to triglycerides, except that phosphoric acid takes the place of one of the fatty acid units. Glucolipids are formed by a combination of carbohydrates, fatty acids, and nitrogen. Lipoproteins are water-soluble aggregates of protein with either triglycerides, phospholipids, or cholesterol. Lipoproteins are used to transport fats (cholesterol and triglycerides) in the blood and have a significant role in the development and prevention of heart disease (see cholesterol and triglycerides in Chapter 12).

Derived Fats are a combination of simple and compound fats. Sterols are an example of derived fats. Although sterols contain no fatty acids, they are viewed as fats because they are insoluble in water. The most often mentioned sterol is cholesterol, which is found in many foods or can be manufactured from saturated fats in the body.

Protein

Proteins are the main substances used to build and repair tissues such as muscles, blood, internal organs, skin, hair, nails, and bones. They are a part of hormones, enzymes, and antibodies and help maintain normal body fluid balance. Proteins can also be used as a source of energy, but only if there are not enough carbohydrates and fats available. Each gram of protein yields four calories of energy, and the primary sources are meats and alternates and milk and other dairy products.

There are approximately twenty **amino acids** or basic building blocks that the human body uses to build different types of protein. Amino acids contain nitrogen, carbon, hydrogen, and oxygen. Nine of the twenty amino acids are referred to as essential amino acids because they cannot be produced in the body. The other eleven can be manufactured by the body if sufficient nitrogen is provided from food proteins in the diet.

Proteins that contain all of the essential amino acids are known as complete or higher-quality protein. These types of proteins are usually of animal source. If one or more of the essential amino acids are missing, the proteins are referred to as incomplete or lower-quality protein.

The only concerns in regard to protein intake is that individuals get enough protein (quantity) in the diet to insure nitrogen for adequate amino acid production, as well as to get enough high-quality protein to obtain the essential amino acids. Protein deficiency is not a significant problem in the American diet.

Vitamins

Vitamins are organic substances essential for normal metabolism, growth, and development of the body. They are classified into two types based on their solubility: fat-soluble vitamins (A, D, E, and K), and water-soluble vitamins (B complex and C). Vitamins cannot be manufactured by the body; hence, they can only be obtained through a well-balanced diet. A description of the functions of each vitamin is presented in Figure 2.5.

Minerals

Minerals are inorganic elements found in the body and in food. They serve several important functions. *Minerals are constituents of all cells, especially those found in hard parts of the body (bones, nails, teeth). They are crucial in the maintenance of water balance and the acid-base balance. They are essential components of respiratory pigments, enzymes, and enzyme systems, and they regulate muscular and nervous tissue excitability.* The specific functions of some of the most important minerals are contained in Figure 2.6.

Water

Approximately 70 percent of total body weight is water. *Water is the most important nutrient and is involved in almost every vital body process. Water is used in digestion and absorption of food, in the circulatory process, in removing waste products, in building and rebuilding cells, and in the transport of other nutrients.* Water is contained in almost all foods but primarily in liquid foods, fruits, and vegetables. Besides the natural content in foods, it is recommended that every person drink at least eight to ten glasses of fluids a day.

Fiber

Dietary *fiber is basically a type of complex carbohydrate made up of plant material that cannot be digested by the human body.* It is mainly present in leaves, skins, roots, and seeds. Processing and refining foods removes almost all of the natural fiber. In our daily diets, the main sources of dietary fiber are whole-grain cereals and breads, fruits, and vegetables.

The most common types of fiber are cellulose and hemicellulose, found in plant cell walls; pectins, found in fruits; and gums, also found in small quantities in foods of plant origin.

Fiber is important in the diet because it binds water, yielding a softer stool that decreases transit time of food residues in the intestinal tract. Many researchers feel that speeding up the passage of food residues through the intestines decreases the risk for colon cancer, primarily because of the decreased time that cancer-causing agents remain in contact with the intestinal wall. The increased water content of the stool may also dilute the cancer-causing agents, decreasing the potency of these substances.

The risk for coronary heart disease may also decrease with increased fiber intake. This decreased risk can be attributed to two factors. First, all too often saturated fats take the place of dietary fiber in the diet, thereby increasing cholesterol absorption and/or formation. Second, some specific water-soluble fibers such as pectin and guar gum found in beans, oat bran, corn, and fruits seem to bind cholesterol in the intestines, thereby preventing its absorption. In addition, several other health disorders have been linked to low fiber intake, including constipation, diverticulitis, hemorrhoids, gallbladder disease, and obesity.

Determining the amount of fiber in your diet can be confusing at times because it can be measured either as crude fiber or dietary fiber. Crude fiber is the smaller portion of the dietary fiber that actually remains after chemical extraction in the digestive tract. The recommended amount of dietary fiber is about twenty-five grams per day, which is the equivalent of seven grams of crude fiber. Since most nutrition labels list the fiber content in terms of dietary fiber, you should be careful to use the twenty-five gram guideline (see Table 2.1). Also, be aware that too much fiber consumption can be detrimental to health, since excessive amounts can lead to increased loss of calcium, phosphorus, and iron, not to mention increased gastrointestinal discomfort. It is also important to increase fluid intake when fiber consumption is increased, since too little fluid can lead to dehydration and/or constipation.

BALANCING THE DIET

Most people would like to live life to its fullest, maintain good health, and lead a productive life. One of the fundamental ways to accomplish this goal is by eating a well-balanced diet. Generally, *daily caloric intake should be distributed in such a way that about 58 percent of the total calories come from carbohydrates (48 percent complex carbohydrates and 10 percent sugar) and less than 30 percent of the total calories from fat. Protein intake should be about .8 grams per kilogram (2.2 pounds) of body weight or about 15 to 20 percent of the total calories.* Saturated fats should constitute less than 10 percent of the total daily caloric intake. In addition, all of the vitamins, minerals, and water must be provided. To accurately rate a diet is difficult without conducting a complete nutrient analysis (see below).

FIGURE 2.5

Major functions of vitamins

NUTRIENT	GOOD SOURCES	MAJOR FUNCTIONS	DEFICIENCY SYMPTOMS
Vitamin A	Milk, cheese, eggs, liver, and yellow/dark green fruits and vegetables	Required for healthy bones, teeth, skin, gums, and hair. Maintenance of inner mucous membranes, thus increasing resistance to infection. Adequate vision in dim light	Night blindness, decreased growth, decreased resistance to infection, rough-dry skin
Vitamin D	Fortified milk, cod liver oil, salmon, tuna, egg yolk	Necessary for bones and teeth. Needed for calcium and phosphorus absorption	Rickets (bone softening), fractures, and muscle spasms
Vitamin E	Vegetable oils, yellow and green leafy vegetables, margarine, wheat germ, whole grain breads and cereals	Related to oxydation and normal muscle and red blood cell chemistry	Leg cramps, red blood cell breakdown
Vitamin K	Green leafy vegetables, cauliflower, cabbage, eggs, peas, and potatoes	Essential for normal blood clotting	Hemorrhaging
Vitamin B_1 (Thiamine)	Whole grain or enriched bread, lean meats and poultry, organ fish, liver, pork, poultry, organ meats, legumes, nuts, and dried yeast	Assists in proper use of carbohydrates. Normal functioning of nervous system. Maintenance of good appetite	Loss of appetite, nausea, confusion, cardiac abnormalities, muscle spasms
Vitamin B_2 (Riboflavin)	Eggs, milk, leafy green vegetables, whole grains, lean meats, dried beans and peas	Contributes to energy release from carbohydrates, fats, and proteins. Needed for normal growth and development, good vision, and healthy skin	Cracking of the corners of the mouth, inflammation of the skin, impaired vision
Vitamin B_6 (Pyridoxine)	Vegetables, meats, whole grain cereals, soybeans, peanuts, and potatoes	Necessary for protein and fatty acids metabolism, and normal red blood cell formation	Depression, irritability, muscle spasms, nausea
Vitamin B_{12}	Meat, poultry, fish, liver, organ meats, eggs, shellfish, milk, and cheese	Required for normal growth, red blood cell formation, nervous system and digestive tract functioning	Impaired balance, weakness, drop in red blood cell count
Niacin	Liver and organ meats, meat, fish, poultry, whole grains, enriched breads, nuts, green leafy vegetables, and dried beans and peas	Contributes to energy release from carbohydrates, fats, and proteins. Normal growth and development, and formation of hormones and nerve-regulating substances	Confusion, depression, weakness, weight loss
Biotin	Liver, kidney, eggs, yeast, legumes, milk, nuts, dark green vegetables	Essential for carbohydrate metabolism and fatty acid synthesis	Inflamed skin, muscle pain, depression, weight loss
Folic Acid	Leafy green vegetables, organ meats, whole grains and cereals, and dried beans	Needed for cell growth and reproduction and red blood cell formation	Decreased resistance to infection
Pantothenic Acid	All natural foods, especially liver, kidney, eggs, nuts, yeast, milk, dried peas and beans, and green leafy vegetables	Related to carbohydrate and fat metabolism	Depression, low blood sugar, leg cramps, nausea, headaches
Vitamin C (Ascorbic Acid)	Fruits and vegetables	Helps protect against infection; formation of collagenous tissue. Normal blood vessels, teeth, and bones	Slow healing wounds, loose teeth, hemorrhaging, rough-scaly skin, irritability

───── *FIGURE 2.6* ─────

Major functions of minerals

NUTRIENT	GOOD SOURCES	MAJOR FUNCTIONS	DEFICIENCY SYMPTOMS
Calcium	Milk, yogurt, cheese, green leafy vegetables, dried beans, sardines, and salmon	Required for strong teeth and bone formation. Maintenance of good muscle tone, heart beat, and nerve function	Bone pain and fractures, periodontal disease, muscle cramps
Iron	Organ meats, lean meats, seafoods, eggs, dried peas and beans, nuts, whole and enriched grains, and green leafy vegetables	Major component of hemoglobin. Aids in energy utilization	Nutritional anemia, and overall weakness
Phosphorus	Meats, fish, milk, eggs, dried beans and peas, whole grains, and processed foods	Required for bone and teeth formation. Energy release regulation	Bone pain and fracture, weight loss, and weakness
Zinc	Milk, meat, seafood, whole grains, nuts, eggs, and dried beans	Essential component of hormones, insulin, and enzymes. Used in normal growth and development	Loss of appetite, slow healing wounds, and skin problems
Magnesium	Green leafy vegetables, whole grains, nuts, soybeans, seafood, and legumes	Needed for bone growth and maintenance. Carbohydrate and protein utilization. Nerve function. Temperature regulation	Irregular heartbeat, weakness, muscle spasms, and sleeplessness
Sodium	Table salt, processed foods, and meat	Body fluid regulation. Transmission of nerve impulse. Heart action	Rarely seen
Potassium	Legumes, whole grains, bananas, orange juice, dried fruits, and potatoes	Heart action. Bone formation and maintenance. Regulation of energy release. Acid-base regulation	Irregular heartbeat, nausea, weakness

───── TABLE 2.1 ─────

Dietary Fiber Content of Selected Foods

Food	Serving Size	Dietary Fiber (gm)	Food	Serving Size	Dietary Fiber (gm)
Almonds	1 oz.	3.0	Fruit Wheats	1 oz.	2.0
Apple	1 medium	4.3	Just Right	1 oz.	2.0
Banana	1 medium	3.3	Wheaties	1 oz.	2.0
Beans — red, kidney	.5 cup	10.2	Corn (cooked)	.5 cup	3.9
Blackberries	.5 cup	4.9	Eggplant (cooked)	.5 cup	3.0
Beets (cooked)	.5 cup	2.0	Lettuce (chopped)	.5 cup	0.4
Brazil nuts	1 oz.	2.5	Orange	1 medium	3.0
Broccoli (cooked)	.5 cup	3.3	Parsnips (cooked)	.5 cup	2.1
Brown rice (cooked)	.5 cup	2.0	Pear	1 medium	5.0
Carrots (cooked)	.5 cup	2.9	Peas (cooked)	.5 cup	3.7
Cauliflower (cooked)	.5 cup	1.7	Popcorn (plain)	1 cup	1.5
Cereal			Potato (baked)	1 medium	3.9
All Bran	1 oz.	8.5	Strawberries	.5 cup	1.6
Cheerios	1 oz.	1.1	Summer squash (cooked)	.5 cup	1.6
Cornflakes	1 oz.	0.5	Watermelon	1 cup	0.8
Fruit and Fibre	1 oz.	4.0			

Nutrient Analysis

The initial step to evaluate your diet is achieved by conducting your own nutrient analysis. This analysis can be quite an educational experience because most people do not realize how detrimental and non-nutritious many common foods are. Lab 2A will provide you with the opportunity to evaluate your own diet.

To analyze your diet, keep a three-day record of everything that you eat using the forms given in Lab 2A — Figure 2A.1. At the end of each day, look up the nutrient content for the foods you ate in the "Nutritive Value of Selected Foods" list given in Appendix A. This information should be recorded in the respective spaces provided in your three-day listing of foods in Figure 2A.1. If you do not find a particular food in the list given in Appendix A, the information is often provided on the food container itself, or you may refer to the references provided at the end of the list.

After recording the nutritive values for each day, add up each column and record the totals at the bottom of the chart. Following the third day, use Figure 2A.2 and compute an average for the three days. To rate your diet, the results of the analysis should be compared against the Recommended Dietary Allowance (RDA) given in Figures 2.7 and 2A.2 (Lab 2A). The results of your analysis will give a good indication of areas of strength and deficiency in your current diet.

The reader should also realize that there is a difference between the RDA (Recommended Dietary Allowance) and the U.S. RDA (U.S. Recommended Daily Allowance). The U.S. RDA was derived from the RDA and was developed as a standard for nutrition labeling. The U.S. RDA usually includes the highest RDA for most nutrients. These standards are given for healthy people between the age of four and adulthood, except pregnant and lactating women. The relative levels of nutrients on a U.S. RDA label are represented as a percentage of the selected standard for each nutrient (see Figure 2.8). For example, the U.S. RDA for calcium is 1,000 mg. If a label shows that a serving of a particular food contains 2 percent of the U.S. RDA, this indicates that there are approximately 20 mg of calcium in that serving.

The process of analyzing your diet by hand is quite time consuming and can be simplified by using the computer software for this analysis (also available through Morton Publishing Company in Englewood, Colorado). If this software is used, you will only need to record the foods by code and the number of servings based on the standard amounts given in the list of selected foods contained in Appendix A (use the form contained in Figure 2A.3 – Lab 2A). A sample nutrient analysis printout is shown in Figures 2.13 and 2.14 at the end of this chapter.

Some of the most revealing information learned in a nutrient analysis is the source of fat intake in the diet. The average fat consumption in the American diet is in excess of 40 percent of the total caloric intake. Less than 30 percent is recommended. Each gram of carbohydrates and protein supplies the body with four calories, while fat provides nine calories per gram consumed (alcohol provides seven calories per gram). In this regard, just looking at the total amount of grams consumed for each type of food can be very misleading. For example, a person who consumes 160 grams of carbohydrates, 100 grams of fat, and 70 grams of protein has a total intake of 330 grams of food. This indicates that 33 percent of the total grams of food are in the form of fat (100 grams of fat ÷ 330 grams of total food × 100).

In reality, the diet consists of almost 50 percent fat calories. In this sample diet, 640 calories are derived from carbohydrates (160 grams × 4 calories/gram), 280 calories from protein (70 grams × 4 calories/gram), and 900 calories from fat (100 grams × 9 calories/gram), for a total of 1,820 calories. If 900 calories are derived from fat, you can easily observe that almost half of the total caloric intake is in the form of fat (900 ÷ 1,820 × 100 = 49.5 percent).

Realizing that each gram of fat yields nine calories is a very useful guideline when attempting to determine the fat content of individual foods. All you need to do is multiply the grams of fat by nine and divide by the total calories in that particular food. The percentage is obtained by multiplying the latter figure by 100 (Figure 2.9). For example, if a food label lists a total of 100 calories and 7 grams of fat, the fat content would be 63 percent of total calories. This simple guideline can help you decrease fat intake in your diet. The fat content of selected foods, expressed in grams and as a percent of total calories, is given in Table 2.2. Beware also of products labeled 97 percent fat free. These products use weight and not percent of total calories as a measure of fat. Many of these foods are still in the range of 30 percent fat calories (see Figure 2.9).

Achieving a Balanced Diet

An individual who has completed a nutrient analysis and has given careful consideration to Figures 2.5 and 2.6 (Vitamins and Minerals) would probably realize that in order to have a well-balanced diet, a variety of foods must be consumed, along with a decreased daily intake in fats and sweets. Although achieving a balanced diet may seem very complex, the basic guidelines to achieve an optimal

FIGURE 2.7

*Recommended Dietary Allowances**

	Calories	Protein	Fat	Sat. Fat	Choles-terol (mg)	Carbo-hydrates	Calcium (mg)	Iron (mg)	Sodium (mg)	Vit. A (I.U.)	Thiamin (Vit. B$_1$) (mg)	Riboflavin (Vit. B$_2$) (mg)	Niacin (mg)	Vit. C (mg)
Men 15-18 years	See below[a]	See below[b]	< 30%[c]	< 10%[c]	< 300	50% >[c]	1,200	12	3,000	5,000	1.5	1.8	20	60
Men 19-24 years			< 30%[c]	< 10%[c]	< 300	50% >[c]	1,200	10	3,000	5,000	1.5	1.7	19	60
Men 25-50 years			< 30%[c]	< 10%[c]	< 300	50% >[c]	800	10	3,000	5,000	1.5	1.7	19	60
Men 51 +			< 30%[c]	< 10%[c]	< 300	50% >[c]	800	10	3,000	5,000	1.2	1.4	15	60
Women 15-18 years			< 30%[c]	< 10%[c]	< 300	50% >[c]	1,200	15	3,000	4,000	1.1	1.3	15	60
Women 19-24 years			< 30%[c]	< 10%[c]	< 300	50% >[c]	1,200	15	3,000	4,000	1.1	1.3	15	60
Women 25-50 years			< 30%[c]	< 10%[c]	< 300	50% >[c]	800	15	3,000	4,000	1.1	1.3	15	60
Women 51 +			< 30%[c]	< 10%[c]	< 300	50% >[c]	800	10	3,000	4,000	1.0	1.2	13	60
Pregnant			< 30%[c]	< 10%[c]	< 300	50% >[c]	1,200	30	3,000	4,000	1.5	1.6	17	70
Lactating			< 30%[c]	< 10%[c]	< 300	50% >[c]	1,200	15	3,000	6,000	1.6	1.8	20	95

[a] Use Table 3.1 for al categories.

[b] Protein intake should be .8 grams per kilogram of body weight. Pregnant women should consume an additional 15 grams of daily protein, while lactating women should have an extra 20 grams.

[c] Percentage of total calories based on recommendations by nutrition experts.

*Adapted from *Recommended Dietary Allowances*, © 1989, by the National Academy of Sciences, National Academy Press, Washington D.C.

―――――― **FIGURE 2.8** ――――――

Food Label and the U.S. RDA (U.S. Recommended Daily Allowance): A standard for nutrition labeling derived from the RDA.

No legal meaning. The product can still contain preservatives, artificial flavoring, and other additives.

Make sure serving sizes are the same when comparing brands.

This number can be within 20% of the actual calorie count.

The amount of saturated and unsaturated fatty acids as well as cholesterol must be listed if health claims are made on the package.

These eight nutrients must be listed.

Ingredients are listed in descending order according to weight. This gives you no idea how much of any ingredient is actually used.

GRANOLA CEREAL
ALL NATURAL

NUTRITION INFORMATION

SERVING SIZE	1 ounce
SERVINGS PER PACKAGE	16
Calories	140
Protein	3g
Carbohydrates	16g
Fat	7g
Sodium	100mg

PERCENTAGE OF U.S. RDA

Protein	4
Vitamin A	*
Vitamin C	*
Thiamine	6
Riboflavin	2
Niacin	2
Calcium	2
Iron	4

*Contains less than 2% of the U.S. RDA of this nutrient.

INGREDIENTS: Rolled oats, brown sugar, corn syrup, sugar, raisins, peanuts, honey, nonfat dry milk, salt, vegetable oil (one or more of the following: soybean, hydrogenated palm, and/or coconut oil), artificial and natural flavors, preservative BHT, MSG.

Sugars, fiber, and complex carbohydrates are lumped together under carbohydrates.

To figure out what percentage of calories comes from fat, multiply the grams of fat by 9 (calories in a gram of fat) and divide by the total number of calories.

The U.S. RDA for calcium is 1,000 mg per day, so 2% is only 20 mg.

―――――― **FIGURE 2.9** ――――――

How to Determine Fat Calories in Food

CALORIC VALUE OF FOOD

Sources of Calories

1 gram of carbohydrate	4 calories
1 gram of protein	4 calories
1 gram of fat	9 calories
1 gram of alcohol	7 calories

COMPUTATION FOR FAT CONTENT IN FOOD

Example: Caloric Distribution for Turkey Breast, 97% Fat Free

Portion size	1 slice (1 oz)
Calories	29
Protein	4 grams × 4 calories = 16 calories
Carbohydrate	1 gram × 4 calories = 4 calories
Fat	1 gram × 9 calories = 9 calories
	Total calories = 29 calories

Percent Fat Calories = (grams of fat × 9) divided by total calories × 100

Percent fat calories in 97% fat free turkey = [(1 × 9) ÷ 29] × 100
= 31%

—— *TABLE 2.2* ——

Fat Content of Selected Foods (expressed in grams and as a Percent of Total Calories)

Food	Amount	Calories	Fat (g)	Percent of Calories
Avocado	.5 medium	185	19	92
Bacon	2 slc.	86	8	84
Beef, ground (lean)	3 oz.	186	10	48
Beef, round steak	3 oz.	222	13	53
Beef, sirloin	3 oz.	329	27	74
Butter	1 tsp.	36	4	100
Cheese, american	1 oz.	100	8	72
Cheese, cheddar	1 oz.	114	9	71
Cheese, cottage (1% fat)	.5 cup	82	1	11
Cheese, cottage (4% fat)	.5 cup	112	5	40
Cheese, cream	1 oz.	99	8	73
Cheese, muenster	2 oz.	208	17	74
Cheese, parmesan	2 oz.	261	17	61
Cheese, swiss	2 oz.	214	16	67
Chicken, light meat, no skin	3 oz.	141	3	17
Chicken, dark meat, no skin	3 oz.	149	5	30
Egg (hard cooked)	1	72	5	63
Frankfurter	1	176	16	82
Halibut	3 oz.	144	6	38
Ice Cream (vanilla)	.5 cup	135	7	47
Ice Milk (vanilla)	.5 cup	100	3	27
Lamb leg, roast, trimmed	3 oz.	237	16	61
Margarine	1 tsp.	34	4	100
Mayonnaise	1 tsp.	36	4	100
Milk, skim	1 cup	88	0	3
Milk, low fat (2%)	1 cup	145	5	31
Milk, whole	1 cup	159	9	51
Nuts (brazil)	1 oz.	186	19	92
Salmon, broiled with butter	3 oz.	156	6	35
Sherbet	.5 cup	135	2	12
Shrimp, boiled	3 oz.	99	1	9
Tuna (canned, oil, drained)	3 oz.	167	7	38
Tuna (canned, water, drained)	3 oz.	126	1	1
Turkey, light and dark	3 oz.	162	5	28

diet are given in Figure 2.10. The rules of this "New American Eating Guide" are:

1. Eat the minimum number of servings required for each one of the four basic food groups:

   (a) four or more servings per day of beans, grains, and nuts;

   (b) four or more servings per day of fruits and vegetables, including one good source of vitamin A (apricots, cantaloupe, broccoli, carrots, pumpkin, and dark leafy vegetables), and one good source of vitamin C (cantaloupe, citrus fruit, kiwi fruit, strawberries, broccoli, cabbage, cauliflower, and green pepper);

   (c) two or more servings per day of milk products;

   (d) two or more servings per day of poultry, fish, meat and eggs.

2. Obtain a final positive ("+") score at the end of each day:

   (a) "anytime" foods get one positive point,

   (b) "in moderation" foods do not get any points,

   (c) "now and then" foods lose one point.

To aid you in balancing your diet, the log given in Lab 2B (Figure 2B.1) can be used to record your daily food intake. This record sheet is much easier to keep than the complete dietary analysis. First, make a copy of Figure 2.10 (or obtain the poster from the Center for Science in the Public Interest — see footnote at the bottom of the figure) and post it

FIGURE 2.10
The New American Eating Guide

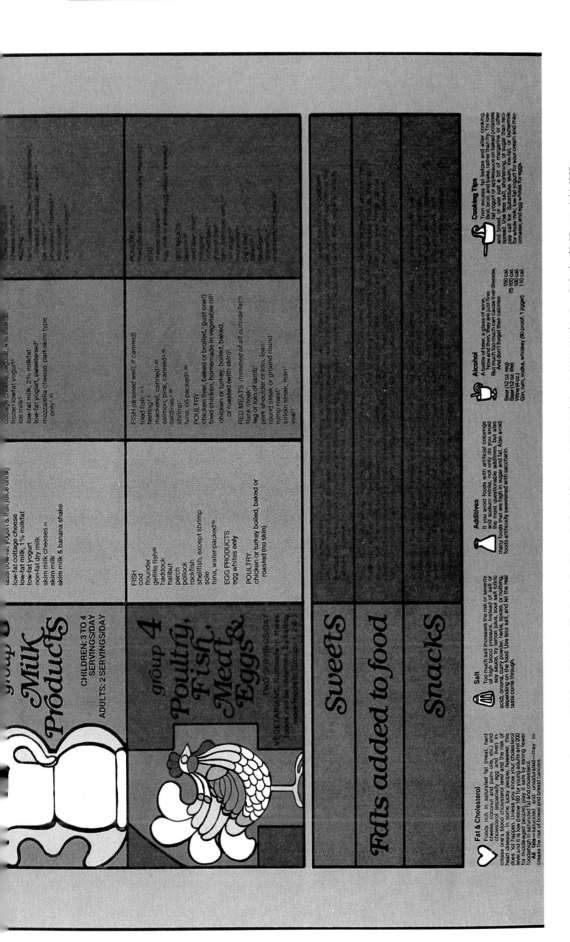

Reprinted from New American Eating Guide poster which is available from the Center for Science in the Public Interest, 1501 16th Street, N.W., Washington, D.C., for $3.95, copyright 1982.

One serving equals: Group 1 = 1 slice of bread, 1 cup ready-to-eat cereal, ½ cup cooked cereal/pasta/grits, or equivalent; Group 2 = ½ cup cooked or juice, 1 cup raw, or 1 medium size fruit; Group 3 = 1 cup milk/yogurt, 1½ oz. cheese, 1 cup pudding/ice cream, 2 cups cottage cheese, or equivalent; Group 4 = 2 oz. cooked lean meat/fish/poultry, 2 eggs, or equivalent.

somewhere visible in the kitchen or keep it accessible at all times.

Figure 2B.1 in Lab 2B can then be used. Whenever you have something to eat, record the code for the food from the list in Appendix A and the " + ", "NP" (no points), or " − " characters in the corresponding spaces provided for each day. Individuals on a weight reduction program should also record the caloric content of each food. This information can be obtained from the list of foods, the food container itself, or some of the references given at the end of the list of foods. The information should be recorded immediately after each meal, since it will be easier to keep track of foods and the amount eaten. If twice the amount of a particular serving is eaten, the calories must be doubled and two " + ", " − ", or "NP" characters should also be recorded.

At the end of the day, the diet is evaluated by checking whether the minimum required servings for each food group were consumed, and by adding up the " + " and " − " points accumulated. If you have met the required servings and end up with a positive score, you have achieved a well-balanced diet for that day.

Vitamin and Mineral Supplementation

Another point of significant interest in nutrition is the unnecessary and sometimes unsafe use of vitamin and mineral supplementation. Even though experts agree that supplements are not necessary, people consume them at a greater rate than ever before. The Food and Drug Administration has indicated that in the United States four out of every ten adults take daily supplements, and one in every seven has a nutrient intake of almost eight times the Recommended Dietary Allowance. Research has clearly demonstrated that *even when a person consumes as few as 1,200 calories per day, no additional supplementation is needed as long as the diet contains the recommended servings from the four basic food groups.*

Although water-soluble vitamins cannot be stored as long as fat-soluble vitamins, they are easily retained for weeks or months in various organs and tissues of the body. Excessive intakes are readily excreted from the body. Fat-soluble vitamins are stored in fatty tissue. Therefore, daily intake of these vitamins is not as crucial. Furthermore, excessive amounts of vitamins A and D can be detrimental to your health. Mineral requirements are provided in sufficient quantities in a normal balanced diet.

For most people, vitamin and mineral supplementation is unnecessary. Iron deficiency (determined through blood testing) is the only exception for women who suffer from heavy menstrual flow.

Some pregnant and lactating women may also require supplements. According to 1990 guidelines by the National Academy of Science, the average pregnant woman who consumes an adequate amount of a variety of foods only needs to take a low-dose of iron supplement daily. Those women who are pregnant with more than one baby may need additional supplements. In all instances, supplements should be taken under a physician's supervision. Other people who may benefit from supplementation are alcoholics and street-drug users who are not consuming a balanced diet, smokers, strict vegetarians, individuals on extremely low-calorie diets, elderly people who don't regularly receive balanced meals, and newborn infants (usually given a single dose of vitamin K to prevent abnormal bleeding).

For healthy people with a balanced diet, supplementation provides no additional health benefits. It will not help a person run faster, jump higher, relieve stress, improve sexual prowess, cure a common cold, or boost energy levels!

Research has shown that not even athletes need vitamin and mineral supplementation, or for that matter, any other special type of diet. The simple truth is that unless the diet is deficient in basic nutrients, there are no special, secret, or magic diets that will help a person perform better or develop faster as a result of what he/she is eating. As long as the diet is balanced, that is, it is based on a large variety of foods from each of the basic food groups, athletes do not need any additional supplements. Even in strength training and body building no additional protein in excess of 20 percent of total daily caloric intake is needed.

The only difference between a sedentary person and a highly trained one is in the total number of calories required on a daily basis. The trained person may consume more calories because of the increased energy expenditure as a result of intense physical training.

The only time that a normal diet should be modified is when an individual is going to participate in long-distance events lasting in excess of one hour (e.g. marathon, triathlon, and road cycling). Athletic performance is increased for these types of events by consuming a regular balanced diet along with exhaustive physical training the fifth and fourth days prior to the event, followed by a diet high in carbohydrates (about 70 percent) and a progressive decrease in training intensity the last three days before the event.

Another fallacy regarding nutrition is that many people who regularly eat fast foods high in fat content and/or excessive sweets feel that vitamin and mineral supplementation is needed to balance their diet. The problem in these cases is not a lack of vitamins and minerals, but rather a diet that is too high in calories, fat, and sodium. Supplementation will not offset such poor eating habits.

If you feel that your diet is not balanced, you first need to determine which nutrients are missing (see Nutrient Analysis). Then use the "New American Eating Guide" and the vitamin and mineral charts given in this chapter, and increase the intake of those foods high in nutrients deficient in your diet.

SPECIAL NUTRITION CONSIDERATIONS FOR WOMEN

Bone Health (Osteoporosis)

Osteoporosis has been defined as the softening, deterioration, or loss of total body bone. Bones become so weak and brittle that fractures, primarily of the hip, wrist, and spine, occur very readily.

Osteoporosis is really a preventable disease. The disease process slowly begins in the third and fourth decade of life, and women are especially susceptible after menopause. This is primarily due to estrogen loss following menopause, which increases the rate at which bone mass is broken down.

Approximately 15 to 20 million women in the United States suffer from osteoporosis and about 1.3 million fractures are attributed to this condition each year. It is further estimated that 30,000 to 60,000 of the 200,000 women with hip fractures die of complications resulting from these fractures. According to Dr. Barbara Drinkwater, a leading researcher in this area, *"shocking as these figures are, they cannot adequately convey the pain and deterioration in the quality of life of women who suffer the crippling effects of osteoporotic fractures."*[4]

The importance of normal estrogen levels, adequate calcium intake, and physical activity cannot be underemphasized in maximizing bone density in young women and decreasing the rate of bone loss later in life. All three factors are crucial in the prevention of osteoporosis (Figure 2.11). The absence of any one of these three factors will lead to bone loss and is never completely compensated for by the other two.

The prevention of osteoporosis begins early in life by providing adequate amounts of calcium in the diet (follow the Recommended Dietary Allowance of 800 to 1,200 mg per day) and by participating in a *lifetime* exercise program. The calcium RDA can easily be met through diet alone. In conjunction with adequate calcium intake, there may be a need for an additional amount of vitamin D, which is necessary for optimal calcium absorption. For your information, a list of selected foods and their respective calcium content is provided in Table 2.3.

Weight-bearing types of exercise such as walking, jogging, and weight training are especially helpful, because not only do they tone up muscles, but also develop stronger and thicker bones. Current studies indicate that people who are active have better bone mineral density than inactive people. Similar to other benefits of exercise participation, there is no such thing as "bone in the bank." To enjoy good bone health, people need to participate in a *regular lifetime exercise* program.

Prevailing research also indicates that estrogen is the most important factor in preventing bone loss. For instance, lumbar bone density in women who had always had regular menstrual cycles exceeded that of women with a history of oligomenorrhea (irregular cycles) and amenorrhea (cessation of menstruation) interspaced with regular cycles. Furthermore, the lumbar density of these two groups of women is higher than that of women who had never had regular cycles.

Following menopause, every woman needs to seriously consider hormone replacement therapy with her physician. Women who use estrogen therapy will not lose bone mineral density at the rate that non-therapy women do. Neither exercise nor calcium supplementation will offset the damaging effects of lower estrogen levels. For instance, research clearly indicates that amenorrheic athletes (who have lower estrogen levels) have lower bone mineral density than even non-athletes with normal estrogen levels. One particular study showed that amenorrheic athletes at age 25 have the bones of 52-year-old women. Furthermore, a sedentary woman with normal estrogen levels has better bone mineral density than an active amenorrheic athlete. Many experts now indicate that the best predictor of bone mineral content is the previous history of menstrual regularity.

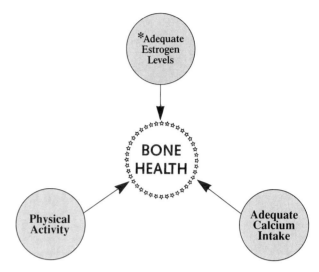

——— *FIGURE 2.11* ———

Variables that Impact the Prevention of Osteoporosis

*Most important factor in the prevention of osteoporosis

——— *TABLE 2.3* ———

Lowfat Calcium-Rich Foods

Food	Amount	Calcium (mg)	Calories	Calories from Fat
Beans, red kidney, cooked	1 cup	70	218	4%
Beet, greens, cooked	1/2 cup	72	13	—
Broccoli, cooked, drained	1 sm stalk	123	36	—
Burrito, bean	1	173	307	28%
Cottage cheese, 2% lowfat	1/2 cup	78	103	18%
Ice milk (vanilla)	1/2 cup	102	100	27%
Inst. breakfast, whole milk	1 cup	301	280	26%
Kale, cooked, drained	1/2 cup	103	22	—
Milk, nonfat, powdered	1 tbsp	52	27	1%
Milk, skim	1 cup	296	88	3%
Okra, cooked, drained	1/2 cup	74	23	—
Shrimp, boiled	3 oz.	99	99	9%
Spinach, raw	1 cup	51	14	—
Yogurt, fruit	1 cup	345	231	8%
Yogurt, lowfat, plain	1 cup	271	160	20%

Iron Deficiency

Iron is a key element of hemoglobin in blood, which carries oxygen from the lungs to all tissues of the body. The Recommended Dietary Allowance of iron for most women is 15 mg per day (10-12 mg for men). Unfortunately, *a recent survey by the Department of Agriculture indicated that 19 to 50 year-old women in the United States consumed only 60 percent of the U.S. RDA for iron.* People who do not have an adequate iron intake can develop iron deficiency anemia, a condition in which the concentration of hemoglobin in the red blood cells is reduced.

Some researchers have indicated that physically active women may also have a higher than average iron need. It is thought that heavy training creates an iron demand higher than the recommended intake because small amounts of iron are lost through sweat, urine, and stools. Mechanical trauma, caused by the pounding of the feet on pavement during extensive jogging, may also lead to the destruction of iron-containing red blood cells. A large percentage of endurance female athletes have been reported to suffer from iron deficiency. Blood ferritin levels, a measure of stored iron in the human body, should be checked frequently in women that participate in intense physical training.

There are also some individuals who have higher rates of iron absorption or faster rates of iron loss. In most cases, nonetheless, adequate iron intake can be achieved by eating more iron-rich foods such as beans, peas, green leafy vegetables, enriched grain products, egg yolk, fish, and lean meats (organ meats are especially good sources, but they are also high in cholesterol). A list of foods high in iron content is given in Table 2.4.

NATIONAL ACADEMY OF SCIENCES' DIETARY RECOMMENDATIONS

Based on the available scientific research on nutrition and health and the current dietary habits of the American people, the National Academy of Sciences' Committee on Diet and Health recently issued dietary recommendations for healthy North American adults and children. These guidelines, released in 1989, have the potential of reducing the risk of developing certain chronic diseases. The committee's recommendations are as follows:

- Reduce total fat intake to 30 percent or less of calories. Reduce saturated fatty acid intake to less than 10 percent of calories, and the intake of cholesterol to less than 300 mg daily. The intake of fat and cholesterol can be reduced by substituting fish, poultry without skin, lean meats and low or nonfat dairy products for fatty meats and whole milk dairy products; by choosing more vegetables, fruits, cereals, and legumes; and by limiting oils, fats, egg yolks, and fried and other fatty foods.

TABLE 2.4

Iron-Rich Foods

Food	Amount	Iron (mg)	Calories	Cholesterol	Calories from Fat
Beans, red kidney, cooked	1 cup	4.4	218	0	4%
Beef, ground lean	3 oz.	3.0	186	81	48%
Beef, sirloin	3 oz.	2.5	329	77	74%
Beef, liver, fried	3 oz.	7.5	195	345	42%
Beet, greens, cooked	1/2 cup	1.4	13	0	—
Broccoli, cooked, drained	1 sm stalk	1.1	36	0	—
Burrito, bean	1	2.4	307	14	28%
Egg, hard, cooked	1	1.0	72	250	63%
Farina (Cream of Wheat), cooked	1/2 cup	6.0	51	0	—
Inst. breakfast, whole milk	1 cup	8.0	280	33	26%
Peas, frozen, cooked, drained	1/2 cup	1.5	55	0	—
Shrimp, boiled	3 oz.	2.7	99	128	9%
Spinach, raw	1 cup	1.7	14	0	—
Vegetables, mixed, cooked	1 cup	2.4	116	0	—

- Every day eat five or more servings of a combination of vegetables and fruits, especially green and yellow vegetables and citrus fruits. Also, increase intake of starches and other complex carbohydrates by eating six or more daily servings of a combination of breads, cereals, and legumes. An average serving is equal to a half cup for most fresh or cooked vegetables, fruits, dry or cooked cereals and legumes, one medium piece of fresh fruit, one slice of bread, or one roll or muffin. The committee also recommends that the intake of carbohydrates be increased to more than 55 percent of total calories.

- Maintain protein intake at moderate levels (not to exceed 1.6 gr/kg or twice the RDA).

- Balance food intake and physical activity to maintain appropriate body weight (see Chapter 3 for a comprehensive weight control program).

- The committee does not recommend alcohol consumption. For those who drink alcoholic beverages, the committee recommends limiting consumption to the equivalent of less than one ounce of pure alcohol in a single day. This is the equivalent of two cans of beer, two small glasses of wine, or two average cocktails. Pregnant women should avoid alcoholic beverages.

- Limit total daily intake of salt (sodium chloride) to six grams or less. Limit the use of salt in cooking and avoid adding it to food at the table. Salty, highly processed salty, salt-preserved, and salt-pickled foods should be consumed sparingly.

- Maintain adequate calcium intake.

- Avoid taking supplements in excess of the RDA in any one day.

- Maintain an optimal intake of fluoride, particularly during the years of primary and secondary tooth formation and growth.

PROPER NUTRITION: A LIFETIME PRESCRIPTION FOR HEALTHY LIVING

Proper nutrition, along with a sound exercise program and smoking cessation (for those who smoke), are the three most significant factors to improve health, longevity, and quality of life. Achieving and maintaining a balanced diet is not as difficult as most people think. If parents and schools did a better job at teaching and reinforcing proper nutrition habits in early youth (Figure 2.12), we would not have the magnitude of nutrition-related health problems that we presently have. The difficult part for most people is retraining themselves to adopt a lifetime healthy nutrition plan; that is, to eat the right type of foods and use moderation with those that are high in fat, sodium, alcohol, or have little or no nutritive value.

Yet, in spite of the ample scientific evidence linking poor dietary habits to early disease and mortality rates, most people are not willing to change their eating patterns. Even when faced with such conditions as obesity, elevated blood lipids, hypertension, etc., people still do not change. The motivating factor seems to be when a major health

———— *FIGURE 2.12* ————

Positive Nutrition Habits Should Be Taught and Reinforced in Early Youth.

breakdown actually occurs (e.g. a heart attack, a stroke, cancer). By this time the damage has already been done. In many cases it is irreversible, and for some, fatal. Keep in mind that "an ounce of prevention is worth a pound of cure." The sooner you implement the dietary guidelines presented in this chapter, the better your chances of preventing the development of chronic diseases and reaching a higher state of wellness.

LABORATORY EXPERIENCES

LAB 2A: Nutrient Analysis

LAB PREPARATION: Prior to your lab, keep a three-day record of all food consumed using Figure 2A.1 from Lab 2. You should also record all of the nutrients from the "Nutritive Values of Selected Foods" list (Appendix A). Please note that if your serving is twice the standard amount, you need to double all of the nutrient contents. If you only have half a serving, then only record half of the contents, and so forth. You should also total your nutrient intake for each day before the lab session. If the computer software available with this book is used, you will only need to record the codes and the number of servings eaten (use Figure 2A.3) prior to your lab session.

LAB 2B: Balancing Your Diet

LAB PREPARATION: None. This lab will be given as homework to follow up the nutrient analysis (see Lab 2B).

References

1. American Medical Association: Council on Scientific Affairs. "Dietary Fiber and Health." *Journal of the American Medical Association* 262:542-546, 1989.

2. Brownell, K., and J. P. Forey. *Handbook of Eating Disorders*. New York: Basic Books, Inc., 1986.

3. Drinkwater, B. L. "Maximizing Bone Mass in the Premenopausal Years: Positive and Negative Factors." In Christiansen, C., J. S. Johansen, B. J. Riis, eds. *Osteoporosis* 1987. Copenhagen: Osteopress 884-888, 1987.

4. Drinkwater, B. L. "Nutrition, Exercise, and Bone Health." Seattle, WA: Pacific Medical Center, 1990.

5. Drinkwater, B.L. "Osteoporosis and the Female Masters Athlete." In Sutton, J. R., and R. M. Brock, eds. *Sports Medicine for the Mature Athlete*. Benchmark Press: 353-359, 1986.

6. Drinkwater, B. L., B. Bruemner, and C. H. III Chestnut. "Menstrual History as a Determinant of Current Bone Density in Young Athletes." *Journal of the American Medical Association* 263:545-548, 1990.

7. Girdano, D. A., D. Dusek, and G. S. Everly. *Experiencing Health*. Englewood Cliffs, NJ: Prentice-Hall, 1985.

8. "How to Balance Your Diet." *Fit* 46-47, April 1983.

9. Hoeger, W. W. K. *Lifetime Physical Fitness & Wellness: A Personalized Program*. Englewood, CO: Morton Publishing Co., 1989.

10. Hoeger, W. W. K. *The Complete Guide for the Development & Implementation of Health Promotion Programs*. Englewood, CO: Morton Publishing Co., 1987.

11. Kanders, B., D. W. Demster, R. Lindsay. "Interaction of Calcium Nutrition and Physical Activity on Bone Mass in Young Women." *Journal of Bone Mineral Research* 3:145-149, 1988.

12. Kirschmann, J. D. *Nutrition Almanac*. New York: McGraw-Hill Book Company, 1989.

13. Kleiner, S. M. "Seafood and Your Heart." *The Physician and Sportsmedicine* 18(4):19-20, 1990.

14. Morgan, B. L. G. *The Lifelong Nutrition Guide*. Englewood Cliffs, NJ: Prentice-Hall, 1983.

15. National Academy of Sciences. "Diet and Health: Implications for Reducing Chronic Disease Risk." Washington, D.C. National Academy Press, 1989.

16. "The Fallacies of Taking Supplementation." *Tufts University Diet & Nutrition Letter*. July 1987.

17. Thornton, J. S. "Feast or Famine: Eating Disorders in Athletes." *The Physician and Sportsmedicine* 18(4):116-122, 1990.

18. "Use a Variety of Fibers." *The Health Letter*. March 1982.

19. Whitney, E. N. and E. M. N. Hamilton. *Understanding Nutrition*. St. Paul, MN: West Publishing Co., 1987.

─────── *FIGURE 2.13* ───────

Computerized Nutritional Analysis. Sample Food List*

NUTRITIONAL ANALYSIS
Based on Chapter Two of the textbook
PRINCIPLES AND LABORATORIES FOR PHYSICAL FITNESS & WELLNESS
by Werner W.K. Hoeger
Morton Publishing Company, 1988.

Jane Doe   Date: 01-12-1988
Age: 22
Body Weight: 124 lbs (56.2 kg)
Activity Rating: Moderate

Food Intake Day One

Food	Amount	Calo-ries	Pro-tein gm	Fat gm	Sat Fat gm	Cho-les-terol mg	Car-bohy-drate gm	Cal-cium mg	Iron mg	Sodium mg	Vit A I.U.	Thi-amin mg	Ribo-fla-vin mg	Nia-cin mg	Vit C mg
Cornflakes	1.5 c	146	3.0	0	0.0	0	32	5	0.9	377	270	0.44	0.83	4.4	14
Milk skim	1 c	88	9.0	0	0.3	5	12	296	0.1	126	10	0.09	0.44	0.2	2
Apple juice	.5 c	59	0.1	0	0.0	0	15	8	0.7	1	0	0.01	0.03	0.1	1
Cheese/cheddar	1 oz.	114	7.0	9	6.0	30	0	204	0.2	171	300	0.01	0.11	0.0	0
Pears/raw	.5 pear(s)	50	0.6	1	0.0	0	13	7	0.3	1	15	0.02	0.04	0.1	4
Bread/whole wheat	2 slice(s)	122	5.2	2	1.2	0	24	50	1.6	264	0	0.12	0.06	1.4	0
Tuna/canned/water	3.5 oz.	126	27.7	1	0.0	55	0	16	1.6	161	0	0.00	0.10	13.2	0
Mayonnaise	2 tsp.	72	0.0	8	1.4	6	0	2	0.0	56	26	0.00	0.00	0.0	0
Pickles/dill	.5 large	8	0.5	0	0.0	0	2	18	0.7	964	70	0.00	0.02	0.0	4
Tomatoes/raw	.5 med	10	0.5	0	0.0	0	2	6	0.3	2	410	0.03	0.02	0.3	11
Milk skim	1 c	88	9.0	0	0.3	5	12	296	0.1	126	10	0.09	0.44	0.2	2
Cookies/vanilla	5 cookies	93	1.0	3	0.8	10	15	8	0.1	50	25	0.00	0.01	0.0	0
Beef/ground/lean	3 oz.	186	23.3	10	5.0	81	0	10	3.0	57	20	0.08	0.20	5.1	0
Noodles/egg/cooked	1 c	200	6.6	2	0.0	0	38	16	1.4	4	110	0.22	0.14	2.0	0
Tomatoes/canned	.5 c	26	1.2	0	0.0	0	5	7	0.6	157	1,085	0.06	0.04	0.9	21
Vegetables/mixed/cooked	1 c	116	5.8	0	0.0	0	24	46	2.4	348	4,505	0.22	0.13	2.0	15
Milk skim	1 c	88	9.0	0	0.3	5	12	296	0.1	126	10	0.09	0.44	0.2	2
Doughnuts/plain	1 doughnut	164	1.9	8	2.0	19	22	17	0.6	210	30	0.07	0.07	0.5	0
Totals Day One		1,755	111.3	44	17.3	216	227	1,307	14.6	3,200	6,896	1.5	3.1	30.6	75

*Computer software available through Morton Publishing Co., Englewood, Colorado.

————— *FIGURE 2.14* —————

Computerized Nutritional Analysis. Sample Daily Analysis, Average, and Recommended Dietary Allowance Comparison*

NUTRITIONAL ANALYSIS: DAILY ANALYSIS, AVERAGE, AND
RECOMMENDED DIETARY ALLOWANCE (RDA) COMPARISON

	Calo-ries	Pro-tein gm	Fat %	Sat Fat %	Cho-les-terol mg	Car-bohy-drate %	Cal-cium mg	Iron mg	Sodium mg	Vit A I.U.	Thi-amin mg	Ribo-fla-vin mg	Nia-cin mg	Vit C mg
Day One	1,755	111.3	22	9	216	52	1,307	14.6	3,200	6,896	1.5	3.1	30.6	75
Day Two	1,618	76.9	27	7	384	54	957	10.2	2,750	3,665	1.3	1.7	18.2	161
Day Three	2,319	127.6	26	7	695	53	1,373	15.8	3,754	5,655	1.7	2.6	30.4	142
Three Day Average	1,897	105.3	25	7	432	53	1,212	13.5	3,235	5,405	1.5	2.5	26.4	126
RDA	1,674*	45.0	<30	<10	<300	50>	800	18.0	1,674	4,000	1.1	1.3	14.0	60

*Estimated caloric value based on gender, current body weight, and activity rating (does not include
additional calories burned through a physical exercise program).

OBSERVATIONS

Daily caloric intake should be distributed in such a way that 50 to 60 percent of the total calories come from carbohydrates and less than 30 percent of the total calories from fat. Protein intake should be about .8 to 1.5 grams per kilogram of body weight or about 15 to 20 percent of the total calories. Pregnant women need to consume an additional 30 grams of daily protein, while lactating women should have an extra 20 grams of daily protein, or about 25 and 22 percent of total calories, respectively (these additional grams of protein are already included in the RDA values for pregnant and lactating women). Saturated fats should constitute less than 10 percent of the total daily caloric intake.

Please note that the daily listings of food intake express the amount of carbohydrates, fat, saturated fat, and protein in grams. However, on the daily analysis and the RDA, only the amount of protein is given in grams. The amount of carbohydrates, fat, and saturated fat are expressed in percent of total calories. The final percentages are based on the total grams and total calories for all days analyzed, not from the average of the daily percentages.

If your average intake for protein, fat, saturated fat, cholesterol, or sodium is high, refer to the daily listings and decrease the intake of foods that are high in those nutrients. If your diet is deficient in carbohydrates, calcium, iron, vitamin A, thiamin, riboflavin, niacin, or vitamin C, refer to the statements below and increase your intake of the indicated foods, or consult Chapter 2 in your textbook Principles and Laboratories for Physical Fitness & Wellness.

Caloric intake may be too high.

Protein intake is high.

Dietary cholesterol intake is too high. An average consumption of dietary cholesterol above 300 mg/day increases the risk for coronary heart disease. Do you know your blood cholesterol level?

Iron intake is low. Iron containing foods include organ meats such as liver, lean meats, poultry, eggs, seafood, dried peas/beans, nuts, whole and enriched grains, and green leafy vegetables.

Sodium intake is high.

*Computer software available through Morton Publishing Co., Englewood, Colorado.

Principles of Weight Control

OBJECTIVES

- Understand the health consequences of obesity.
- Learn about fad diets and other myths and fallacies regarding weight control.
- Define eating disorders, identify medical problems and behavior patterns associated with eating disorders, and understand the need for professional help in the treatment of these conditions.
- Understand the physiology of weight loss, including setpoint theory and the effects of diet on basal metabolic rate.
- Recognize the role of a lifetime exercise program as the key to a successful weight loss and maintenance program.
- Learn to implement a physiologically sound weight reduction and weight maintenance program.
- Learn behavior modification techniques that help adhere to a lifetime weight maintenance program.

Patty Neavill is a typical example of someone who often tried to change her life around, but was unable to do so because she did not know how to implement a sound exercise and weight control program. At age 24, Patty, a college sophomore, was discouraged with her weight, level of fitness, self-image, and quality of life in general. She had struggled with her weight for most of her life. Like thousands of other people, she had made many unsuccessful attempts to lose weight. Patty put her fears aside and decided it was time to enroll in a fitness course. As part of the course requirement, a battery of fitness tests was administered at the beginning of the semester. Patty's cardiovascular fitness and strength ratings were poor, her flexibility classification was average, she weighed over 200 pounds, and her percent body fat was 41 (percent body fat or body composition assessment is discussed in detail in Chapter 6).

Following the initial fitness assessment, Patty met with her course instructor who prescribed an exercise and nutrition program such as is presented in this book. Patty fully committed to carry out the prescription. She walked or jogged five times per week, worked out with weights twice a week, and played volleyball or basketball two to four times per week. Her daily caloric intake was in the range of 1,500 to 1,700 calories. Care was taken to meet the minimum required servings from the four food groups each day, which contributed about 1,200 calories to her diet. The remainder of the calories came primarily from complex carbohydrates. At the end of the sixteen-week semester, Patty's cardiovascular fitness, strength, and flexibility ratings had all improved to the good category, she lost 50 pounds, and her percent body fat had decreased to 22.5!

A thank you note from Patty to the course instructor at the end of the semester read:

> "Thank you for making me a new person. I truly appreciate the time you spent with me. Without your kindness and motivation, I would have never made it. It is great to be fit and trim. I've never had this feeling before and I wish everyone could feel like this once in their life.
> Thank you,
> Your trim Patty!"

Patty was never taught the principles for implementing a sound weight loss program. *The information presented in this chapter, along with the chapters on exercise prescription, will help the reader understand the fundamental principles involved in the implementation of a healthy lifetime weight management program.*

In Patty's case, not only did she need to obtain this knowledge, but like most Americans who have never experienced the *"process of becoming physically fit,"* she needed to be in a structured exercise setting to truly feel the *"joy of fitness."* Even of greater significance, Patty has maintained her aerobic and strength-training programs. A year after ending her calorie-restricted diet, her weight increased by ten pounds, but her body fat decreased from 22.5 to 21.2 percent. As will be pointed out later in this chapter, the weight increase is primarily related to changes in lean tissue, lost during the weight reduction phase. In spite of only a slight drop in weight during the second year following the calorie-restricted diet, the two-year follow-up revealed a further decrease in body fat to 19.5 percent. Patty now understands the new quality of life reaped through a sound fitness program, and at the same time, she has finally learned how to apply the principles that regulate weight maintenance.

Unfortunately, obesity is a health hazard of epidemic proportions in most developed countries around the world. Statistical estimates indicate that 35 percent of the adult population in industrialized nations is obese. *Current estimates in the United States indicate that over 50 percent of all adults have a weight problem.* The evidence further shows that the prevalence is still increasing. When Yankee stadium in New York was renovated several years ago, total seating capacity had to be reduced in order to accommodate the wider bodies of our adult population. In the last decade, the average weight of American adults increased by about fifteen pounds. In 1990, Americans spent about $40 billion attempting to lose weight. Over $10 billion went to memberships in weight reduction centers and another $30 billion were spent on diet food sales.

Obesity by itself has been associated with several serious health problems and accounts for 15 to 20 percent of the annual mortality rate in the United States. Obesity has long been recognized as a major risk factor for diseases of the cardiovascular system, including coronary heart disease, hypertension, congestive heart failure, elevated blood lipids, atherosclerosis, strokes, thromboembolitic disease, osteoarthritis, varicose veins, and intermittent claudication.

Subsequent research has indicated that the way in which people store fat may also affect the risk for disease. Some individuals have a tendency to store high amounts of fat in the abdominal area, while others store it primarily around the hips and thighs (gluteal/femoral fat). Data indicates that obese individuals with high abdominal fat are clearly at higher risk for coronary heart disease, congestive heart failure, hypertension, strokes, and diabetes

than obese people with similar amounts of total body fat, but stored primarily in the hips and thighs. Relatively new evidence also indicates that among individuals with high abdominal fat, those whose fat deposits are around internal organs (visceral fat) are at even greater risk for disease than those whose abdominal fat is primarily beneath the skin (subcutaneous fat).

A *waist-to-hip ratio test* designed by a panel of scientists appointed by the National Academy of Sciences and the Dietary Guidelines Advisory Council for the U.S. Departments of Agriculture and Health and Human Services recommends that *men need to lose weight if the waist-to-hip ratio is 1.0 or higher. Women need to lose weight if the ratio is .85 or higher.* For instance, the waist-to-hip ratio for a man with a 36-inch waist and a 35-inch hip would be 1.03 (36 ÷ 35). Such a ratio may be indicative of increased risk for disease.

Other research points toward a possible link between obesity and cancer of the colon, rectum, prostate, gallbladder, breast, uterus, and ovaries. It is interesting to note that if all deaths from cancer could be eliminated, the average life span would increase by approximately two years. If obesity was eliminated, life span could increase by as many as seven years. In addition, obesity has been associated with osteoarthritis, ruptured intervertebral discs, gallstones, gout, respiratory insufficiency, and comlications during pregnancy and delivery. Furthermore, it can lead to psychological maladjustment and increased accidental death rate. Life insurance companies are also quick to point out that there is a 150 percent greater mortality rate among overweight males as compared to the average mortality rate.

While there is little disagreement regarding a greater mortality rate among obese people, scientific evidence also points to the fact that the same is true for underweight people. Although a slight change has been seen in recent years, *the social pressure to achieve model-like thinness is still with us and continues to cause a gradual increase in the number of people who develop eating disorders* (anorexia nervosa and bulimia, which will be discussed later in this chapter). *Extreme weight loss can cause the development of such medical conditions as heart damage, gastrointestinal problems, shrinkage of internal organs, immune system abnormalities, disorders of the reproductive system, loss of muscle tissue, damage to the nervous system, and even death.*

Achieving and maintaining recommended body weight is a major objective of a good physical fitness and wellness program (Figure 3.1). The assessment of recommended body weight is discussed in detail in Chapter 6. Next to poor cardiovascular fitness, obesity is the most common problem encountered in fitness and wellness assessments.

Approximately 65 million Americans are either overweight or considered themselves to be

—————— *FIGURE 3.1* ——————

Recommended body weight is best determined through the assessment of body composition.

overweight. About 50 percent of all women and 25 percent of all men are on diets at any given moment. Unfortunately, only 5 to 10 percent of all people who ever initiate a traditional weight loss program are able to lose the desired weight, and worse yet, only one in 200 is able to keep the weight off for a significant period of time. You may ask why the traditional diets have failed. The answer is simply because very few diets teach the importance of lifetime changes in food selection and the role of exercise as the keys to successful weight loss. The 40 billion-dollar diet industry tries to capitalize on the idea that weight can be lost quickly without taking into consideration the consequences of fast weight loss or the importance of lifetime behavioral changes to insure proper weight loss and maintenance.

FAD DIETING

There are several reasons why fad diets continue to deceive people and can claim that weight will indeed be lost if "all" instructions are followed. Most diets are very low in calories and/or deprive the body of certain nutrients, creating a metabolic imbalance that can even cause death. Under such conditions, a lot of the weight loss is in the form of water and protein and not fat. On a crash diet, close to 50 percent of the weight loss is in lean (protein) tissue. When the body uses protein instead of a combination of fats and carbohydrates as a source

of energy, weight is lost as much as ten times faster. A gram of protein yields half the amount of energy that fat does. In the case of muscle protein, one-fifth of protein is mixed with four-fifths water. In other words, each pound of muscle yields only one-tenth the amount of energy of a pound of fat. As a result, most of the weight loss is in the form of water, which on the scale, of course, looks good. Nevertheless, when regular eating habits are resumed, most of the lost weight comes right back.

Some diets only allow the consumption of certain foods. If people would only realize that there are no "magic" foods that will provide all of the necessary nutrients, and that a person has to eat a variety of foods to be well nourished, the diet industry would not be as successful. The unfortunate thing about most of these diets is that they create a nutritional deficiency which at times can be fatal. The reason why some of these diets succeed is because in due time people get tired of eating the same thing day in and day out and eventually start eating less. If they happen to achieve the lower weight, once they go back to old eating habits without implementing permanent dietary changes, weight is quickly gained back again.

A few diets recommend exercise along with caloric restrictions, which, of course, is the best method for weight reduction. A lot of the weight lost is due to exercise; hence, the diet has achieved its purpose. Unfortunately, if no permanent changes in food selection and activity level take place, once dieting and exercise are discontinued, the weight is quickly gained back.

EATING DISORDERS

Anorexia nervosa and bulimia have been classified as physical and emotional problems usually developed as a result of individual, family, and/or social pressures to achieve thinness. These medical disorders are steadily increasing in most industrialized nations, where low-calorie diets and model-like thinness are normal behaviors encouraged by society. Individuals who suffer from eating disorders have an intense fear of becoming obese, which does not disappear even as extreme amounts of weight are lost.

Anorexia nervosa is a condition of self-imposed starvation to lose and then maintain very low body weight. Approximately nineteen of every twenty anorexics are young women. It is estimated that 1 percent of the female population in the United States suffers from this disease. The anorexic seems to fear weight gain more than death from starvation. Furthermore, these individuals have a distorted image of their body and perceive themselves as being fat even when critically emaciated.

Although a genetic predisposition may exist, the anorexic patient often comes from a mother-dominated home, with other possible drug addictions in the family. The syndrome may start following a stressful life event and the uncertainty of the ability to cope efficiently. Because the female role in society is changing more rapidly, women seem to be especially susceptible. Life events such as weight gain, start of menstrual periods, beginning of college, loss of a boyfriend, poor self-esteem, social rejection, start of a professional career, and/or becoming a wife or mother may trigger the syndrome. The person usually begins a diet and may initially feel in control and happy about weight loss, even if not overweight. To speed up the weight loss process, severe dieting is frequently combined with exhaustive exercise and overuse of laxatives and/or diuretics. The individual commonly develops obsessive and compulsive behaviors and emphatically denies the condition. There also appears to be a constant preoccupation with food, meal planning, grocery shopping, and unusual eating habits. As weight is lost and health begins to deteriorate, the anorexic feels weak and tired and may realize that there is a problem but will not discontinue starvation and refuses to accept the behavior as abnormal.

Once significant weight loss and malnutrition begin, typical physical changes become more visible. Some of the more common changes exhibited by anorexics are amenorrhea (cessation of menstruation), digestive difficulties, extreme sensitivity to cold, hair and skin problems, fluid and electrolyte abnormalities (which may lead to an irregular heartbeat and sudden stopping of the heart), injuries to nerves and tendons, abnormalities of immune function, anemia, growth of fine body hair, mental confusion, inability to concentrate, lethargy, depression, skin dryness, and decreased skin and body temperature.

Many of the changes of anorexia nervosa are by no means irreversible. Treatment almost always requires professional help, and the sooner it is started, the higher the chances for reversibility and cure. A combination of medical and psychological techniques is used in therapy to restore proper nutrition, prevent medical complications, and modify the environment or events that triggered the syndrome. *Seldom are anorexics able to overcome the problem by themselves.* Unfortunately, there is strong denial among anorexics, and they are able to hide their condition and deceive friends and relatives quite effectively. Based on their behavior, many individuals meet all of the characteristics of anorexia nervosa, but the condition goes undetected because both thinness and dieting are socially acceptable behaviors. Only a well-trained clinician is able to make a positive diagnosis.

Bulimia, a pattern of binge eating and purging, is more prevalent than anorexia nervosa. For many years it was thought to be a variant of anorexia nervosa, but it is now identified as a separate disease. It afflicts primarily young people, and estimates indicate that as many as one in every five women

on college campuses is affected by it. Bulimia is also more frequent in males than anorexia nervosa.

Bulimics are usually healthy-looking people, well educated, near recommended body weight, who enjoy food and often socialize around it. However, they are emotionally insecure, rely on others, and lack self-confidence and esteem. Maintenance of recommended weight and food are both important to them. As a result of stressful life events or simple compulsion to eat, they periodically engage in binge eating that may last an hour or longer, during which several thousand calories may be consumed. A feeling of deep guilt and shame then follows, along with intense fear of gaining weight. Purging seems to be an easy answer to the problem, and the binging cycle continues without the fear of gaining weight. The most common form of purging is self-induced vomiting, although strong laxatives and emetics are frequently used. Overuse of the latter caused the death of Karen Carpenter in 1983. Near-fasting diets and strenuous bouts of exercise are also commonly seen in bulimics.

Medical problems associated with bulimia include cardiac arrhythmias, amenorrhea, kidney and bladder damage, ulcers, colitis, tearing of the esophagus and/or stomach, tooth erosion, gum damage, and general muscular weakness.

Unlike anorexics, bulimics realize that their behavior is abnormal and feel great shame for their actions. Fearing social rejection, the binge-purging cycle is primarily carried out in secrecy and during unusual hours of the day. Nevertheless, bulimia can be treated successfully when the person realizes that such destructive behavior is not the solution to life's problems. Hopefully, the change in attitude will grasp the individual before permanent or fatal damage is done.

Treatment for anorexia nervosa and bulimia can be initiated on most school campuses by contacting either the school's counseling center or the health center. Local hospitals also offer treatment for these conditions. Support groups, frequently led by professional personnel, are available in many communities. The latter are usually provided free of charge.

PHYSIOLOGY OF WEIGHT LOSS

Even though only a few years ago the principles that govern a weight loss and maintenance program seemed to be pretty clear, we now know that the final answers are not yet in. The traditional concepts related to weight control have been centered around three assumptions: (1) that balancing food intake against output allows a person to achieve recommended weight; (2) that fat people just eat too much; and (3) that it really does not matter to the human body how much (or little) fat is stored. While there may be some truth to these statements, they are still open to much debate and research.

The Energy-Balancing Equation

The energy-balancing equation basically states that as long as caloric input equals caloric output, the person will not gain or lose weight. If caloric intake exceeds the output, the individual will gain weight. When output exceeds input, weight is lost. This principle is simple, and if daily energy requirements could be accurately determined, it seems reasonable that the conscious mind could be used to balance caloric intake versus output. Unfortunately, this is not always the case because there are large individual differences, genetic and lifestyle related, which determine the number of calories required to maintain or lose body weight. Some general guidelines for estimating daily caloric intake according to lifestyle patterns are given in Table 3.1. Remember that this is only an estimated figure and, as will be discussed later on in this chapter, it only serves as a starting point from whence individual adjustments will have to be made.

Perhaps some examples may help explain this. It is well known that *one pound of fat equals 3,500 calories*. Assuming that the basic daily caloric expenditure for a given person is 2,500 calories, if this person decreased the daily intake by 500 calories per day, one pound of fat should be lost in seven days ($500 \times 7 = 3,500$). Research has shown, however, and many dieters have probably experienced, that *even when caloric input is carefully balanced against caloric output, weight loss does not always come as predicted*. Furthermore, *two people with similar measured caloric intake and output will not necessarily lose weight at the same rate*.

The most common explanation given by many in the past regarding individual differences in weight loss or weight gain was variations in human metabolism from one person to the other. We have all seen people who can eat "all day long" and yet not gain an ounce of weight, while others cannot even "dream" about food without gaining weight.

Since many experts did not believe that such extreme differences could be accounted to human metabolism alone, several theories have been developed that may better explain these individual variations.

Setpoint Theory

Results of several research studies seem to indicate that there is a weight-regulating mechanism (WRM) located in the hypothalamus of the brain that regulates how much the body should weigh. This mechanism has a setpoint that controls both appetite and the amount of fat stored. It is hypothesized that the setpoint works like a thermostat for body fat, maintaining body weight fairly constantly because it knows at all times the exact amount of adipose tissue stored in the fat cells. Some people have high settings, and others are low. If body weight decreases (as in dieting), this change is sensed by the setpoint which, in turn, triggers the WRM to increase the person's appetite or make the body conserve energy to maintain the "set" weight. The opposite may also be true. Some people who consciously try to gain weight have an extremely difficult time in doing so. In this case, the WRM decreases appetite or causes the body to waste energy to maintain the lower weight.

Dieting Makes People Fat!

Every person has his/her own certain body fat percentage (as established by the setpoint) that the body attempts to maintain. The genetic instinct to survive tells the body that fat storage is vital, and therefore it sets an inherently acceptable fat level. This level remains pretty constant or may gradually climb due to poor lifestyle habits. For instance, under strict caloric reductions, the body may make extreme metabolic adjustments in an effort to maintain its setpoint for fat. The basal metabolic rate may drop dramatically against a consistent negative caloric balance, and a person may be on a plateau for days or even weeks without losing much weight. Dietary restriction alone will not lower the setpoint even though weight and fat may be lost. When the dieter goes back to the normal or even below normal caloric intake, at which the weight may have been stable for a long period of time, the fat loss is quickly regained as the body strives to regain a comfortable fat store.

Let's use a practical illustration. A person would like to lose some body fat and assumes that a stable body weight has been reached at an average daily caloric intake of 1,800 calories (no weight gain or loss occurs at this daily intake). This person now starts a strict low-calorie diet, or even worse, a near-fasting diet in an attempt to achieve rapid

---

TABLE 3.1

Average Caloric Requirement Per Pound of Body Weight Based on Lifestyle Patterns and Gender

	Calories per pound	
	Men	Women*
Sedentary — Limited physical activity	13.0	12.0
Moderate physical activity	15.0	13.5
Hard Labor — Strenuous physical effort	17.0	15.0

*Pregnant or lactating women add three calories to these values.

weight loss. Immediately the body activates its survival mechanism and readjusts its metabolism to a lower caloric balance. After a few weeks of dieting at less than 400 to 600 calories per day, the body can now maintain its normal functions at 1,000 calories per day. Having lost the desired weight, the person terminates the diet but realizes that the original caloric intake of 1,800 calories per day will need to be decreased to maintain the new lower weight. Therefore, to adjust to the new lower body weight, the intake is restricted to about 1,500 calories per day, but the individual is surprised to find that even at this lower daily intake (300 fewer calories), weight is gained back at a rate of one pound every one to two weeks. This new lowered metabolic rate may take a year or more after terminating the diet to kick back up to its normal level.

From this explanation, it is clear that individuals should never go on very low-calorie diets. Not only will this practice decrease resting metabolic rate, but it will also deprive the body of the basic daily nutrients required for normal physiological functions. Under no circumstances should a person ever engage in diets below 1,200 and 1,500 calories for women and men, respectively. Remember that weight (fat) is gained over a period of months and years and not overnight. Equally, weight loss should be accomplished gradually and not abruptly. Daily caloric intakes of 1,200 to 1,500 calories will still provide the necessary nutrients if properly distributed over the four basic food groups (meeting the daily required servings from each group). Of course, the individual will have to learn which foods meet the requirements and yet are low in fat and sugar. This can be easily learned after only a few days of following the "New American Eating Guide" explained in Chapter 2.

Setpoint and Nutrition

Other researchers feel that a second way in which the setpoint may work is by keeping track of the nutrients and calories that are consumed on a daily basis. The body, like a cash register, records the daily food intake, and the brain will not feel satisfied until the calories and nutrients have been "registered."

For some people this setpoint for calories and nutrients seems to work regardless of the amount of physical activity that they do, as long as it is not too exhausting. Numerous studies have shown that hunger does not increase with moderate physical activity. In such cases, people can choose to lose weight by either going hungry or by increasing daily physical (aerobic) activity. The increased number of calories burned through exercise will help decrease body fat.

The most common question that individuals seem to have regarding the setpoint is how can it be lowered so that the body will feel comfortable at a lower fat percentage. Several factors seem to have a direct effect on the setpoint. *Aerobic exercise, a diet high in complex carbohydrates,* nicotine, and amphetamines all have *been shown to decrease the fat thermostat.* The last two, however, are more destructive than the overfatness, thereby eliminating themselves as reasonable alternatives (it has been said that as far as the extra strain on the heart is concerned, smoking one pack of cigarettes per day is the equivalent of carrying fifty to seventy-five pounds of excess body fat). On the other hand, *a diet high in fats and refined carbohydrates, near-fasting diets, and perhaps even artificial sweeteners seems to increase the setpoint.* Therefore, it looks as though the only practical and effective way to lower the setpoint and lose fat weight is through a combination of aerobic exercise and a diet high in complex carbohydrates and low in fat and sugar.

Because of the effects of proper food management on the body's setpoint, many nutritionists now believe that the total number of calories should not be a concern in a weight control program, but rather the source of those calories. In this regard, most of the effort is spent in retraining eating habits, increasing the intake of complex carbohydrates and high-fiber foods, and decreasing the use of refined carbohydrates (sugars) and fats. In addition, *a "diet" is no longer viewed as a temporary tool to aid in weight loss, but rather as a permanent change in eating behaviors to insure adequate weight management and health enhancement.* The role of increased physical activity must also be considered, because successful weight loss, maintenance, and recommended body composition are seldom achieved without a regular exercise program.

Yellow Fat Versus Brown Fat

For years it has been known that there are two different types of fat — yellow and brown. The proportion of yellow to brown could be another factor that influences weight regulation. The average ratio is about 99 percent yellow fat to 1 percent brown fat. The difference between the two is that yellow fat simply stores energy in the form of fat, while brown fat has a high amount of the iron-containing hemoglobin pigment found in red blood cells. The brown cells do not store fat, but rather have the capacity to produce body heat by burning the fat. Under resting conditions, brown fat produces an estimated 25 percent of the total body heat, and, according to Dr. George A. Bray of the Los Angeles Medical Center at Harbour University of California, the brown fat can actually produce as much heat as the entire rest of the body.

The fact that brown fat converts food energy to heat may also explain why some individuals simply do not gain weight. Even though the amount of brown fat is genetically determined and cannot be changed throughout life, people with only slightly higher levels may have an advantage when it comes to weight control. It is also possible that some individuals may have more active brown cells that generate more heat. Perhaps you have come across thin people who are warm even when everyone else seems comfortable. On the contrary, since one of the basic functions of fat is body heat preservation, obese people who are successful in losing weight but have a lower proportion of or less active brown fat may feel cold when it is actually pleasantly warm.

Diet and Metabolism

Fat can be lost using proper food selection, aerobic exercise, and/or caloric restrictions. However, when weight loss is pursued by means of dietary restrictions alone, there will always be a decrease in lean body mass (muscle protein, along with vital organ protein). The amount of lean body mass lost depends exclusively on the caloric restriction of your diet. *In near-fasting diets, up to 50 percent of the weight loss can be lean body mass, and the other 50 percent will be actual fat loss. When diet is combined with exercise, close to 100 percent of the weight loss will be in the form of fat*, and there may actually be an increase in lean tissue. Lean body mass loss is never desirable because it weakens the organs and muscles and slows down the metabolism.

Contrary to some beliefs, metabolism does not decrease with age. It has been shown that basal metabolism is directly related to lean body weight. The greater the lean tissue, the higher the metabolic rate. What happens is that as a result of sedentary living and less physical activity, the lean component decreases and fat tissue increases. The organism, though, continues to use the same amount of oxygen per pound of lean body mass. Since fat is considered metabolically inert from the point of view of caloric use, the lean tissue uses most of the oxygen even at rest. Consequently, as muscle and organ mass decreases, the energy requirements at rest also decrease.

Decreases in lean body mass are commonly seen with aging (due to physical inactivity) and severely restricted diets. The loss of lean body mass may also account for the lower metabolic rate described under "dieting makes people fat" and the lengthy period of time that it takes to kick back up. There are no diets with caloric intakes below 1,200 to 1,500 calories that can insure no loss of lean body mass. Even at this intake, there is some loss unless the diet is combined with exercise. Many diets have claimed that the lean component is unaltered with their particular diet, but the simple truth is that regardless of what nutrients may be added to the diet, if caloric restrictions are too severe, there will always be a loss of lean tissue.

Unfortunately, too many people constantly engage in low-calorie diets, and every time they do so, the metabolic rate keeps slowing down as more lean tissue is lost. It is not uncommon to find individuals in the forties or older who weigh the same as they did when they were twenty and feel that they are at recommended body weight. Nevertheless, during this span of twenty years or more, they have "dieted" all too many times without engaging in an exercise program. The weight is regained shortly after terminating each diet, but most of that gain is in fat. Perhaps at age twenty they weighed 150 pounds and only had 15 to 16 percent body fat. Now at age forty, even though they still weigh 150 pounds, they may have 30 percent body fat. They may feel that they are at recommended body weight and wonder why they are eating very little and still have a difficult time maintaining that weight.

Exercise: The Key to Successful Weight Loss and Weight Maintenance

Based on the preceding discussion on weight control, it can be easily concluded that exercise is the key to weight loss and weight maintenance (Figure 3.2). Not only will exercise maintain lean tissue, but advocates of the setpoint theory also indicate that exercise resets the fat thermostat to a new lower level. For a lot of people this change occurs rapidly, but in some instances it may take time. There are overweight individuals who have faithfully exercised on an almost daily basis, sixty minutes at a time, for a whole year before significant weight changes started to occur. Individuals who have a very "sticky" setpoint will need to be patient and persistent.

For individuals who are trying to lose weight, a combination of aerobic and strength-training exercises works best. Aerobic exercise is the key to offset

FIGURE 3.2

Regular participation in a lifetime exercise program is the key to successful weight management.

the setpoint, and because of the continuity and duration of these types of activities, many calories are burned in the process. On the other hand, strength-training exercises have the greatest impact in increasing lean body mass. *Each additional pound of muscle tissue can raise the basal metabolic rate between 50 and 100 calories per day. Using the conservative estimate of 50 calories per day, an individual who adds five pounds of muscle tissue as a result of strength training would increase the basal metabolic rate by 250 calories per day, or the equivalent of 91,250 calories per year.*

Strength training is especially recommended for people who feel that they are at optimal body weight, but yet the body fat percentage is higher than recommended. Nevertheless, the number of calories burned during an "average" hour of strength training is significantly less than during an hour of aerobic exercise. Due to the high intensity of weight training, frequent rest intervals are required to recover from each set of exercise. The average individual only engages in actual lifting a total of ten to twelve minutes out of every hour of exercise. Weight loss can occur with a regular strength-training program but at a much slower rate. However, the benefits of increments in lean tissue are enjoyed in the long run. The guidelines for developing aerobic and strength-training programs are given in Chapters 5 and 8 and their respective labs.

Since exercise leads to an increase in lean body mass, it is not uncommon for body weight to remain the same or increase when you initiate an exercise program, while inches and percent body fat decrease. The increase in lean tissue results in an increased functional capacity of the human body. With exercise, most of the weight loss is seen after a few weeks of training, when the lean component has stabilized.

"Skinny" people should also realize that the only healthy manner to gain weight is through exercise, primarily strength-training exercises, and a slight increase in caloric intake. Attempting to gain weight by just overeating will increase the fat component and not the lean component, which is not conducive to better health. Consequently, exercise is the best solution to weight (fat) reduction as well as weight (lean) gain.

A strength-training program such is outlined in Chapter 8 is the best approach to increase body weight. To produce the greatest amount of muscle hypertrophy, the training program should include at least two exercises of three to five sets for each major body part (see Principles Involved in Strength Training, Chapter 8). Each set should consist of about 10 repetitions maximum.

While the metabolic cost of synthesizing one pound of muscle tissue is still unclear, it has been estimated that an additional daily 500 calories, including 15 grams of protein above the RDA, are

required to gain an average of one pound of muscle tissue per week. Based on the typical American diet, the extra 15 grams of protein are not necessary. The average American already consumes 30 to 60 grams of daily protein above the RDA. The additional 500 calories should be provided in the form of complex carbohydrates because most diets are already too high in fat. Keep in mind, though, that if the increased caloric intake is not accompanied by a strength-training program, the increase in body weight will be in the form of fat and not muscle tissue.

It is also important to clarify that research has shown that there is no such thing as spot reducing or losing "cellulite" from certain body parts. Some people use the term cellulite in reference to fat deposits that "bulge out." These deposits are nothing but enlarged fat cells due to excessive accumulation of body fat. Just doing several sets of daily sit-ups will not help to get rid of fat in the midsection of the body. When fat comes off, it does so from throughout the entire body, and not just the exercised area. The greatest proportion of fat may come off the largest fat deposits, but the caloric output of a few sets of sit-ups is practically nil to have a real effect on total body fat reduction. The amount of exercise has to be much longer to have a real impact on weight reduction.

Other common fallacies regarding quick weight loss are the use of rubberized sweatsuits, steam baths, and/or mechanical vibrators. When an individual wears a sweatsuit or steps into a sauna, there is a significant amount of water loss and not fat. Sure, it looks nice immediately after when you step on the scale, but it is just a false loss of weight. As soon as you replace body fluids, the weight is quickly gained back. Wearing rubberized sweatsuits not only increases the rate of body fluid loss, which is vital during prolonged exercise, but also increases core temperature. Dehydration through these methods leads to impaired cellular function and in extreme cases even death. Similarly, mechanical vibrators are worthless in a weight control program. Vibrating belts and turning rollers may feel good but require no effort whatsoever on the part of the muscles. Fat cannot be "shaken off" — it has to be burned off in muscle tissue.

Although we now know that a negative caloric balance of 3,500 calories will not always result in an exact loss of one pound of fat, the role of exercise in achieving a negative balance by burning additional calories is significant in weight reduction and maintenance programs. Sadly, some individuals claim that the amount of calories burned during exercise is hardly worth the effort. These individuals feel that it is easier to cut the daily intake by some 200 calories, rather than participate in some sort of exercise that would burn the equivalent amount of calories. The only problem is that the willpower to cut those 200 calories only lasts a few weeks, and then it is right back to the old eating patterns. If a person gets into the habit of exercising regularly, say three times per week, running three miles per exercise session (about 300 calories burned), this would represent 900 calories in one week, 3,600 in one month, or 43,200 calories per year. This apparently insignificant amount of exercise could mean as many as twelve extra pounds of fat in one year, twenty-four in two, and so on. We tend to forget that our weight creeps up gradually over the years, and not just overnight. Hardly worth the effort? And we have not even taken into consideration the increase in lean tissue, the possible resetting of the setpoint, the benefits to the cardiovascular system, and most important, the improved quality of life! There is very little argument that the fundamental reasons for overfatness and obesity are lack of physical activity and sedentary living.

—————— *FIGURE 3.3* ——————
Water Aerobics: A relatively new form of aerobic exercise that is conducive to weight loss without the fear of injuries.

LOSING WEIGHT THE SOUND AND SENSIBLE WAY

Dieting has never been fun and never will be. *Individuals who have a weight problem and are serious about losing weight will have to make exercise a regular part of their daily life, along with proper food management, and perhaps even sensible adjustments in caloric intake.* Some precautions are necessary, since excessive body fat is a risk factor for cardiovascular disease. Depending on the extent of the weight problem, a medical examination and possibly a stress ECG (see Figure 1.9, Chapter 1) may be required prior to initiating the exercise program. A physician should be consulted in this regard.

Significantly overweight individuals may also have to choose activities where they will not have to support their own body weight, but that will still be effective in burning calories. Joint and muscle injuries are very common among overweight individuals who participate in weight-bearing exercises such as walking, jogging, and aerobic dancing. Swimming may not be a good exercise either. The increased body fat makes the person more buoyant, and most people do not have the skill level to swim fast enough to get an optimal training effect. The tendency is to just "float" along, limiting the amount of calories burned as well as the benefits to the cardiovascular system. Some better alternatives are riding a bicycle (either road or stationary), walking in a shallow pool, water aerobics (Figure 3.3), or running in place in deep water (treading water). The latter forms of water exercise are quickly gaining in popularity and has proven to be effective in achieving weight reduction without the "pain" and fear of injuries. The caloric expenditure of selected physical activities is given in Table 3.2, and you will be able to determine your own daily caloric requirement in Lab 3A.

How long should each exercise session last? To develop and maintain cardiovascular fitness, twenty to thirty minutes of exercise at the ideal target rate, three to five times per week is sufficient (see Chapter 5). For weight loss purposes, many experts recommend exercising for at least 45 minutes at a time, five to six times per week. Nevertheless, a person should not try to increase the duration and frequency of exercise too fast. It is recommended that unconditioned beginners start with about fifteen minutes three times per week, and then gradually increase the duration by approximately five minutes each week and the frequency by one day per week during the next three to four weeks.

One final benefit of exercise as related to weight control is that fat can be burned more efficiently. Since both carbohydrates and fats are sources of energy, when the glucose levels begin to decrease during prolonged exercise, more fat is used as energy substrate. Equally important is the fact that fat-burning enzymes increase with aerobic training. The role of these enzymes is significant, because fat can only be lost by burning it in muscle. As the concentration of the enzymes increases, so does the ability to burn fat.

In addition to exercise and adequate food management, many experts still recommend that individuals take a look at their daily caloric intake and compare it against the estimated daily requirement. The daily caloric intake is determined through the nutritional analysis (see Lab 2A). While this intake may not be as crucial if proper food

———— *TABLE 3.2* ————

Caloric Expenditure of Selected Physical Activities (expressed in calories per pound of body weight per minute of activity)

Activity*	Cal/lb/min	Activity	Cal/lb/min
Aerobic Dance		Running	
Moderate	0.075	11.0 min/mile	0.070
Vigorous	0.095	8.5 min/mile	0.090
Archery	0.030	7.0 min/mile	0.102
Badminton		6.0 min/mile	0.114
Recreation	0.038	Deep water[a]	0.100
Competition	0.065	Skating (moderate)	0.038
Baseball	0.031	Skiing	
Basketball		Downhill	0.060
Moderate	0.046	Level (5 mph)	0.078
Competition	0.063	Soccer	0.059
Bowling	0.030	Strength Training	0.050
Calisthenics	0.033	Swimming (crawl)	
Cycling (level)		20 yds/min	0.031
5.5 mph	0.033	25 yds/min	0.040
10.0 mph	0.050	45 yds/min	0.057
13.0 mph	0.071	50 yds/min	0.070
Dance		Table Tennis	0.030
Moderate	0.030	Tennis	
Vigorous	0.055	Moderate	0.045
Golf	0.030	Competition	0.064
Gymnastics		Volleyball	0.030
Light	0.030	Walking	
Heavy	0.056	4.5 mph	0.045
Handball	0.064	Shallow pool	0.090
Hiking	0.040	Water Aerobics	
Judo/Karate	0.086	Moderate	0.080
Racquetball	0.065	Vigorous	0.100
Rope Jumpiing	0.060	Wrestling	0.085
Rowing (vigorous)	0.090		

*Values are only for actual time engaged in the activity.   [a]Treading water

Adapted from:
  Allsen, P. E., J. M. Harrison, and B. Vance. *Fitness for Life: An Individualized Approach.* Dubuque, IA: Wm. C. Brown, 1989.
  Bucher, C. A., and W. E. Prentice, *Fitness for College and Life.* St. Louis: Times Mirror/Mosby College Publishing, 1989.
  Consolazio, C. F., R. E. Johnson, and L. J. Pecora. *Physiological measurements of Metabolic Functions in Man.* New York: McGraw-Hill, 1963.
  Hockey, R. V. *Physical Fitness: The Pathway to Healthful Living.* St. Louis: Times Mirror/Mosby College Publishing, 1989.

management and exercise are incorporated into the person's lifestyle, it is still beneficial in certain circumstances. All too often the nutritional analysis reveals that "faithful" dieters are not consuming enough calories and actually need to increase the daily caloric intake (combined with an exercise program) in order to get the metabolism to kick back up to a normal level.

There are other cases where knowledge of the daily caloric requirement is needed for successful weight control. The reasons for prescribing a certain caloric figure to either maintain or lose weight are: (a) it takes time to develop new behaviors and some individuals have difficulty in changing and adjusting to the new eating habits; (b) many individuals are in such poor physical condition that it takes them a long time to increase their activity level so as to have a significant impact in offsetting

the setpoint and in burning enough calories to aid in body fat loss; (c) some dieters find it difficult to succeed unless they can count calories; and (d) some individuals will simply not alter their food selection. All of these people can benefit from caloric intake guidelines, and in many instances a sensible caloric decrease is helpful in the early stages of the weight reduction program. For the latter group, that is, those who will not alter their food selection (which will still increase the risk for chronic diseases), a significant increase in physical activity, a negative caloric balance, or a combination of both are the only solutions for successful weight loss.

An estimated daily caloric requirement can be determined by using Tables 3.1 and 3.2. This activity will be conducted in Lab 3A. Keep in mind that this is only an estimated value, and individual adjustments related to many of the factors discussed in this chapter may be required to establish a more precise value. Nevertheless, the estimated value will provide an initial guideline for weight control and/or reduction.

The average daily caloric requirement without exercise is based on typical lifestyle patterns, total body weight, and gender. Individuals who hold jobs that require heavy manual labor burn more calories during the day as opposed to those who hold sedentary jobs (such as working behind a desk). To determine the activity level, refer to Table 3.1 and rate yourself accordingly. Since the number given in Table 3.1 is per pound of body weight, you will need to multiply your current weight by that number. For example, the typical caloric requirement to maintain body weight for a moderately active male who weighs 160 pounds would be 2,400 calories (160 lbs × 15 cal/lb).

The second step is to determine the average number of calories that are burned on a daily basis as a result of exercise. To obtain this number, you will need to figure out the total number of minutes in which you engage in exercise on a weekly basis, and then determine the daily average exercise time. For instance, a person cycling at thirteen miles per hour, five times per week, for thirty minutes each time, exercises a total of 150 minutes per week (5 × 30). The average daily exercise time would be twenty-one minutes (150 ÷ 7 and round off to the lowest unit). Next, using Table 3.2, determine the energy requirement for the activity (or activities) that have been chosen for the exercise program. In the case of cycling (thirteen miles per hour), the requirement is .071 calories per pound of body weight per minute of activity (cal/lb/min). With a body weight of 160 pounds, each minute this man would burn 11.4 calories (body weight × .071 or 160 × .071). In twenty-one minutes, he would burn approximately 240 calories (21 × 11.4).

The third step is to determine the estimated total caloric requirement, with exercise, needed to maintain body weight. This value is obtained by adding the typical daily requirement (without exercise) and the average calories burned through exercise. In our example, it would be 2,640 calories (2,400 + 240).

If a negative caloric balance is recommended to lose weight, this person would have to consume less than 2,640 daily calories to achieve the objective. Because of the many different factors that play a role in weight control, the previous value is only an estimated daily requirement. Furthermore, to lose weight, it would be difficult to say that exactly one pound of fat would be lost in one week if daily intake was reduced by 500 calories (500 × 7 = 3,500 calories, or the equivalent of one pound of fat). Nevertheless, the estimated daily caloric figure will provide a target guideline for weight control. Periodic readjustments are necessary because there can be significant differences among individuals, and the estimated daily cost will change as you lose weight and modify your exercise habits.

The recommended number of calories to be subtracted from the daily intake to obtain a negative caloric balance depends on the typical daily requirement. At this point, the best recommendation is to moderately decrease the daily intake, never below 1,200 calories for women and 1,500 for men. A good rule to follow is to restrict the intake by no more than 500 calories if the daily requirement is below 3,000 calories. For caloric requirements in excess of 3,000, as many as 1,000 calories per day may be subtracted from the total intake. Remember also that the daily distribution should be approximately 60 percent carbohydrates (mostly complex carbohydrates), less than 30 percent fat, and about 15 percent protein.

The time of day when food is consumed may also play a role in weight reduction. A study conducted at the Aerobics Research Center in Dallas, Texas, indicated that when a person is on a diet, weight is lost most effectively if the majority of the calories are consumed before 1:00 p.m. and not during the evening meal. The recommendation made at this center is that when a person is attempting to lose weight, a minimum of 25 percent of the total daily calories should be consumed for breakfast, 50 percent for lunch, and 25 percent or less at dinner. Other experts have indicated that if most of your daily calories are consumed during one meal, the body may perceive that something is wrong and will slow down your metabolism so that it can store a greater amount of calories in the form of fat. Also, eating most of the calories in one meal causes you to go hungry the rest of the day, making it more difficult to adhere to the diet.

The principle of consuming most of the calories earlier in the day not only seems to be helpful in losing weight, but also in the management of atherosclerosis. According to research, the time of day when most of the fats and cholesterol are consumed can have an impact on blood lipids and coronary heart disease. Peak digestion time following a heavy meal takes place about seven hours after that meal. If most lipids are consumed during the evening meal, digestion peaks while the person is sound asleep, at a time when the metabolism is at its lowest rate. Consequently, the body may not be able to metabolize fats and cholesterol as effectively, leading to higher blood lipids and increasing the risk for atherosclerosis and coronary heart disease.

To monitor daily progress, you may use a form similar to Figure 2B.1 (Lab 2B). Meeting the basic requirements from each food group should be given top priority. The caloric content for each food is found in the Nutritive Value of Selected Foods list in Appendix A, Table A.1. The information should be recorded immediately after each meal to obtain a more precise record. According to the person's progress, adjustments can be made in the typical daily requirement and/or the exercise program.

TIPS TO HELP CHANGE BEHAVIOR AND ADHERE TO A LIFETIME WEIGHT MANAGEMENT PROGRAM

Achieving and maintaining recommended body composition is by no means an impossible task, but it does require desire and commitment. *If adequate weight management is to become a priority in life, people must realize that some retraining of behavior is crucial for success*. Modifying old habits and developing new positive behaviors take time. The following list of management techniques has been successfully used by individuals to change detrimental behavior and adhere to a positive lifetime weight control program. People are not expected to use all of the strategies listed, but they should check the ones that would apply and help them in developing a retraining program.

1. **Commitment to change.** The first ingredient to modify behavior is the desire to do so. The reasons for change must be more important than those for carrying on with present lifestyle patterns. People must accept the fact that there is a problem and decide by themselves whether they really want to change. If a sincere commitment is there, the chances for success are already enhanced.

2. **Set realistic goals.** Most people with a weight problem would like to lose weight in a relatively short period of time but fail to realize that the weight problem developed over a span of several years. A sound weight reduction and maintenance program can only be accomplished by establishing new lifetime eating and exercise habits, both of which take time to develop.

   In setting a realistic long-term goal, short-term objectives should also be planned. The long-term goal may be a decrease in body fat to 20 percent of total body weight. The short-term objective may be a 1 percent decrease in body fat each month. Such objectives allow for regular evaluation and help maintain motivation and renewed commitment to achieve the long-term goal.

3. **Incorporate exercise into the program.** Selecting enjoyable activities, places, times, equipment, and people to work with enhances exercise adherence. Details on developing a complete exercise program are found in Chapters 5 (cardiovascular), 7 (strength), and 9 (flexibility).

4. **Develop healthy eating patterns.** Plan on eating three regular meals per day consistent with the body's nutritional requirements. Learn to differentiate between hunger and appetite. Hunger is the actual physical need for food. Appetite is a desire for food, usually triggered by factors such as stress, habit, boredom, depression, food availability, or just the thought of food itself. Eating only when there is a physical need is wise weight management. In this regard, developing and sticking to a regular meal pattern helps control hunger.

5. **Avoid automatic eating.** Many people associate certain daily activities with eating. For example, people eat while cooking, watching television, reading, talking on the telephone, or visiting with neighbors. Most of the time, the foods consumed in such situations lack nutritional value or are high in sugar and fat.

6. **Stay busy.** People tend to eat more when they sit around and do nothing. Keeping the mind and body occupied with activities not associated with eating helps decrease the desire to eat. Try walking, cycling, playing sports, gardening, sewing, or visiting a library, a museum, a park, etc. Develop other skills and interests or try something new and exciting to break the routine of life.

7. **Plan your meals ahead of time.** Wise shopping is required to accomplish this objective (by the way, when shopping, do so on a full stomach, since such a practice will decrease impulsive buying of unhealthy foods — and then snacking on the way home). Include whole-grain breads and cereals, fruits and vegetables, low-fat milk and dairy products, lean meats, fish, and poultry.

8. **Cook wisely.** Decrease the use of fat and refined foods in food preparation. Trim all visible fat off meats and remove skin off poultry prior to cooking. Skim the fat off gravies and soups. Bake, broil, and boil instead of frying. Use butter, cream, mayonnaise, and salad dressings sparingly. Avoid shellfish, coconut oil, palm oil, and cocoa butter. Prepare plenty of bulky foods. Add whole-grain breads and cereals, vegetables, and legumes to most meals. Try fruits for dessert. Beware of soda pop, fruit juices, and fruit-flavored drinks. Drink plenty of water — at least six glasses a day.

9. **Do not serve more food than can or should be eaten.** Measure the food portions and keep serving dishes away from the table. In this manner,

less food is consumed, seconds are more difficult to obtain, and appetite is decreased because food is not visible. People should not be forced to eat when they are satisfied (including children after they have already had a healthy, nutritious serving).

10. **Learn to eat slowly and at the table only.** Eating is one of the pleasures of life, and we need to take time to enjoy it. Eating on the run is detrimental because the body is not given sufficient time to "register" nutritive and caloric consumption, and overeating usually occurs before the fullness signal is perceived. Always eating at the table also forces people to take time out to eat and will decrease snacking between meals, primarily because of the extra time and effort that are required to sit down and eat. When done eating, do not sit around the table. Clean up and put the food away to avoid unnecessary snacking.

11. **Avoid social binges.** Social gatherings are a common place for self-defeating behavior. Practice visual imagery prior to attending any social gatherings. That is, plan ahead and visualize yourself in that particular gathering. Do not feel pressured to eat or drink, nor rationalize in these situations. Choose low-calorie foods and entertain yourself with other activities such as dancing and talking.

12. **Beware of raids on the refrigerator and the cookie jar.** When such occur, attempt to take control of the situation. Stop and think what is taking place. For those who have difficulty in avoiding such raids, environmental management is recommended. Do not bring high-calorie, high-sugar, and/or high-fat foods into the house. If they are brought into the house, they ought to be stored in places where they are difficult to get to or are less visible. If they are unseen or not readily available, there will be less temptation. Keeping them in places like the garage and basement may be sufficient to discourage many people from taking the time and effort to go get them. By no means should treats be completely eliminated, but all things should be done in moderation.

13. **Practice adequate stress management techniques.** Many people snack and increase food consumption when confronted with stressful situations. Eating is not a stress-releasing activity and can in reality aggravate the problem if weight control is an issue. Several stress management techniques are discussed in Chapter 14.

14. **Monitor changes and reward accomplishments.** Feedback on fat loss, lean tissue gain, and/or weight loss is a reward in itself. Awareness of changes in body composition also helps reinforce new behaviors. Furthermore, being able to exercise uninterruptedly for fifteen, twenty, thirty, sixty minutes, or swimming a certain distance, running a mile, etc., are all accomplishments that deserve recognition. When certain objectives are met, rewards that are not related to eating are encouraged. Buy new clothing, a tennis racquet, a bicycle, exercise shoes, or something else that is special and would have not been acquired otherwise.

15. **Think positive.** Avoid negative thoughts on how difficult it might be to change past behaviors. Instead, think of the benefits that will be reaped, such as feeling, looking, and functioning better, plus enjoying better health and improving the quality of life. Attempt to stay away from negative environments and people who will not be supportive. Those who do not have the same desires and/or encourage self-defeating behaviors should be avoided.

IN CONCLUSION

There is no simple and quick way to take off excessive body fat and keep it off for good. *Weight management is accomplished through a lifetime commitment to physical activity and adequate food selection.* When engaged in a weight (fat) reduction program, people may also have to moderately decrease caloric intake and implement appropriate strategies to modify unhealthy eating behaviors.

During the process of behavior modification, it is almost inevitable to relapse and engage in past negative behaviors. The three most common factors leading to relapse are: (a) stress-related factors (major life changes, depression, job changes, and illness); (b) social reasons (entertaining, eating out, business travel); and (c) self-enticing behaviors (placing yourself in a situation to see how much you can get away with; e.g., "one small taste will not hurt;" leading to "I will just eat one slice;" and finally, "I have not done so well, I might as well eat some more."

Keep in mind, nevertheless, that making mistakes is human and does not necessarily mean failure. Failure comes to those who give up and do not use previous experiences to build upon and, in turn, develop appropriate skills that will prevent self-defeating behaviors in the future. "If there is a will, there is a way," and those who persist will reap the rewards.

LABORATORY EXPERIENCES

LAB 3A: Estimation of Daily Caloric Requirement.

LAB PREPARATION: None.

LAB 3B: Behavioral Objectives for Weight Management.

LAB PREPARATION: Read Chapters 2 and 3 of this textbook.

References

1. Adams, T. D., et. al. *Fitness for Life*. Salt Lake City, UT: Intermountain Health Care, Inc., 1983.

2. Anderson, A. J., et. al. "Body Fat Distribution, Plasma Lipids and Lipoproteins." *Arteriosclerosis* 8:88-94, 1988.

3. Bennett, W., and J. Gurin. "Do Diets Really Work?" *Science* 42-50, March 1982.

4. Bouchard, C., and F. E. Johnson (Editors). *Fat Distribution During Growth and Later Health Outcomes*. New York: Alan R. Liss, 1988.

5. "Brown Fat is Good Fat." *The Health Letter*. December 11, 1981.

6. "Brown Fat/White Fat." *Aviation Medical Bulletin*. June, 1981.

7. Cumming, C., and V. Newman. *Eater's Guide: Nutrition Basis for Busy People*. Englewood Cliffs, NJ: Prentice-Hall, 1981.

8. Hafen, B. Q., A. L. Thygerson, K.J. Frandsen. *Behavioral Guidelines for Health & Wellness*. Englewood, CO: Morton Publishing Company, 1988.

9. Hoeger, W. W. K. *The Complete Guide for the Development & Implementation of Health Promotion Programs*. Englewood, CO: Morton Publishing Company, 1987.

10. Morgan, B. L. G. *The Lifelong Nutrition Guide*. Englewood Cliffs, NJ: Prentice-Hall, 1983.

11. National Academy of Sciences. "Diet and Health: Implications for Reducing Chronic Disease Risk." Washington, D.C. National Academy Press, 1989.

12. Jenkins, D. J. A., et. al. "Nibbling versus Gorging: Metabolic Advantages of Increased Meal Frequency." *The New England Journal of Medicine* 321(14):929-934, 1989.

13. Perkins, K. A., L. H. Epstein, B. L. Marks, R. L. Stiller, and R. G. Jacob. "The Effect of Nicotine on Energy Expenditure During Light Physical Activity." *The New England Journal of Medicine* 320(14):898-903, 1989.

14. Remington, D., A. G. Fisher, and E. A. Parent. *How to Lower Your Fat Thermostat*. Provo, UT: Vitality House International, Inc., 1983.

15. Steen, S. N., R. A. Oppliger, and K. D. Brownell. "Metabolic Effects of Repeated Weight Loss and Regain in Adolescent Wrestlers." *Journal of the American Medical Association* 260:47-50, 1988.

16. Stunkard, A. J., T. I. A. Sorensen, C. Hanis, T. W. Teasdale, R. Chakraborty, W. J. Schull, and F. Schulsinger. "An Adoption Study of Human Obesity." *The New England Journal of Medicine* 314(4):193-198, 1986.

17. Wadden, T. A., T. B. Van Itallie, and G. L. Blackburn. "Responsible and Irresponsible Use of Very-Low-Calorie Diets in the Treatment of Obesity." *Journal of the American Medical Association* 263:83-85, 1990.

18. Whitney, E. N., and E. V. N. Hamilton. *Understanding Nutrition*. St. Paul, MN: West Publishing Co., 1987.

19. Wolf, M.D. "The Battle Against Body Fat." *Fitness Management* 3(3):48-49, 1987.

Cardiovascular Endurance Assessment

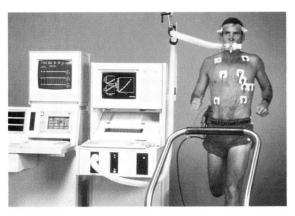

Photo Courtesy of Quinton Instrument Co., 2121 Terry Avenue, Seattle, Washington 98121-2791.

OBJECTIVES

- Understand the importance of adequate cardiovascular endurance in the maintenance of good health and well-being.
- Define cardiovascular endurance and the benefits of cardiovascular endurance training.
- Define aerobic and anaerobic exercise.
- Be able to assess cardiovascular endurance through the use of four different maximal oxygen uptake estimation protocols (1.5-Mile Run Test, Step Test, Astrand-Rhyming Test, and Houston Non-Exercise Test).
- Learn to interpret cardiovascular endurance assessment test results according to health fitness and physical fitness standards.

Introduction.

The most important component of physical fitness and best indicator of overall health is cardiovascular endurance. Physical activity, however, is no longer a natural part of our existence. We live in an automated world, where most of the activities that used to require strenuous physical exertion can be accomplished by machines with the simple pull of a handle or push of a button. For instance, if there is a need to go to a store that may only be a couple of blocks away, most people drive their automobiles and then spend several minutes driving around the parking lot in an effort to find a spot ten yards closer to the store's entrance. The groceries do not even have to be carried out anymore. They are usually taken out in a cart and placed in the vehicle by a youngster working at the store. Similarly, during a normal visit to a multi-level shopping mall, it can easily be observed that almost everyone chooses to ride the escalators instead of taking the stairs (Figure 4.1). Automobiles, elevators, escalators, telephones, intercoms, remote controls, electric garage door openers, etc. are all modern-day commodities that minimize the amount of movement and effort required of the human body. Lack of adequate physical activity is a fact of modern life that most people can no longer avoid, but to enjoy these twentieth-century commodities and still expect to live life to its fullest, a personalized lifetime exercise program must also become a part of daily living.

———— *FIGURE 4.1* ————

Advances in modern technology have almost completely eliminated the need for physical activity, significantly enhancing the deterioration rate of the human body.

49

The primary detrimental effect of modern-day technology is a decrement in the level of *cardiovascular endurance,* or *the ability of the lungs, heart, and blood vessels to deliver adequate amounts of oxygen to the cells to meet the demands of prolonged physical activity* (Figure 4.2). As a person breathes, part of the oxygen contained in ambient air is taken up in the lungs and transported in the blood to the heart. The heart is then responsible for pumping the oxygenated blood through the circulatory system to all organs and tissues of the body. At the cellular level, oxygen is used to convert food substrates, primarily carbohydrates and fats, into energy necessary to conduct body functions and maintain a constant internal equilibrium. As was discussed in Chapter 1, the "typical" American is not exactly a good role model when it comes to cardiovascular endurance. *Only 10 to 20 percent of the adult population exercises vigorously enough to develop the cardiovascular system.*

During physical exertion, a greater amount of energy is needed to carry out the work. As a result, the heart, lungs, and blood vessels have to deliver more oxygen to the cells to supply the required energy to accomplish the task. During prolonged physical activity, an individual with a high level of cardiovascular endurance is able to deliver the required amount of oxygen to the tissues with relative ease. The cardiovascular system of a person with a low level of endurance would have to work much harder, since the heart would have to pump more often to supply the same amount of oxygen to the tissues, and consequently would fatigue faster. Hence, a higher capacity to deliver and utilize oxygen (oxygen uptake) indicates a more efficient cardiovascular system.

Cardiovascular endurance activities are also frequently referred to as "aerobic" exercises. The word "aerobic" means "with oxygen." Whenever an activity is carried out where oxygen is utilized to produce energy, it is considered an aerobic exercise. Examples of cardiovascular or aerobic exercises are walking, jogging, swimming, cycling, cross-country skiing, water aerobics, rope skipping, aerobic dancing, etc. On the other hand, *"anaerobic" activities are carried out "without oxygen." The intensity of anaerobic exercise is so high that oxygen is not utilized to produce energy. Since energy production is very limited in the absence of oxygen, these activities can only be carried out for short periods of time* (two to three minutes). The higher the intensity, the shorter the duration. Such activities as the 100, 200, and 400 meters in track and field, the 100 meters in swimming, gymnastics routines, and weight training are good examples of anaerobic activities. Only aerobic activities will help increase cardiovascular endurance. Anaerobic activities will not significantly contribute toward the development of the cardiovascular system. The basic guidelines for cardiovascular exercise prescription are discussed in Chapter 5.

———— *FIGURE 4.2* ————

Cardiovascular Endurance. The ability of the lungs, heart, and blood vessels to deliver adequate amounts of oxygen to the cells to meet the demands of prolonged physical activity.

Benefits of Cardiovascular Endurance Training

Every individual who initiates a cardiovascular or aerobic exercise program can expect a number of physiological adaptations that result from training. Among these benefits are:

1. *An increase in the oxygen-carrying capacity of the blood.* As a result of training, there is an increase in the red blood cell count, which contains hemoglobin that is responsible for transporting oxygen in the blood.

2. *A higher maximal oxygen uptake (Max VO$_2$).* The amount of oxygen that the body is able to utilize during physical activity is significantly increased. This allows the individual to exercise longer and at a higher rate before becoming fatigued. Depending on the initial fitness level, Max VO$_2$ may increase as much as 30 percent.

3. *A decrease in resting heart rate and an increase in cardiac muscle strength.* During resting conditions, the heart ejects between five and six quarts of blood per minute. This amount of blood is sufficient to meet the energy demands in the resting state. As any other muscle, the heart responds to training by increasing in strength and size. As the heart gets stronger, the muscle can produce a more forceful contraction that causes a greater ejection of blood with each beat (stroke volume), yielding a decreased heart rate. This reduction in heart rate also allows the heart to rest longer between beats.

Resting heart rates are frequently decreased by 10 to 20 beats per minute (bpm) after only six to eight weeks of training. A reduction of 20 bpm would save the heart about 10,483,200 beats per year. The average heart beats between 70 and 80 bpm. In highly trained athletes, however, resting heart rates are commonly found around 40 bpm.

4. *A lower heart rate at given work loads.* When compared with untrained individuals, a trained person has a lower heart rate response to a given task. This is due to the increased efficiency of the cardiovascular system. Individuals are also surprised to find that following several weeks of training, a given work load (let's say a 10-minute mile) elicits a much lower heart rate response as compared to the initial response when training first started.

5. *An increase in the number and size of the mitochondria.* All energy necessary for cell function is produced in the mitochondria. As the size and number increase, so does the potential to produce energy for muscular work.

6. *An increase in the number of functional capillaries.* These smaller vessels allow for the exchange of oxygen and carbon dioxide between the blood and the cells. As more vessels open up, a greater amount of gas exchange can take place, therefore decreasing the onset of fatigue during prolonged exercise. This increase in capillaries also speeds up the rate at which waste products of cell metabolism can be removed. Increased capillarization is also seen in the heart, which enhances the oxygen delivery capacity to the heart muscle itself.

7. *A decrease in recovery time.* Trained individuals enjoy a faster recovery time following exercise. A fit system is able to restore at a greater speed any internal equilibrium that was disrupted during exercise.

8. *A decrease in blood pressure and blood lipids.* A regular aerobic exercise program will cause a reduction in blood pressure and fats such as cholesterol and triglycerides, all of which have been linked to the formation of the atherosclerotic plaque that obstructs the arteries. This reduction decreases the risk of coronary heart disease. (see Chapter 12). High blood pressure is also a leading risk factor for strokes.

9. *An increase in fat-burning enzymes.* The role of these enzymes is significant, because fat can only be lost by burning it in muscle. As the concentration of the enzymes increases, so does the ability to burn fat.

CARDIOVASCULAR ENDURANCE ASSESSMENT

The level of cardiovascular endurance, cardiovascular fitness, or aerobic capacity is determined by the maximal amount of oxygen (Max VO₂) that the human body is able to utilize per minute of physical activity. This value can be expressed in liters per minute (L/min) or milliliters per kilogram per minute (ml/kg/min). The latter is most frequently used because it takes into consideration total body mass (weight). When comparing two individuals with the same absolute value, the one with the lesser body mass will have a higher relative value, indicating that a greater amount of oxygen is available to each kilogram (2.2 pounds) of body weight. Since all tissues and organs of the body utilize oxygen to function, a higher amount of oxygen consumption indicates a more efficient cardiovascular system.

The most precise way to determine maximal oxygen uptake is through direct gas analysis. This is done with the use of a metabolic cart through which the amount of oxygen consumption can be directly measured (see photo at the beginning of this chapter). This type of equipment, however, is not readily available in most health/fitness centers. As a result, several alternate methods of estimating maximal oxygen uptake using limited equipment have been developed.

Even though most cardiovascular endurance tests are probably safe to administer to apparently healthy individuals, that is, those with no major coronary risk factors, the American College of Sports Medicine recommends that a physician be present for all maximal exercise tests on individuals over the age of thirty-five (regardless of state of health). A maximal test can be described as any test that requires an all-out effort, to the point of complete fatigue, on the part of the participant. For submaximal tests, a physician should be present when testing higher risk/asymptomatic individuals over the age of thirty-five or any symptomatic or diseased people regardless of age.

Three common exercise tests frequently used to assess cardiovascular fitness will now be introduced. These tests are the 1.5-mile run test, the step test, and the Astrand-Ryhming test. The specific test protocols are explained in Figures 4.3, 4.4, and

4.7. Depending on time and equipment limitations, you may perform one or more of these tests in Lab 4A. However, keep in mind that these are different testing protocols and each test will not necessarily yield the exact same results. Therefore, to make valid comparisons, the same test should be used when doing pre- and post-assessments. A fourth test, the University of Houston Non-Exercise Test, will also be discussed at the end of this chapter.

The 1.5-Mile Run Test

This test is most frequently used to predict cardiovascular fitness according to the time it takes to run/walk a 1.5-mile course (see Figure 4.3). Maximal oxygen uptake is estimated based on the time it takes to cover the distance (see Table 4.1).

--------- *FIGURE 4.3* ---------

Procedures for the 1.5-Mile Run Test

1. Make sure that you qualify for this test. This test is contraindicated for unconditioned beginners, individuals with symptoms of heart disease, and those with known heart disease and/or risk factors.

2. Select the testing site. Find a school track (each lap is one-fourth of a mile) or a premeasured 1.5-mile course.

3. Have a stopwatch available to determine your time.

4. Conduct a few warm-up exercises prior to the test. Do some stretching exercises, some walking, and slow jogging.

5. Initiate the test and try to cover the distance in the fastest time possible (walking or jogging). Time yourself during the run to see how fast you have covered the distance. If any unusual symptoms arise during the test, do not continue. Stop immediately and retake the test after another six weeks of aerobic training.

6. At the end of the test, cool down by walking or jogging slowly for another three to five minutes. Do not sit or lie down after the test.

7. According to your performance time, look up your estimated maximal oxygen uptake in Table 4.1.

8. Example: A twenty-year-old female runs the 1.5-mile course in 12 minutes and 40 seconds. Table 4.1 shows a maximal oxygen uptake of 39.8 ml/kg/min for a time of 12:40. According to Table 4.6, this maximal oxygen uptake would place her in the good cardiovascular fitness category.

--------- *TABLE 4.1* ---------

Estimated Maximal Oxygen (Max VO$_2$) in ml/kg/min for the 1.5-Mile Run Test

Time	Max VO$_2$	Time	Max VO$_2$
6:10	80.0	12:40	39.8
6:20	79.0	12:50	39.2
6:30	77.9	13:00	38.6
6:40	76.7	13:10	38.1
6:50	75.5	13:20	37.8
7:00	74.0	13:30	37.2
7:10	72.6	13:40	36.8
7:20	71.3	13:50	36.3
7:30	69.9	14:00	35.9
7:40	68.3	14:10	35.5
7:50	66.8	14:20	35.1
8:00	65.2	14:30	34.7
8:10	63.9	14:40	34.3
8:20	62.5	14:50	34.0
8:30	61.2	15:00	33.6
8:40	60.2	15:10	33.1
8:50	59.1	15:20	32.7
9:00	58.1	15:30	32.2
9:10	56.9	15:40	31.8
9:20	55.9	15:50	31.4
9:30	54.7	16:00	30.9
9:40	53.5	16:10	30.5
9:50	52.3	16:20	30.2
10:00	51.1	16:30	29.8
10:10	50.4	16:40	29.5
10:20	49.5	16:50	29.1
10:30	48.6	17:00	28.9
10:40	48.0	17:10	28.5
10:50	47.4	17:20	28.3
11:00	46.6	17:30	28.0
11:10	45.8	17:40	27.7
11:20	45.1	17:50	27.4
11:30	44.4	18:00	27.1
11:40	43.7	18:10	26.8
11:50	43.2	18:20	26.6
12:00	42.3	18:30	26.3
12:10	41.7	18:40	26.0
12:20	41.0	18:50	25.7
12:30	40.4	19:00	25.4

Adapted from: Cooper, K. H. "A Means of Assessing Maximal Oxygen Intake." *JAMA* 203:201-204, 1968. Pollock, M. L., et al. *Health and Fitness Through Physical Activity.* New York: John Wiley and Sons, 1978. Wilmore, J. H. *Training for Sport and Activity.* Boston: Allyn and Bacon, Inc., 1982.

The only equipment necessary to conduct this test is a stopwatch and a track or premeasured 1.5-mile course. It is perhaps the easiest test to administer, but caution should be taken when conducting the test. Since the objective is to cover the distance in the shortest period of time, it is considered to be a maximal exercise test. The use of this test should be limited to conditioned individuals who have been cleared for exercise. At least six weeks of aerobic training are recommended before a person should be allowed to take the test. It is contraindicated for unconditioned beginners, symptomatic individuals, and those with known disease and/or coronary heart disease risk factors.

The Step Test

This test requires little time and equipment and can be administered to most everyone, since submaximal workloads are used to estimate maximal oxygen uptake. This test should not be administered to symptomatic and diseased individuals, or those at high risk (no symptoms) over the age of thirty-five. Significantly overweight individuals and those with joint problems in the lower extremities may have a difficult time performing this test.

The actual test only takes three minutes. A fifteen-second recovery heart rate is taken between five and twenty seconds following the test (see Figure 4.4). The equipment required is a bench or gymnasium bleacher 16¼ inches high, a stopwatch, and a metronome. You will need to know how to take your heart rate by counting your pulse (see Lab 1B). This can be done on the wrist by placing two fingers over the radial artery (inside of the wrist on the side of the thumb) or over the carotid artery in the neck just below the jaw next to the voice box (see Figures 4.5 and 4.6). If individuals are taught to take their own heart rate, a large group of people can be tested at once when using gymnasium bleachers.

FIGURE 4.4

Procedures for the Step Test

1. The test is conducted with a bench or gymnasium bleachers 16¼ inches high.

2. The stepping cycle is performed to a four-step cadence (up-up-down-down). Men should perform twenty-four complete step-ups per minute, regulated with a metronome set at 96 beats per minute. Women perform twenty-two step-ups per minute, or 88 beats per minute on the metronome.

3. Allow a brief practice period of five to ten seconds to familiarize yourself with the stepping cadence.

4. Begin the test and perform the step-ups for exactly three minutes.

5. Upon completion of the three minutes, remain standing and take your heart rate for a fifteen-second interval from five to twenty seconds into recovery. Convert recovery heart rate to beats per minute (multiply 15-second heart rate by 4).

6. Maximal oxygen uptake in ml/kg/min is estimated according to the following equations:

   Men:
   maximal oxygen uptake = 111.33 − (0.42 × recovery heart rate in bpm)

   Women:
   maximal oxygen uptake = 65.81 − (0.1847 × recovery heart rate in bpm)

7. Example: The recovery fifteen-second heart rate for a male subject following the three-minute step test is found to be 39 beats. Maximal oxygen uptake is estimated as follows:

   Fifteen-second heart rate = 39 beats
   Minute heart rate = 39 × 4 = 156 bpm

   Maximal oxygen uptake = 111.33 − (0.42 × 156) = 45.81 ml/kg/min

8. Maximal oxygen uptake can also be obtained according to recovery heart rates in Table 4.2.

From McArdle, W. D., et al. *Exercise Physiology: Energy, Nutrition, and Human Performance.* Philadelphia: Lea & Febiger, 1986.

——— *FIGURE 4.5* ———

Pulse taken at the radial artery.

——— *TABLE 4.2* ———

Predicted Maximal Oxygen Uptake (Max VO₂) for the Step Test in ml/kg/min

15-Sec HR	HR-bpm	Max VO$_2$ Men	Max VO$_2$ Women
30	120	60.9	43.6
31	124	59.3	42.9
32	128	57.6	42.2
33	132	55.9	41.4
34	136	54.2	40.7
35	140	52.5	40.0
36	144	50.9	39.2
37	148	49.2	38.5
38	152	47.5	➤ 37.7
39	156	45.8	37.0
40	160	44.1	36.3
41	164	42.5	35.5
42	168	40.8	34.8
43	172	39.1	34.0
44	176	37.4	33.3
45	180	35.7	32.6
46	184	34.1	31.8
47	188	32.4	31.1
48	192	30.7	30.3
49	196	29.0	29.6
50	200	27.3	28.9

——— *FIGURE 4.6* ———

Pulse taken at the carotid artery.

Astrand-Ryhming Test

Because of its simplicity and practicality, the Astrand-Ryhming test has become one of the most popular protocols used in estimating maximal oxygen uptake in the laboratory setting. The test is conducted on a bicycle ergometer, and, similar to the step test, it only requires submaximal workloads and little time to administer. The contraindications given for the step test also apply for the Astrand-Ryhming test. Nevertheless, since the participant does not have to support his/her own body weight while riding the bicycle, the test can be used with overweight individuals and those with limited joint problems in the lower extremities.

The bicycle ergometer to be used on this test should allow for the regulation of workloads (see test procedures in Figure 4.7). Besides the bicycle ergometer, a stopwatch and an additional technician to monitor the heart rate are needed to conduct the test (Figure 4.8). The duration of the test is six minutes, and the heart rate is taken every minute. At the end of the test, the heart rate should be in the range given for each workload in Table 4.4 (primarily between 120 and 170 beats per minute).

—————— *FIGURE 4.7* ——————
Procedures for the Astrand-Rhyming Test

1. Adjust the bike seat so that the knees are almost completely extended as the foot goes through the bottom of the pedaling cycle.

2. During the test, the speed should be kept constant at fifty revolutions per minute. Test duration is six minutes.

3. Select the appropriate work load for the bike based on age, weight, health, and estimated fitness level. For unconditioned individuals: women, use 300 kpm (kilopounds per meter) or 450 kpm; men, 300 kpm or 600 kpm. Conditioned adults: women, 450 kpm or 600 kpm; men, 600 kpm or 900 kpm.[a]

4. Ride the bike for six minutes and check the heart rate every minute, during the last ten seconds of each minute. Heart rate should be determined by recording the time it takes to count thirty pulse beats, and then converting to beats per minute using Table 4.3.

5. Average the final two heart rates (fifth and sixth minutes). If these two heart rates are not within five beats per minute of each other, continue the test for another few minutes until this is accomplished. If the heart rate continues to climb significantly after the sixth minute, stop the test and rest for fifteen to twenty minutes. You may then retest, preferably at a lower work load. The final average heart rate should also fall between the ranges given for each work load in Table 4.4 (e.g., men: 300 kpm = 120 to 140 beats per minute; 600 kpm = 120 to 170 beats per minute).

6. Based on the average heart rate of the final two minutes and your work load, look up the maximal oxygen uptake in Table 4.4 (e.g., men: 600 kpm and average heart rate = 145, maximal oxygen uptake = 2.4 liters/minute).

7. Correct maximal oxygen uptake using the correction factors found in Table 4.5 (e.g., maximal oxygen uptake = 2.4 and age thirty-five, correction factor = .870. Multiply 2.4 × .870 and final corrected maximal oxygen uptake = 2.09 liters/minute).

8. To obtain maximal oxygen uptake in ml/kg/min, multiply the maximal oxygen uptake by 1,000 (to convert liters to milliliters) and divide by body weight in kilograms (to obtain kilograms, divide your body weight in pounds by 2.2046).

9. Example: Corrected maximal oxygen uptake = 2.09 liters/minute
   Body weight = 132 pounds or 60 kilograms (132 ÷ 2.2046 = 60)

   Maximal oxygen uptake in ml/kg/min =
   2.09 × 1,000 = 2,090
   2,090 divided by 60 = 34.8 ml/kg/min

[a] On the Monarch bicycle ergometer when riding at a speed of fifty revolutions per minute, a load of 1 kp = 300 kpm, 1.5 kp = 450, 2 kp = 600 kpm, and so forth, with increases of 150 kpm to each ½ kp.

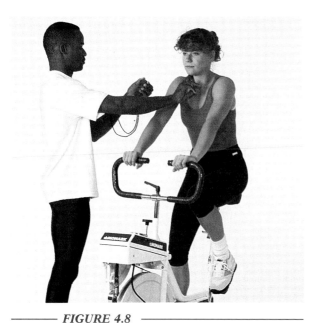

─────── *FIGURE 4.8* ───────

Monitoring heart rate on the carotid artery during the Astrand-Ryhming Test.

Good judgment is essential when administering the test to older people. Low workloads should be used, because if the higher heart rates are reached (around 150 to 170 bpm), these individuals could be working near or at their maximal capacity, making it an unsafe test to perform without adequate medical supervision. When choosing workloads for older people, final exercise heart rates should not exceed 130 to 140 bpm.

University of Houston Non-Exercise Test

The University of Houston Non-Exercise Test (N-Ex) is a method used to estimate maximal oxygen uptake (Max VO_2) that does not involve any form of exercise testing. This protocol can be used: (a) as an initial estimate of maximal oxygen uptake and (b) for mass screening because the required information is collected through a self-reported method. The test is especially useful when testing individuals on high blood pressure medication. Hypertensive medication lowers heart rate, therefore, heart

─────── TABLE 4.3 ───────

Conversion of the Time for 30 Pulse Beats to Pulse Rate Per Minute

Sec.	bpm	Sec.	bpm	Sec.	bpm	Sec.	bpm	Sec.	bpm	Sec.	bpm
22.0	82	19.6	92	17.2	105	14.8	122	12.4	145	10.0	180
21.9	82	19.5	92	17.1	105	14.7	122	12.3	146	9.9	182
21.8	83	19.4	93	17.0	106	14.6	123	12.2	148	9.8	184
21.7	83	19.3	93	16.9	107	14.5	124	12.1	149	9.7	186
21.6	83	19.2	94	16.8	107	14.4	125	12.0	150	9.6	188
21.5	84	19.1	94	16.7	108	14.3	126	11.9	151	9.5	189
21.4	84	19.0	95	16.6	108	14.2	127	11.8	153	9.4	191
21.3	85	18.9	95	16.5	109	14.1	128	11.7	154	9.3	194
21.2	85	18.8	96	16.4	110	14.0	129	11.6	155	9.2	196
21.1	85	18.7	96	16.3	110	13.9	129	11.5	157	9.1	198
21.0	86	18.6	97	16.2	111	13.8	130	11.4	158	9.0	200
20.9	86	18.5	97	16.1	112	13.7	131	11.3	159	8.9	202
20.8	87	18.4	98	16.0	113	13.6	132	11.2	161	8.8	205
20.7	87	18.3	98	15.9	113	13.5	133	11.1	162	8.7	207
20.6	87	18.2	99	15.8	114	13.4	134	11.0	164	8.6	209
20.5	88	18.1	99	15.7	115	13.3	135	10.9	165	8.5	212
20.4	88	18.0	100	15.6	115	13.2	136	10.8	167	8.4	214
20.3	89	17.9	101	15.5	116	13.1	137	10.7	168	8.3	217
20.2	89	17.8	101	15.4	117	13.0	138	10.6	170	8.2	220
20.1	90	17.7	102	15.3	118	12.9	140	10.5	171	8.1	222
20.0	90	17.6	102	15.2	118	12.8	141	10.4	173	8.0	225
19.9	90	17.5	103	15.1	119	12.7	142	10.3	175		
19.8	91	17.4	103	15.0	120	12.6	143	10.2	176		
19.7	91	17.3	104	14.9	121	12.5	144	10.1	178		

—— *TABLE 4.4* ——

Maximal Oxygen Uptake (Max VO₂) Estimates for the Astrand-Rhyming Test in Liters per Minute (L/min)

Heart Rate	Men					Women				
	300	600	900	1200	1500	300	450	600	750	900
120	2.2	3.4	4.8			2.6	3.4	4.1	4.8	
121	2.2	3.4	4.7			2.5	3.3	4.0	4.8	
122	2.2	3.4	4.6			2.5	3.2	3.9	4.7	
123	2.1	3.4	4.6			2.4	3.1	3.9	4.6	
124	2.1	3.3	4.5	6.0		2.4	3.1	3.8	4.5	
125	2.0	3.2	4.4	5.9		2.3	3.0	3.7	4.4	
126	2.0	3.2	4.4	5.8		2.3	3.0	3.6	4.3	
127	2.0	3.1	4.3	5.7		2.2	2.9	3.5	4.2	
128	2.0	3.1	4.2	5.6		2.2	2.8	3.5	4.2	4.8
129	1.9	3.0	4.2	5.6		2.2	2.8	3.4	4.1	4.8
130	1.9	3.0	4.1	5.5		2.1	2.7	3.4	4.0	4.7
131	1.9	2.9	4.0	5.4		2.1	2.7	3.4	4.0	4.6
132	1.8	2.9	4.0	5.3		2.0	2.7	3.3	3.9	4.5
133	1.8	2.8	3.9	5.3		2.0	2.6	3.2	3.8	4.4
134	1.8	2.8	3.9	5.2		2.0	2.6	3.2	3.8	4.4
135	1.7	2.8	3.8	5.1		2.0	2.6	3.1	3.7	4.3
136	1.7	2.7	3.8	5.0		1.9	2.5	3.1	3.6	4.2
137	1.7	2.7	3.7	5.0		1.9	2.5	3.0	3.6	4.2
138	1.6	2.7	3.7	4.9		1.8	2.4	3.0	3.5	4.1
139	1.6	2.6	3.6	4.8		1.8	2.4	2.9	3.5	4.0
140	1.6	2.6	3.6	4.8	6.0	1.8	2.4	2.8	3.4	4.0
141		2.6	3.5	4.7	5.9	1.8	2.3	2.8	3.4	3.9
142		2.5	3.5	4.6	5.8	1.7	2.3	2.8	3.3	3.9
143		2.5	3.4	4.6	5.7	1.7	2.2	2.7	3.3	3.8
144		2.5	3.4	4.5	5.7	1.7	2.2	2.7	3.2	3.8
145		2.4	3.4	4.5	5.6	1.6	2.2	2.7	3.2	3.7
146		2.4	3.3	4.4	5.6	1.6	2.2	2.6	3.2	3.7
147		2.4	3.3	4.4	5.5	1.6	2.1	2.6	3.1	3.6
148		2.4	3.2	4.3	5.4	1.6	2.1	2.6	3.1	3.6
149		2.3	3.2	4.3	5.4		2.1	2.6	3.0	3.5
150		2.3	3.2	4.2	5.3		2.0	2.5	3.0	3.5
151		2.3	3.1	4.2	5.2		2.0	2.5	3.0	3.4
152		2.3	3.1	4.1	5.2		2.0	2.5	2.9	3.4
153		2.2	3.0	4.1	5.1		2.0	2.4	2.9	3.3
154		2.2	3.0	4.0	5.1		2.0	2.4	2.8	3.3
155		2.2	3.0	4.0	5.0		1.9	2.4	2.8	3.2
156		2.2	2.9	4.0	5.0		1.9	2.3	2.8	3.2
157		2.1	2.9	3.9	4.9		1.9	2.3	2.7	3.2
158		2.1	2.9	3.9	4.9		1.8	2.3	2.7	3.1
159		2.1	2.8	3.8	4.8		1.8	2.2	2.7	3.1
160		2.1	2.8	3.8	4.8		1.8	2.2	2.6	3.0
161		2.0	2.8	3.7	4.7		1.8	2.2	2.6	3.0
162		2.0	2.8	3.7	4.6		1.8	2.2	2.6	3.0
163		2.0	2.8	3.7	4.6		1.7	2.2	2.6	2.9
164		2.0	2.7	3.6	4.5		1.7	2.1	2.5	2.9
165		2.0	2.7	3.6	4.5		1.7	2.1	2.5	2.9
166		1.9	2.7	3.6	4.5		1.7	2.1	2.5	2.8
167		1.9	2.6	3.5	4.4		1.6	2.1	2.4	2.8
168		1.9	2.6	3.5	4.4		1.6	2.0	2.4	2.8
169		1.9	2.6	3.5	4.3		1.6	2.0	2.4	2.8
170		1.8	2.6	3.4	4.3		1.6	2.0	2.4	2.7

From Astrand, I. *Acta Physiologica Scandinavica* 49(1960). Supplementum 169:45-60.

TABLE 4.5

Age-Based Correction Factors for Maximal Oxygen Uptake

Age	Correction Factor	Age	Correction Factor	Age	Correction Factor	Age	Correction Factor
14	1.11	40	.830	27	.974	53	.726
15	1.10	41	.820	28	.961	54	.718
16	1.09	42	.810	29	.948	55	.710
17	1.08	43	.800	30	.935	56	.704
18	1.07	44	.790	31	.922	57	.698
19	1.06	45	.780	32	.909	58	.692
20	1.05	46	.774	33	.896	59	.686
21	1.04	47	.768	34	.883	60	.680
22	1.03	48	.762	35	.870	61	.674
23	1.02	49	.756	36	.862	62	.668
24	1.01	50	.750	37	.854	63	.662
25	1.00	51	.742	38	.846	64	.656
26	.987	52	.734	39	.838	65	.650

Adapted from Astrand, I. *Acta Physiologica Scandinavica* 49 (1960). Supplementum 169:45-60.

rate based tests (step test and Astrand-Ryhming) cannot be used with such individuals. Maximal exercise tests (1.5-mile run) are also contraindicated for hypertensive people. The N-Ex equations to predict maximal oxygen uptake have been found to maintain a high degree of accuracy with men on anti-hypertensive medication.

The non-exercise test is based on research findings in exercise physiology which indicates that maximal oxygen uptake is negatively related to age and body composition, but positively related to exercise habits. Based on these variables multiple regression equations were developed to estimate maximal oxygen uptake in ml/kg/min. The procedures for the Houston Non-Exercise Test are outlined in Figures 4.9 and 4.10. The test is suitable for both men and women.

INTERPRETING YOUR MAXIMAL OXYGEN UPTAKE RESULTS

After obtaining your maximal oxygen uptake, you can determine your current level of cardiovascular fitness in Table 4.6. Locate the maximal oxygen uptake in your respective age category, and on the top row you will find your present level of cardiovascular fitness. For example, a nineteen-year-old male with a maximal oxygen uptake of 35 ml/kg/min would be classified in the average cardiovascular fitness category. After you initiate your personal cardiovascular exercise program (see Chapter 5), you may wish to retest yourself periodically to evaluate your progress.

——————— *FIGURE 4.9* ———————

Procedures for the University of Houston Non-Exercise Test*

Multiple regression equations have been developed to estimate maximal oxygen uptake in ml/kg/min according to physical activity rating (PAR), age (A), and percent body fat (%Fat) or body mass index (BMI). The first equation uses percent body fat determined through skinfolds (N-EX %Fat). The procedures to determine percent body fat through skinfolds are outlined in Figure 6.4 in Chapter 6. The second equation uses body mass index (N-Ex BMI). The N-Ex %Fat equation is slightly more accurate than the N-Ex BMI equation. The physical activity rating code provided in Figure 4.10 is used for a global, self-rating of physical activity. The subject uses the code to rate his or her physical activity during the past month. The selected number is a global rating of the subject's exercise habits. This value is used in the equation. The regression equations are as follows:

N-Ex %Fat Model

Men $Max VO_2 = 56.370 - (.289 \times A) - (.552 \times \%Fat) + (1.589 \times PAR)$

Women $Max VO_2 = 50.513 - (.289 \times A) - (.552 \times \%Fat) + (1.589 \times PAR)$

N-Ex BMI Model (BMI = Weight in kg ÷ Height^2 in meters)

Men $Max VO_2 = 67.350 - (.381 \times A) - (.754 \times BMI) + (1.951 \times PAR)$

Women $Max VO_2 = 56.363 - (.381 \times A) - (.754 \times BMI) + (1.951 \times PAR)$

Examples

The N-Ex %fat model is illustrated with a 40-year-old man with 17 percent body fat and an activity rating of 6. Estimated Max VO$_2$ for the man would be:

$Max VO_2 = 56.37 - (.289 \times 40) - (.552 \times 17) + (1.589 \times 6)$

$Max VO_2 = 45.0$ ml/kg/min

The N-Ex BMI for a 30-year-old woman who weighs 130 pounds, with a height of 64 inches, and a physical activity rating of 5 would be:

BMI = Weight in kg ÷ Height^2 in meters

Weight in kg = weight in pounds ÷ 2.2046 = 130 ÷ 2.2046 = 59

Height in meters = height in inches × .0254 = 64 × .0254 = 1.626

$BMI = 59 \div (1.626)^2 = 22.32$

$Max VO_2 = 56.363 - (.381 \times 30) - (.754 \times 22.32) + (1.951 \times 5)$

$Max VO_2 = 37.9$ ml/kg/min

*University of Houston Non-Exercise Test reproduced with permission from *Exercise Concepts, Calculations, & Computer Applications* by R. M. Ross and A. S. Jackson; Benchmark Press, Inc., pp. 108-110, 1990.

——————— *FIGURE 4.10* ———————

Physical Activity Code for the University of Houston Non-Exercise Test

Use the appropriate number (0-7) which best describes your general physical activity rating (PAR) for the previous month:

I. **Do not participate regularly in programmed recreation sport or physical activity.**
    - 0   Avoid walking or exertion, e.g., always use elevator, drive whenever possible instead of walking.
    - 1   Walk for pleasure, routinely use stairs, occasionally exercise sufficiently to cause heavy breathing or perspiration.

II. **Participated regularly in recreation or work requiring modest physical activity, such as golf, horseback riding, calisthenics, gymnastics, table tennis, bowling, weight lifting, yard work.**
    - 2   10 to 60 minutes per week.
    - 3   Over one hour per week.

III. **Participate regularly in heavy physical exercise such as running or jogging, swimming, cycling, rowing, skipping rope, running in place or engaging in vigorous aerobic activity type exercise such as tennis, basketball or handball.**
    - 4   Run less than one mile per week or spend less than 30 minutes per week in comparable physical activity.
    - 5   Run 1 to 5 miles per week or spend 30 to 60 minutes per week in comparable physical activity.
    - 6   Run 5 to 10 miles per week or spend 1 to 3 hours per week in comparable physical activity.
    - 7   Run over 10 miles per week or spend over 3 hours per week in comparable physical activity.

TABLE 4.6

Cardiovascular Fitness Classification According to Maximal Oxygen Uptake (Max VO_2) in ml/kg/min

		Fitness Classification				
Sex	**Age**	**Poor**	**Fair**	**Average**	**Good**	**Excellent**
Men	<29	<25	25-33	34-43	44-52	53+
	30-39	<23	23-30	31-41	42-49	50+
	40-49	<20	20-26	27-38	39-44	45+
	50-59	<18	18-24	25-37	38-42	43+
	60-69	<16	16-22	23-35	36-40	41+
Women	<29	<24	24-30	31-38	39-48	49+
	30-39	<20	20-27	28-36	37-44	45+
	40-49	<17	17-24	25-34	35-41	42+
	50-59	<15	15-21	22-33	34-39	40+
	60-69	<13	13-20	21-32	33-36	37+

High physical fitness standard

Health fitness standard

See Chapter 1, Fitness Standards: Health vs. Physical Fitness Standards, p. 4.

LABORATORY EXPERIENCE

LAB 4A: Cardiovascular Endurance Assessment Protocols

LAB PREPARATION: Wear exercise clothing, including jogging shoes. Be prepared to take the step test, the Astrand-Ryhming test, and/or the 1.5-mile run test. Avoid vigorous physical activity twenty-four hours prior to this lab.

References

1. American College of Sports Medicine. *Guidelines for Graded Exercise Testing and Exercise Prescription*. Philadelphia: Lea & Febiger, 1986.
2. American Heart Association Committee on Exercise. *Exercise Testing and Training of Apparently Healthy Individuals: A Handbook for Physicians*. New York: The Association, 1972.
3. Astrand, I. *Acta Physiologica Scandinavica* 49, 1960. Supplementum 169:45-60, 1960.
4. Astrand, P. O., and K. Rodahl. *Textbook of Work Physiology*. New York: McGraw-Hill, 1977.
5. Cooper, K. H. "A Means of Assessing Maximal Oxygen Intake." *Journal of the American Medical Association* 203:201-204, 1968.
6. Cooper, K. H. *The Aerobics Program for Total Well-Being*. New York: Mount Evans and Co., 1982.
7. Jackson, A. S., et al. "Prediction of VO_2 Max Without Exercise Testing." *Medicine and Science in Sports and Exercise* 21(2):S115, 1989.
8. McArdle, W. D., F. I. Katch, and V. L. Katch. *Exercise Physiology: Energy, Nutrition and Human Performance*. Philadelphia: Lea & Febiger, 1986.
9. Pollock, M. L., J. H. Wilmore, and S. M. Fox III. *Health and Fitness Through Physical Activity*. New York: John Wiley & Sons, 1978.
10. Ross, R. M. and A. S. Jackson. *Exercise Concepts, Calculations, & Computer Applications*. Carmel, IN: Benchmark Press, Inc., 1990.
11. Wilmore, J. H., and D. L. Costill. *Training for Sport and Activity*. Dubuque, IA: Wm. C. Brown Publishers, 1988.

Principles of Cardiovascular Exercise Prescription

OBJECTIVES

- Teach the principles that govern cardiovascular exercise prescription (intensity, mode, duration, and frequency).
- Clarify misconceptions related to cardiovascular endurance training.
- Introduce concepts for injury prevention and treatment.
- Learn basic skills to enhance exercise adherence.
- Learn to predict oxygen uptake and caloric expenditure from exercise heart rate.

A sound cardiovascular endurance program greatly contributes toward the enhancement and maintenance of good health. Although there are four components of physical fitness, cardiovascular endurance is the single most important factor. Certain amounts of muscular strength and flexibility are necessary in daily activities to lead a normal life. However, a person can get away without large amounts of strength and flexibility but cannot do without a good cardiovascular system. Aerobic exercise is especially important in the prevention of coronary heart disease. A poorly conditioned heart that has to pump more often just to keep a person alive is subject to more wear-and-tear than a well-conditioned heart. In situations where strenuous demands are placed on the heart, such as doing yard work, lifting heavy objects or weights, or running to catch a train, the unconditioned heart may not be able to sustain the strain. Additionally, regular participation in cardiovascular endurance activities helps achieve and maintain recommended body weight, the fourth component of health-related physical fitness.

All too often, individuals who exercise regularly and then take a cardiovascular endurance test are surprised to find that their maximal oxygen uptake is not as good as they think it is. Although these individuals may be exercising regularly, they most likely are not following the basic principles for cardiovascular exercise prescription; therefore, they do not reap significant improvements in cardiovascular endurance.

For a person to develop the cardiovascular system, the heart muscle has to be overloaded like any other muscle in the human body. Just as the biceps muscle in the upper arm is developed with strength-training exercises, the heart muscle also has to be exercised to increase in size, strength, and efficiency. *To better understand how the cardiovascular system can be developed, the four basic principles that govern this development will be discussed. These principles are intensity, mode, duration, and frequency of exercise.*

INTENSITY OF EXERCISE

The intensity of exercise is perhaps the most commonly ignored factor when trying to develop the cardiovascular system. This principle refers to how hard a person has to exercise to improve cardiovascular endurance. Muscles have to be overloaded to a given point for them to develop. While the training stimuli to develop the biceps muscle can be accomplished with curl-up exercises, the stimuli for the cardiovascular system is provided by making the heart pump at a higher rate for a certain period of time. *Research has shown that cardiovascular development occurs when working between 50 and 85 percent of heart rate reserve* (see Determining Training Intensity below). Many experts, however, prescribe exercise between 70 and 85 percent of this capacity. This is done to insure better and faster development. The 70 and 85 percentages can be easily calculated and training can be monitored by checking your pulse.

Determining Training Intensity

The following steps are used to determine the intensity of exercise or cardiovascular training zone:

1. Estimate your maximal heart rate (MHR). The maximal heart rate is dependent on the person's age and can be estimated according to the following formula:

   MHR = 220 minus age (220 − age)

2. Check your resting heart rate (RHR) sometime after you have been sitting quietly for fifteen to twenty minutes. You may take your pulse for thirty seconds and multiply by two or take it for a full minute.

3. Determine the heart rate reserve (HRR). This is done by subtracting the resting heart rate from the maximal heart rate (HRR = MHR − RHR). The heart rate reserve indicates the amount of beats available to go from resting conditions to an all-out maximal effort.

4. The cardiovascular training zone is determined by computing the training intensities (TI) at 70 and 85 percent. Multiply the heart rate reserve by the respective 70 and 85 percentages and then add the resting heart rate to both of these figures (70 percent TI = HRR + .70 × RHR, and 85 percent TI = HRR + .85 × RHR). Your cardiovascular training zone is found between these two target heart rates.

5. Example. The cardiovascular training zone for a twenty-year-old person with a resting heart rate of 72 bpm would be:

   MHR: 220 − 20 = 200 beats per minute (bpm)
   RHR = 72 bpm
   HRR: 200 − 72 = 128 beats
   70 Percent TI = (128 × .70) + 72 = 162 bpm
   85 Percent TI = (128 × .85) + 72 = 181 bpm
   Cardiovascular training zone: 162 to 181 bpm

The cardiovascular training zone indicates that whenever you exercise to improve the cardiovascular system, you should maintain the heart rate between the 70 and 85 percent training intensities to obtain adequate development (Figure 5.1). If you have been physically inactive, you may want to use a 60 percent training intensity during the first few weeks of your exercise program. Older adults should use 50 percent during the initial weeks of the exercise program (older adults should always have a medical examination prior to initiating an exercise program).

Following a few weeks of training, you may experience a significant reduction in resting heart rate (ten to twenty beats in eight to twelve weeks); therefore, you should recompute your target zone periodically. Once you have reached an ideal level of cardiovascular endurance, training in the 70 to 85 percent range will allow you to maintain your fitness level.

Exercise heart rate should be monitored regularly during exercise to make sure that you are training in the respective zone. Wait until you are about five minutes into your exercise session before taking your first rate. When you check the heart rate, count your pulse for ten seconds and then multiply by six to get the per-minute pulse rate. Exercise heart rate will remain at the same level for about fifteen seconds following exercise. After fifteen seconds, heart rate will drop rapidly. Do not hesitate to stop during your exercise bout to check your pulse. If the rate is too low, increase the intensity of the exercise. If the rate is too high, slow down.

To develop the cardiovascular system you do not have to exercise above the 85 percent rate. From a fitness standpoint, training above this percentage will not add any extra benefits and may actually be unsafe for some individuals. For unconditioned adults, it is recommended that cardiovascular training be conducted around the 70 percent rate. This lower rate is recommended to reduce potential problems associated with high-intensity exercise.

Training Intensity: Health Fitness vs Physical Fitness

The reader should also be aware that training benefits can be obtained by exercising between the 50 and 60 percent training intensities. Training at these lower percentages, however, may only be sufficient to place a person in an average or "moderately fit" category (see Table 4.6, Chapter 4). As will be discussed later in this chapter (see Special Exercise Considerations — question 1), exercising at this lower intensity may be adequate to significantly decrease the risk for cardiovascular mortality (health fitness), but will not allow the person to

FIGURE 5.1

Typical Cardiovascular or Aerobic Training Pattern

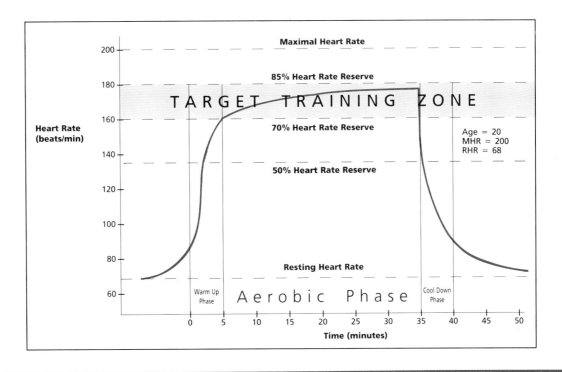

achieve a high cardiovascular fitness rating (physical fitness). The latter ratings are obtained by exercising above the 70 percent threshold.

Rate of Perceived Exertion

Since many people do not check their heart rate during exercise, an alternate method of prescribing intensity of exercise has become more popular in recent years. *This method uses a rate of perceived exertion (RPE) scale* developed by Gunnar Borg. Using the scale shown in Figure 5.2, *a person subjectively rates the perceived exertion or difficulty of exercise when training in the appropriate target zone. The exercise heart rate is then associated with the corresponding RPE value.* For example, if the training intensity requires a heart rate zone between 150 and 170 bpm, the person would associate this with training between "hard" and "very hard." However, some individuals may perceive less exertion than others when training in the correct zone. Therefore, associate your own inner perception of the task with the phrases given on the scale. You may then proceed to exercise at that rate of perceived exertion. It is important that you cross-check your target zone with your perceived exertion in the initial weeks of your exercise program. To help you

develop this association, keep a regular record of your activities using the form provided in Figure 5.4. After several weeks of training, you should be able to predict your exercise heart rate just by your own perceived exertion of the exercise session.

Whether you monitor the intensity of exercise by checking your pulse or through rate of perceived exertion, be aware that changes in normal exercise conditions will affect the training zone. For example, exercising on a hot and/or humid day, or at

FIGURE 5.2

Rate of Perceived Exertion Scale

6		14	
7	Very, very light	15	Hard
8		16	
9	Very light	17	Very hard
10		18	
11	Fairly light	19	Very, very hard
12		20	
13	Somewhat hard		

From Borg, G. "Perceived Exertion: A Note on History and Methods." *Medicine and Science in Sports and Exercise* 5:90-93, 1983.

altitude, increases the heart rate response to a given task. Consequently, make the necessary adjustments in the intensity of your exercise.

MODE OF EXERCISE

In Chapter 4, it was mentioned that the type of exercise that develops the cardiovascular system has to be aerobic in nature. *Once you have established your cardiovascular training zone, any activity or combination of activities that will get your heart rate up to that training zone and keep it there for as long as you exercise will yield adequate development.* Examples of such activities are walking, jogging, aerobic dancing, swimming, water aerobics, cross-country skiing, rope skipping, cycling, racquetball, stair climbing, and stationary running or cycling (Figure 5.3).

The activity that you choose should be based on your personal preferences, what you enjoy doing best, and your physical limitations. There may be a difference in the amount of strength or flexibility developed through the use of different activities, but as far as the cardiovascular system is concerned, the heart doesn't know whether you are walking, swimming, or cycling. All the heart knows is that it has to pump at a certain rate, and as long as that rate is in the desired range, cardiovascular development will occur.

DURATION OF EXERCISE

Regarding the duration of exercise, *the general recommendation is that a person train between twenty and sixty minutes per session*. The duration is based on how intensely a person trains. If the training is done around 85 percent, twenty minutes are sufficient. At 70 percent intensity, the person should train for at least thirty minutes. As mentioned earlier under intensity of training, unconditioned adults should train at lower percentages; therefore, the activity should be carried out over a longer period of time.

FIGURE 5.3

Aerobic activities promote cardiovascular development and help decrease the risk for chronic diseases.

readin
ity, it
ance t
few w
ever, "
begin
ficult.
cise th
sense
gestior

1. **Se**
   Pic
   de
   Do
   ev

2. **Us**
   car
   act
   de
   act
   en
   ba
   cor
   pro

3. **Se**
   do
   ing
   adl

4. **Ob**
   po
   the
   rig

5. **Fin**
   wi
   mo
   sor

6. **Se**
   tou
   you
   a |
   pa

7. **Do**
   list
   chr
   enj
   "st

8. **Ex**
   pra

9. **Ke**
   ma
   res
   yea

---

fit you comfortably
ment of the differe
also select your clo
temperature and h
rubberized materia
will interfere with
the human body an
flow. Proper-fitting s
ically for your choic
mended to prevent l

9. **How long should a
   before engaging in s**
   The length of time
   wait before exercisir
   the amount of food c
   after a regular mea
   about two hours bef
   uous physical activ
   reason why the indiv
   take a walk or do s
   activity following a
   practice helps burn
   help the body metab

10. **What time of the day**
    cise can be carried ou
    day with the exceptic
    following a regular m
    afternoon hours on h
    people enjoy exercisi
    because it gives them
    day. Others prefer th
    control reasons. By e
    not eat as big a luncl
    caloric intake down.
    seem to like the even
    relaxing effects of exe

11. **Why is it unsafe to e
    conditions?** When a pe
    40 percent of the ener
    is used for mechanica
    rest of the energy (60 t
    into heat. If this heat
    pated because it is eith
    humidity is too high,
    increase, and in extren
    The specific heat o
    required to raise the t
    by one degree Centigr
    pound of body weigh
    grade (.38 cal/lb/°C). T
    body heat is dissipate
    would only need to bt
    .38) to increase total b
    degree Centigrade. If t
    exercise session that
    (about three miles rur
    dissipation, the inner t
    increase by 5.3 degrees

While most experts recommend twenty to thirty minutes of aerobic exercise per session, 1990 research published in *The American Journal of Cardiology* indicates that three, ten-minute bouts of exercise per day (separated by at least four hours), at approximately 70 percent of maximal heart rate, also produce significant training benefits. Although the increases in maximal oxygen uptake were not as large (57 percent) as those found in a group of subjects performing a continuous thirty-minute bout of exercise per day; the researchers concluded that moderate-intensity exercise training, conducted for ten-minutes, three times per day, provides significant benefits to the cardiovascular system. The results of this study are meaningful because lack of time is frequently mentioned by people as the reason for not participating in an exercise program. Many individuals feel that they must exercise for at least twenty minutes to derive any benefits at all. While twenty to thirty minutes are ideal, short-intermittent bouts of exercise are also beneficial to the cardiovascular system.

As a part of the training session, always include a five-minute warm-up and a five-minute cool-down period (see Figure 5.1). Your warm-up should consist of general calisthenics, stretching exercises, or exercising at a lower intensity level than the actual target zone. To cool down, gradually decrease the intensity of exercise. Do not stop abruptly. This will cause blood to pool in the exercised body parts, thereby diminishing the return of blood to the heart. A decreased blood return can cause dizziness and faintness or even induce cardiac abnormalities.

FREQUENCY OF EXERCISE

Ideally, a person should engage in aerobic exercise three to five times per week. When initiating an exercise program, research indicates that three training sessions per week, done on nonconsecutive days, produce significant improvements in maximal oxygen uptake. Better results can be obtained by training up to five times per week. Improvements in maximal oxygen uptake, nonetheless, are minimal when training is conducted more than five days per week. For individuals on a weight loss program, 30 to 60-minute exercise sessions of low to moderate intensity conducted five to six days per week are recommended (see Chapter 3). Three twenty- to thirty-minute training session per week, done on nonconsecutive days, will maintain cardiovascular fitness as long as the heart rate is in the appropriate target zone.

SPECIFIC EXERCISE CONSIDERATIONS

In addition to many of the exercise-related issues already discussed up to this point, there are many other concerns which have not always been completely clear or have been somewhat controversial. Let's examine some of these issues:

1. **Does aerobic exercise make a person immune to heart and blood vessel disease?** Although aerobically fit individuals have a lower incidence of cardiovascular disease, a regular aerobic exercise program by itself is not an absolute guarantee against cardiovascular disease. Overall risk factor management is the best guideline to minimize the risk for cardiovascular disease (see Chapter 12). There are many factors that increase the person's risk, including a genetic predisposition. Experts, however, believe that a regular aerobic exercise program will not only delay the onset of cardiovascular problems, but the chances of surviving a heart attack are much greater for those who exercise regularly.

   Even moderate increases in aerobic fitness significantly decrease premature cardiovascular deaths. Data from the Aerobics Research Institute in Dallas, Texas (see Figure 1.4 in Chapter 1) indicates that the greatest decrease in cardiovascular mortality is seen between the unfit (group 1) and the moderate fitness (2 and 3) groups. A further decrease in cardiovascular mortality is observed between the moderate and the highly fit groups (4 and 5), but the difference is not as pronounced as that shown between the unfit and moderate fitness groups.

2. **How much aerobic exercise is required to decrease the risk for cardiovascular disease?** While research has not yet indicated the exact amount of aerobic exercise required to decrease the risk for cardiovascular disease, general recommendations have been made in this regard. Dr. Thomas K. Cureton, in his book, *The Physiological Effects of Exercise Programs Upon Adults*, reports that 300 calories per exercise session provide the necessary stimuli to control blood lipids (cholesterol and triglycerides), which are a primary risk factor for atherosclerosis, coronary heart disease, and strokes. Dr. Ralph Paffenbarger and co-researchers in their study "Cause-Specific Death Rates per 10,000 Man-Years of Observation Among 16,936 Harvard Alumni, 1962 to 1968, by Physical Activity Index" showed that 2,000 calories expended per week as a result of physical activity yielded the lowest risk for cardiovascular disease among this group of almost 17,000 Harvard alumni (see Chapter 1, Table 1.1). Two thousand calories per week represents about 300 calories per daily exercise session.

3. **Do people experience a "physical high" during aerobic exercise?** During vigorous exercise, morphine-like substances referred to as

"endorphines" are r
gland in the brain. T
killer, but can also i
and natural well-beir
phines are commonl
endurance activities
for as long as thirty
exercise. Many exp
higher levels explai
high" that people ex
prolonged exercise p
  Endorphine levels
be elevated during
Since endorphines a
higher levels coul
increased tolerance t
experienced during r
pleasant feelings exp
birth of the baby. Si
shown shorter and c
conditioned women,
these women may ac
levels during deli
childbirth less trau
untrained women.

4. **Is it safe to exercise (**
is no reason why wo
during pregnancy. If
that women do so to
prepare for delivery.
experience shorter la
faster recovery as com
  Among Indian tr
observed that pregna
carry out all of their ha
very day of delivery, a
birth of the baby the
activities. There have a
athletes who have com
during the early stage
1952 Olympic games, a
and field was won b
Nevertheless, the final c
ticipation should be ma
and her personal physi
  Experts have recom
who has been exercisi
tinue to carry out the sa
fifth month of pregnanc
be taken not to exceed a
of 38.5 Centigrade (101..
adequate oxygen deliver
heart rates should be ke
minute and training sess
15 minutes. After the fif
tionary cycling, and/oi
and water aerobics are
tion with some light si
For women who have r

labored
ness, h
excessiv
muscles
signs o
things t
body. If
should
your ex

  Your
of overe
rate is
cardiova
rate wil
rule of t
per min
rate is a
yourself
abnorm
duration
heart ra
consult

Side S

Side sti
stages o
this sha
cise is u
it could
respirat
exertion
ditioned
they ex
you imp
will disa
intensit
you nee
altogeth

Shin S

One of
limbs ar
terized l
the leg
the follc
tioning,
surfaces
asphalt)
(e) musc
shoes, a
particip

  Shin
or reduc
surfaces
ports, c
shin spl
cises bet

On the other end of the spectrum, some people who weigh very little and are viewed by many as "skinny" or underweight can actually be classified as obese because of their high body fat content. Not at all uncommon are cases of people weighing as little as 100 pounds who are over 30 percent fat (about one-third of their total body weight). Such cases are more readily observed among sedentary people and those who are constantly dieting. Both physical inactivity and constant negative caloric balance lead to a loss in lean body mass. It is clear from these examples that body weight alone does not always tell the true story.

ESSENTIAL AND STORAGE FAT

Total fat in the human body is classified into two types, essential fat and storage fat. The essential fat is needed for normal physiological functions, and without it, human health begins to deteriorate. This essential fat constitutes about 3 percent of the total fat in men and 12 percent in women. The percentage is higher in women because it includes sex-specific fat, such as that found in the breast tissue, the uterus, and other sex-related fat deposits.

  Storage fat constitutes the fat that is stored in adipose tissue, mostly beneath the skin (subcutaneous fat) and around major organs in the body. This fat serves three basic functions: (a) as an insulator to retain body heat, (b) as energy substrate for metabolism, and (c) as padding against physical trauma to the body. The amount of storage fat does not differ between men and women, except that men tend to store fat around the waist, and women more so around the hips and thighs.

TECHNIQUES FOR ASSESSING BODY COMPOSITION

There are several different procedures whereby body composition can be determined. The most common techniques are: (a) hydrostatic or underwater weighing, (b) bioelectrical impedance, (c) skinfold thickness, and (d) girth measurements.

  Hydrostatic weighing (Figure 6.1) is the most accurate technique available to assess body composition, but it also requires a considerable amount of time, skill, space, equipment, and complex procedures. The person's residual lung volume (the amount of air left in the lungs following complete forceful exhalation) must also be measured while the person is in the water. If the residual volume cannot be measured, as is the case in many health/fitness centers, the volume is estimated using predicting equations, which may sacrifice the accuracy of hydrostatic weighing. The psychological factor of being weighed while submerged underwater

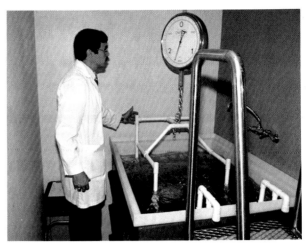

——— *FIGURE 6.1* ———
Hydrostatic weighing technique for body composition assessment.

also makes hydrostatic weighing difficult to administer to the aqua-phobic.

  The bioelectrical impedance technique is much simpler to administer but does require costly equipment. This technique requires the subject to be hooked up to a machine, and a weak electrical current (totally painless) is run through the body to analyze body composition (body fat, lean body mass, and body water). This technique is based on the principle that fat tissue is not as good a conductor of an electrical current as is lean tissue. The easier the conductance, the leaner the individual.

  Because of cost, time, and/or complexity of test procedures, most health and fitness programs prefer the use of anthropometric measurement techniques that correlate quite well with hydrostatic weighing. These techniques, primarily skinfold thickness and girth measurements, provide a quick, simple, and inexpensive estimate of body composition. Both of these techniques will now be introduced in this chapter.

The Skinfold Thickness Technique

The assessment of body composition using skinfold thickness is based on the principle that approximately 50 percent of the fatty tissue in the body is deposited directly beneath the skin. If this tissue is estimated validly and reliably, a good indication of percent body fat can be obtained. This test is regularly performed with the aid of pressure calipers (see Figures 6.2 and 6.3), and several sites must be measured to reflect the total percentage of fat. These sites are triceps, suprailium, and thigh skinfolds for women; and chest, abdomen, and thigh for men. All measurements should be taken on the right side of the body.

post-measurements be conducted by the same technician. Furthermore, measurements should be taken at the same time of the day, preferably in the morning, since water hydration changes due to activity and exercise can increase skinfold girth up to 15 percent. The procedures for assessing percent body fat using skinfold thickness are outlined in Figure 6.4. If skinfold calipers* are available to you, you may proceed to assess your percent body fat with the help of your instructor or an experienced technician.

Girth Measurements Technique

A simpler method to determine body fat is by measuring circumferences at various body sites. All this technique requires is the use of a standard measuring tape, and with little practice good accuracy can be achieved. The limitation of this procedure is that it may not be valid for athletic individuals (men or women) who actively participate in strenuous physical activity, or subjects who can visually be classified as thin or obese. The required procedures for this technique are given in Figure 6.6. The girth measurements for women include the upper arm, hip, and wrist; and for men, the waist and wrist are used.

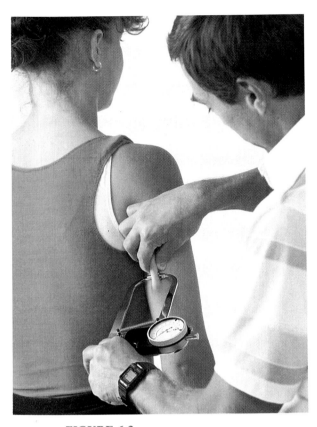

FIGURE 6.2

Skinfold thickness technique for body composition assessment.

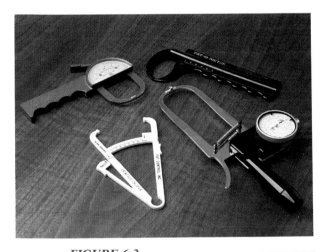

FIGURE 6.3

Various types of skinfold calipers used to assess skinfold thickness.

Nevertheless, even with the skinfold technique, a minimum amount of training is necessary to achieve accurate measurements. Also, small variations in measurements on the same subject may be found when these are taken by different observers. Therefore, it is recommended that pre- and

Waist-to-Hip Ratio

In Chapter 3 it was mentioned that the way in which people store fat may also affect the risk for disease. Obese individuals with a tendency to store high amounts of fat in the abdominal area, instead of around the hips and thighs, are clearly at higher risk for coronary heart disease, congestive heart failure, hypertension, strokes, and diabetes. Therefore, a waist-to-hip ratio test was recently designed by a panel of scientists appointed by the National Academy of Sciences and the Dietary Guidelines Advisory Council for the U.S. Departments of Agriculture and Health and Human Services. The panel recommends that men need to lose weight if the waist-to-hip ratio is 1.0 or higher. Women need to lose weight if the ratio is .85 or higher. The waist-to-hip ratio for a man with a 40-inch waist and a 38-inch hip would be 1.05 (40 ÷ 38). Such a ratio may be indicative of increased risk for disease.

---

*This instrument is available at most colleges and universities around the country. If unavailable, you can purchase an inexpensive, but yet reliable Skinfold Caliper from Fat Control Inc., P.O. Box 10117, Towson, MD 21204 — Phone (301) 296-1993

sedentary living, which, in
...e resting metabolic rate. If
...ng at the same rate, body fat
...rage decrease in resting
...y-year-old individual is about
...as compared to a twenty-six-
...e, participating in a strength-
...an important factor in the
...ion of obesity.

WOMEN AND STRENGTH TRAINING

One of the most common misconceptions about physical fitness is related to women and strength training. Due to the increase in muscle mass commonly seen in men, many women feel that strength-training programs are counterproductive because they will make them look muscular and less feminine. *While the quality of muscle in men and women is the same, endocrinological differences will not allow women to achieve the same amount of muscle hypertrophy (size) as men.*

The thought that strength training will make women less feminine is as false as to think that playing basketball will turn them into giants. Masculinity and femininity are established by genetic inheritance and not by the amount of physical activity. *Variations in the degree of masculinity and femininity are determined by individual differences in hormonal secretions of androgen, testosterone, estrogen, and progesterone.* Women with a bigger-than-average build are often inclined to participate in sports because of their natural physical advantage. As a result, many women have associated sports and strength participation with increased masculinity.

As the number of women who participate in sports has steadily increased in the last few years, the myth that strength training masculinizes women has gradually been disappearing (Figure 7.1). For example, per pound of body weight, women gymnasts are considered to be among the strongest athletes in the world. These athletes engage in very serious strength-training programs and for their body size are most likely twice as strong as the average male. Yet, women gymnasts are among the most graceful and feminine of all women. In recent years, increased femininity has become the rule rather than the exception for women who participate in strength-training programs.

On the other hand, you may ask yourself "if weight training does not masculinize women, why do so many women body builders develop such heavy musculature?" In the sport of body building, the athletes follow intense training routines consisting of two or more hours of constant weight lifting with very short rest intervals between sets.

FIGURE 7.1

Female gymnast performing a strength skill on the floor exercise event. Contrary to some beliefs, high levels of strength do not masculinize women.

Many times during the training routine, back-to-back exercises that require the use of the same muscle groups are performed. The objective of this type of training is to "pump" extra blood into the muscles, which makes the muscles appear much bigger than they really are in resting conditions. Based on the intensity and the length of the training session, the muscles can remain filled with blood, appearing measurably larger for several hours after completing the training session. Therefore, in real life, these women are not as muscular as they seem when they are "pumped up" for a contest.

In the sport of body building, a big point of controversy is the use of anabolic steroids and human growth hormones, even among women participants. Anabolic steroids are synthetic versions of the male sex hormone testosterone, which promotes muscle development and hypertrophy. The use of these hormones, however, can produce detrimental and undesirable side effects, which some women deem tolerable (e.g., hypertension, fluid retention, decreased breast size, deepening of the voice, facial whiskers, and body hair growth). The use of these steroids among women is definitely on the increase, and according to several sportsmedicine physicians and women body builders, about 80 percent of women body builders have used steroids. Furthermore, several women's track-and-field coaches have indicated that as many as 95 percent of women athletes around the world in this sport will use anabolic steroids in order to remain competitive at the international level.

There is no doubt that women who take steroids will indeed build heavy musculature like men, and if taken long enough, will lead to masculinizing effects. As a result, the International Federation of Body Building recently instituted a mandatory steroid-testing program among women participating in the Miss Olympia contest. When drugs are not used to promote development, increased health and femininity are the rule rather than the exception among women who participate in body building, strength training, or sports in general.

Another benefit of strength training, which is accentuated even more when combined with aerobic exercise, is a decrease in adipose or fatty tissue around the muscle fibers themselves. Research has shown that in women the decrease in fatty tissue is greater than the amount of muscle hypertrophy. Therefore, it is not at all uncommon to lose inches and yet not lose body weight (see Figure 7.2). However, since muscle tissue is more dense than fatty tissue, and in spite of the fact that inches are being lost, women often become discouraged because the results cannot be readily seen on the scale. This discouragement can be easily offset by regularly determining body composition to monitor changes in percent body fat as opposed to simply measuring total body weight changes.

MUSCULAR STRENGTH AND ENDURANCE ASSESSMENT

Although muscular strength and endurance are interrelated, a basic difference exists between the two. *Strength is defined as the ability to exert maximum force against resistance. Endurance is the ability of a muscle to exert submaximal force repeatedly over a period of time.* Muscular endurance depends to a large extent on muscular strength, and to a lesser extent on cardiovascular endurance. Weak muscles cannot repeat an action several times, nor sustain it for a prolonged period of time. Keeping these two principles in mind, strength tests and training programs have been designed to measure and develop absolute muscular strength, muscular endurance, or a combination of both.

Muscular strength is usually determined by the maximal amount of resistance (one repetition maximum or 1 RM) *that an individual is able to lift in a single effort.* This assessment gives a good measure of absolute strength, but it does require a considerable amount of time since the 1 RM is determined through trial and error. For example, the strength of the chest muscles is frequently measured with the bench press exercise. If the individual has not trained with weights, he/she may try 100 pounds and find out that this resistance is lifted quite easily. Then 50 pounds is added, but the person fails to lift the resistance. The resistance is then decreased by ten or twenty pounds, and finally, after several trials the 1 RM is established. Fatigue also becomes a factor, because by the time the 1 RM is established, several maximal, or near-maximal attempts have already been performed. *Muscular endurance is commonly established by the number of repetitions that an individual can perform against a submaximal resistance or by the length of time that a given contraction can be sustained.*

In Lab 7A you will have the opportunity to assess your own level of muscular strength and/or endurance. Two tests are given in this lab. You may take either or both of these tests according to time and/or facilities available. Since muscular strength and endurance are highly specific and a high degree in one body part does not necessarily indicate a high degree in other parts, the exercises for these tests were selected to obtain a profile that would include

-------- FIGURE 7.2 --------

Changes in Body Composition as a Result of a Combined Aerobic and Strength Training Program.

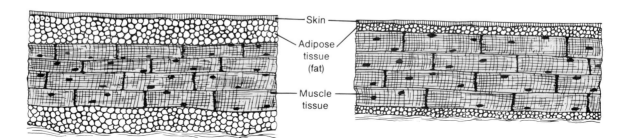

PRE-TRAINING   **POST-TRAINING**

Skin
Adipose tissue (fat)
Muscle tissue

FIGURE 8.1
Strength Training Record Form (Continued)

Date												
Exercise	**St/Reps/Res***	**St/Reps/Res**	**St/Reps/Res**	**St/Reps/Res**	**St/Reps/Res**	**St/Reps/Res**	**St/Reps/Res**	**St/Reps/Res**	**St/Reps/Res**	**St/Reps/Res**	**St/Reps/Res**	**St/Reps/Res**

Name _____

*St/Reps/Res = Sets, Repetitions, and Resistance (e.g., 1/6/125 = 1 set of 6 repetitions with 125 pounds).

Principles of Muscular Flexibility Prescription

OBJECTIVES

- Define ballistic stretching, slow-sustained stretching, and proprioceptive neuromuscular facilitation stretching.
- Explain the factors that contibute to the development of muscular flexibility.
- Introduce a complete set of exercises for an overall body flexibility-development program.
- Present a program for the prevention and rehabilitation of low back pain.

The development and maintenance of good joint range of motion (flexibility) is important to enhance health and quality of life. *Although genetics play a role in body flexibility, adequate range of joint mobility can be increased and maintained through a regular flexibility exercise program.* Since range of motion is highly specific to each body part (ankle, trunk, shoulder), a comprehensive stretching program that includes all body parts and follows the basic guidelines for flexibility development should be followed to obtain the desired benefits.

GUIDELINES FOR FLEXIBILITY DEVELOPMENT

The overload and specificity of training principles discussed in conjunction with strength development in Chapter 9 also apply to the development of muscular flexibility. To increase the total range of motion of a given joint, the specific muscles that surround that particular joint have to be progressively stretched beyond their normal accustomed length. Principles of mode, intensity, repetitions, and frequency of exercise can also be used for the prescription of flexibility programs.

Mode of Exercise

Three modes of stretching exercises can be used to increase flexibility: (a) ballistic stretching, (b) slow-sustained stretching, and (c) proprioceptive neuromuscular facilitation stretching. Although research has indicated that all three types of stretching are effective in developing better flexibility, there are certain advantages to each technique.

Ballistic or dynamic stretching exercises are performed using jerky, rapid, and bouncy movements that provide the necessary force to lengthen the muscles. In spite of the fact that studies have indicated that this type of stretching helps to develop flexibility, the *ballistic actions may lead to increased muscle soreness and injury due to small tears to the soft tissue.* In addition, proper precautions must be taken not to overstretch ligaments, since they undergo plastic or permanent elongation. If the magnitude of the stretching force cannot be adequately controlled, as in fast, jerky movements, ligaments can be easily overstretched. This, in turn, leads to excessively loose joints, increasing the risk for injuries, including joint dislocation and subluxation (partial dislocation). Consequently, most authorities do not recommend ballistic exercises for flexibility development.

With the slow-sustained stretching technique, muscles are gradually lengthened through a joint's complete range of motion, and the final position is held for a few seconds. Using a slow-sustained stretch causes the muscles to relax; hence, greater length can be achieved. This type of stretch causes relatively little pain and has a very low risk of injury. *Slow-sustained stretching exercises are the most frequently used and recommended for flexibility development programs.*

Proprioceptive neuromuscular facilitation (PNF) stretching (Figure 10.1) has become more popular in the last few years. This technnique is based on a "contract and relax" method and requires the assistance of another person. The procedure used is as follows:

A. The person assisting with the exercise provides an initial force by slowly pushing in the direction of the desired stretch. The initial stretch does not cover the entire range of motion.

B. The person being stretched then applies force in the opposite direction of the stretch, against the assistant, who will try to hold the initial degree of stretch as close as possible. In other words, an isometric contraction is being performed at that angle.

C. After four or five seconds of isometric contraction, the muscle(s) being stretched are completely relaxed. The assistant then slowly increases the degree of stretch to a greater angle.

FIGURE 10.1
Proprioceptive neuromuscular facilitation stretching technique.

D. The isometric contraction is then repeated for another four or five seconds, following which the muscle(s) is relaxed again. The assistant can then slowly increase the degree of stretch one more time. This procedure is repeated anywhere from two to five times until mild discomfort occurs. On the last trial, the final stretched position should be held for several seconds.

Theoretically, with the PNF technique, the isometric contraction aids in the relaxation of the muscle(s) being stretched, which results in greater muscle length. While some researchers have indicated that PNF is more effective than slow-sustained stretching, the disadvantages are that the degree of pain incurred with PNF is greater, a second person is required to perform the exercises, and a greater period of time is needed to conduct each session.

Intensity of Exercise

Before starting any flexibility exercises, always warm up the muscles adequately with some calisthenic exercises. A good time to do flexibility exercises is following aerobic workouts. Increased body temperature can significantly increase joint range of motion. Failing to conduct a proper warm-up increases the risk for muscle pulls and tears.

The intensity or degree of stretch when doing flexibility exercises should only be to a point of mild discomfort. Pain does not have to be a part of the stretching routine. Excessive pain is an indication that the load is too high and may lead to injury. Stretching should only be done to slightly below the pain threshold. As participants reach this point, they should try to relax the muscle(s) being stretched as much as possible. After completing the stretch, the body part is brought gradually back to the original starting point.

Repetitions

The duration of an exercise session for flexibility development is based on the repetitions performed for each exercise and the length of time that each repetition (final stretched position) is held. *The general recommendations are that each exercise be done four or five times, and each time the final position should be held for about ten seconds.* As the flexibility levels increase, the subject can progressively increase the time that each repetition is held, up to a maximum of one minute.

Frequency of Exercise

Flexibility exercises should be conducted five to six times per week in the initial stages of the program. After a minimum of six to eight weeks of almost daily stretching, flexibility levels can be maintained with only two or three sessions per week, using about three repetitions of ten to fifteen seconds each.

FLEXIBILITY EXERCISES

To improve body flexibility at least one stretching exercise should be used for each major muscle group. *A complete set of exercises for the development of muscular flexibility is presented at the end of this chapter.* For some of these exercises (e.g., lateral head tilts and arm circles) you may not be able to hold a final stretched position, but you should still perform the exercise through the joint's full range of motion. Depending on the number and the length of the repetitions performed, a complete workout will last between fifteen and thirty minutes.

PREVENTION AND REHABILITA-TION OF LOW BACK PAIN

Very few people make it through life without suffering from low back pain at some point. Current estimates indicate that 75 million Americans suffer from chronic low back pain each year. Unfortunately, *approximately 80 percent of the time, backache syndrome is preventable and is caused by: (a) physical inactivity, (b) poor postural habits and body mechanics, and (c) excessive body weight.*

Lack of physical activity is the most common cause contributing to chronic low back pain. The deterioration or weakening of the abdominal and gluteal muscles, along with a tightening of the lower back (erector spine) muscles, bring about an unnatural forward tilt of the pelvis (see Figure 10.2). This tilt puts extra pressure on the spinal vertebrae, causing pain in the lower back. In addition, excessive accumulation of fat around the midsection of the body contributes to the forward tilt of the pelvis, which further aggravates the condition.

Low back pain is also frequently associated with faulty posture and improper body mechanics. This refers to the use of correct body positions in all of life's daily activities, including sleeping, sitting, standing, walking, driving, working, and exercising. Incorrect posture and poor mechanics, as explained in Figure 10.3, lead to increased strain not only on the lower back, but on many other bones, joints, muscles, and ligaments.

The incidence and frequency of low back pain can be greatly reduced by including some specific stretching and strengthening exercises as a part of the regular fitness program. When suffering from backache,

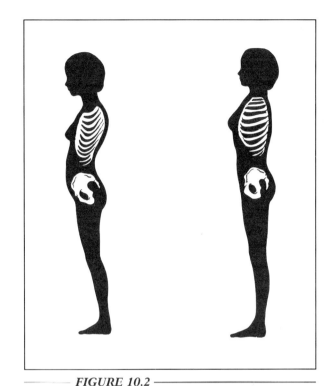

——— *FIGURE 10.2* ———
A comparison of incorrect (left) and correct (right) pelvic alignment.

in most cases pain is only present with movement and physical activity. If the pain is severe and persists even at rest, the initial step is to consult a physician, who can rule out any disc damage and most likely prescribe correct bed rest using several pillows under the knees for adequate leg support (see Figure 10.3). This position helps release muscle spasms by stretching the muscles involved. Additionally, a physician may prescribe a muscle relaxant, and/or anti-inflammatory medication, and/or some type of physical therapy. Once the individual is pain-free in the resting state, he/she needs to start correcting the muscular imbalance by stretching the tight muscles and strengthening weak ones (stretching exercises are always performed first).

Several exercises for the prevention and rehabilitation of the backache syndrome are given at the end of this Chapter. These exercises can be conducted twice or more daily when a person suffers from backache. Under normal circumstances, three to four times per week is sufficient to prevent the syndrome.

LABORATORY EXPERIENCES

LAB 10A: Sample Flexibility Development Program

LAB PREPARATION: Wear exercise clothing and be prepared to participate in a sample flexibility development session.

LAB 10B: Exercises for the Prevention and Rehabilitation of Low Back Pain

LAB PREPARATION: Wear exercise clothing and prepare to perform all of the exercises for the prevention and rehabilitation of low back pain outlined in this Chapter.

References

1. Heyward, V.H. *Advanced Methods for Physical Fitness Assessment and Exercise Prescription.* Champaign, IL: Human Kinetic Publishers, 1991.

2. Hoeger, W.W.K. *The Complete Guide for the Development & Implementation of Health Promotion Programs.* Englewood, CO: Morton Publishing Company, 1987.

3. "Your Back and How to Care For It." Kenilworth, NJ: Schering Corporation, 1965.

FIGURE 10.3

Your back
and how to care for it

Whatever the cause of low back pain, part of its treatment is the correction of faulty posture. But good posture is not simply a matter of "standing tall." It refers to correct use of the body at all times. In fact, for the body to function in the best of health it must be so used that no strain is put upon muscles, joints, bones, and ligaments. To prevent low back pain, avoiding strain must become a way of life, practiced while lying, sitting, standing, walking, working, and exercising. When body position is correct, internal organs have enough room to function normally and blood circulates more freely.

With the help of this guide, you can begin to correct the positions and movements which bring on or aggravate backache. Particular attention should be paid to the positions recommended for resting, since it is possible to strain the muscles of the back and neck even while lying in bed. By learning to live with good posture, under all circumstances, you will gradually develop the proper carriage and stronger muscles needed to protect and support your hard-working back.

COPYRIGHT © 1965, SCHERING CORPORATION   ALL RIGHTS RESERVED

HOW TO STAY ON YOUR FEET WITHOUT TIRING YOUR BACK
To prevent strain and pain in everyday activities, it is restful to change from one task to another before fatigue sets in. Housewives can lie down between chores; others should check body position frequently, drawing in the abdomen, flattening the back, bending the knees slightly.

Use of a footrest relieves swayback.

Bend the knees and hips, not the waist.

Hold heavy objects close to you.

Never bend over without bending the knees.

Not this way

CHECK YOUR CARRIAGE HERE
In correct, fully erect posture, a line dropped from the ear will go through the tip of the shoulder, middle of hip, back of kneecap, and front of anklebone.

Incorrect:
Lower back is arched or hollow.

Incorrect:
Upper back is stooped, lower back is arched, abdomen sags.

Incorrect:
Note how, in strained position, pelvis tilts forward, chin is out, and ribs are down, crowding internal organs.

Correct:
In correct position, chin is in, head up, back flattened, pelvis held straight.

To find the correct standing position: Stand one foot away from wall. Now sit against wall, bending knees slightly. Tighten abdominal and buttock muscles. This will tilt the pelvis back and flatten the lower spine. Holding this position, inch up the wall to standing position, by straightening the legs. Now walk around the room, maintaining the same posture. Place back against wall again to see if you have held it.

HOW TO SIT CORRECTLY
A back's best friend is a straight, hard chair. If you can't get the chair you prefer, learn to sit properly on whatever chair you get. To correct sitting position from forward slump: Throw head well back, then bend it forward to pull in the chin. This will straighten the back. Now tighten abdominal muscles to raise the chest. Check position frequently.

Relieve strain by sitting well forward, flatten back by tightening abdominal muscles, and cross knees.

Use of footrest relieves swayback. Aim is to have knees higher than hips.

Correct way to sit while driving, close to pedals. Use seat belt or hard backrest, available commercially.

TV slump leads to "dowager's hump," strains neck and shoulders.

If chair is too high, swayback is increased.

Keep neck and back in as straight a line as possible with the spine. Bend forward from hips.

Driver's seat too far from pedals emphasizes curve in lower back.

Strained reading position. Forward thrusting strains muscles of neck and head.

FIGURE 10.3

(Continued)

HOW TO PUT YOUR BACK TO BED

For proper bed posture, a firm mattress is essential. Bedboards, sold commercially, or devised at home, may be used with soft mattresses. Bedboards, preferably, should be made of ¾ inch plywood. Faulty sleeping positions intensify swayback and result not only in backache but in numbness, tingling, and pain in arms and legs.

Incorrect:	Correct:
Lying flat on back makes swayback worse.	Lying on side with knees bent effectively flattens the back. Flat pillow may be used to support neck, especially when shoulders are broad.

Use of high pillow strains neck, arms, shoulders.	Sleeping on back is restful and correct when knees are properly supported.

Sleeping face down exaggerates swayback, strains neck and shoulders.	Raise the foot of the mattress eight inches to discourage sleeping on the abdomen.

Bending one hip and knee does not relieve swayback.	Proper arrangement of pillows for resting or reading in bed.

A straight-back chair used behind a pillow makes a serviceable backrest.

WHEN DOING NOTHING, DO IT RIGHT

Rest is the first rule for the tired, painful back. The following positions relieve pain by taking all pressure and weight off the back and legs.

Note pillows under knees to relieve strain on spine.

For complete relief and relaxing effect, these positions should be maintained from 5 to 25 minutes.

EXERCISE—WITHOUT GETTING OUT OF BED

Exercises to be performed while lying in bed are aimed not so much at strengthening muscles as at teaching correct positioning. But muscles used correctly become stronger and in time are able to support the body with the least amount of effort.

Do all exercises in this position. Legs should not be straightened.

Bring knee up to chest. Lower slowly but do not straighten leg. Relax. Repeat with each leg 10 times.

Bring both knees slowly up to chest. Tighten muscles of abdomen, press back flat against bed. Hold knees to chest 20 seconds, then lower slowly. Relax. Repeat 5 times. This exercise gently stretches the shortened muscles of the lower back, while strengthening abdominal muscles. Clasp knees, bring them up to chest, at the same time coming to a sitting position. Rock back and forth.

RULES TO LIVE BY—FROM NOW ON

1. Never bend from the waist only; bend the hips and knees.
2. Never lift a heavy object higher than your waist.
3. Always turn and face the object you wish to lift.
4. Avoid carrying unbalanced loads; hold heavy objects close to your body.
5. Never carry anything heavier than you can manage with ease.
6. Never lift or move heavy furniture. Wait for someone to do it who knows the principles of leverage.
7. Avoid sudden movements, sudden "overloading" of muscles. Learn to move deliberately, swinging the legs from the hips.
8. Learn to keep the head in line with the spine, when standing, sitting, lying in bed.
9. Put soft chairs and deep couches on your "don't sit" list. During prolonged sitting, cross your legs to rest your back.
10. Your doctor is the only one who can determine when low back pain is due to faulty posture. He is the best judge of when you may do general exercises for physical fitness. When you do, omit any exercise which arches or overstrains the lower back: backward bends, or forward bends, touching the toes with the knees straight.

EXERCISE—WITHOUT ATTRACTING ATTENTION

Use these inconspicuous exercises whenever you have a spare moment during the day, both to relax tension and improve the tone of important muscle groups.

1. Rotate shoulders, forward and backward.
2. Turn head slowly side to side.
3. Watch an imaginary plane take off, just below the right shoulder. Stretch neck, follow it slowly as it moves up, around and down, disappearing below the other shoulder. Repeat, starting on left side.
4. Slowly, slowly, touch left ear to left shoulder; right ear to right shoulder. Raise both shoulders to touch ears, drop them as far down as possible.
5. At any pause in the day—waiting for an elevator to arrive, for a specific traffic light to change—pull in abdominal muscles, tighten, hold it for the count of eight without breathing. Relax slowly. Increase the count gradually after the first week, practice breathing normally with the abdomen flat and contracted. Do this sitting, standing, and walking.

11. Wear shoes with moderate heels, all about the same height. Avoid changing from high to low heels.
12. Put a footrail under the desk, and a footrest under the crib.
13. Diaper the baby sitting next to him or her on the bed.
14. Don't stoop and stretch to hang the wash; raise the clothesbasket and lower the washline.
15. Beg or buy a rocking chair. Rocking rests the back by changing the muscle groups used.
16. Train yourself vigorously to use your abdominal muscles to flatten your lower abdomen. In time, this muscle contraction will become habitual, making you the envied possessor of a youthful body-profile!
17. Don't strain to open windows or doors.
18. For good posture, concentrate on strengthening "nature's corset"—the abdominal and buttock muscles. The pelvic roll exercise is especially recommended to correct the postural relation between the pelvis and the spine.

SCHERING CORPORATION · KENILWORTH, N.J

PRINTED IN U.S.A   CE 504 11868000 8 78

Flexibility Exercises

Exercise 1: LATERAL HEAD TILT

Action: Slowly and gently tilt the head laterally. Repeat several times to each side.

Areas Stretched: Neck flexors and extensors and ligaments of the cervical spine.

Exercise 2: ARM CIRCLES

Action: Gently circle your arms all the way around. Conduct the exercise in both directions.

Areas Stretched: Shoulder muscles and ligaments.

Exercise 3: SIDE STRETCH

Action: Stand straight up, feet separated to shoulder width, and place your hands on your waist. Now move the upper body to one side and hold the final stretch for a few seconds. Repeat on the other side.

Areas Stretched: Muscles and ligaments in the pelvic region.

Exercise 4: BODY ROTATION

Action: Place your arms slightly away from your body and rotate the trunk as far as possible, holding the final position for several seconds. Conduct the exercise for both the right and left sides of the body. You can also perform this exercise by standing about two feet away from the wall (back toward the wall), and then rotate the trunk, placing the hands against the wall.

Areas Stretched: Hip, abdominal, chest, back, neck, and shoulder muscles. Hip and spinal ligaments.

Exercise 5:   CHEST STRETCH

Action: Kneel down behind a chair and place both hands on the back of the chair. Gradually push your chest downward and hold for a few seconds.

Areas Stretched: Chest (pectoral) muscles and shoulder ligaments.

Exercise 6:   SHOULDER HYPEREXTENSION STRETCH

Action: Have a partner grasp your arms from behind by the wrists and slowly push them upward. Hold the final position for a few seconds.

Areas Stretched: Deltoid and pectoral muscles, and ligaments of the shoulder joint.

Exercise 7:   SHOULDER ROTATION STRETCH

Action: With the aid of an aluminum or wood stick or surgical tubing, place the stick or tubing behind your back and grasp the two ends using a reverse (thumbs-out) grip. Slowly bring the stick over your head, keeping the elbows straight. Repeat several times (bring the hands closer together for additional stretch).

Areas Stretched: Deltoid, latissimus dorsi, and pectoral muscles. Shoulder ligaments.

Exercise 8:   QUAD STRETCH

Action: Stand straight up and bring up one foot, flexing the knee. Grasp the front of the ankle and pull the ankle toward the gluteal region. Hold for several seconds. Repeat with the other leg.

Areas Stretched: Quadriceps muscle, and knee and ankle ligaments.

Exercise 9:
HEEL CORD STRETCH

Action: Stand against the wall or at the edge of a step and stretch the heel downward, alternating legs. Hold the stretched position for a few seconds.

Areas Stretched: Heel cord (Achilles tendon), gastrocnemius, and soleus muscles.

Exercise 10:
ADDUCTOR STRETCH

Action: Stand with your feet about twice shoulder width and place your hands slightly above the knee. Flex one knee and slowly go down as far as possible, holding the final position for a few seconds. Repeat with the other leg.

Areas Stretched: Hip adductor muscles.

Exercise 11:
SITTING ADDUCTOR STRETCH

Action: Sit on the floor and bring your feet in close to you, allowing the soles of the feet to touch each other. Now place your forearms (or elbows) on the inner part of the thigh and push the legs downward, holding the final stretch for several seconds.

Areas Stretched: Hip adductor muscles.

Exercise 12:
SIT-AND-REACH STRETCH

Action: Sit on the floor with legs together and gradually reach forward as far as possible. Hold the final position for a few seconds. This exercise may also be performed with the legs separated, reaching to each side as well as to the middle.

Areas Stretched: Hamstrings and lower back muscles, and lumbar spine ligaments.

Exercise 13: TRICEPS STRETCH

Action: Place the right hand behind your neck. Grasp the right arm above the elbow with the left hand. Gently pull the elbow backward. Repeat the exercise with the opposite arm.

Areas Stretched: Back of upper arm (triceps muscle) and shoulder joint.

Exercises for the Prevention and Rehabilitation of Low Back Pain

Exercise 14: SINGLE-KNEE TO CHEST STRETCH

Action: Lie down flat on the floor. Bend one leg at approximately 100 degrees and gradually pull the opposite leg toward your chest. Hold the final stretch for a few seconds. Switch legs and repeat the exercise.

Areas Stretched: Lower back and hamstring muscles, and lumbar spine ligaments.

Exercise 15: DOUBLE-KNEE TO CHEST STRETCH

Action: Lie flat on the floor and then slowly curl up into a fetal position. Hold for a few seconds.

Areas Stretched: Upper and lower back and hamstring muscles. Spinal ligaments.

Exercise 16: UPPER AND LOWER BACK STRETCH

Action: Sit in a chair with feet separated greater than shoulder width. Place your arms to the inside of the thighs and bring your chest down toward the floor. At the same time, attempt to reach back as far as you can with your arms.

Areas Stretched: Upper and lower back muscles and ligaments.

Exercise 17: SIT-AND-REACH STRETCH

(see Exercise 12 in this chapter)

Exercise 18: GLUTEAL STRETCH

Action: Sit on the floor, bend the right leg and place your right ankle slightly above the left knee. Grasp the left thigh with both hands and gently pull the leg toward your chest. Repeat the exercise with the opposite leg.

Areas Stretched: Buttock area (gluteal muscles).

Exercise 19: SIDE AND LOWER BACK STRETCH

Action: As illustrated in the photograph, sit on the floor with knees bent, feet to the right side, the left foot touching the right knee, and both legs flat on the floor. Place the right hand on the left knee and the left hand next to the right hand slightly above the knee. Gently pull the right shoulder toward the left knee and at the same time you may rotate the upper body counterclockwise. Switch sides and repeat the exercise (do not arch your back while performing this exercise).

Areas Stretched: Side and lower back muscles and lower back ligaments.

Note: The stretch is felt primarily when people experience low back pain due to muscle spasm or contracture.

Exercise 20: TRUNK ROTATION AND LOWER BACK STRETCH

Action: Sit on the floor and bend the left leg, placing the left foot on the outside of the right knee. Place the right elbow on the left knee and push against it, as illustrated in the photograph. At the same time, try to rotate the trunk to the left (counterclockwise). Hold the final position for a few seconds. Repeat the exercise with the other side.

Areas Stretched: Lateral side of the hip and thigh, trunk, and lower back.

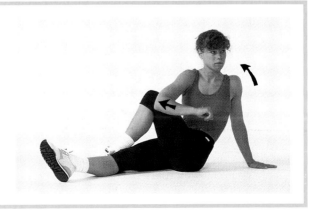

Exercise 21:   PELVIC TILT

Action: Lie flat on the floor with the knees bent at about a 70-degree angle. Tilt the pelvis by tightening the abdominal muscles, flattening your back against the floor, and raising the lower gluteal area ever so slightly off the floor. Hold the final position for several seconds. The exercise can also be performed against a wall as shown in illustration c.

Areas Stretched:
Low back muscles and ligaments.

Areas Strengthened:
Abdominal and gluteal muscles.

Note: This is perhaps the most important exercise for the care of the lower back. It should be included as a part of your daily exercise routine and should be performed several times throughout the day when pain the lower back is present as a result of muscle imbalance.

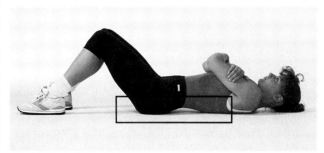

a

b

c

Exercise 22:   ABDOMINAL CURL-UP (see Exercise 4 in Chapter 8)

It is important that you do not stabilize your feet when performing this exercise, because doing so decreases the work of the abdominal muscles. Also, remember not to "swing up" but rather curl up as you perform the exercise.

Skill-Related Components of Physical Fitness

OBJECTIVES

- Describe the benefits of good skill-related fitness.
- Identify and define the six components of skill-related fitness.
- Introduce performance tests to assess skill-related fitness.

Skill-related fitness is important for successful motor performance in athletic events and in such lifetime sports and activities as basketball, racquetball, golf, hiking, soccer, and water skiing. Good skill-related fitness also enhances overall quality of life by helping people cope more effectively in emergency situations.

The components of skill-related fitness are agility, balance, coordination, power, reaction time, and speed. All of these are important to a certain extent in sports and athletics. For example, outstanding gymnasts must achieve good skill-related fitness in all components. Let's look at some of the elements required in this sport. A significant amount of agility is necessary to perform a double back somersault with a full twist, a skill during which the athlete must simultaneously rotate around one axis and twist around a different one. Static balance is essential for maintaining a handstand or a scale, while dynamic balance is needed to perform many of the gymnastic routines (e.g., balance beam, parallel bars, pommel horse). Coordination is important to successfully integrate various skills that require different degrees of difficulty into one routine. Power and speed are needed to propel the body into the air such as when tumbling or vaulting. Reaction time is used in determining when to terminate rotation upon a visual clue such as spotting the floor on a dismount.

As with the health-related fitness components, the principle of specificity of training also applies to skill-related components. This principle states that to
develop a given component, the training program must be specific to the type of development that the individual is trying to achieve. *In the case of agility, balance, coordination, and reaction time, research indicates that the development of these components is very task-specific. That is, to develop a certain task or skill, the individual must practice that same specific task many times over. There seems to be very little cross-over learning effect. For instance, proper practice of a handstand (balance) will eventually lead to successful performance of the skill, but complete mastery of this skill does not insure that the individual will find immediate success when attempting to perform other static balance positions in gymnastics. Power and speed may be improved with a specific strength-training program and/or frequent repetition of the specific task that is to be improved.*

The rate of learning in skill-related fitness varies among individuals, primarily because these components seem to be determined to a large extent by hereditary factors. Individuals with good skill-related fitness tend to do better and learn faster when performing a wide variety of skills. Nevertheless, few individuals enjoy complete success in all skill-related components. Furthermore, while skill-related fitness can be improved with practice, improvements in reaction time and speed are limited and seem to be primarily related to genetic endowment.

Although it is unknown how much skill-related fitness is desirable, everyone should attempt to develop and maintain a better than "average" level.

151

As pointed out earlier, this type of fitness is not only crucial for athletes, but it is also important to lead a better and happier life. *Improvements in skill-related fitness will allow an individual greater enjoyment and success in lifetime sports* (e.g., tennis, racquetball, basketball). Perhaps even more important, it can help a person cope more effectively in emergency situations. Good reaction time, balance, coordination, and/or agility can help you avoid a fall or break a fall so as to minimize injury. The ability to generate maximum force in a short period of time (power) could be crucial to decrease injury or even preserve life in a situation where you may be called upon to lift a heavy object that has fallen on another person or even yourself. In our society where the average lifespan continues to increase, maintenance of speed can be especially crucial for the elderly. Many of these individuals, and for that matter, many unfit/overweight young people, no longer possess the speed to safely cross an intersection prior to the light change for oncoming traffic.

Regular participation in a health-related fitness program can help increase performance of skill-related components and vice-versa. For example, significantly overweight individuals do not enjoy good agility or speed. Since participation in a cardiovascular endurance program helps decrease body fat, an overweight individual who loses weight through such an exercise program can improve agility and speed. A sound flexibility program will decrease resistance to motion about body joints, which may increase agility, balance, and overall coordination. Improvements in strength most definitely help develop power. On the other hand, people that possess good skill-related fitness usually participate in lifetime sports and games, which in turn helps develop health-related fitness.

PERFORMANCE TESTS FOR SKILL-RELATED FITNESS

Several performance tests have been developed over the years to assess the various components of skill-related fitness. Each component will now be introduced, along with the description of a performance test that can be used to obtain a general rating for each component. The results of the performance tests, expressed in percentile ranks, are given in Tables 11.1 (men) and 11.2 (women). As with muscular strength and endurance, and muscular flexibility, the various fitness categories are given based on the following standards: 81 percentile and above is excellent, 61 to 80 percentile is good, 41 to 60 percentile is average, 21 to 40 percentile is fair, and less than 21 percentile is poor (see Table 11.3.).

AGILITY

Agility is defined as the ability to quickly and efficiently change body position and direction. Agility is important in sports such as basketball, racquetball, and soccer (see Figure 11.1); where the participant must change direction rapidly and also maintain proper body control.

――――― **FIGURE 11.1** ―――――

Successful soccer players demonstrate high levels of skill-fitness.

Agility Test: SEMO Agility Test.

Objective. To measure general body agility.

Procedures. The free throw area of a basketball court or any other smooth area 12 by 19 feet with adequate running space around it can be used for this test. Four plastic cones or similar objects are placed on each corner of the free throw lane as shown in Figure 11.2. The participant starts on the

――――― **FIGURE 11.2** ―――――

Graphic description of the SEMO (agility) test

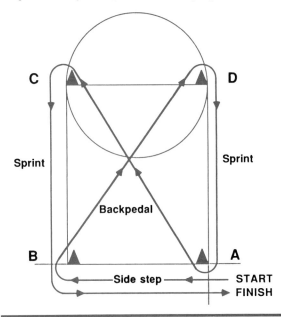

outside of the free throw lane at point A, with his back to the free throw line. When given the "go" command, the person should side step from A to B (a crossover step cannot be used), backpedal from B to D, sprint forward from D to A, again backpedal from A to C, sprint forward from C to D, and side-step from B to the finish line at A. The subject must always go around (outside) each corner cone. The stopwatch is started at the "go" command and stopped when the subject crosses the finish line. The best of two trials preceded by a practice trial is used as the final test score. Record the time to the nearest tenth of a second.

BALANCE

Balance is the ability to maintain the body in proper equilibrium. Balance is crucial in activities such as gymnastics, diving, ice skating, skiing (Figure 11.3), or even football and wrestling, where the athlete attempts to upset the opponent's equilibrium.

———— *FIGURE 11.3* ————
Nordic skiing requires good balance, a skill-related component of fitness.

Balance Test: One Foot Stand Test (preferred foot, without shoes).

Objective. To measure the static balance of the participant.

Procedures. A flat, smooth floor — not carpeted — is used for this test. Remove the shoes and socks and stand on your preferred foot, placing the other foot on the inside of the supporting knee, and the

hands on the sides of the hips. When the "go" command is given, raise your heel off the floor and balance yourself as long as possible without moving the ball of the foot from its initial position (see Figure 11.4). The test is terminated when any of the following conditions occur:

1. The supporting foot moves (shuffles)
2. The raised heel touches the floor
3. The hands are removed from the hip
4. Sixty seconds time has elapsed

The test is scored by recording the amount of time balance is maintained on the selected foot, starting with the "go" command. The best of two trials preceded by a practice trial is used as the final performance score. Record the time to the nearest tenth of a second.

———— *FIGURE 11.4* ————
Balance test.

COORDINATION

Coordination can be defined as the integration of the nervous and the muscular systems to produce correct, graceful, and harmonious body movements. This component is important in a wide variety of motor activities such as golf, baseball, karate, soccer, and racquetball where hand-eye and/or foot-eye movements must be properly integrated.

Coordination Test: "Soda Pop" Test.

Objective. To assess overall motor/muscular control and movement time.

Procedures. The following homemade equipment is necessary to perform this test. Draw a straight line lengthwise through the center of a piece of cardboard approximately 32 inches long by 5 inches wide. Draw six marks exactly 5 inches away from each other on this line (draw the first mark about 2½ inches from the edge of the cardboard). Using a compass, draw six circles 3¼ inches in diameter (a radius of 1 centimeter larger than a can of soda pop) which must be centered on the six marks along the line. For the purposes of this test, each circle is assigned a number starting with 1 for the first circle on the right of the subject, all the way to 6 for the last circle on the left. The previously described cardboard, three unopened (full) cans of soda pop, a table, a chair, and a stopwatch are needed to perform the test.

To administer the test, place the cardboard on a table and have the subject sit in front of it with the center of the cardboard bisecting the body. The preferred hand is used for this test. If the right hand is used, place the three cans of pop on the cardboard in the following manner: can one is centered in circle 1 (farthest to the right), can two in circle 3, and can three in circle 5. To start the test, the right hand, with the thumb up, is placed on can one and the elbow joint should be at about 100-120 degrees. When the tester gives the signal, the stopwatch is started and the subject proceeds to turn the cans of pop upside down, placing can one inside circle 2, followed by can two inside circle 4, and then can three inside circle 6; immediately the subject returns all three cans, **starting with can one** (see Figure 11.6), then can two, and can three — turning them right side up — to their original placement. On this "return trip", the cans are grasped with the

hand in a thumb down position. This entire procedure is done twice, without stopping, and counted as one trial. In other words, two "trips" down and up are required to complete one trial. The watch is stopped when the last can of pop is returned to its original position, following the second trip back. The preferred hand (in this case the right hand) is used throughout the entire task, and the object of the test is to perform the task as fast as possible, making sure that the cans are always placed within each circle. If the person misses a circle at any time during the test (a can placed on a line or outside a circle), the trial must be repeated from the start. A graphic illustration of this test is provided in Figure 11.6.

FIGURE 11.6

Graphic illustration of the "Soda Pop" (coordination) Test

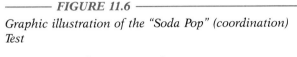
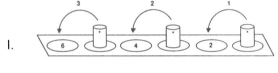
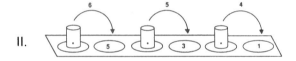
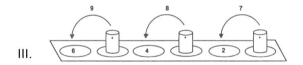
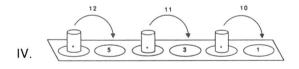

If the participant chooses to use the left hand, the same procedures are used, except that the cans are placed starting from the left, with can one in circle 6, can two in circle 4, and can three in circle 2. The procedure is initiated by turning can one upside down onto circle 5, can two onto circle 3, and so on...

Two practice trials are allowed prior to initiating the test. Two test trials are then given, and the best time, recorded to the nearest tenth of a second, is used as the test score. If the person has a mistrial (misses a circle), repeat the test until two successful trials are accomplished.

FIGURE 11.5

"Soda pop" (coordination) test.

Car
F

■ Present a com
disease risk re

*Cardiovascular
death in the United
half of the total m
refers to any path
heart and the cir
Some examples of
nary heart disea
congenital heart c
atherosclerosis, st
congestive heart f
vessel disease is s
lem in the country
percent in the last
for this dramatic
tion. More people
for cardiovascular
cant changes in th
potential risk of su*

*The major form
nary heart disease
arteries that supply
nutrients are narr
cholesterol and tri
coronary arteries d
heart muscle, whi
attack (see Figure
cause of death in t
approximately on*

POWER

Power is the ability to produce maximum force in the shortest period of time. The two components of power are speed and force (strength). An effective combination of these two components allows a person to produce explosive movements such as in jumping, putting the shot, and spiking/throwing/hitting a ball.

Power Test. Standing Long Jump Test.

Objective: To measure leg power.

Procedures. Draw a takeoff line on the floor and place a ten foot-long tape measure perpendicular to this line. The student stands with the feet several inches apart, centered with the tape measure, and toes just behind the takeoff line (see Figure 11.7). Prior to the jump, the participant swings the arms backward and bends the knees. The jump is performed by extending the knees and swinging the arms forward at the same time. The distance is recorded from the takeoff line to the heel or other body part that touches the floor nearest the takeoff line. Three trials are allowed and the best trial measured to the nearest inch is used as the final test score.

─────── *FIGURE 11.7* ───────

Correct placement of the feet for the start of the standing broad jump (power test)

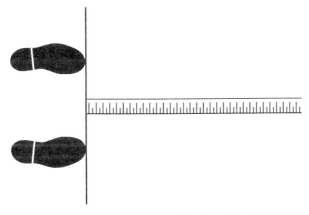

REACTION TIME

Reaction time can be defined as the length of time required by an individual to initiate a response to a given stimulus. Good reaction time is important for starts in track and swimming, to react quickly when playing tennis at the net, or in sports like ping pong, boxing, and karate.

Reaction Time Test: "Yard stick" Test (preferred hand).

Objective. To measure the participants hand reaction time in response to a visual stimulus.

Procedures. For this test you will need a regular yard stick with a shaded "concentration zone" marked on the first two inches of the stick. The test is administered with the subject sitting in a chair adjacent to a table and the preferred forearm and hand resting on the table. As illustrated in Figure 11.8, the tips of the thumb and fingers are held in a "ready to pinch" position, about one inch apart and two inches beyond the edge of the table, with the upper edges of the thumb and index finger parallel to the floor.

The person administering the test should hold the yardstick near the end and the zero point of the stick must be even with the upper edge of the subject's thumb and index finger. The tester may steady the middle of the stick with the other hand. The participant is instructed to look at the "concentration zone" and react by catching the stick when it is dropped. He/she may not look at the tester's hand nor move the hand up or down while trying to catch the stick. Twelve trials are given, each preceded by the preparatory command "ready." A random one- to three-second count is used between the "ready" command and each stick drop. Each trial is scored to the nearest one-half of an inch, read just above the upper edge of the thumb. Three practice trials are given prior to initiating the actual test to be sure that the subject understands the procedures. The three lowest and the three highest scores are discarded, and the average of the middle six is used as the final test score. The testing area should be as free from distractions as possible.

SPEED

Speed is the ability to rapidly propel the body or a part of the body from one point to another. Sprints in track, stealing a base in baseball, soccer, and basketball are all examples of activities that require good speed for success.

Speed Test: Fifty-Yard Dash.

Objective. To measure the participant's speed.

Procedures. It is recommended that the fifty-yard dash test be administered to two students at a time. Both students should take their positions behind the starting line. A starter will raise one arm and give the instruction "are you ready," followed by the command "go," simultaneously swinging the arm downward for the timer(s), who stand at the finish line to start the stopwatch(s). The score is the time elapsed between the starting signal and the moment the participant crosses the finish line, recorded to the nearest tenth of a second.

and the moderately fit (2 and 3) groups. It, therefore, appears that even small improvements in cardiovascular endurance, to approximately 35 and 32.5 ml/kg/min in men and women respectively, will significantly decrease the risk for cardiovascular mortality. Such fitness levels can be easily achieved by most adults who engage in a moderate exercise program.

Caution should be taken, however, not to ignore the other risk factors. Although aerobically fit individuals have a lower incidence of cardiovascular disease, a regular aerobic exercise program by itself is not an absolute guarantee for a lifetime free of cardiovascular problems. Poor lifestyle habits, such as smoking, eating excessive fatty/salty/sweet foods, excess body fat, and high levels of stress increase cardiovascular risk and will not always be completely eliminated through aerobic exercise. Overall risk factor management is the best guideline to minimize the risk for cardiovascular disease. Yet, *aerobic exercise is one of the most important aspects in the prevention and reduction of cardiovascular problems*. The basic principles for cardiovascular exercise prescription were given in Chapter 5 and Lab 5A.

RESTING AND STRESS ELECTROCARDIOGRAMS

The electrocardiogram, or ECG, is a valuable record of the heart's function. *It is a record of the electrical impulses that stimulate the heart to contract* (see Figure 12.3). In the actual reading of an ECG, five general areas are interpreted: heart rate, the heart's rhythm, the heart's axis, enlargement or hypertrophy of the heart, and myocardial infarction or heart attack.

─────── *FIGURE 12.3* ───────

Normal electrocardiogram (P wave= atrial depolarization, QRS complex= ventricular depolarization, T wave= ventricular repolarization)

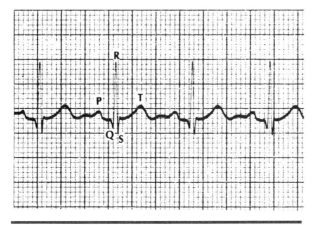

On a standard twelve-lead ECG, ten electrodes are placed on the person's chest. From these ten electrodes, twelve "pictures" or leads of the electrical impulses as they travel through the heart muscle (myocardium) are studied from twelve different positions. By looking at the tracings of an ECG, it is possible to identify abnormalities in the functioning of the heart (see Figure 12.4). Based on the findings, the ECG may be interpreted as normal, equivocal, or abnormal. Since not all problems will always be identified by an ECG, a normal tracing is not an absolute problem-free guarantee, nor does an abnormal tracing necessarily mean the presence of a serious condition.

─────── *FIGURE 12.4* ───────

Abnormal electrocardiogram showing a depressed S-T segment. This abnormality is commonly seen during exercise in patients with coronary disease.

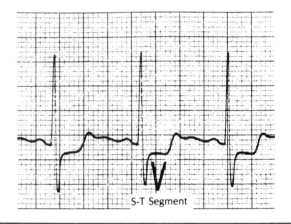

ECGs are taken at rest, during stress of exercise (see Figure 12.5), and during recovery. A stress ECG is also known as a maximal exercise tolerance test. Similar to a high-speed road test on a car, *a stress ECG reveals the tolerance of the heart to high-intensity exercise. As compared to a resting ECG, a stress ECG is a much better test for the discovery of coronary heart disease.*It is also used to determine cardiovascular fitness levels, to screen persons for preventive and cardiac rehabilitation programs, to detect abnormal blood pressure response during exercise, and to establish actual or functional maximal heart rate for exercise prescription purposes. The recovery ECG also becomes an important diagnostic tool in the monitoring of the return of the heart's activity to normal conditions.

While not every adult who wishes to start or continue in an exercise program needs a stress ECG, the following guidelines can be used to determine when this type of test should be administered:

1. Adults forty-five years or older.

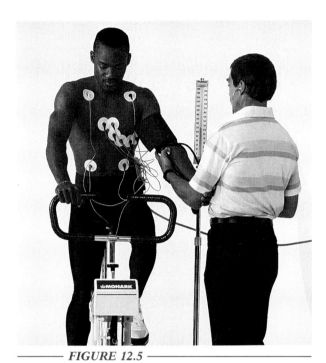

———— *FIGURE 12.5* ————

Exercise Tolerance Test with Twelve-Lead Electro-cardiographic Monitoring (exercise stress-ECG)

2. A total cholesterol level above 200 mg/dl, or an HDL-cholesterol below 45 mg/dl.

3. Hypertensive and diabetic patients.

4. Cigarette smokers.

5. Individuals with a family history of coronary heart disease, syncope, or sudden death before age sixty.

6. People with an abnormal resting ECG.

7. All individuals with symptoms of chest discomfort, dysrhythmias, syncope, or chronotropic incompetence (a heart rate that increases slowly during exercise and never reaches maximum).

Although the predictive value of a stress ECG has been at times questioned, it must be remembered that at present it is the most practical, inexpensive, noninvasive procedure available in diagnosing latent coronary heart disease. On the average, the test is accurate in diagnosing coronary heart disease about 65 percent of the time. Part of the problem is that many times those who administer stress ECGs are doing it without a clear understanding of the indications and limitations of this test. Nonetheless, the sensitivity of the test is increased as the severity of the disease increases. It is also more accurate in people who are at high risk for cardiovascular disease, in particular men over 45 and women over 55 with a poor cholesterol profile, high blood pressure, and/or a family history of heart disease. Test protocols, number of leads, electrocardiographic criteria, and the quality of the

technicians administering the test further increase its sensitivity. It therefore still remains a very useful tool in identifying those at high risk for exercise-related sudden death.

CHOLESTEROL

The term "blood lipids" (fats) is mainly used in reference to cholesterol and triglycerides. These lipids are carried in the bloodstream by molecules of protein known as high-density lipoproteins, low-density lipoproteins, very low-density lipoproteins, and chylomicrons. A significant elevation in blood lipids has long been associated with heart and blood vessel disease.

Cholesterol has received considerable attention in the last few years. This fatty or lipid substance is essential for certain metabolic functions in the body. However, *high levels of blood cholesterol contribute to the formation of the atherosclerotic plaque, or the buildup of fatty tissue in the walls of the arteries* (see Figure 12.6). *In the case of the heart, as the plaque builds up it obstructs the coronary vessels. Since these arteries supply the heart muscle (myocardium) with oxygen and nutrients, a myocardial infarction or heart attack will follow when obstruction occurs* (see Figure 12.1). Unfortunately, the heart disguises its problems quite effectively, and typical symptoms of heart disease, such as angina pectoris or chest pain, do not start until the arteries are about 75 percent occluded; in many cases, the first symptom is sudden death.

The general recommendation is to keep total blood cholesterol levels below 200 mg/dl (milligrams per deciliter). For individuals thirty and younger it is now recommended that the total cholesterol count should not exceed 180 mg/dl. Cholesterol levels between 200 and 239 mg/dl are thought to be borderline high, while levels of 240 mg/dl and above are indicative of high risk for disease. Based on research conducted at the Institute for Aerobics Research in Dallas, Texas, the relative risk for all-cause mortality by physical fitness and serum cholesterol levels is given in Figure 12.7.

Another important factor in the development of heart disease seems to be the way in which cholesterol is "packaged" or carried in the bloodstream. *Cholesterol is primarily transported in the form of high-density lipoprotein cholesterol (HDL-cholesterol) and low-density lipoprotein cholesterol (LDL-cholesterol). The high-density molecules have a high affinity for cholesterol and tend to attract cholesterol, which is then carried to the liver to be metabolized and excreted.* In other words, they act as "scavengers" removing cholesterol from the body, thus preventing plaque formation in the arteries. On the other hand, *LDL-cholesterol tends to release cholesterol, which may then penetrate the lining of the arteries, enhancing the process of atherosclerosis.*

──────── *FIGURE 12.6* ────────

The Atherosclerotic Process

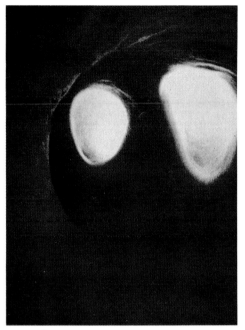

Normal artery

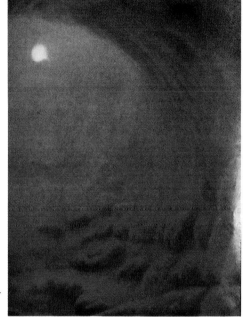

*Early
stage of
atherosclerosis*

*Advanced stage of
atherosclerosis*

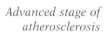

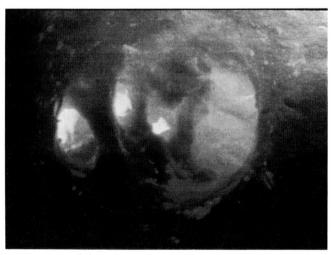

Progression of the atherosclerotic plaque

From the previous discussion, it can easily be seen that the more HDL-cholesterol present, the better. HDL-cholesterol is the so called "good cholesterol" and offers a certain degree of protection against heart disease. *New evidence indicates that low levels of HDL-cholesterol could be the best predictor of coronary heart disease,* and seems to be more significant than the total value itself.

Researchers at the 1988 annual American Heart Association meeting indicated that people with low total cholesterol (less than 200 mg/dl) and also low HDL-cholesterol (under 40 mg/dl) may have three times the heart disease risk of those with high cholesterol but with good HDL-cholesterol levels. Another researcher presented data on 797 patients whose total cholesterol was less than 200 mg/dl.

──────── *FIGURE 12.7* ────────

Relative Risks of All-Cause Mortality by Physical Fitness and Serum Cholesterol Level. Numbers on top of the bars are all-cause death rates per 10,000 person-years of follow-up for each cell — 1 person-year indicates one person that was followed-up one year later (least fit group = 1, most fit group = 5).

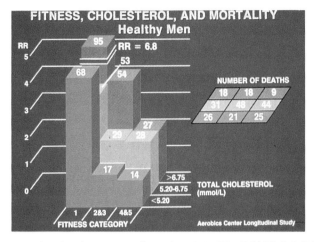
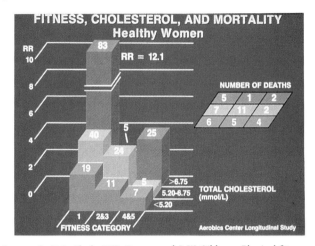

Reproduced with permission from Blair, S.N., H.W. Kohl III, R.S. Paffenbarger, Jr, D.G. Clark, K.H. Cooper, and L.W. Gibbons. *Physical fitness and all-cause mortality: a prospective study of healthy men and women.* JAMA 262:2395-2401, 1989. Copyright 1989, American Medical Association.

Their work showed that 60 percent of the patients had heart disease, and almost 75 percent of this group had HDL-cholesterol levels below 40 mg/dl. *The recommended HDL-cholesterol values to minimize the risk for disease are 45 and 55 mg/dl (or higher) for men and women respectively.*

Many authorities believe that the ratio of total cholesterol to HDL-cholesterol is also a strong indicator of potential risk for cardiovascular disease. It is generally accepted that a 4.5 or lower ratio (total cholesterol/HDL-cholesterol) is excellent for men, and 4.0 or lower is best for women. For instance, 50 mg/dl of HDL-cholesterol as compared to 200 mg/dl of total cholesterol yields a ratio of 4.0 (200 ÷ 50 = 4.0). The lower the ratio, the greater the protection. In another instance, a person's total cholesterol could also be 200 mg/dl, but if the HDL-cholesterol is only 20 mg/dl, the ratio would be 10.0. Such a ratio is extremely dangerous and is very conducive to atherosclerosis and coronary disease.

Although the average American consumes between 400 and 600 mg of daily cholesterol, the body actually manufactures more cholesterol than is consumed in the diet. Approximately 700 mg of cholesterol per day are produced from saturated fats. These fats are found primarily in meats and dairy products but are seldom found in foods of plant origin (see Table 12.2). Poultry and fish also contain less saturated fat than beef. Unsaturated fats are mainly of plant origin and cannot be converted to cholesterol. There are individual differences as to how much cholesterol can be manufactured by the body. Some people can have higher-than-normal intakes of saturated fats and still maintain normal blood levels, while others with a lower intake can have abnormally high levels.

If the total cholesterol or the total cholesterol/HDL-cholesterol ratio is higher than ideal, certain guidelines should be followed to lower these figures. This can be accomplished by lowering the LDL-cholesterol component. *A diet low in fat and saturated fat* (Figure 12.8) *and high in fiber* is recommended to decrease LDL-cholesterol. *Total fat consumption on a daily basis should not exceed 30 percent of the total caloric intake, and saturated fat consumption should be less than 10 percent of the total caloric intake. The average intake of cholesterol should also be limited to less than 300 mg per day.* LDL-cholesterol can also be lowered by losing excess body fat and using medication. As a general rule of thumb, *the following dietary guidelines are recommended to lower LDL-cholesterol levels: (a) egg consumption should be limited to less than three eggs per week; (b) red meats should be eaten less than three times per week, and organ meats (e.g., liver and kidneys), sausage, bacon, hot dogs, and canned meats should be avoided; (c) low-fat milk (1 percent or less preferably) and low-fat dairy products are recommended; (d) coconut oil, palm oil, and cocoa butter should be avoided; (e) fish, especially those high in Omega-3 fatty acids (fresh or frozen mackerel, herring, tuna, salmon, and lake trout) should be eaten twice a week; and (f) recommended body weight should be achieved.*

The second factor involved in improving the cholesterol profile is increasing the *HDL-cholesterol component. HDL-cholesterol is genetically determined, and women have higher values than men.*

TABLE 12.2

Cholesterol and Saturated Fat Content of Selected Foods

Food	Serving Siz	Cholesterol (mg.)	Sat. Fat (gr)
Avocado	1/8 med.	—	3.2
Bacon	2 slc.	30	2.7
Beans (all types)	any	—	—
Beef — Lean, fat trimmed off	3 oz.	75	6.0
Beef — Heart (cooked)	3 oz.	150	1.6
Beef — Liver (cooked)	3 oz.	255	1.3
Butter	1 tsp.	12	0.4
Caviar	1 oz.	85	—
Cheese — American	2 oz.	54	11.2
Cheese — Cheddar	2 oz.	60	12.0
Cheese — Cottage (1% fat)	1 cup	10	0.4
Cheese — Cottage (4% fat)	1 cup	31	6.0
Cheese — Cream	2 oz.	62	6.0
Cheese — Muenster	2 oz.	54	10.8
Cheese — Parmesan	2 oz.	38	9.3
Cheese — Swiss	2 oz.	52	10.0
Chicken (no skin)	3 oz.	45	0.4
Chicken — Liver	3 oz.	472	1.1
Chicken — Thigh, Wing	3 oz.	69	3.3
Egg (yolk)	1	250	1.8
Frankfurter	2	90	11.2
Fruits	any	—	—
Grains (all types)	any	—	—
Halibut, Flounder	3 oz.	43	0.7
Ice Cream	1/2 cup	27	4.4
Lamb	3 oz.	60	7.2
Lard	1 tsp.	5	1.9
Lobster	3 oz.	170	0.5
Margarine (all vegetable)	1 tsp.	—	0.7
Mayonnaise	1 tbsp.	10	2.1
Milk — Skim	1 cup	5	0.3
Milk — Low Fat (2%)	1 cup	18	2.9
Milk — Whole	1 cup	34	5.1
Nuts	1 oz.	—	1.0
Oysters	3 oz.	42	—
Salmon	3 oz.	30	0.8
Scallops	3 oz.	29	—
Sherbet	1/2 cup	7	1.2
Shrimp	3 oz.	128	0.1
Trout	3 oz.	45	2.1
Tuna (canned — drained)	3 oz.	55	—
Turkey — Dark Meat	3 oz.	60	0.6
Turkey — Light Meat	3 oz.	50	0.4
Vegetables (except avocado)	any	—	—

——— *FIGURE 12.8* ———

Substituting low fat for high fat products in the diet significantly decreases the risk for disease.

This is probably one of the reasons why heart disease is less common among women. *Research has indicated that increases in HDL-cholesterol values are almost completely dependent upon a very regular aerobic exercise program.* There is a clear relationship between HDL-cholesterol and aerobic exercise. The greater the amount of exercise, the higher the HDL-cholesterol. A cardiovascular exercise program, if properly prescribed, should yield positive results. *A combination of adequate nutrition and aerobic exercise is the best prescription for achieving a good cholesterol profile.*

You should also be aware that several other factors can lower the HDL-cholesterol levels. Beta-blocker type medications (used in treating heart disease and hypertension), tobacco usage, and birth control pills all have a negative effect on HDL-cholesterol levels. A combination of two or three of these is even worse.

TRIGLYCERIDES

Triglycerides are also known as free fatty acids, and in combination with cholesterol, they accelerate the formation of plaque. Triglycerides are carried in the bloodstream primarily by very low-density lipoproteins (VLDL) and chylomicrons. *These fatty acids are found in poultry skin, lunch meats, and shellfish. However, they are mainly manufactured in the liver from refined sugars, starches, and alcohol.* High intake of alcohol and sugars (honey included) will significantly increase triglyceride levels. Thus, they can be lowered by decreasing the consumption of the above-mentioned foods along with weight reduction (if overweight) and aerobic exercise. *An optimal blood triglyceride level is less than 100 mg/dl.*

Individuals who have never had a blood chemistry test should probably have one done in the near future. An initial test is always useful to establish a baseline for future reference. Make sure that the blood test does include the HDL-cholesterol component, since many clinics and hospitals still do not include this factor in their regular analyses. While no definite guidelines have yet been given, following an initial normal baseline test, and as long as the recommended dietary and exercise guidelines are kept, a blood analysis every three to five years prior to the age of thirty-five should suffice. After the age of thirty-five, a blood lipid test should be conducted every year in conjunction with a regular preventive medicine physical examination.

DIABETES

Diabetes is a condition in which the blood glucose is unable to enter the cells because of insufficient insulin production by the pancreas. Several studies have shown that the incidence of cardiovascular disease among diabetic patients is quite high. Cardiovascular disease is also the leading cause of death among these patients.

Individuals with chronically elevated blood glucose levels may also have problems in metabolizing fats. This, in turn, can increase susceptibility to atherosclerosis, increasing the risk for coronary disease and other conditions such as vision loss and kidney damage. Fasting blood glucose levels over 120 mg/dl may be an early sign of diabetes and should be brought to the attention of a physician. Blood glucose levels around 150 to 160 mg/dl are considered by many health care practitioners as borderline diabetes.

Although there is a genetic predisposition to diabetes, adult-onset diabetes is closely related to obesity. In most cases, this type of condition can be corrected by following a special diet, a weight loss program, and exercise. If you have elevated blood glucose levels, you should consult your physician and let him/her decide on the best approach to treat this condition.

BLOOD PRESSURE

There are some 60,000 miles of blood vessels running through the human body. As the heart forces the blood through these vessels, the fluid is under pressure. Hence, *blood pressure is but a measure of the force exerted against the walls of the vessels by the blood flowing through them.* Blood pressure is measured in milliliters of mercury and is usually expressed in two numbers. *Ideal blood pressure should be 120/80 or below.* The higher number reflects the pressure exerted during the forceful contraction of the heart or systole (therefore, the name "systolic" pressure), and the lower pressure is taken during the heart's relaxation, or diastolic phase, when no blood is being ejected.

When Is Blood Pressure Considered Too High?

A few years ago, a systolic pressure of 100 plus your age was the acceptable standard. However, this is no longer the case. Hypertension has been viewed as the point where the pressure doubles the mortality risk. This pressure has been determined at about 160/96. Traditionally, the upper limits of normal were established at 140/90, a reading that by today's standards is considered by many as borderline hypertension. Readings between 140/90 and 160/96 (either number being in that range) were classified as mild hypertension. However, statistical evidence clearly indicates that *blood pressure readings above 140/90 increase the risk of disease and premature death*. Consequently, in 1986, the American Heart Association revised its standards and now considers all blood pressures over 140/90 as hypertension.

While the threshold for hypertension has been set at 140/90, many experts believe that the lower the blood pressure, the better. Even if the pressure is around 90/50, as long as that person does not have any symptoms of low blood pressure or hypotension, he/she does not need to be concerned. Typical hypotension symptoms are dizziness, lightheadedness, and fainting.

Blood pressure may also fluctuate during a regular day. Many factors affect blood pressure, and one single reading may not be a true indicator of your real pressure. For example, physical activity and stress increase blood pressure, while rest and relaxation decrease it. Consequently, several measurements should be made before a diagnosis of elevated pressure is suggested.

Based on 1988 estimates by the American Heart Association, almost 61 million adults and 2.7 million children (six to seventeen years old) in the United States are hypertensive. As a disease, hypertension has been referred to as the silent killer. It does not hurt, it does not make you feel sick, and unless you check it, years may go by before you even realize that you have a problem. *Elevated blood pressure is a risk factor not only for coronary heart disease, but also for congestive heart failure, strokes, and kidney failure*. The relative risk for all-cause mortality by systolic blood pressure and various fitness levels is illustrated in Figure 12.9.

What Makes Hypertension A Killer?

All inner walls of arteries are lined by a layer of smooth endothelial cells. The nature of this lining is such that blood lipids cannot penetrate it and build up unless damage is done to the cells. High blood pressure is thought to be a leading factor contributing to the destruction of this lining. As blood pressure rises, so does the risk for atherosclerosis or the development of fatty-cholesterol deposits in the walls of the arteries. The higher the pressure, the greater the damage that is done to the arterial wall, allowing a faster occlusion of the vessels, especially if serum cholesterol is also elevated. Occlusion of the coronary vessels decreases the blood supply to

---

FIGURE 12.9

Relative Risks of All-Cause Mortality by Physical Fitness and Systolic Blood Pressure. Numbers on top of the bars are all-cause death rates per 10,000 person-years of follow-up for each cell — 1 person-year indicates one person that was followed-up one year later (least fit group = 1, most fit group = 5).

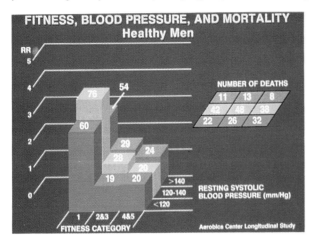
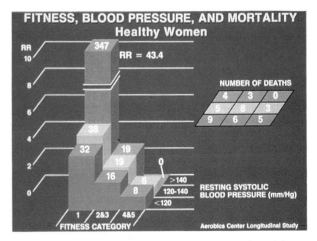

Reproduced with permission from Blair, S.N., H.W. Kohl III, R.S. Paffenbarger, Jr, D.G. Clark, K.H. Cooper, and L.W. Gibbons. *Physical fitness and all-cause mortality: a prospective study of healthy men and women.* JAMA 262:2395-2401, 1989. Copyright 1989, American Medical Association.

the heart muscle and can lead to heart attacks. When brain arteries are involved, strokes may follow.

A clear example of the role of elevated pressure in the development of atherosclerosis can be seen by comparing blood vessels in the human body. Even when significant atherosclerosis is present throughout major arteries in the body, fatty plaques are rarely seen in the pulmonary artery, which goes from the right heart to the lungs. The pressure in this artery is normally below 40 mmHg, and at such low pressure significant deposits do not occur. This is one of the reasons why people with low blood pressure have a lower incidence of cardiovascular disease.

Constantly elevated blood pressure also causes the heart to work much harder. Initially the heart does well, but in time, this constant strain results in a pathologically enlarged heart and subsequent congestive heart failure. Furthermore, high blood pressure damages blood vessels to the kidneys and eyes, leading to eventual kidney failure and loss of vision.

How Can Hypertension Be Controlled?

Ninety percent of all hypertension has no definite cause. This type of hypertension is referred to as essential hypertension and is treatable. *Aerobic exercise, weight reduction, a low-sodium/high-potassium diet, stress reduction, smoking cessation, a decrease in blood lipids, a lower caffeine and alcohol intake, and antihypertensive medication have all been used effectively in treating essential hypertension.* The other 10 percent is caused by such pathological conditions as narrowing of the kidney arteries, glomerulonephritis (a kidney disease), tumors of the adrenal glands, and narrowing of the aortic artery. With this type of hypertension, the pathological cause has to be treated first in order to correct the blood pressure problem.

Antihypertensive medications are often the first choice of treatment modality, but they also produce multiple side effects, such as lethargy, somnolence, sexual difficulties, increased blood cholesterol and glucose levels, lower potassium levels, and elevated uric acid levels. Often, a physician may end up treating these side effects as much as the hypertension problem itself. Because of the multiple side effects, approximately 50 percent of the patients will stop taking the medication within the first year of treatment.

Perhaps one of the most significant factors contributing to elevated blood pressure is excessive sodium in the diet (salt is sodium chloride and contains approximately 40 percent sodium). Water retention increases with high sodium intake. As water retention increases, so does the blood volume, which, in turn, drives the pressure up. On the other hand, high intake of potassium seems to regulate water retention and therefore appears to lower the pressure slightly.

While sodium is essential for normal physiological functions, only 200 mg or one-tenth of a teaspoon of salt is required on a daily basis. *Even under very strenuous conditions, such as jobs and sports participation where heavy sweating is involved, the amount of sodium required by the organism seldom exceeds 3,000 mg per day.* Yet, in the typical American diet, sodium intake ranges between 6,000 and 20,000 mg per day! No wonder hypertension is so prevalent today.

In underdeveloped countries and Indian tribes where no salt is used in cooking or added at the table, and the only sodium consumed comes from food in its natural form, daily intake seldom exceeds 2,000 mg. Blood pressure among these people does not increase with age, and hypertension is practically unknown. These findings seem to indicate that the human body may be able to handle 2,000 mg per day, but higher intakes than that on a regular basis may cause a gradual rise in blood pressure over the years.

Many people ask themselves, where does all the sodium come from? The answer is found in Table 12.3. Most individuals do not realize the amount of sodium contained in various foods, and the list in Table 12.3 does not include the salt added at the table. Even if you do not have a blood pressure problem now, you need to be concerned about sodium intake — otherwise blood pressure may sneak up on you.

New research studies have also indicated that there may be a link between hypertension and calcium and magnesium deficiencies. The connection between calcium and hypertension isn't quite clear, but a recent national dietary survey linked calcium deficiency to high blood pressure. Magnesium supplementation has been used effectively to lower blood pressure in patients suffering from hypertensive encephalopathy and in patients affected by diuretic-induced low magnesium levels. However, no evidence at this point shows a decrease in blood pressure in patients with normal magnesium levels.

When treating high blood pressure, prior to using medication (unless elevation is extremely high), many sports medicine physicians prefer a combination of aerobic exercise, weight loss, and sodium reduction. In most instances this treatment modality will bring blood pressure under control.

The link between hypertension and obesity has been well established. Not only does blood volume increase with excess body fat, but every additional pound of fat requires an estimated extra mile of blood vessels to feed this tissue. Furthermore, blood capillaries are constricted by the adipose tissue as these vessels run through them. As a result, the heart muscle must work harder to pump

────── *TABLE 12.3* ──────

Sodium, Potassium, Calcium, and Magnesium Levels of Selected Foods

Food	Serving Size	Sodium (mg)	Potassium (mg)	Calcium (mg)	Magnesium (mg)
Apple	1 med.	1	182	10	6
Asparagus	1 cup	2	330	26	24
Avocado	1/2	4	680	11	39
Banana	1 med.	1	440	8	33
Bologna	3 oz.	1,107	133	6	12
Bouillon Cube	1	960	4	0	0
Cantaloupe	1/4	17	341	20	22
Carrot (raw)	1	34	225	27	12
Cheese					
American	2 oz.	614	93	376	16
Cheddar	2 oz.	342	56	408	16
Muenster	2 oz.	356	77	406	16
Parmesan	2 oz.	1,056	53	672	24
Swiss	2 oz.	148	64	410	16
Chicken (light meat)	6 oz.	108	700	20	20
Corn (canned)	1/2 cup	195	80	4	15
Corn (natural)	1/2 cup	3	136	2	29
Frankfurter	1	627	136	4	5
Haddock	6 oz.	300	594	66	41
Hamburger (reg)	1	500	321	63	25
Lamb (leg)	6 oz.	108	700	18	22
Milk (whole)	1 cup	120	351	288	33
Milk (skim)	1 cup	126	406	296	28
Orange	1 med.	1	263	54	13
Orange Juice	1 cup	1	200	26	27
Peach	1 med.	2	308	14	9
Pear	1 med.	2	130	13	9
Peas (canned)	1/2 cup	200	82	22	20
Peas (boiled-natural)	1/2 cup	2	178	18	24
Pizza (cheese - 14" diam.)	1/8	456	85	110	25
Potato	1 med.	6	763	14	75
Potato Chips	10	150	226	8	25
Potato (french fries)	10	5	427	12	40
Pork	6 oz.	96	438	17	25
Roast Beef	6 oz.	98	448	15	27
Salami	3 oz.	1,047	170	12	5
Salmon (canned)	6 oz.	198	756	262	50
Salt	1 tsp.	2,132	0	14	7
Soups					
Chicken Noodle	1 cup	979	55	17	5
Clam Chowder					
(New England)	1 cup	914	146	43	7
Cream of Mushroom	1 cup	955	98	191	5
Vegetable Beef	1 cup	1,046	162	12	6
Soy Sauce	1 tsp.	1,123	22	13	2
Spaghetti (tomato sauce					
and cheese)	6 oz.	648	276	54	20
Strawberries	1 cup	1	244	31	16
Tomato (raw)	1 med.	3	444	12	11
Tuna (drained)	3 oz.	38	255	7	0

the blood through a longer, constricted network of blood vessels.

The role of aerobic exercise in the management of blood pressure is becoming more important each day. On the average, cardiovascularly fit individuals have lower blood pressures than unfit people. An 18-year follow-up study on exercising and nonexercising subjects showed considerably lower blood pressures in the active group. The exercise group had an average resting blood pressure of 120/79 as compared to 150/90 for the nonexercise group (see Table 12.4).

Aerobic exercise is also frequently used in the treatment of hypertensive patients. Several well-documented studies have shown that *nearly 90 percent of hypertensive patients who initiate a moderate aerobic exercise program can expect a significant decrease in blood pressure after only a few weeks of training.* The research data also shows that exercise, and not weight loss, is the major contributor to the decrease in blood pressure seen in exercising subjects. These changes, however, are not maintained if aerobic exercise is discontinued.

New research presented by Dr. Larry W. Gibbons (Cooper Clinic, Dallas, Texas) at the 1990 American College of Sports Medicine meeting also indicates that *exercise programs for hypertensive patients should be of moderate intensity.* Training at about 50 percent of heart rate reserve seems to have the same effect in lowering blood pressure as training at a 70 percent heart rate reserve. Furthermore,

high intensity training in hypertensive patients may actually cause a new rise in blood pressure. It may be better, nonetheless, to be highly fit and have high blood pressure, than to be unfit and have low blood pressure. As illustrated in Figure 12.9, the death rates for unfit individuals (group 1) with low systolic blood pressure are much higher than in highly fit people (groups 4 and 5) with high systolic blood pressure.

The best tip, though, is to use a preventive approach. It is easier to keep blood pressure under control rather than try to bring it down once it is elevated. Blood pressure should be checked regularly, regardless of whether elevation is present or not. Regular physical exercise, weight control, a low-salt diet, smoking cessation, and stress management are the basic guidelines for blood pressure control. Those who suffer from hypertension should not stop using the medication unless their personal physician so indicates. Remember — high blood pressure kills people if not treated properly. Combining the medication with the other treatment modalities may eventually lead to a reduction or complete elimination of the drug therapy.

BODY COMPOSITION

Body composition refers to the ratio of lean body weight to fat weight. If too much fat is accumulated, the person is considered to be obese. *Obesity has been long recognized as a primary risk factor for coronary heart disease.* Until a few years ago, experts felt that the disease was actually brought on by some of the other risk factors that usually deteriorate with increased body fat (higher cholesterol and triglycerides, hypertension, diabetes, lower level of cardiovascular fitness). Recent evidence, however, suggests that excess body fat, in and of itself, is a serious coronary risk factor. Even when all of the other risk factors are in good range, individuals with body fat percentages higher than the recommended standard have a higher incidence of coronary disease.

Attaining recommended body composition is not only important in decreasing cardiovascular risk, but also in achieving a better state of health and wellness. The only positive thing that can be said about excess body fat accumulation is that it can be lost through a combination of diet and exercise. Dieting by itself very seldom works. If you have a weight problem and you desire to achieve recommended weight, three things must take place: (a) an increase in the level of physical activity; (b) a diet low in fat and refined sugars, and high in complex carbohydrates and fiber; and (c) a moderate reduction in total caloric intake that will still provide all of the necessary nutrients to sustain normal physio-

--- *TABLE 12.4* ---

Effects of a Regular Aerobic Exercise Program* on Resting Blood Pressure: An 18-Year Follow-up Study**

	Initial	Final
Exercise Group		
Age	44.6	68.0
Blood Pressure	120/79	120/78
Nonexercise Group		
Age	51.6	69.7
Blood Pressure	135/85	150/90

*The aerobic exercise program consisted of an average four training sessions per week, each 66 minutes long, at about 76 percent of heart rate reserve.

**Based on data from Kash, F. W., J. L. Boyer, S. P. Van Camp, L. S. Verity, and J. P. Wallace. "The Effect of Physical Activity on Aerobic Power in Older Men (A Longitudinal Study)." *The Physician and Sports Medicine* 18(4):73-83, 1990.

logical body functions. Additional recommendations for weight reduction and weight control were discussed in Chapter 3.

SMOKING

Cigarette smoking is the single largest preventable cause of illness and premature death in the United States. Smoking has been linked to cardiovascular disease, cancer, bronchitis, emphysema, and peptic ulcers. In relation to coronary disease, not only does it speed up the process of atherosclerosis, but there is also a threefold increase in the risk of sudden death following a myocardial infarction.

Smoking causes the release of nicotine and some other 1,200 toxic compounds into the bloodstream. Similar to hypertension, many of these substances are destructive to the inner membrane that protects the walls of the arteries. As mentioned before, once the lining is damaged, cholesterol and triglycerides can be readily deposited in the arterial wall. As the plaque builds up, blood flow is significantly decreased as obstruction of the arteries occurs. Furthermore, smoking enhances the formation of blood clots, which can completely obstruct an already narrowed artery due to atherosclerosis. In addition, carbon monoxide, a byproduct of cigarette smoke, significantly decreases the oxygen-carrying capacity of the blood. A combination of obstructed arteries, decreased oxygen, and the presence of nicotine in the heart muscle greatly increases the risk for a serious heart problem.

Smoking also increases heart rate, blood pressure, and the irritability of the heart, which can trigger fatal cardiac arrhythmias. Another harmful effect is a decrease in HDL-cholesterol, or the "good type" that helps control your blood lipids. There is no question that smoking actually causes a much greater risk of death from heart disease than from lung disease.

Pipe and/or cigar smoking and chewing tobacco also increase the risk for heart disease. Even if no smoke is inhaled, certain amounts of toxic substances can be absorbed through the mouth membranes and end up in the bloodstream. Individuals who use tobacco in any of these three forms also have a much greater risk for cancer of the oral cavity.

Cigarette smoking, along with low levels of fitness, a poor cholesterol profile and high blood pressure, are the four most significant risk factors for coronary disease. Nevertheless, the risk for both cardiovascular disease and cancer starts to decrease the moment you quit. The risk approaches that of a lifetime nonsmoker ten and fifteen years, respectively, following cessation. A more thorough discussion of the harmful effects of cigarette smoking, the benefits of quitting, and a complete program for smoking cessation are outlined in Chapter 15.

TENSION AND STRESS

Tension and stress have become a normal part of every person's life. Everyone has to deal with goals, deadlines, responsibilities, pressures, etc. in daily life. Almost everything in life (whether positive or negative) is a source of stress. However, it is not the stressor itself that creates the health hazard, but rather the individual's response to it that may pose a health problem.

The way in which the human body responds to stress is by increasing the amount of catecholamines (hormones) to prepare the body for the so-called "fight or flight" mechanism. These hormones increase heart rate, blood pressure, and blood glucose levels, preparing the individual to take action. If the person "fights or flees," the increased levels of catecholamines are metabolized and the body is able to return to a "normal" state. However, if a person is under constant stress and unable to take action (such as in the case of the death of a close relative or friend, loss of a job, trouble at work, financial insecurity, etc.), the catecholamines will remain elevated in the bloodstream. *People who are unable to relax will experience a constant low-level strain on the cardiovascular system that could manifest itself in the form of heart disease. Additionally, when a person is in a stressful situation, the coronary arteries that feed the heart muscle constrict (clamp down), reducing the oxygen supply to the heart. If significant arterial occlusion due to atherosclerosis is present, abnormal rhythms of the heart or even a heart attack may follow.*

Individuals who feel that they are under a lot of stress, and do not cope well with it, need to begin to take appropriate measures to reduce the effects of stress in their lives. One of the best recommendations to overcome stress is to identify the sources of stress and learn how to cope with those events. People need to take control of themselves and examine and act upon the things of greatest importance in their lives. Less significant or meaningless details should be ignored.

Physical exercise has been found to be one of the best ways to relieve stress. When a person engages in physical activity, excess catecholamines are metabolized, and the body is able to return to a normal state. Exercise also increases muscular activity, which causes muscular relaxation upon completion of physical activity. Many executives in large cities are choosing the evening hours for their physical activity programs, stopping right after work at the health or fitness club. This way they are able to "burn up" the excess tension built up during the day and better enjoy the evening hours. This has proven to be one of the best stress management techniques. Additional information on several stress management techniques commonly used is presented in Chapter 14.

PERSONAL AND FAMILY HISTORY

Individuals who have suffered from cardiovascular problems are at higher risk than those who have never had a problem. People with such a history should be strongly encouraged to maintain the other risk factors as low as possible. Since most risk factors are reversible, this practice significantly decreases the risk for future problems. The longer it has been since the incidence of the cardiovascular problem, the lower the risk for recurrence.

The genetic predisposition toward heart disease has been clearly demonstrated and seems to be gaining in importance each day. All other factors being equal, a person who has had blood relatives who suffered from heart disease prior to age sixty runs a greater risk than someone who has no such history. The younger the age at which the incident happened to the relative, the greater the risk for the disease.

In many cases there is no way of knowing whether there is a true genetic predisposition or simply poor lifestyle habits that led to a particular problem. It is quite possible that a person may have been physically inactive, overweight, have smoked, have had bad dietary habits, etc., leading to a heart attack, and therefore all blood relatives would fall in the family history category. Since there is no definite way of telling them apart, a person with a family history should keep a close watch on all other factors and maintain them at as low a risk level as possible. In addition, an annual blood chemistry analysis is strongly recommended to make sure that blood lipids are being handled properly by the body.

ESTROGEN USE

Only recently was estrogen (found in oral contraceptives and certain other drugs) added to the list of risk factors for coronary disease. *Estrogen can cause an increase in blood pressure, enhance the clotting mechanism of the blood, but it may help raise HDL-cholesterol* (the "good guys"). High blood pressure by itself will increase the susceptibility to atherosclerosis. As plaque builds up, complete obstruction may occur from a blood clot enhanced by the use of estrogen. *Following menopause, estrogen therapy is crucial for the prevention of osteoporosis (see Chapter 2). Therefore, women who are at high risk for heart disease should carefully discuss and weigh the risks and benefits of estrogen therapy with their personal physician.*

AGE

Age is a risk factor because of the greater incidence of heart disease among older people. This tendency may be partly induced by an increased risk among the other factors due to changes in lifestyle as we get older (less physical activity, poor nutrition, obesity, etc.).

Young people, however, should not feel that heart disease will not affect them. The disease process begins early in life. This was clearly shown among American soldiers who died during the Korean and Vietnam conflicts. Autopsies conducted on soldiers killed at twenty-two years of age and younger revealed that approximately 70 percent of them showed early stages of atherosclerosis. Other studies have found elevated blood cholesterol levels in children as young as ten years old.

While the aging process cannot be stopped, it can certainly be slowed down. *The concept of physiological versus chronological age is certainly an important concept in the prevention of disease. It has often been said that certain individuals in their sixties or older possess the bodies of twenty-year-olds. The opposite also holds true: twenty-year-olds often are in such poor condition and health that they almost seem to have the bodies of sixty-year-olds.* Adequate risk factor management and positive lifestyle habits are the best ways to slow down the natural aging process.

A FINAL WORD ON CORONARY RISK REDUCTION

As was mentioned at the beginning of this chapter, most of the risk factors for coronary heart disease are reversible and preventable. The fact that a person has a family history of heart disease and possibly some of the other risk factors because of neglect in lifestyle does not signify by any means that this person is doomed. The objective of this chapter was to provide the guidelines and recommendations to decrease the risk of suffering from cardiovascular disease (particularly coronary heart disease). As has been discussed, *a healthier lifestyle — free of cardiovascular problems — is something that you can pretty much control by yourself.* You are encouraged to be persistent. It requires willpower and commitment to develop positive patterns that will eventually turn into healthy habits conducive to total well-being. *Only you can act on it by taking control of your lifestyle and thereby reaping the benefits of wellness.*

LABORATORY EXPERIENCE

LAB 12A: Self-Evaluation of Cardiovascular Risk

LAB PREPARATION: If time allows, reassess cardiovascular endurance, body composition, and blood pressure during this lab (wear appropriate exercise clothing for this reassessment — see Labs 1B, 4A, and 6A). Also, if you have had a blood chemistry analysis performed in the past that included total cholesterol, HDL-cholesterol, triglycerides, and glucose levels, you may use the results for this laboratory experience.

References

1. American Heart Association. *Coronary Risk Handbook: Estimating Risk of Coronary Heart Disease in Daily Practice*. Dallas, TX: The Association, 1973.

2. American Heart Association. *Heart Facts*. Dallas, TX: The Association, 1988.

3. Blair, S. N., K. H. Cooper, L. W. Gibbons, L. R. Gettman, S. Lewis, and N. N. Goodyear. "Changes in Coronary Heart Disease Risk Factors Associated with Increased Treadmill Time in 753 Men." *American Journal of Epidemiology* 3:352-359, 1983.

4. Blair, S. N., N. N. Goodyear, L. W. Gibbons, and K. H. Cooper. "Physical Fitness and Incidence of Hypertension in Healthy Normotensive Men and Women." *Journal of the American Medical Association* 252:487-490, 1984.

5. Blair, S. N., H. W. Kohl III, R. S. Paffenbarger, Jr, D. G. Clark, K. H. Cooper, and L. W. Gibbons. "Physical Fitness and All-Cause Mortality: A Prospective Study of Healthy Men and Women." *Journal of the American Medical Association* 262:2395-2401, 1989.

6. Cooper, K. H. *Running Without Fear*. New York: Mount Evans and Co., 1985.

7. Cooper, K. H. *The Aerobics Way*. New York: Mount Evans and Co., 1977.

8. Cooper, K. H. *The Aerobics Program for Total Well-Being*. New York: Mount Evans and Co., 1982.

9. Diethrich, E. B. *The Arizona Heart Institute's Heart Test*. New York, NY: International Heart Foundation, 1981.

10. Gibbons, L. W., S. Blair, K. H. Cooper, and M. Smith. "Association Between Coronary Heart Disease Risk Factors and Physical Fitness in Healthy Adult Women." *Circulation* 5:977-983, 1983.

11. Guss, S. B. *Heart Attack Risk Score*. Cardiac Alert, 1983.

12. Hoeger, W. W. K. *Ejercicio, Salud y Vida [Exercise, Health and Life]*. Caracas, Venezuela: Editorial Arte, 1980.

13. Hoeger, W. W. K. *The Complete Guide for the Development & Implementation of Health Promotion Programs*. Englewood, CO: Morton Publishing Company, 1987.

14. Hoeger, W. W. K. "Self-Assessment of Cardiovascular Risk." *Corporate Fitness & Recreation* 5(6):13-16, 1986.

15. "How Good is 'Good' Cholesterol?" *The Health Letter*. April 9, 1982.

16. Hubert, H. B., M. Feinleib, P. M. MacNamara, and W. P. Castelli. "Obesity as an Independent Risk Factor for Cardiovascular Disease: A 26-year Follow-up of Participants in the Framingham Heart Study." *Circulation* 5:968-977, 1983.

17. Johnson, L. C. *Interpreting Your Test Results*. Chattanooga, TN: Blue Cross Blue Shield of Tennessee, 1990.

18. Kannel, W. B., D. McGee, and T. Gordon. "A General Cardiovascular Risk Profile: The Framingham Study." *The American Journal of Cardiology* 7:46-51, 1976.

19. Kash, F. W., J. L. Boyer, S. P. Van Camp, L. S. Verity, and J. P. Wallace. "The Effect of Physical Activity on Aerobic Power in Older Men (A Longitudinal Study)." *The Physician and Sports Medicine* 18(4):73-83, 1990.

20. Kostas, G. "Three Nutrients May Help Control Blood Pressure." *The Aerobics News* 1(7):6, 1986.

21. Leon, A., J. Connett, D. R. Jacobs, and R. Rauramaa. "Leisure-time Physical Activity Levels and Risk of Coronary Heart Disease and Death: The Multiple Risk Factor Intervention Trial". *Journal of the American Medical Association* 258:2388-2395, 1987.

22. Multiple Risk Factor Intervention Trial. "Risk Factor Changes and Mortality Results." Multiple risk factor intervention trial research group. *Journal of the American Medical Association* 248:1465-1477, 1982.

23. Neufeld, H. N., and U. Gouldbourt. "Coronary Heart Disease: Genetic Aspects." *Circulation* 5:943-954, 1983.

24. Page, L. B. "On Making Sense of Salt and Your Blood Pressure." *Executive Health*. August 1982.

25. Peters, R. K., L. D. Cady, Jr, D. P. Bischoff, L. Bernstein, and M. C. Pike. "Physical Fitness and Subsequent Myocardial Infarction in Healthy Workers." *Journal of the American Medical Association* 249:3052-3056, 1983.

26. Powell, K. E., P. D. Thompson, C. J. Caspersen, and J. S. Kendrick. "Physical Activity and the evidence of Coronary Heart Disease." *Public Health Reviews* 8:253-287, 1987.

27. Sobolski, J., et al. "Protection Against Ischemic Heart Disease in the Belgian Physical Fitness Study: Physical Fitness Rather than Physical Activity." *American Journal of Epidemiology* 125:601-610, 1987.

28. Van Camp, S. P. "The Fixx Tragedy: A Cardiologist's Perspective." *Physician and Sportsmedicine* 12:153-155, 1984.

29. Wiley, J. A., and T. C. Camacho. "Lifestyle and Future Health: Evidence from the Alameda County Study." *Preventive Medicine* 9:1-21, 1980.

Cancer Risk Management

OBJECTIVES

- Define cancer and how it starts and spreads.
- Discuss the importance of health education in a cancer prevention program.
- Learn the American Cancer Society's guidelines for cancer prevention.
- Learn to recognize early warning signs of possible serious illness.
- Review major risk factors that lead to the development of specific types of cancer.
- Assess your own risk for the development of certain types of cancer.

The human body has approximately 100 trillion cells, and under normal conditions these cells reproduce themselves in an orderly manner. The growth of cells occurs so that old, worn-out tissue can be replaced and injuries can be repaired. However, in some instances certain cells grow in an uncontrolled and abnormal manner. Some cells will grow into a mass of tissue called a tumor, which can be either benign or malignant. A malignant tumor is considered to be a "cancer." Cancer cells grow for no reason and multiply uncontrollably, destroying normal tissue. The rate at which cancer cells grow varies from one type to another. Certain types grow fast, while others may take years to do so.

Over 100 types of cancer can develop in any tissue or organ of the body. Cancer probably starts with the abnormal growth of one cell, which can then multiply into billions of cancerous cells. It takes approximately one billion cells, or the equivalent of a one-centimeter tumor, before cancer can be detected. Through metastasis (the movement of bacteria or body cells from one part of the body to

another), cells break away from a malignant tumor and migrate to other parts of the body where they can cause new cancer. Although most cancer cells are destroyed by the immune system, it only takes one abnormal cell to lodge elsewhere and start a new cancer. In contrast, benign tumors do not invade other tissue. They can interfere with normal bodily functions but rarely cause death. (*see* Figure 13.1).

CANCER INCIDENCE

The 1987 report by the National Center for Health Statistics indicated that 22.4 percent of all deaths in the United States were caused by cancer. It is the second leading cause of death in the country and the leading cause among children between the ages of three and fourteen. About 500,000 people died of the disease in 1989, and approximately 1,040,000 new cases were expected the same year. The 1990 statistical estimates of cancer incidence and deaths

175

──────── *FIGURE 13.1* ────────

How Cancer Starts and Spreads. Illustration by John Stone Quinan and Jo Ellen Murphy of the Washington Post *(edited by Cancer News, American Cancer Society, Texas Division, Inc., Winter 1986).*

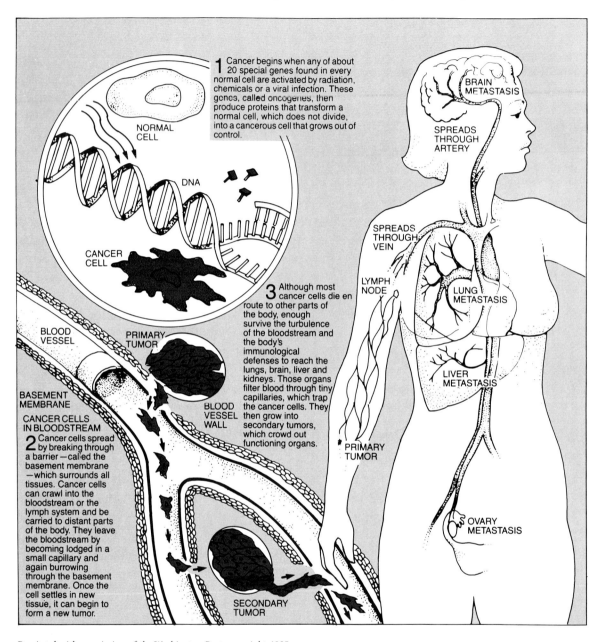

Reprinted with permission of the Washington Post, copyright 1985.

by sex and site are given in Figure 13.2 (these estimates exclude nonmelanoma skin cancer and carcinoma in situ). Estimates also indicated that 76 million Americans, based on the total 1990 population, would suffer from cancer in their lifetime, striking approximately three out of every four families.

As with coronary heart disease, cancer is largely a preventable disease. As much as 80 percent of all human cancers are related to lifestyle or environmental factors (includes diet, tobacco use, excessive use of alcohol, overexposure to sunlight, and exposure

to occupational hazards). *Most of these cancers could be prevented through positive lifestyle habits.* The proportion of cancers related to environmental factors was carefully studied in the Birmingham and West Midland regions of England. The report indicated that only 6 percent of cancers in men and 2 percent in women originated in the workplace. Approximately 85 to 90 percent were lifestyle-related (see Figure 13.3).

Research sponsored by the American Cancer Society and the National Cancer Institute showed that individuals who adhere to a healthy lifestyle

FIGURE 13.2

FIGURE 13.2

Cancer Incidence and Deaths by Site and Sex: 1990 Estimates. From 1990 Cancer Facts & Figures. *New York: American Cancer Society.*

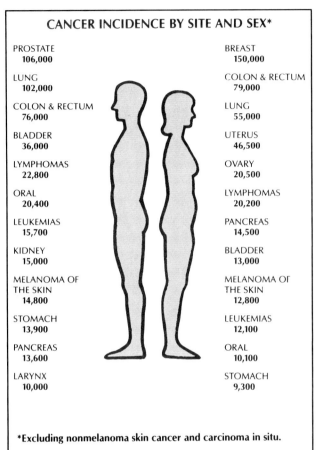

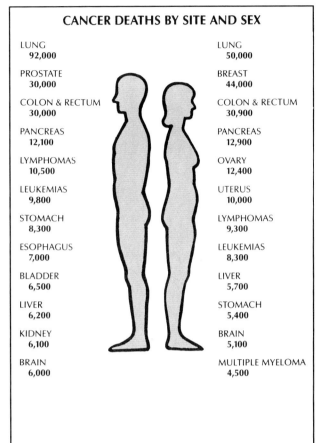

CANCER INCIDENCE BY SITE AND SEX*

PROSTATE **106,000**	BREAST **150,000**
LUNG **102,000**	COLON & RECTUM **79,000**
COLON & RECTUM **76,000**	LUNG **55,000**
BLADDER **36,000**	UTERUS **46,500**
LYMPHOMAS **22,800**	OVARY **20,500**
ORAL **20,400**	LYMPHOMAS **20,200**
LEUKEMIAS **15,700**	PANCREAS **14,500**
KIDNEY **15,000**	BLADDER **13,000**
MELANOMA OF THE SKIN **14,800**	MELANOMA OF THE SKIN **12,800**
STOMACH **13,900**	LEUKEMIAS **12,100**
PANCREAS **13,600**	ORAL **10,100**
LARYNX **10,000**	STOMACH **9,300**

*Excluding nonmelanoma skin cancer and carcinoma in situ.

CANCER DEATHS BY SITE AND SEX

LUNG **92,000**	LUNG **50,000**
PROSTATE **30,000**	BREAST **44,000**
COLON & RECTUM **30,000**	COLON & RECTUM **30,900**
PANCREAS **12,100**	PANCREAS **12,900**
LYMPHOMAS **10,500**	OVARY **12,400**
LEUKEMIAS **9,800**	UTERUS **10,000**
STOMACH **8,300**	LYMPHOMAS **9,300**
ESOPHAGUS **7,000**	LEUKEMIAS **8,300**
BLADDER **6,500**	LIVER **5,700**
LIVER **6,200**	STOMACH **5,400**
KIDNEY **6,100**	BRAIN **5,100**
BRAIN **6,000**	MULTIPLE MYELOMA **4,500**

FIGURE 13.3

Cancer Deaths from Presumed and Environmental Factors in the Birmingham and West Midland Regions of England in 1968-1972.

Factor	Percentages of Cancer	
	Males	Females
Tobacco*	30	7
Tobacco/alcohol*	5	3
Sunlight*	10	10
Occupation*	6	2
Radiation*	1	1
Iatrogenic*	1	1
Other "Lifestyle" Factors**	30	63
Congenital**	2	2
Unknown	15	11

*Defined environmental factors.
**Presumed environmental factors.
Adapted from Higginson, J., and C. S. Muir. "Environmental Carcinogenesis: Misconceptions and Limitations to Cancer Control" *JNCL* 63(6):1291-1297, 1979.

have some of the lowest cancer mortality rates ever reported in scientific studies (also see Physical Fitness in Chapter 1). A group of about 10,000 members from The Church of Jesus Christ of Latter Day Saints (commonly refered to as the Mormon Church) in California was reported to have only about one third (men) to one half (women) the rate of cancer mortality of the general white population. The investigators in this study looked at three general health habits among the participants: lifetime abstinence from smoking, regular physical activity, and sleep. Additionally, healthy lifestyle guidelines instituted by the church in 1833 (also referred to as the "word of wisdom") include abstention from tobacco, alcohol, caffeine, drugs, and adherence to a well-balanced diet. Nutrition recommendations include a diet based on grains, fruits, vegetables, and moderate use of poultry and red meat.

Equally important is the fact that cancer is now viewed as the most curable of all chronic diseases. Over half of all cancers are curable. Over 6 million Americans were alive in 1990 who had a history of cancer. Close to 3 million of them were considered cured. *The biggest factor in fighting cancer today is health education.* People need to be informed regarding the risk factors for cancer and the guidelines for early detection.

GUIDELINES FOR CANCER PREVENTION

The most effective way to protect against cancer is by changing negative lifestyle habits and behaviors that have been practiced for years. The American Cancer Society has issued the following recommendations in regard to cancer prevention (also see Lab 13A):

1. **Dietary changes**. The diet should be low in fat and high in fiber, and with ample amounts of vitamins A and C from natural sources (see Figure 13.4). Cruciferous vegetables (plants that produce cross-shaped leaves) are encouraged in the diet, alcohol should be used in moderation, and obesity should be avoided.

   High fat intake has been linked primarily to breast, colon, and prostate cancers. Low fiber intake seems to increase the risk of colon cancer. Foods high in vitamins A and C may help decrease the incidence of larynx, esophagus, and lung cancers. Additionally, salt-cured, smoked, and nitrite-cured foods should be avoided. These foods have been linked to cancer of the esophagus and stomach. Vitamin C seems to help decrease the formation of nitrosamines (cancer-causing substances that are formed when cured meats are eaten). Cruciferous vegetables (cauliflower, broccoli, cabbage, Brussels sprouts, and kohlrabi) should be included in the diet, since they seem to decrease the risk for the development of certain cancers (Figure 13.5).

Alcohol should be used in moderation. Alcoholism increases the risk of certain cancers, especially when combined with tobacco smoking or smokeless tobacco. In combination, they significantly increase the risk of mouth, larynx, throat, esophagus, and liver cancers. According to some research, the synergistic action of heavy use of alcohol and tobacco yields a fifteen-fold increase in cancer of the oral cavity.

Maintenance of recommended body weight is also recommended. Obesity has been associated with colon, rectum, breast, prostate, gallbladder, ovary, and uterine cancers.

2. **Abstinence from cigarette smoking.** It has been reported that 83 percent of all lung cancers and 30 percent of all cancers are attributed to smoking. Smokeless tobacco also increases the risk of mouth, larynx, throat, and esophagus cancers. About 138,600 annual cancer deaths are attributed to the use of tobacco. However, cigarette smoking by itself is a major health hazard. When considering all related deaths, cigarette smoking is responsible for 350,000 unnecessary deaths per year. The average life expectancy for a chronic smoker is seven years less than for a nonsmoker.

3. **Avoid sun exposure.** Sunlight exposure is a major factor in the development of skin cancer. Almost 100 percent of the 600,000 nonmelanoma skin cancer cases reported annually in the United States are related to sun exposure. Sunscreen lotion should be used at all times when the skin is going to be exposed to sunlight for extended periods of time. Tanning of the skin is the body's natural reaction to cell damage taking place as a result of excessive sun exposure.

4. **Avoid estrogen use, radiation exposure, and occupational hazard exposure.** Estrogen use has

---
FIGURE 13.4

Nutrition guidelines for a cancer prevention program include a diet low in fat and high in fiber, with ample amounts of vitamins A and C from natural sources.

FIGURE 13.5

Cruciferous vegetables are recommended in a cancer-prevention diet.

been linked to endometrial cancer but can be taken safely under careful physician supervision. Radiation exposure also increases cancer risk. Many times, however, the benefits of X-ray use outweigh the risk involved, and most medical facilities use the lowest dose possible to decrease the risk to a minimum. Occupational hazards, such as asbestos fibers, nickel and uranium dusts, chromium compounds, vinyl chloride, bischlormethyl ether, etc., increase cancer risk. The risk of occupational hazards is significantly magnified by the use of cigarette smoking.

A more active lifestyle and lower stress levels also seem to offer a protective effect against cancer (Figure 13.6). Although the mechanism is not clear,

FIGURE 13.6

Research studies examining the association between physical activity and health point toward a strong, graded, and consistent inverse relationship between physical fitness and cancer mortality in men and women.

research studies examining the association between physical activity and health point toward a graded and consistent inverse relationship between physical fitness and cancer mortality in men and women (see Table 1.1 and Figure 1.4 in Chapter 1). Relatively recent studies on specific cancer sites have indicated that a moderately intense-lifetime exercise program lowers the risk for breast, colon, and reproductive system cancers. Additionally, there is growing evidence that the body's auto-immune system may play a role in preventing cancer. Studies have indicated that exercise improves the auto-immune system. On the other hand, high levels of tension and stress and/or poor coping may have a negative effect on this system and consequently reduce the body's effectiveness in dealing with the various cancers.

The contribution of many of the other much publicized factors is not as significant as the above factors. *The contribution to total cancer incidence of intentional food additives, saccharin, processing agents, pesticides, and packaging materials in current use in the United States and other developed countries appears to be minimal.*

Genetics plays a role in susceptibility in only 2 percent of all cancers. Most of it is seen in early childhood years. Some cancer can be seen as a combination of genetic and environmental liability. Genetics may act to enhance environmental risks of certain types of cancers. The biggest carcinogenic exposure in the workplace is cigarette smoke. However, environment means more than pollution, smoke, etc. It includes diet, lifestyle-related events, viruses, and physical agents such as X-rays and sun exposure.

Equally important is the fact that through early detection, many cancers can be controlled or cured. The real problem is the spreading of cancerous cells. Once spreading occurs, it becomes very difficult to wipe the cancer out. It is therefore crucial to practice effective prevention or at least catch cancer when the possibility of cure is greatest. Herein lies the importance of proper periodic screening for prevention and/or early detection.

The following are the seven warning signals for cancer. Every individual should become familiar with these warning signals and bring them to the attention of a physician if any of them are present:

1. Change in bowel or bladder habits.
2. A sore that does not heal.
3. Unusual bleeding or discharge.
4. Thickening or lump in breast or elsewhere.
5. Indigestion or difficulty in swallowing.
6. Obvious change in wart or mole.
7. Nagging cough or hoarseness.

In addition to the seven warning signals, the American Medical Association has developed an "early warning signs of possible serious illness" questionnaire to help alert people to symptoms that may indicate a serious health problem. This questionnaire is given in Lab 13B. Although in most cases there is nothing seriously wrong, if any of the described symptoms arise, a physician should be consulted as soon as possible. Furthermore, the Guidelines for Screening Recommendations by the American Cancer Society outlined in Figure 13.7 should be included in regular physical examinations as part of a cancer prevention program.

Scientific evidence and testing procedures for prevention and/or early detection of cancer do change. Results of current clinical and epidemiologic studies provide constant new information about cancer prevention and detection. The purpose of cancer prevention programs is to educate and guide individuals toward a lifestyle that will aid them in the prevention and/or early detection of malignancy. Treatment of cancer should always be left to specialized physicians and cancer clinics.

CANCER HEALTH PROTECTION PLAN*

The Health Protection Plan for Cancer outlined at the end of this chapter (see Figure 13.8) was designed by The Preventive Medicine Institute/ Strang Clinic in New York to help people assess their risk for certain common types of cancer. People who may have more than the average risk of developing certain cancers can be identified by some of the risk factors for these cancer sites. The questions to be answered under each cancer site make reference to the major risk factors and by no means represent the only ones that might be involved. The questions have been grouped into four categories: (a) symptoms that may indicate that something is wrong, (b) family history, (c) personal history, and (d) preventive measures that can

*Questionnaire published by The Preventive Medicine Institute/ Strang Clinic. New York, 1982. Reproduced with permission.

FIGURE 13.7

Guidelines for Cancer Screening

Test	Patient age	Frequency
Breast physical examination	20-40 Over 40	Every 3 yrs Annually
Breast self-examination	Over 20	Monthly
Chest X-ray	No specific recommendation	No specific recommendation
Digital rectal examination	Over 40	Annually
Endometrial tissue examination	At menopause[a]	At menopause
Mammography	35-40 40-49 Over 50	One baseline Every 1-2 yrs Annually
Pap smear	20-65 and sexually active teenagers	2 consecutive yrs, then every 3 yrs
Pelvic examination	20-40 Over 40 At menopause	Every 3 yrs Annually
Sigmoidoscopy	Over 50	2 consecutive yrs, then every 3-5 yrs
Sputum cytology	No specific recommendation	No specific recommendation
Stool guaiac	Over 50	Annually
Health counseling and cancer check-up[b]	Over 20 Over 40	Every 3 yrs Every yr

From *Guidelines for the Cancer-Related Checkup: Recommendations and Rationale.* New York: American Cancer Society, July/August 1980. Reproduced with permission.
[a] Recommended for obese women with a history of involuntary infertility, failure of ovulation, abnormal uterine bleeding, or estrogen therapy.
[b] To include examinations for cancers of the thyroid, testicles, prostate, ovaries, lymph nodes, oral region, and skin.

help to protect you from certain health hazards. In Lab 13C you will be required to complete this questionnaire. Nevertheless, the questionnaire is included at the end of this chapter so that it can be retained for future reference.

OTHER CANCER SITES

Risk factors and prevention techniques for other types of cancer not contained in the cancer questionnaire have also been outlined in the Cancer Book published by the American Cancer Society, as well as in a series of pamphlets on "Facts on Cancer" (one each for selected cancer sites). Some of these types of cancer are listed next, along with the risk factors associated with each type and preventive techniques to help decrease risk.

Pancreatic Cancer

The pancreas is a thin gland that lies behind the stomach. This gland releases insulin and pancreatic juice. Insulin regulates blood sugar and pancreatic juice contains enzymes that aid in food digestion.

POSSIBLE RISK FACTORS

1. The incidence increases between the ages of thirty-five and seventy but is significantly higher around the age of fifty-five.
2. Cigarette smoking.
3. High cholesterol diet.
4. Exposure to unspecified environmental agents.

PREVENTION AND WARNING SIGNALS

Detection of pancreatic cancer is difficult because (a) no symptoms are evoked in the early disease process and (b) advanced disease symptoms are similar to those of other diseases. Warning signals that may be related to pancreatic cancer include pain in the abdomen or lower back, jaundice, loss of weight and appetite, nausea, weakness, agitated depression, loss of energy and feeling weary, dizziness, chills, muscle spasms, double vision, and coma.

Oral Cancer

Oral cancer includes cancer of the mouth, lips, tongue, salivary glands, pharynx, larynx, and floor of the mouth. Most of these cancers seem to be related to cigarette smoking and excessive alcohol consumption.

RISK FACTORS

1. Heavy smoking and/or drinking.
2. Broken or ill-fitting dentures.
3. A broken tooth that irritates the inside of the mouth.
4. Chewing and dipping tobacco.
5. Excessive sun exposure (lip cancer).

PREVENTION AND WARNING SIGNALS

Regular examinations and good dental hygiene help in the prevention and early detection of oral cancer. Warning signals may include the following: a nonhealing sore or white patch in the mouth, the presence of a lump, problems with chewing and swallowing, and a constant feeling of having "something" in the throat. A person with any of these conditions should be evaluated by a physician or dentist. A tissue biopsy is normally conducted to diagnose the presence of cancer.

Thyroid Cancer

The thyroid gland is located in the lower portion of the front of the neck and helps to regulate growth and metabolism. Thyroid cancer among women occurs almost twice as often as in men, and the incidence is also higher in whites as compared to blacks.

RISK FACTORS

1. Risk increases with age.
2. Radiation therapy of the head and neck region received in childhood or adolescence.
3. A family history of thyroid cancer.

PREVENTION AND WARNING SIGNALS

Regular inspection for thyroid tumors is done by palpation of the gland and surrounding areas during a physical examination. Thyroid cancer is a slow growing process; therefore, this malignancy is highly treatable. However, any unusual lumps in front of the neck should be promptly reported to a physician. Although thyroid cancer is quite asymptomatic, warning signals (besides a lump) may include: difficulty in swallowing or choking, labored breathing, and persistent hoarseness.

Liver Cancer

The incidence of liver cancer in the United States is very low. Men are more prone to liver cancer, and the disease is more common after the age of sixty.

RISK FACTORS

1. A history of cirrhosis of the liver.

2. A history of hepatitis B virus.

3. Exposure to vinyl chloride (industrial gas used when plastics are manufactured) and aflotoxin (natural food contaminant).

4. Heavy alcohol consumption.

PREVENTION AND WARNING SIGNALS

Prevention is primarily accomplished by avoidance of the risk factors and awareness of warning signals. Possible signs and symptoms are a lump or pain in the upper right abdomen (which may radiate into the back and the shoulder), fever, nausea, rapidly deteriorating health, jaundice, and liver tenderness.

Leukemia

Leukemia is a type of cancer that interferes with blood-forming tissues (bone marrow, lymph nodes, and spleen), bringing about the production of too many immature white blood cells. Consequently, people afflicted by leukemia cannot fight infection effectively. For the most part, the causes of leukemia are unknown, although suspected risk factors have been identified.

RISK FACTORS

1. Inherited susceptibility, but not directly transmitted from parent to child.

2. An increased incidence is observed among children with Down's syndrome (mongolism) and a few other genetic abnormalities.

3. Excessive exposure to ionizing radiation.

4. Environmental exposure to chemicals such as benzene.

PREVENTION AND WARNING SIGNALS

Detection is not easy, because early symptoms may be attributed to less serious ailments. Early warning signals may include fatigue, pallor, weight loss, easy bruising, nosebleeds, paleness, loss of appetite, repeated infections, hemorrhages, night sweats, bone and joint pain, and fever. At a more advanced stage, fatigue increases, hemorrhages become more severe, pain and high fever continue, and swelling of the gums and various skin disorders occur.

A FINAL WORD ON CANCER RISK MANAGEMENT

Individuals who are at high risk for any of the cancer sites are advised to discuss any particular problems with a physician. An ounce of prevention is worth a pound of cure! Although cardiovascular disease is the number one killer in the United States, cancer is the number one fear. Keep in mind that 60 to 80 percent of all cancers are preventable and about 50 percent are curable. Since most cancers are lifestyle related, awareness of the risk factors and implementation of the screening guidelines (Figure 13.7), along with the basic recommendations for cancer prevention, will significantly decrease cancer risk.

LABORATORY EXPERIENCES

LAB 13A: Cancer Prevention: Are You Taking Control?

LAB PREPARATION: None.

LAB 13B: Early Warning Signs of Possible Serious Illness

LAB PREPARATION: None.

LAB 13C: Health Protection Plan for Cancer

LAB PREPARATION: None.

References

1. American Cancer Society, Texas Division. *Cancer: Assessing Your Risk.* Dallas, TX: The Society, 1982.

2. American Cancer Society. 1987 *Cancer Facts and Figures.* New York: The Society, 1987.

3. American Cancer Society. *Cancer Book.* New York: The Society, 1986.

4. American Cancer Society. *Guidelines for the Cancer-Related Checkup: Recommendations and Rationale.* New York: The Society, 1980.

5. American Cancer Society. Pamphlets on facts on "Selected" Cancer Sites. New York: The Society, pamphlets published between 1978 and 1983.

6. Blair, S.N., H.W. Kohl III, R.S. Paffenbarger, Jr., D.G. Clark, K.H. Cooper, and L. W. Gibbons. "Physical Fitness and All-Cause Mortality: A Prospective Study of Healthy Men and Women." *Journal of the American Medical Association* 262:2395-2401, 1989.

7. Enstrom, J.E. "Health Practices and Cancer Mortality Among Active California Mormons." *Journal of the National Cancer Institute* 81:1807-1814, 1989.

8. Greenwald, P. "Assessment of Risk Factors for Cancer." *Preventive Medicine* 9:260-263, 1980.

9. Hammond, E.C., and H. Seidman. "Smoking and Cancer in the United States." *Preventive Medicine* 9:169-173, 1980.

10. Higginson, J. "Proportion of Cancers Due to Occupation." *Preventive Medicine* 9:180-188, 1980.

11. Paffenbarger, R.S., R.T. Hyde, A.L. Wing, and C.H. Steinmetz. "A Natural History of Athleticism and Cardiovascular Health." *Journal of the American Medical Association* 252:491-495, 1984.

12. Rothman, K.J. "The Proportion of Cancer Attributable to Alcohol Consumption." *Preventive Medicine* 9:174-179, 1980.

13. Weisburger, J.H., D.M. Hegsted, G.B. Gori, and B. Lewis. "Extending the Prudent Diet to Cancer Prevention." *Preventive Medicine* 9:297-304, 1980.

14. Williams, C.L. "Primary Prevention of Cancer Beginning in Childhood." *Preventive Medicine* 9:275-280, 1980.

15. Williams, P.A. "A Productive History and Physical Examination in the Prevention and Early Detection of Cancer." *Cancer* 47:1146-1150, 1981.

LABORATORY EXPERIENCES

LAB 14A: The Life Experiences Survey

LAB PREPARATION: None.

LAB 14B: Type A Personality Assessment Form and Behavioral Objectives for Stress Reduction and Personality Change.

LAB PREPARATION: None.

LAB 14C: Stress Management Techniques

LAB PREPARATION: None.

References

1. Andrasik, F., D. Coleman, and L. H. Epstein. "Biofeedback: Clinical and Research Considerations." In *Behavioral Medicine: Assessment and Treatment Strategies*. Edited by D. M. Doleys, R. L. Meredith, and A. R. Ciminero. New York: Plenum Press, 1982.

2. Blanchard, E. B., and L. H. Epstein. *A Biofeedback Primer*. Reading, MA: Addison-Wesley, 1978.

3. Blue Cross Association. *Stress*. Chicago: The Association, 1974.

4. Brown, B. *New Mind, New Body*. New York: Harper & Row, 1974.

5. Chesney, M. A., J. R. Eagleston, and R. H. Roseman. "Type A Assessment and Intervention." In *Medical Psychology: Contributions to Behavioral Medicine*. Edited by C. K. Prokop and L. A. Bradley. New York: Academic Press, 1981.

6. Gauron, E. F. *Mental Training for Peak Performance*. Lansing, NY: Sport Science Associates, 1984.

7. Girdano,D., and G. Everly. *Controlling Stress and Tension: A Holistic Approach*. Englewood Cliffs, NJ: Prentice-Hall, Inc., 1990.

8. Greenberg, J. S. *Comprehensive Stress Management*. Dubuque, IA: Wm. C. Brown Company Publishers, 1987.

9. Kriegel, R. J., and M. H. Kriegel. *The C Zone: Peak Performance Under Stress*. Garden City, NY: Anchor Press/Doubleday, 1984.

10. Luthe, W. "Autogenic Training: Method, Research and Applications in Medicine." *American Journal of Psychotherapy* 17:174-195, 1963.

11. McKay, M., M. Davis, and P. Fanning. *Thoughts and Feelings: The Act of Cognitive Stress Intervention*. Richmond, CA: New Harbinger Publications, 1981.

12. Miller, L. H., and A. D. Smith. "Vulnerability Scale." *Stress Audit, 1983*.

13. Sarason, I. G., J. H. Johnson, and J. M. Siegel. "Assessing the Impact of Life Changes: Development of the Life Experiences Survey." *Journal of Consulting and Clinical Psychology* 46:932- 946, 1978.

14. Selye, H. *Stress Without Distress*. New York: Signet, 1974.

15. Selye, H. *The Stress of Life*. New York: McGraw-Hill Book Co., 1978.

16. Staff. "How Running Relieves Stress." *The Runner* 8(11):38-43, 82, 1986.

17. Turk, D. C., and R. D. Kerns. "Assessment in Health Psychology: A Cognitive-Behavioral Perspective." In *Measurement Strategies in Health Psychology*. Edited by P. Karoly. New York: John Wiley & Sons, 1985.

Smoking Cessation

OBJECTIVES

- Understand the detrimental health effects of tobacco use in general.
- Recognize cigarette smoking as the largest preventable cause of premature illness and death in the United States.
- Learn the fundamental reasons for which people smoke.
- Understand the benefits and the significance of a smoking cessation program.
- Learn how to implement a smoking cessation program, either for yourself (if you smoke), or to help others go through the quitting process.

Tobacco has been used throughout the world for hundreds of years. Prior to the eighteenth century, it was smoked primarily in the form of pipes or cigars. Cigarette smoking per se did not become popular until the mid-1800s, and its use started to increase dramatically at the turn of the century. In 1915, 18 billion cigarettes were consumed in the United States, as compared to 640 billion in 1981. This figure dropped to 538 billion in 1989. There are, nonetheless, more than 50 million Americans over the age of seventeen who still smoke an average of one and one-half packs of cigarettes per day.

The harmful effects of cigarette smoking and tobacco usage in general were not exactly known until the early 1960s, when researchers began to show a positive link between tobacco usage and disease. In 1964, the United States Surgeon General issued the first major report presenting scientific evidence that cigarettes were indeed a major health hazard in our society.

The use of tobacco in all forms is now considered a significant threat to life. Estimates indicate that 10 percent of the 5 billion people presently living on the earth will die as a result of smoking related illnesses, killing approximately three million people each year. *Cigarette smoking is also the largest preventable cause of illness and premature death in the United States. When considering all related deaths, smoking is responsible for over 350,000 unnecessary deaths each year.* There is a definite increase in death rates from heart disease, cancer, stroke, aortic aneurysm, chronic bronchitis, emphysema, and peptic ulcers. Maternal cigarette smoking has been linked to retarded fetal growth, increased risk for spontaneous abortion, and prenatal death. Smoking is also the most common cause of fire deaths and injuries. The average life expectancy for a chronic smoker is up to eighteen years less than a nonsmoker, and the death rate among chronic smokers during the most productive years of life, between the ages of twenty-five and sixty-five, is twice that of the national average. The relative risk for all-cause mortality by cigarette smoking status and various fitness levels is illustrated in Figure 15.1.

In spite of the length of time elapsed since the 1964 report by the Surgeon General on the detrimental effects of smoking on health, the Federal Trade Commission reported in 1986 that 40 percent of Americans still did not know that smoking caused lung cancer, and 20 percent were unaware that it caused any type of cancer at all. This same report indicated that 30 percent of the population did not know that smoking increased the risk for heart disease, and that approximately half of all women in the country did not know that smoking during pregnancy increased the risk for miscarriage and spontaneous abortion.

─────── *FIGURE 15.1* ───────

Relative Risks of All-Cause Mortality by Physical Fitness and Cigarette Smoking Status. Numbers on top of the bars are all-cause death rates per 10,000 person-years of follow-up for each cell — 1 person-year indicates one person that was followed-up one year later (least fit group = 1, most fit group = 5).

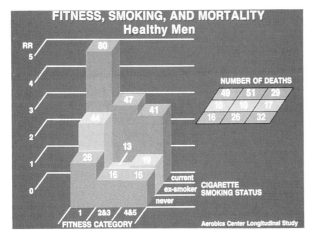
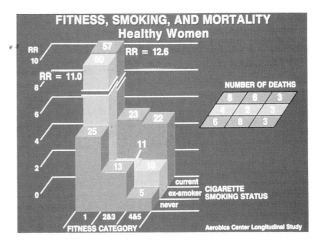

Reproduced with permission from Blair, S. N., H. W. Kohl III, R. S. Paffenbarger, Jr, D. G. Clark, K. H. Cooper, and L. W. Gibbons. *Physical fitness and all-cause mortality: a prospective study of healthy men and women. JAMA* 262:2395-2401, 1989. Copyright 1989, American Medical Association.

According to American Heart Association estimates, over 30 percent or 120,000 fatal heart attacks annually are due to smoking. Heart attack risk is 50 to 100 percent greater for smokers as compared to nonsmokers. There is also an increased mortality rate following heart attacks, since they are usually more severe and the risk for deadly arrhythmias is much greater. Cigarette smoking affects the cardiovascular system by increasing heart rate, blood pressure, susceptibility to atherosclerosis, and blood clots. Evidence also indicates that it decreases high-density lipoprotein cholesterol, or the so-called "good" cholesterol, which decreases the risk for heart disease. Finally, carbon monoxide found in smoke decreases the oxygen delivery capacity of the blood to the tissues of the body.

Also known is the fact that the biggest carcinogenic exposure in the workplace is cigarette smoke. *The American Cancer Society reports that 83 percent of lung cancer and 30 percent of all cancers are due to smoking. It kills about 142,000 people each year.* Lung cancer (Figure 15.2) is the leading cancer killer and is responsible for 30 percent of all cancer deaths. According to a 1990 report by the Environmental Protection Agency (EPA), secondhand smoke is also a killer. Secondhand smoke is responsible for 3,000 or more lung cancer deaths annually. While it is encouraging to note that over 50 percent of all cancers are now curable, the five-year survival rate for lung cancer is less than 10 percent. Tobacco usage also increases cancer risk of the oral cavity, larynx, esophagus, bladder, pancreas, and kidneys.

New research presented at the 1990 World Conference on Lung Health also indicates that non-smokers who live with smokers have a 20 to 30 percent higher risk of dying from heart disease than do other non-smokers. The results of this research further suggested that the number of heart disease deaths due to passive smoking is ten times that of cancer.

While many tobacco users are aware of the health consequences of cigarette smoking, many fail to realize the risk of pipe smoking, cigar smoking, and tobacco chewing. As a group in general, the risk for heart disease and lung cancer is lower than for cigarette smokers. However, blood nicotine levels in pipe and cigar smokers have been shown to approach those of cigarette smokers, since nicotine is still absorbed through the membranes of the mouth. Therefore, there is still a higher risk for heart disease as compared to nonsmokers. Cigarette smokers who substitute pipe or cigar smoking for cigarettes usually continue to inhale the smoke, which actually results in a greater amount of nicotine and tar being brought into the lungs. Consequently, the risk for disease is even greater if pipe or cigar smoke is inhaled. The risk and mortality rates for lip, mouth, and larynx cancer for pipe smoking, cigar smoking, or tobacco chewing are actually higher than for cigarette smoking.

The economical impact of cigarette smoking among American business and industry is also staggering. Companies pay in excess of $16 billion each year as a direct result of smoking at the workplace and another $37 billion in lost productivity and earnings because of illness, disability, and death. Heavy smokers have been shown to use the health care system, especially hospitals, over 50 percent more than nonsmokers. The yearly cost to a given company has been estimated between $624 and $4,611 per smoking employee. These costs include employee health care, absenteeism, additional

FIGURE 15.2

Normal Lung (left) and Diseased Lung (right). The white growth near the top of the diseased lung is cancer; the dark appearance on the bottom half is emphysema.

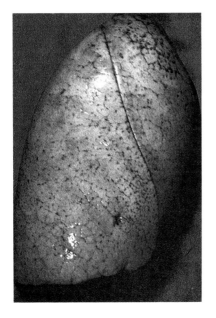

Reproduced with permission from *"If You Smoke"* slide show by Gordon Hewlett.

health insurance, morbidity/disability and early mortality, on-the-job lost time, property damage/maintenance and depreciation, Workmen's Compensation, and involuntary smoking impact.

In spite of the fact that the ill effects of tobacco have been well documented, not enough is being done to decrease and eradicate its use. Consider the following example. In the summer of 1985, over 1,500 people died around the world in major airplane accidents. These accidents resulted in a tremendous amount of worldwide media attention, and planes were grounded for safety reasons. Now imagine what the coverage and concern would be if 350,000 people each year died in the United States alone because of airplane accidents. People would not even consider flying anymore. Most individuals would think of it as a form of suicide.

Similarly, think of the public outrage if close to 350,000 Americans were to die annually in a meaningless war, or if a single nonprescription drug would cause over 138,000 cancer deaths and 120,000 fatal heart attacks. The American public would never tolerate such situations. We would probably mount a very intense fight to prevent these deaths. Yet, are we not committing a form of slow suicide by smoking cigarettes? Isn't tobacco a nonprescription drug available to most anyone who wishes to smoke, killing in excess of 350,000 people each year?

We may ask ourselves, why isn't there a greater campaign against all forms of tobacco use? There are primarily two reasons. First, it is extremely difficult to fight an industry that has as great a financial and political influence in a country as the tobacco industry has in the United States. The tobacco industry is the sixth largest cash-crop in the United States. It produces 2.5 percent of the gross national product and has cleverly influenced elections by emphasizing the individual's right to smoke, avoiding the fact that so many people die because of its use. Second, tobacco had been socially accepted for so many years that many people just learned to live with it. However, in the 1980s, cigarette smoking was no longer acceptable in many social circles. Nonsmokers and ex-smokers alike are fighting for their right to clean air and health. Estimates indicate that if every smoker gave up cigarettes, in one year alone, sick time would be decreased by approximately 90 million days, there would be 280,000 fewer heart conditions and 1 million fewer cases of chronic bronchitis and emphysema, and total death rates from

FIGURE 15.3

Tips for Smoking Cessation (continued)

23. Keep your hands occupied. Try playing a musical instrument, knitting, or fiddling with hand puzzles.

24. Take a shower. You cannot smoke in the shower.

25. Brush your teeth frequently to get rid of the tobacco taste and stains.

26. If you have a sudden craving for a cigarette, take ten deep breaths, holding the last breath while you strike a match. Exhale slowly, blowing out the match. Pretend the match was a cigarette by crushing it out in an ashtray. Now immediately get busy on some work or activity.

27. Only smoke half a cigarette.

28. After you quit, start using your lungs. Increase your activities and indulge in moderate exercise, such as short walks before or after a meal.

29. Bet with someone that you can quit. Put the cigarette money in a jar each morning and forfeit it if you smoke. You keep the money if you don't smoke by the end of the week. Try to extend this period for a month.

30. If you gain weight because you are not smoking, wait until you get over the craving before you diet. Dieting is easier then.

31. If you are depressed or have physical symptoms that might be related to your smoking, relieve your mind by discussing this with your physician. It is easier to quit when you know your health status.

32. Visit your dentist after you quit and have your teeth cleaned to get rid of the tobacco stains.

33. If the cost of cigarettes is your motivation for quitting, try purchasing a money order equivalent to a year's supply of cigarettes. Give it to a friend. If you smoke in the next year, he cashes the money order and keeps the money. If you don't smoke, he gives back the money order at the end of the year.

34. After you quit, never face the confusion of "craving a cigarette" alone. Find someone you can call or visit at this critical time.

35. When you feel irritable or tense, shut your eyes and count backward from ten to zero as you imagine yourself descending a flight of stairs, or imagine that you are looking at the horizon as the sun sets in the west.

36. Get out of your old habits. Seek new activities or perform old activities in a new way. Don't rely on the old ways of solving problems. Do things differently.

37. If you are a "kitchen smoker" in the morning, volunteer your services to schools or nonprofit organizations to get you out of the house.

38. Stock up on light reading materials, crossword puzzles, and vacation brochures that you can read during your coffee breaks.

39. Frequent places where you can't smoke, such as libraries, buses, theatres, swimming pools, department stores, or just going to bed during the first weeks you are off cigarettes.

40. Give yourself time to think and get fit by walking one-half hour each day. If you have a dog, take him for a walk with you.

From *TIPS*. American Cancer Society, Texas Division, Inc., with permission.

Relevant Fitness and Wellness Issues

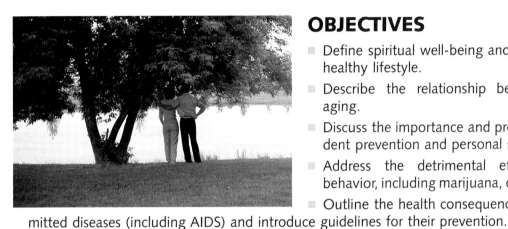

OBJECTIVES

- Define spiritual well-being and its relationship to a healthy lifestyle.
- Describe the relationship between fitness and aging.
- Discuss the importance and present a plan for accident prevention and personal safety.
- Address the detrimental effects of addictive behavior, including marijuana, cocaine, and alcohol.
- Outline the health consequences of sexually transmitted diseases (including AIDS) and introduce guidelines for their prevention.
- Provide guidelines to review health/fitness accomplishments and to help you chart a wellness program for the future.

The purpose of this last chapter is to address six additional wellness issues that are a part of twentieth-century living and may directly influence your personal well-being. These current issues are: (a) spirituality, (b) exercise and aging, (c) accident prevention and personal safety, (d) addiction, (e) adherence to health-promoting behaviors, and (f) prevention of sexually transmitted diseases. In addition, in this chapter you will have the opportunity to determine how well you achieved the objectives that you accomplished this semester, and general guidelines are introduced to help you chart your personal wellness program for the future.

SPIRITUAL WELL-BEING

The scientific association between spirituality and health is more difficult to establish than that of other lifestyle factors such as alcohol, smoking, physical inactivity, seat belt use, etc. Several research studies, nonetheless, have reported a positive relationship between spiritual well-being, emotional well-being, life's satisfaction, and health. One particular study indicated a much higher rate of heart attacks among nonreligious people as compared to a religious sample attending church. Other studies suggest that religious support may

act as a buffer against disease and that the social support encourages preventive health.

Spiritual well-being is defined by the National Interfaith Coalition on Aging as an affirmation of life in a relationship with God, self, community, and environment that nurtures and celebrates wholeness (Figure 16.1). Because this definition includes Christians and non-Christians alike, it assumes that all people are spiritual in nature.

Wellness requires a balance between physical, mental, spiritual, emotional, and social well-being. The relationship between spirituality and wellness, therefore, is meaningful in man's quest for a better quality of life. Religion has been a major part of cultures since the beginning of time. While not everyone in the United States claims affiliation to a certain religion or denomination, current surveys indicate that 94 percent of the U.S. population believes in God or a Universal spirit who functions as God. People, furthermore, believe to different extents that (a) a relationship with God is meaningful; (b) God can grant help, guidance, and assistance in daily living; and (c) that there is a purpose to the mortal existence. If we accept any or all of these statements, then attaining the proper degree of spirituality will have a definite effect on life's happiness and well-being.

———— *FIGURE 16.1* ————

Spiritual Well-being. An affirmation of life in a relationship with God, self, community, and environment that nurtures and celebrates wholeness.

Spiritual

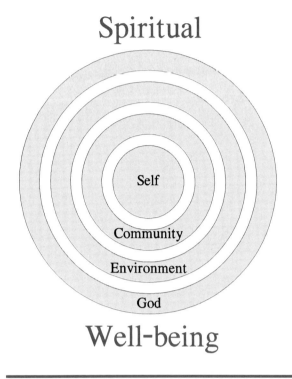

Self

Community

Environment

God

Well-being

EXERCISE AND AGING

Unlike any previous time in American society, the elderly constitute the fastest growing segment of our population. In 1880, less than three percent of the total population, or fewer than two million people, were over the age of 65. By 1980, the elderly population had reached approximately 25 million, representing over 11.3 percent of the population. It has been estimated that the elderly will make up more than 20 percent of the total population by the year 2035.

Historically, the older adults have been neglected in the development of fitness programs. Adequate fitness is just as important for older individuals as it is for young people. While much research remains to be done in this area, studies indicate that older individuals who are physically fit also enjoy better health and a higher quality of life.

The main objective of fitness programs for older adults should be to improve the functional capacity of the participant. *A committee of the American Alliance of Health, Physical Education, Recreation, and Dance (AAHPERD) recently defined functional fitness for older adults as "the physical capacity of the individual to meet ordinary and unexpected demands of daily life safely and effectively."* This definition

clearly indicates the need for fitness programs that closely relate to activities normally encountered by this population. The AAHPERD committee encourages participation in programs that will help develop cardiovascular endurance, localized muscular endurance, muscular flexibility, agility and balance, and motor coordination. A copy of a recently developed battery of fitness tests for older adults can be obtained from the AAHPERD national office in Reston, Virginia.

Relationship Between Fitness and Aging

While previous research studies have documented declines in physiological functioning and motor capacity as a result of aging, at present there is no hard evidence which proves that declines in physical work capacity are primarily related to the aging process. Lack of physical activity, a common phenomena seen in our society as people age, may cause decreases in physical work capacity that are by far greater than the effects of aging itself.

Data on individuals who have engaged in systematic physical activity throughout life indicate that these groups of people maintain a higher level of functional capacity and do not experience the typical declines in later years. Dr. George Sheehan, cardiologist and runner, states that, from a functional point of view, the typical American is 30 years older than his/her chronological age indicates. In other words, an active sixty-year-old person can have a similar work capacity as a sedentary thirty-year-old individual.

Physical Training in the Older Adult

The trainability of both elderly men and women and the effectiveness of physical activity as a relative modality has been demonstrated in prior research. Older adults who increase their level of physical activity will experience significant changes in cardiovascular endurance, strength, and flexibility. The extent of the changes depends on their initial fitness level and the types of activities selected for their training (walking, cycling, strength training, etc.).

Current studies show that relative changes in maximal oxygen uptake in older adults are similar to younger people, although a longer training period seems to be required to achieve these changes. In terms of decrements, some earlier studies have shown a 10 to 15 percent decline in endurance (maximal oxygen uptake) per decade of life after age 25. Relatively new research, however, has shown declines of about 9 percent for sedentary adults and 5 percent or less in active people. The average decline in maximal oxygen uptake is thought to be in the range of 0.4 to 0.6 ml/kg/min per year in sedentary groups, while the decline is only about 0.2 ml/kg/min in active people.

Results from a recent study on the effects of aging (an 18-year follow-up) on the cardiovascular system of male exercisers versus nonexercisers, published in *The Physician and Sportsmedicine*, showed that the maximal oxygen uptake of regular exercisers is almost twice that of the nonexercisers (see Table 16.1). *The study demonstrated a decline in maximal oxygen uptake of only 13 percent in the active group as compared to 41 percent in the inactive group.* These changes seem to indicate that one third of the loss in maximal oxygen uptake is due to aging, whereas two thirds of the loss is due to inactivity. *Blood pressure was significantly lower in the exercising group. Contrary to common assumptions, the data shows that in active individuals, blood pressure does not increase with age. Heart rate and body weight values were also significantly better in the exercising group.*

In regard to strength development, research has shown that although older adults can significantly increase their strength levels, the amount of muscle hypertrophy achieved decreases with age. In terms of body composition, after the age of 60, inactive adults continue to gain body fat despite the fact that body weight tends to decrease.

Older adults who wish to initiate or continue an exercise program are strongly encouraged to have a complete medical exam, including a stress electro-cardiogram test (see Chapter 12, Figure 12.5). Recommended activities for older adults include calisthenics, walking, jogging, swimming, cycling, and water aerobics. Isometric and other intense weight training exercises should be avoided. Activities that require an all-out effort and/or require participants to hold their breath (valsalva maneuver) tend to

decrease blood flow to the heart and cause a significant increase in blood pressure and the load placed on the heart. Older adults should participate in activities that require continuous and rhythmic muscular activity (about 50 to 70 percent of functional capacity). Such activities do not cause large increases in blood pressure or place an intense overload on the heart.

ACCIDENT PREVENTION AND PERSONAL SAFETY

Most people do not perceive accidents as being a health problem, but accidents are the third leading cause of death in the United States, affecting the total well-being of millions of Americans each year. Accident prevention and personal safety are also part of a health enhancement program aimed at achieving a higher quality of life. Proper nutrition, exercise, abstinence from cigarette smoking, and stress management are of little help if the person is involved in a disabling or fatal accident due to distraction, a single reckless decision, or not properly wearing safety seat belts.

Accidents do not just happen. We cause accidents and we are victims of accidents. Although some factors in life are completely beyond our control, such as earthquakes, tornadoes, or airplane crashes, *more often than not, personal safety and accident prevention are a matter of common sense.* A majority of accidents are the result of poor judgment and confused mental states. Accidents frequently happen when we are upset, not paying attention to the task with which we are involved, or by abusing alcohol and other drugs.

Alcohol abuse is the number-one cause of all accidents. Statistics clearly show that alcohol intoxication is the leading cause of most fatal automobile accidents. Other drugs commonly abused in society alter feelings and perceptions, lead to mental confusion, and impair judgment and coordination, thereby greatly enhancing the risk for accidental morbidity and mortality.

To help improve your personal safety, you are encouraged to fill out the "Health Protection Plan for Environmental Hazards, Crime Prevention, and Personal Safety" given in Lab 16A. Keep in mind that you control most actions in your life, and by following the recommendations given in this questionnaire, you can further enhance your personal safety and well-being.

ADDICTION

When most people think of addiction, they probably think of dark/dirty alleys, an addict shooting drugs into the veins, or the "junkie" passed out next to a garbage can after an evening bout with alcohol.

TABLE 16.1

Effects of Physical Activity and Inactivity on Selected Physiological Parameters in Older Men[1]

	Exercisers	Nonexercisers
Age (yrs)	68.0	69.8
Weight (lbs)	160.3	186.3
Resting Heart Rate (bpm)	55.8	66.0
Maximal heart Rate (bpm)	157.0	146.0
Heart Rate Reserve[2] (bpm)	101.2	80.0
Blood Pressure (mmHg)	120/78	150/90
Maximal Oxygen Uptake (ml/kg/min)	38.6	20.3

[1] Data from Kash, F. W., J. L. Boyer, S. P. Van Camp, L. S. Verity, and J. P. Wallace. "The Effect of Physical Activity on Aerobic Power in Older Men (A Longitudinal Study)." The Physician and Sports Medicine 18(4):73-83, 1990.
[2] Heart rate reserve = maximal heart rate − resting heart rate.

Jacquelyn Small, psychotherapist and author, defines addiction as a problem of imbalance or unease within the body and mind. *While some addictive behaviors are worse than others, there are many types of addiction, including food, television, work, compulsive shopping, even exercise, and most seriously, chemical dependency* (e.g., tobacco, coffee, alcohol, cocaine, heroin, marijuana, prescription drugs).

Some people become addicted to food. They eat to release stress, boredom, or to reward themselves for every small personal achievement. A great number of people are addicted to television. Estimates indicate that the average adult in the United States spends seven hours per day watching television.

Other individuals become addicted to their jobs in such a manner that all they think about is work. Although work starts out as an enjoyable leisure activity, when it totally consumes a person's life, work can become an unhealthy behavior. If you find that you are readily irritated, moody, grouchy, constantly tired, not as alert as you used to be, or making more mistakes than usual, you are probably becoming a workaholic and need to slow down and/or take time off work.

Exercise has enhanced the health and quality of life of millions of people, but for a very small group of individuals, exercise can become an obsessive behavior with potential addictive and overuse properties. Compulsive exercisers often express feelings of guilt and discomfort when a day's workout is missed. These individuals continue to exercise even during periods of injury and sickness that require proper rest for adequate recovery. People who exceed the recommended guidelines for fitness development and maintenance (see Chapters 5, 8, and 10) are exercising for reasons other than health, including addictive behavior.

Caffeine addiction can also produce undesirable side effects. Caffeine doses in excess of 200 to 500 mg can produce an abnormally rapid heart rate, abnormal heart rhythms, increased blood pressure, birth defects, increased body temperature, and increased secretion of gastric acids leading to stomach problems. It may also induce symptoms of anxiety, depression, nervousness, and dizziness. The caffeine content of different drinks varies depending upon the product. For six ounces of coffee, the content varies from 65 mg for instant coffee to as high as 180 mg for drip coffee. Soft drinks, mainly colas, range in caffeine content from 30 to 60 mg per twelve-ounce can.

The previous examples, as well as more serious forms of chemical dependency, are by no means the only types of addiction, but are used only to illustrate addictive behaviors. Other examples are gambling, pornography, sex, people, places, etc. While all forms of addiction are unhealthy, this chapter will focus on three of the most serious, self-destructive forms of addiction in our society:

marijuana, cocaine, and alcohol (the addiction to cigarette smoking and tobacco in general has already been discussed in detail in Chapter 15).

DRUGS AND DEPENDENCE

Approximately 60 percent of the world's production of illegal drugs is consumed in the United States. Each year Americans spend over $100 billion on illegal drugs, an amount that surpasses the total amount taken in from all crops by United States farmers. *According to the U.S. Department of Education, today's drugs are stronger, more addictive, and pose a greater risk than ever before.* Drugs lead to physical and psychological dependence. With regular use, they integrate into the body's chemistry, increasing drug tolerance and forcing the user to constantly increase the dosage to obtain similar results. Drug abuse leads not only to serious health problems, but over half of all adolescent suicides are drug-related.

Marijuana

Marijuana (pot or grass, as it is commonly referred to), is the most widely used illegal drug in the United States. Estimates indicate that 64 percent of Americans between the ages of eighteen and twenty-five and 23 percent of those twenty-six and over have smoked marijuana. Approximately 20 million people in the country regularly use marijuana. This psychoactive drug is prepared from a mixture of crushed leaves, flowers, small branches, stems, and seeds from the hemp plant, cannabis sativa.

Marijuana in small doses has a sedative effect, while larger doses produce physical and psychic changes. Earlier studies in the 1960s indicated that the potential effects of marijuana were exaggerated and that the drug was relatively harmless. However, the drug as it is used today is as much as ten times stronger than when the initial studies were conducted. *Ninety percent of research today shows marijuana to be a dangerous and harmful drug.*

The major and most active psychoactive and mind-altering ingredient of marijuana is thought to be delta-9-tetrahydrocannabinol (THC). In the 1960s, THC content in marijuana ranged from .02 to 2 percent. The latter was labeled by users as the "real good grass." Today's THC content averages 4 to 6 percent, although it has been reported as high as 20 percent. The THC content in sinsemilla, a seedless variety of high-potency marijuana grown from the seedless female cannabis plant, is approximately 8 percent. THC reaches the brain within 30 seconds of inhalation of marijuana smoke, and the psychic and physical changes reach their peak in about two or three minutes. THC is then metabolized in the liver to waste metabolites, but 30 percent of it remains in the body one week after marijuana was first smoked. In fact, studies indicate that thirty days or longer are required to completely eliminate THC following an initial dose of the drug. For regular users the drug will always remain in the system.

Some of the short-term effects of marijuana include tachycardia (increased heart rate, sometimes as high 180 beats per minute), *dryness of the mouth, reddening of the eyes, increased appetite, decrease in coordination and tracking* (following a moving stimulus), *difficulty in concentration, intermittent confusion, impairment of short-term memory and continuity of speech, and interference with the physical and mental learning process during periods of intoxication.* Another common effect seen with marijuana use is the amotivational syndrome, a condition characterized by a loss of motivation, dullness, apathy, and no interest in the future. This syndrome persists even after periods of intoxication, but usually disappears a few weeks after the individual stops using the drug.

Long-term harmful effects include atrophy of the brain, leading to irreversible brain damage, decreased resistance to infectious diseases, chronic bronchitis, lung cancer (may contain as much as 50 percent more cancer-producing hydrocarbons than cigarette smoke), *and possible sterility and impotence.*

One of the most common myths about marijuana use is that it does not lead to addiction. Ample scientific evidence clearly shows that regular marijuana users do develop physical and psychological dependence. Similar to cigarette smoking, when regular users go without the drug, they crave the substance, experience changes in mood, irritability, and nervousness, and develop an obsession to get more "pot."

Cocaine

Similar to marijuana, cocaine was thought for many years to be a relatively harmless drug. This misconception came to an abrupt halt in 1986 when two well-known athletes, Len Bias (basketball) and Don Rogers (football), died a sudden death following a cocaine overdose. Estimates indicate that between four and eight million Americans use cocaine, 96 percent of whom had previously used marijuana.

Cocaine (2-beta-carbomethoxy-3-betabenozoxy-tropane) is the primary psychoactive ingredient derived from coca plant leaves. Over the years it has been given several different names, including coke, C, snow, blow, toot, flake, Peruvian lady, white girl, and happy dust. The drug is commonly sniffed or snorted, but it can be smoked or injected. Cocaine is an expensive drug. Some users pay in excess of $2000 per ounce. Cocaine used in medical therapy sells for about $100 per ounce. Because of the high cost, cocaine is viewed as a luxury drug. Many users are well-educated, affluent, upwardly mobile professionals who are otherwise law-abiding citizens.

Cocaine has become the fastest growing drug problem in the United States. About 5,000 people try cocaine for the first time each day. The addiction begins with a desire to get high, oftentimes at social gatherings with the assurance that occasional use is harmless. About one in five will continue to use the drug now and then, and for some of them it's the beginning of a lifetime nightmare. The popularity of cocaine is based on the almost universal guarantee that the user will be placed in an immediate state of euphoria and well-being. When cocaine is snorted, it is quickly absorbed through the mucous membranes of the nose into the bloodstream. The drug is usually arranged in fine powder lines one to two inches long. Each line results in about thirty minutes of central and autonomic nervous system stimulation. The drug seems to help relieve fatigue and increase energy levels, as well as decrease the need for appetite and sleep. Following this stimulation comes a "crash," or a state of physiological and psychological depression, oftentimes leaving the user with the desire to get more. This can lead to a constant craving for the drug. *Researchers indicate that addiction becomes a lifetime illness, and, similar to alcoholism, the individual recovers only through complete abstinence from the drug. A single pitfall often results in renewed addiction.*

Light to moderate use of cocaine is commonly associated with feelings of pleasure and well-being. *Sustained cocaine snorting can lead to a constant runny nose, nasal congestion and inflammation, and perforation of the nasal septum. Long-term consequences of cocaine use in general result in a loss of appetite, digestive disorders, weight loss, malnutrition, insomnia, confusion, anxiety, and cocaine psychosis.* The latter is characterized by paranoia and hallucinations. In a particular type of hallucination, referred to as formication or "coke bugs," the chronic user perceives imaginary insects or snakes crawling on or underneath the skin.

High doses of cocaine can cause nervousness, dizziness, blurred vision, vomiting, tremors, seizures, high blood pressure, strokes, angina, and cardiac arrhythmias. Freebase users (a purer, more potent smokable form of cocaine) increase their risk for lung disease, while intravenous users are at risk for hepatitis, AIDS, and other infectious diseases. *Large overdoses of cocaine can lead to sudden death as a result of respiratory paralysis, cardiac arrhythmias, and severe convulsions.* However, some individuals may lack an enzyme used in metabolizing cocaine, and as little as two to three lines of cocaine may be fatal. Chronic users who constantly crave the drug often turn to crime, including murder, to sustain their habit. Some users view suicide as the only solution to this sad syndrome.

Alcohol

Drinking alcohol has been a socially acceptable behavior for centuries. Alcohol is frequently used at parties, ceremonies, dinners, sport contests, the establishment of kingdoms or governments, and the signing of peace treaties. Alcohol has also been used for medical reasons as a mild sedative or as a pain killer for surgery. Nevertheless, for a short period of fourteen years, from 1920 to 1933, by constitutional amendment, the sale and use of alcohol were declared illegal in the United States. This amendment was repealed because both drinkers and nondrinkers questioned the right of the government to pass judgment on individual moral standards. In addition, the country experienced a tremendous growth in organized crime to smuggle and illegally sell alcohol.

The alcohol contained in drinks is known as ethyl alcohol, a depressant drug that affects the brain and slows down central nervous system activity. As with most drugs that affect the brain, it has strong addictive properties and therefore can be easily abused. In fact, alcohol is one of the most significant health-related drug problems in the United States today. Estimates indicate that seven in ten adults, or over 100 million Americans eighteen years and older, are drinkers. Approximately 10 million of them will experience a drinking problem, including alcoholism, in their lifetime. Another 3 million teenagers are thought to have a drinking problem.

The addiction to alcohol develops slowly. Most people feel that they are in control of their drinking habits and do not realize that there is a problem until they become alcoholics; that is, when they develop a physical and emotional dependence on the drug, characterized by excessive use and constant preoccupation with drinking. Alcohol abuse in turn leads to mental, emotional, physical, and social problems.

Alcohol intake reduces peripheral vision, decreases visual and hearing acuity, decreases reaction time, impairs concentration and motor performance (including increased swaying and impaired judgment of distance and speed of moving objects), *decreases fear, increases risk-taking behaviors, increases urination, and induces sleep. A single large dose of alcohol may also decrease sexual function. One of the most unpleasant, dangerous, and life-threatening effects of drinking is the synergistic action of alcohol when combined with other drugs, particularly central nervous system depressants. The effects of mixing alcohol with another drug can be much greater than the sum of two drug actions by themselves.* While there are individual differences as to how the body will react to a combination of alcohol and other drugs, the effects range from loss of consciousness to death.

Long-term effects of alcohol abuse lead to serious and often life-threatening problems. Some of these detrimental effects are cirrhosis of the liver (scarring of the liver which is often fatal); *increased risk for oral, esophageal, and liver cancer; cardiomyopathy* (a disease that affects the heart muscle); *elevated blood pressure; increased risk for strokes; inflammation of the esophagus, stomach, small intestine, and pancreas; stomach ulcers; sexual impotence; malnutrition; brain cell damage leading to loss of memory; psychosis; depression; and hallucinations.*

How To Cut Down Your Drinking*

To find out if drinking is a problem in your life, refer to the questionnaire "Alcohol Abuse: Are You Drinking Too Much" given in Lab 16B. If you give two or more "yes" answers on this questionnaire, you may be jeopardizing your health through excessive consumption of alcohol. Now is the time to start limiting your intake of alcohol. For many people who are determined to control the problem, it is not that hard to do. The first and most important step is to want to cut down. If you want to cut down but find you cannot, you had better accept the probability that alcohol is becoming a serious problem for you, and you should seek guidance from your physician or from an organization such as Alcoholics Anonymous. The next few suggestions may also help you cut down alcohol intake.

1. Set reasonable limits for yourself. Decide not to exceed a certain number of drinks on a given occasion, and stick to your decision. No more than two beers or two cocktails a day is a reasonable limit. You have proven to yourself that you can control your drinking if you set such a target and regularly do not exceed it.

2. Learn to say no. Many people have "just one more" drink because others in the group are having one or because someone puts pressure on them, not because they really want a drink. When you reach the sensible limit you have set for yourself, politely but firmly refuse to exceed it. If you are being the generous host, pour yourself a glass of water or juice "on the rocks." Nobody will notice the difference.

3. Drink slowly. Never gulp down a drink. Choose your drinks for their flavor, not their "kick," and savor the taste of each sip.

4. Dilute your drinks. If you prefer cocktails to beer, try having long drinks. Instead of downing your gin or whiskey neat or nearly so, drink it diluted with a mixer such as tonic, water, or soda water,

*Reproduced with permission from Family Medical Guide by The American Medical Association. New York: Random House, 1982.

in a tall glass. That way, you can enjoy the flavor as well as the act of drinking, but it will take longer to finish each drink. Also, you can make your two-drink limit last all evening or switch to the mixer by itself.

5. Do not drink on your own. Make a point of confining your drinking to social gatherings. It is sometimes hard to resist the urge to pour yourself a relaxing drink at the end of a hard day, but many formerly heavy drinkers have found that a cup of coffee or a soft drink satisfies the need as well as alcohol did, and that it was just a habit. What may help you really to unwind, even with no drink at all, is a comfortable chair, loosened clothing, and perhaps a soothing record, a television program or a good book to read.

Treatment of Addiction

Treatment of drug addiction (including alcohol) is seldom accomplished without professional guidance and support. Of course the initial step is to recognize that there is a problem. The questionnaire given in Lab 16B can help you recognize possible addictive behavior either in yourself or someone you know. If your answers to more than half of these questions is positive, you may have a problem and should speak to your doctor or contact the local mental health clinic for a referral (see the Yellow Pages in your phone book).

SEXUALLY TRANSMITTED DISEASES*

Sexually transmitted diseases (STDs) have become an epidemic of national proportions in the United States. There are now over twenty-five known STDs, some of which are still incurable. According to the Centers for Disease Control in Atlanta, in 1986 more than 10 million new people were infected with STDs, including 4.6 million cases of chlamydia, 1.8 million of gonorrhea, 1 million of genital warts, half a million of herpes, 90,000 of syphilis, and attracting most of the attention because of its life-threatening potential were 15,000 new cases of AIDS or Acquired Immune Deficiency Syndrome. *The American Social Health Association indicates that 25 percent of all Americans will acquire at least one STD in their lifetime.*

Chlamydia is a bacterial infection that can cause significant damage to the reproductive system and *may occur without symptoms.* The disease is considered to be a major factor in male and female infertility. Because of its asymptomatic condition, victims frequently don't even know that they are infected. When symptoms do occur, they tend to mimic other STDs; therefore, the disease can often be mistreated. The Centers for Disease Control indicate that about 20 percent of all college students are infected with chlamydia. The disease can be effectively treated with oral antibiotics, but successful treatment will not reverse any damage that has already occurred to the reproductive system.

One of the oldest STDs is gonorrhea. This disease is also caused by a bacterial infection. If left untreated, it can lead to pelvic inflammation in women, infertility, widespread bacterial infection, heart damage, arthritis in men and women, and blindness in children born to infected women. Gonorrhea is successfully treated with penicillin and other antibiotics.

Genital warts are caused by a viral infection and appear anywhere from a month and a half to eight months following exposure. Genital warts may be flat or raised and are usually found on the penis, around the vulva and the vagina, but can also be found in the mouth, throat, rectum, on the cervix, or around the anus. *Health problems associated with genital warts include an increased risk of cervical cancer and enlargement and spread of the warts leading to obstruction of the urethra, vagina, and anus.* Babies born to infected mothers commonly develop warts over their bodies; therefore, Cesarean sections are recommended in such cases. Treatment requires complete removal of all warts and can be accomplished by freezing them with liquid nitrogen, dissolving them with chemicals, or removing them with electrosurgery or laser surgery.

Herpes is also caused by a viral infection (herpes simplex virus types I and II), *and no known cure is yet available for the disease.* Herpes is characterized by the appearance of sores on the mouth, genitals, rectum, or other parts of the body. The symptoms usually disappear within a few weeks, causing some individuals to believe that they are cured. Nevertheless, herpes is presently incurable and these victims do remain infected. Repeated outbreaks are common. The disease is very contagious and can be transmitted through simple finger contact from the mouth to the genitals. Victims are most contagious when outbreaks occur. In conjunction with the appearance of sores, victims usually experience a mild fever, swollen glands, and headaches.

Another common type of STD, also caused by bacterial infection, is syphilis. Approximately three weeks following infection, a painless sore appears where the bacteria entered the body. This sore disappears on its own in a few weeks. If untreated, additional sores may appear within six months of the initial outbreak, but will again disappear by

*Adapted with permission from Hafen, B.Q., A.L. Thygerson, and K.J. Frandsen. *Behavioral Guidelines for Health & Wellness.* Englewood, CO: Morton Publishing Company, 1988.

themselves. A latent stage, during which the victim is not contagious, may last up to thirty years, leading the victim to believe that he/she is healed. *During the last stage of the disease, some people will suffer from paralysis, crippling, blindness, heart disease, brain damage, insanity, and even death.* One of the oldest STDs known to man, syphilis used to kill its victims prior to the discovery of penicillin and other antibiotics which are used in its treatment.

AIDS is the most frightening of all STDs because there is no known cure and few victims have survived the disease. Anywhere from 1.5 to 4 million Americans are thought to carry the HIV or AIDS virus. *This virus attacks cells, weakening their immune system.* Although there is much debate as to how many carriers will actually get AIDS, it is thought that one-third to one-half of them will develop the disease. Nevertheless, even if the person doesn't develop AIDS, he/she can still pass the virus on to others who could easily develop the disease (including pregnant women to their unborn babies). It is projected that by the year 2000 more than 200,000 people will die from AIDS, making it the third leading cause of death behind cardiovascular disease and cancer.

Based on 1986 estimates, almost all of the AIDS cases have occurred in the following groups of people:

■ Gay and bisexual men: 66 percent

■ Heterosexual intravenous drug users: 17 percent

■ Gay and bisexual men who abuse intravenous drugs: 8 percent

■ Heterosexual sex partners of the above groups: 4 percent

■ Hemophiliacs and people who have had blood transfusions: 3 percent

As shown by the previous estimates, high-risk individuals for AIDS are primarily homosexual males with multiple sexual partners and intravenous drug users, but health experts feel that in future years the disease may become just as common among heterosexuals. The virus is transmitted through blood and semen during sexual intercourse or by using hypodermic needles previously used by an infected individual. The AIDS virus, however, cannot live long outside the human body. Small concentrations of the virus have also been found in saliva and tear drops. Unlike some people think, AIDS cannot be caught by spending time or shaking hands with an infected person, or from a toilet seat, dishes, or silverware used by an AIDS patient, using a towel or clothes from a person with AIDS, or from donating blood.

Once a person becomes infected with the AIDS virus, there will be an incubation period ranging from a few months to six years during which no symptoms appear. *The virus weakens and incapacitates the immune system, leaving the victim vulnerable to all types of infectious diseases and certain types of cancer. Initial symptoms of the disease include unexplained weight loss, constant fatigue, mild fever, swollen lymph glands, diarrhea, and sore throats. Advanced symptoms include loss of appetite, skin diseases, night sweats, and deterioration of the mucous membranes.* The AIDS virus itself doesn't kill, but rather the ineffectiveness of the immune system in dealing with the various illnesses is what leads to death. Most of these illnesses are usually harmless and rare among the general population but prove to be fatal to the AIDS patient. *The two most common fatal conditions seen in AIDS victims are pneumocystis carinii pneumonia* (a parasitic infection of the lungs) *and kaposis sarcoma* (a certain type of skin cancer). *The AIDS virus may also attack the nervous system, leading to brain and spinal cord damage.*

What about dating? Dating and getting to know other people is a normal part of life. Dating, however, does not mean the same thing as having sex. Sexual intercourse as a part of dating can be risky. One of the risks is AIDS. There is no way for you to tell if someone you are dating or would like to date has been exposed to the AIDS virus. The good news, nonetheless, is that as long as sexual activity and sharing drug needles are avoided, it does not matter who you date.

Although several drugs are being tested to treat and slow down the disease process, there is presently no known cure for AIDS. Nonetheless, at the Sixth International Conference on AIDS held in San Francisco in June 1990, researchers showed some optimism. For the first time scientists predicted that a vaccine to prevent the disease could be available for the general population by the mid- to late 1990s. Approximately 30 different approaches to an AIDS vaccine are being explored, with two approved for testing in humans. Although still quite controversial and perhaps somewhat premature, a drug referred to as Compound Q appears to have reversed AIDS in eight of 46 patients. Because of these reports, there is hope and optimism for the future. The best advice at this point, however, is a preventive approach. The recommended guidelines for prevention of STDs, including AIDs, will now be discussed.

Guidelines for the Prevention of Sexually Transmitted Diseases

With all the grim news about STDs, there is also some very good news: There are things you can do to prevent their spread, and precautions you can take to keep yourself from becoming a victim.

The facts are in: The best prevention technique is a mutually monogamous sexual relationship. In other words, you have sexual relationships with only one person, who has sexual relationships only with you. That one behavior, says Dr. James Mason, director of the Centers for Disease Control in Atlanta, will almost completely remove you from any risk of developing a STD.

What about those who do not have — or do not desire — a monogamous relationship? There are still other things that can be done to lower the risk of developing sexually transmitted diseases in general:

1. Know your partner. The days are gone when anonymous bathhouse or singles bars sex is safe. You should limit your sexual relationships or you should be able to reassure your partner that you are infection-free, and you deserve the same right from your partner.

2. Limit the number of sexual partners you have. Having one partner lowers your chance of infection. The greater your number of partners, the greater your chance of infection.

3. If you are sexually promiscuous, consider having periodic checkups from your physician. It is easy to get exposed to a STD by a person who does not have any symptoms and who is unaware of the infection. Sexually promiscuous men and women between the ages of fifteen and thirty-five are considered to be in a particularly high-risk group for developing STDs.

4. Use "barrier" methods of contraception to help prevent the spread of disease. Condoms, diaphragms, the contraceptive sponge, and spermicidal suppositories, foams, and jellies can all help prevent the spread of STDs; spermicidal agents may help act as a disinfectant as well. Many physicians are especially encouraging promiscuous teenagers to use condoms; traditionally, teenagers do not use any birth-control methods at all and remain at high risk for STDs.

5. Be responsible enough to abstain from sexual activity if you know that you have an infection. Go to a physician or clinic for appropriate treatment, and ask your doctor when it will be safe to resume sexual activity. Abstain until it is safe.

6. Urinate immediately following sexual intercourse. While it is not a foolproof method, it may help (especially among men) flush bacteria and viruses from the urinary tract.

7. Wash thoroughly immediately following sexual activity; while washing with hot soapy water will not provide a guaranteed measure of safety against STDs, such washing can prevent you from spreading certain germs on your fingers and may wash away bacteria and viruses that have not yet entered the body.

8. If you suspect that your partner is infected, ask. He or she may not even be aware of the infection, so look for signs of infection, such as sores, redness, inflammations, a rash, growths, warts, or discharge. If you are unsure, abstain.

9. Consider abstaining from sexual relations if you have any kind of an illness or disease, even a common cold. Any kind of illness makes you more susceptible to other illnesses, and a lowered immunity can make you extra vulnerable to STDs. The same holds true for times when you are under extreme stress, when you are fatigued, and when you are overworked. Drugs and alcohol can also lower your resistance to disease.

10. Wear loose-fitting clothes made of natural fibers; tight-fitting clothing made of synthetic fibers (especially underwear and nylon pantyhose) can create conditions that encourage the growth of bacteria and can actually aggravate STDs.

AIDS: Risk Reduction

Observance of the following precautions, which are based upon reports and recommendations from the U.S. Public Health Service, can help reduce your risk of getting AIDS.

1. Avoid having multiple and/or anonymous sexual partners.

2. Don't have sexual contact (this includes open-mouthed or French kissing, since the AIDS virus may be present in saliva; it should be noted, however, that there is no evidence that AIDS has been transmitted in this way) with anyone who has symptoms of AIDS or who is a member of a high-risk group for AIDS.

3. Avoid sexual contact with anyone who has had sex with people at risk of getting AIDS.

4. Don't have sex with prostitutes.

5. If you do have sex with someone who might be infected with the AIDS virus or whose history is unknown to you, avoid exchange of body fluids and receptive anal intercourse. Unless you know with absolute certainty that your partner is not infected, a condom should be used during each sexual act, from start to finish, to help prevent contact with the AIDS virus. Use of a spermicidal agent may also provide some protection.

6. Don't share toothbrushes, razors, or other implements that could become contaminated with blood with anyone who is, or who might be, infected with the AIDS virus.

7. Exercise caution regarding procedures, such as acupuncture, tattooing, ear piercing, etc., in which needles or other unsterile instruments may be used repeatedly to pierce the skin and/or mucous membranes. Such procedures are safe if

proper sterilization methods are employed or disposable needles are used. Ask what precautions are being taken before undergoing such procedures.

8. If you are planning to undergo artificial insemination, insist on frozen sperm obtained from a laboratory that tests all donors for infection with the AIDS virus. Donors should be tested twice before the sperm is used — once at the time of donation and again a few months later.

9. If you know that you will be having surgery in the near future, and you are able, consider donating blood for your own use. This will eliminate completely the already small risk of contracting AIDS through a blood transfusion. It will also eliminate the more substantial risk of contracting other bloodborne diseases, such as hepatitis, from a transfusion.

THE PREVENTION INDEX*

The Prevention Index is an annual measure of the effort Americans are making to prevent disease and accidents and to promote good health and longevity. This nationwide index of the American Public is commissioned by *Prevention Magazine* and it has been developed from information collected by Louis Harris and Associates, Inc. in two national surveys:

1. Self reported practice of preventive health and safety behaviors based on a national probability sample of 1,250 adults in the continental United States 18 years of age and older.

2. Ratings on the relative importance of each of these behaviors for preventing disease and disability in the general population (scale of 1 to 10), as determined by a sample of 103 representative experts in disease prevention and health promotion.

Twenty-one of the behaviors measured in the Harris national probability survey of adults were selected for inclusion in the Prevention Index according to the following criteria:

1. A documented relationship between the health behavior and disease or disability as published in the professional literature.

2. Behaviors that are relevant to the entire adult population.

3. Behaviors that can be controlled or affected by individuals (therefore, the exclusion of important environmental determinants of health such as exposure to air pollution or industrial toxins).

Currently accepted standards of practice for each behavior were determined by thorough review of the professional literature and consultation with experts. For continuous variables (for example, moderate alcohol consumption, exercise or frequency of dental examination), practice was determined by the prevailing consensus in the relevant professional literature and from personal consultation with researchers and spokespersons of professional organizations. For those behaviors with no clear consensus on a minimum compliance level (for example, taking steps to control stress or restricting cholesterol intake), practice was defined in terms of either always engaging in the behavior (taking steps to control stress) or of trying a lot (restricting cholesterol intake). The 1990 percentages of the adult population practicing these 21 major health-promoting behaviors are given in Table 16.2.

A detailed description of the development and computation of the Prevention Index and related analyses is presented in the technical report, "The Prevention Index: A Report Card on the Nation's Health," available from *Prevention Magazine*. Although the Prevention Index takes stock of the nation's health, you can score your own prevention profile by taking the test in Lab 16C.

——————— *TABLE 16.2* ———————

The Prevention Index 1990 Results

Health-Promoting Behavior	% of Adults Practicing
1. Annual blood pressure test	84
2. Annual dental exam	75
3. Limit sodium in the diet	52
4. Limit fat in the diet	58
5. Consume adequate fiber	60
6. Limit cholesterol in the diet	50
7. Adequate vitamins/minerals	58
8. Limit sugar in the diet	46
9. Maintain proper weight	24
10. Frequent strenuous exercise	35
11. Do not smoke	72
12. Control stress	65
13. Sleep 7-8 hours per night	64
14. Socialize regularly	85
15. Drink alcohol moderately	91
16. Wear seat belts	63
17. Obey speed limit	54
18. Avoid driving after drinking	81
19. Smoke detector in home	85
20. Avoid smoking in bed	90
21. Avoid home accidents	80
	Average 65.3

Data from The Prevention Index '90. Consumers' survey conducted for *Prevention Magazine* by Louis Harris & Associates, Inc. *Prevention Magazine*. The Prevention Index '90: Summary Report. Emmaus, PA: Prevention Magazine, 1990.

*The Prevention Index: A Louis Harris & Associates, Inc. survey conducted for *Prevention Magazine*. With permission.

SELF-EVALUATION AND BEHAVIORAL OBJECTIVES FOR THE FUTURE

The main objective of this course was to provide the information and experiences necessary to implement your personal fitness and wellness program. If you have read and successfully completed all of the assignments in this course, including your regular exercise program, you should be convinced of the value of exercise and healthy lifestyle habits in the achievement of a new quality of life. For most people who engage in a personal fitness and wellness program, this new quality of life is experienced after only a few weeks of training and practicing healthy lifestyle patterns. In some instances, however, especially for individuals who have led a poor lifestyle for a long time, it may take a few months before positive habits are established and feelings of well-being are experienced. But in the end, everyone who applies the principles of fitness and wellness will reap the desired benefits.

Self-Evaluation

In various laboratory experiences you have had an opportunity to assess different fitness and wellness components and write behavioral objectives to improve your quality of life. You should now take the time to evaluate how well you achieved your own objectives. Ideally, if time allows, and facilities and technicians are available, you should reassess at least the health-related components of physical fitness. If you are unable to reassess these components, subjectively determine how well you accomplished your objectives. You will find a self-evaluation form in part A of Lab 16D.

Behavioral Objectives for the Future

The real challenge will come now that you are about to finish this course: a lifetime commitment to fitness and wellness. It is a lot easier to adhere to a program while in a structured setting, but from now on you will be on your own. Realizing that you may not have achieved all of your objectives during this course, or perhaps you need to reach beyond your current achievements, a final assignment should be conducted to help you chart the future. To complete this assignment, you will need to use the Wellness Compass given in Figure 16D.1 in part B of Lab 16D. This compass provides a list of various wellness components, each illustrating a scale from five to one. A five indicates a low or poor rating, while a one would indicate an excellent or "wellness" rating for that particular component. Using the

Wellness Compass, rate yourself for each component according to the following instructions:

1. Color in red a number from five to one to indicate where you stood on each component at the beginning of the semester. For example, if at the start of this course you rated poor in cardiovascular endurance, you would color the number five in red.

2. Color in blue a second number from five to one to indicate where you stand on each component at the present time. If your level of cardiovascular endurance improved to average by the end of the semester, color the number three in blue. If you were not able to work on a given component, simply color in blue on top of the previous red.

3. Select one or two components that you intend to work on in the next two months. It takes time to develop new behavioral patterns, and trying to do too much at once will most likely decrease your chances for success. In addition, start with components where you feel you will have a high chance for success. Next, color in yellow the intended objective (number) to accomplish by the end of this period. If your objective in the next two months is to achieve a "good" level of cardiovascular endurance, color the number two in yellow. Once you achieve this level, you may later color the number one, also in yellow, to indicate your next objective.

Once you have completed the previous exercise, you will need to write behavioral objectives for the two components that you intend to work on during the next two months. As you write and work on these objectives, keep in mind the following guidelines:

1. Objectives can be general and specific. The general objective is the ultimate goal that you intend to achieve, while the specific objectives are the necessary steps required to reach this general objective. For example, a general objective could be to achieve recommended body weight. Several specific objectives could be: (a) to lose an average of one pound (or one fat percentage point) per week, (b) to monitor body weight prior to breakfast every morning, (c) to assess body composition every two weeks, (d) to decrease fat intake to less than 30 percent of total calories, (e) to eliminate all pastries from the diet during this time, and (f) to exercise in the appropriate target zone for thirty minutes, five times per week.

2. Whenever possible, objectives (general and specific) should be measurable. To simply state "to lose weight" is not measurable. In the previous general objective, recommended body weight implies lowering your body weight (fat) to the recommended percent body fat standards given

in Chapter 6 (Table 6.6). If this person was a nineteen-year-old female, recommended fat percent would be 17 percent. To be more descriptive, you could reword your general objective as follows: To reduce body weight until 17 percent body fat is achieved. The sample specific objectives given above in number 1 are also measurable. For instance, you can easily determine whether you are losing one pound per week, you can conduct a nutrient analysis to assess the average fat intake, or you can monitor your weekly exercise sessions to make sure that this specific objective is being met.

3. Objectives must be realistic. If you currently weigh 170 pounds and your target weight at 17 percent is 120 pounds, it would be unsound if not impossible to implement a weight loss program to lose fifty pounds in two months. Such a program would not allow implementation of adequate behavior modification techniques and insure weight maintenance at the target weight.

4. Objectives can be either short-term or long-term. If the general objective is to achieve recommended body weight and you are fifty pounds overweight, it would be a lot easier to set a general short-term objective of losing ten pounds, and write specific objectives to accomplish this goal. In this manner, the task will not seem as overwhelming and will be easier to accomplish.

5. Set a specified date by which you plan to achieve your objective. To simply state "I will lose weight" is not time-specific enough to accomplish the objective. It is a lot easier to work on a task if a deadline is established.

6. Educate yourself with regard to the objective that you plan to work on. You cannot lose weight if you do not know the principles that govern weight loss and maintenance. This is the reason why only three in ten individuals achieve the target weight loss, and only one in those three is able to keep it off thereafter.

7. Think positive and reward yourself for your accomplishments. As difficult as some tasks may seem, "if there is a will, there is a way." If you prepare an adequate plan of action according to these guidelines, there is no reason why you shouldn't achieve your objective. Also remember to reward yourself for your accomplishments. Buy yourself new clothing, exercise shoes, or something special that you have wanted for some time.

8. Seek environmental support. It becomes very difficult to lose weight if meal planning and cooking are shared with other roommates who enjoy foods high in fat and refined carbohydrates. This can be even worse if they also have a weight problem and do not desire nor have the willpower to lose weight. Surround yourself with people who will help and encourage you along the way. If necessary, plan and prepare your own meals.

9. Recognize that there will be obstacles. It is almost inevitable that you will make mistakes. Making mistakes is human and does not indicate failure. Failure comes only to those who give up. Use your mistakes and learn from them by preparing a plan that will help you get around self-defeating behaviors in the future.

10. Monitor your progress regularly. There will be times when the specific objectives are not being met. In such cases you will need to evaluate your objectives and perhaps make changes in the general and/or the specific objectives. Also recognize that there are individual differences and that you may not be able to progress as fast as someone else. Be flexible with yourself and reconsider your plan of action.

In Conclusion

Keep in mind that adequate fitness and wellness is a process and you need to put forth a constant and deliberate effort to achieve and maintain a higher quality of life. To make your journey easier, remember to enjoy yourself and have fun along the way. Implement your program based on your interests and what you enjoy doing most. If such is the case, adhering to your new lifestyle will not be difficult. Hopefully, the activities that you have conducted over the last few months have helped you develop positive "addictions" that will carry on throughout life. If you have truly experienced this "new quality of life," you know that there is no looking back. But, if you have not been there, it is difficult to know what it is like. Improving the quality and most likely the longevity of your life is now in your hands. For some it may require persistence and commitment, but only you can take control of your lifestyle and thereby reap the benefits of wellness.

LABORATORY EXPERIENCES

(all three of these laboratories may be conducted as homework assignments)

LAB 16A: Health Protection Plan for Environmental Hazards, Crime Prevention, and Personal Safety

LAB PREPARATION: None.

LAB 16B: Addictive Behavior Questionnaires

LAB PREPARATION: None

LAB 16C: The Prevention Index

LAB PREPARATION: None

LAB 16D: Self-Evaluation and Behavioral Objectives for the Future

LAB PREPARATION: None

References

1. "Addiction." *Aerobics News*. Dallas: The Institute for Aerobics Research, July 1987.

2. American Medical Association. *Family Medical Guide*. New York: Random House, 1982.

3. Carroll, C. R. *Drugs in Modern Society*. Dubuque, IA: Wm.C. Brown Publishers, 1985.

4. Channing L. Bete Co., Inc. *About AIDS and Shooting Drugs*. South Deerfield, MA: The Company, 1986.

5. Clark, B., W. Osness, W. W. K. Hoeger, M. Adrian, D. Raab, R. Wiswell, & R. Ciszek. Tests for fitness in older adults: AAHPERD fitness task force. *Journal of Physical Education, Recreation, and Dance* 60(3):66-71, 1989.

6. Gordon, E. and E. Golanty. *Health & Wellness*. Boston: Jones and Bartlett Publishers, Inc., 1985.

7. Hafen, B. Q., A. L. Thygerson, and K. J. Frandsen. *Behavioral Guidelines for Health & Wellness*. Englewood, CO: Morton Publishing Company, 1988.

8. Hagberg, J. M., J. E. Graves, M. Limacher, et al. "Cardiovascular Responses of 70-79 Year Old Men and Women to Exercise Training." *Journal of Applied Physiology* 66:2589-2594, 1989.

9. Kash, F. W., J. L. Boyer, S. P. Van Camp, L. S. Verity, and J. P. Wallace. "The Effect of Physical Activity on Aerobic Power in Older Men (A Longitudinal Study)." *The Physician and Sports Medicine* 18(4):73-83, 1990.

10. Kemper, D. W., J. Giuffre, and G. Drabinski. *Pathways: A Success Guide for a Healthy Life*. Boise, ID: Healthwise, Inc., 1985.

11. Osness, W., W. W. K. Hoeger, B. Clark, M. Adrian, D. Raab, R. Wiswell, & R. Ciszek. (1989). The AAHPERD fitness task force, history and philosophy. *Journal of Physical Education, Recreation, and Dance* 60(3):64-65, 1989.

12. Prevention Magazine. *The Prevention Index '90: Summary Report*. Emmaus, PA: Prevention Magazine, 1990.

13. Schlaadt, R. G., and P. T. Shannon. *Drugs*. Englewood Cliffs, NJ: Prentice Hall, 1990.

Labs

LAB 1A
CLEARANCE FOR EXERCISE PARTICIPATION

Name: _____ Date: _____ Grade: _____

Instructor: _____ Course: _____ Section: _____

Necessary Lab Equipment: None.

Objective: To determine the safety of exercise participation.

Introduction

While exercise testing and/or exercise participation is relatively safe for most apparently healthy individuals under the age of forty-five, the reaction of the cardiovascular system to increased levels of physical activity cannot always be totally predicted. Consequently, there is a small but real risk of certain changes occurring during exercise testing and/or participation. Some of these changes may include abnormal blood pressure, irregular heart rhythm, fainting, and in rare instances a heart attack or cardiac arrest. Therefore, it is imperative that you provide honest answers to this questionnaire. Exercise may be contraindicated under some of the conditions listed below, while others may simply require special consideration. **If any of the conditions apply, you should consult your physician before you participate in an exercise program.** You should also promptly report to your instructor any exercise-related abnormalities that you may experience during the course of the semester.

A. Have you ever had or do you now have any of the following conditions:

☐ 1. A myocardial infarction.

☐ 2. Coronary artery disease.

☐ 3. Congestive heart failure.

☐ 4. Elevated blood lipids (cholesterol and triglycerides).

☐ 5. Chest pain at rest or during exertion.

☐ 6. Shortness of breath.

☐ 7. An abnormal resting or stress electrocardiogram.

☐ 8. Uneven, irregular, or skipped heartbeats (including a racing or fluttering heart).

☐ 9. A blood embolism.

☐ 10. Thrombophlebitis.

☐ 11. Rheumatic heart fever.

☐ 12. Elevated blood pressure.

☐ 13. A stroke.

☐ 14. Diabetes.

☐ 15. A family history of coronary heart disease, syncope, or sudden death before age sixty.

☐ 16. Any other heart problem that makes exercise unsafe.

B. Do you suffer from any of the following conditions:

☐ 1. Arthritis, rheumatism, or gout.

☐ 2. Chronic low back pain.

☐ 3. Any other joint, bone, or muscle problems.

☐ 4. Any respiratory problems.

☐ 5. Obesity (more than 30 percent overweight).

☐ 6. Anorexia.

☐ 7. Bulimia.

☐ 8. Mononucleosis.

☐ 9. Any physical disability that could interfere with safe exercise participation.

C. Do any of the following conditions apply:

☐ 1. Do you smoke cigarettes?

☐ 2. Are you taking any prescription drug?

☐ 3. Are you forty-five years or older?

D. Do you have any other concern regarding your ability to safely participate in an exercise program? If so, explain:

_____

_____

Student's Signature: _____ Date: _____

LAB 1B
HEART RATE AND BLOOD PRESSURE ASSESSMENT

Name:_____ Date:_____ Grade:_____

Instructor:_____ Course:_____ Section:_____

Necessary Lab Equipment: Stopwatches, stethoscopes, and blood pressure sphygmomanometers.

Objective: To determine resting heart rate and blood pressure.

Preparation: The instructions to determine heart rate and blood pressure are given at the end of Chapter 1. Many factors can affect heart rate and blood pressure. Such factors as excitement, nervousness, stress, food, smoking, pain, temperature, and physical exertion can all significantly alter heart rate and blood pressure. Therefore, whenever possible, readings should be taken in a quiet, comfortable room following a few minutes of rest in the recording position. Avoid any form of exercise several hours prior to the assessment. Wear exercise clothing, including a shirt with short or loose-fitting sleeves to allow for the placement of the blood pressure cuff around the upper arm.

Resting Heart Rate and Blood Pressure

Determine your resting heart rate and blood pressure in the right and left arms while sitting comfortably in a chair.

Resting Heart Rate:_____ bpm   Rating:*_____

Blood Pressure:	Right Arm	Risk Rating**	Left Arm	Risk Rating
Systolic	_____	_____	_____	_____
Diastolic	_____	_____	_____	_____

Standing, Walking, and Jogging Heart Rate and Blood Pressure

Have one individual measure your heart rate and another individual your blood pressure immediately after standing for one minute, after walking for one minute, and after jogging in place for one minute. For blood pressure assessment use the arm with the highest reading in the sitting position.

Activity	Heart Rate (bpm)	Systolic/Diastolic Blood Pressure (mmHg)
Standing	_____	_____ / _____
Walking	_____	_____ / _____
Jogging	_____	_____ / _____

Conclusions. Draw conclusions based on your observed resting and activity heart rates and blood pressures.

_____

_____

_____

_____

---

*See Table 1.4, Chapter 1
**See Table 1.5, Chapter 1

LAB 2A
NUTRITIONAL ANALYSIS

Name:_____ Date:_____ Grade:_____

Instructor:_____ Course:_____ Section:_____

Necessary Lab Equipment: List of "Nutritive Value of Selected Foods," Appendix A. An IBM-PC or Apple IIe computer, if the computer software for use with this book is used. Otherwise, only a small calculator is needed.

Objective: To evaluate your present diet using the Recommended Daily Allowances (RDA).

Instructions

To conduct the following nutritional analysis, you need a record of all foods eaten during a three-day period (use the list of "Nutritive Value of Selected Foods" given in Appendix A). This information should be recorded prior to this lab session in the forms provided in Figure 2A.1. After recording the nutritive values for each day, add up the values in each column and record the totals at the bottom of the form. This work should also be done before the lab session. During your lab, you should proceed to compute an average for the three days. The percentages for carbohydrates, fat, saturated fat, and the protein requirements can be computed by using the instructions at the bottom of Figure 2A.2. The results can then be compared against the Recommended Daily Allowances (RDA).

The analysis can be simplified by using the computer software for this lab.* When using this software, Figure 2A.3 should be used (instead of 2A.1), and you only need to record the code for each food and the amount of servings eaten (.5 for half a serving, 2 for twice the standard serving, and so forth).

---

*Up to seven days may be analyzed when using the computer software available through Morton Publishing Company.

FIGURE 2A.1
Daily Nutrient Intake

Date: _____

Foods	Amount	Calories	Protein (gm)	Fat (total) (gm)	Sat. Fat (gm)	Chol-esterol (mg)	Carbo-hydrates (gm)	Cal-cium (mg)	Iron (mg)	Sodium (mg)	Vit. A (I.U.)	Vit. B$_1$ (mg)	Vit. B$_2$ (mg)	Niacin (mg)	Vit. C (mg)
Totals															

FIGURE 2A.1

Daily Nutrient Intake (Continued)

Date: _____

Foods	Amount	Calories	Protein (gm)	Fat (total) (gm)	Sat. Fat (gm)	Chol-esterol (mg)	Carbo-hydrates (gm)	Cal-cium (mg)	Iron (mg)	Sodium (mg)	Vit. A (I.U.)	Vit. B_1 (mg)	Vit. B_2 (mg)	Niacin (mg)	Vit. C (mg)
Totals															

FIGURE 2A.1
Daily Nutrient Intake (Continued)

Date: _____

Foods	Amount	Calories	Protein (gm)	Fat (total) (gm)	Sat. Fat (gm)	Chol-esterol (mg)	Carbo-hydrates (gm)	Cal-cium (mg)	Iron (mg)	Sodium (mg)	Vit. A (I.U.)	Vit. B$_1$ (mg)	Vit. B$_2$ (mg)	Niacin (mg)	Vit. C (mg)
Totals															

Figure 2A.2.
Three-Day Nutritional Analysis

Name: _____

Day	Calories	Protein (gm)	Fat (gm)	Sat. Fat (gm)	Choles-terol (mg)	Carbo-hydrates (gm)	Calcium (mg)	Iron (mg)	Sodium (mg)	Vit. A (I.U.)	Thiamin (Vit. B$_1$) (mg)	Riboflavin Vit. B$_2$ (mg)	Niacin (mg)	Vit. C (mg)
One														
Two														
Three														
Totals														
Average[a]														
Percentages[b]														

Recommended Dietary Allowances*

	Calories	Protein	Fat	Sat. Fat	Choles-terol (mg)	Carbo-hydrates (gm)	Calcium (mg)	Iron (mg)	Sodium (mg)	Vit. A (I.U.)	Thiamin (Vit. B$_1$) (mg)	Riboflavin Vit. B$_2$ (mg)	Niacin (mg)	Vit. C (mg)
Men 15-18 yrs.	See below[c]	See below[d]	<30%[e]	<10%[e]	<300[e]	50% >[e]	1,200	12	3,000[e]	5,000	1.5	1.8	20	60
Men 19-24 yrs.			<30%	<10%	<300	50% >	1,200	10	3,000	5,000	1.5	1.7	19	60
Men 25-50 yrs.			<30%	<10%	<300	50% >	800	10	3,000	5,000	1.5	1.7	19	60
Men 51+ yrs.			<30%	<10%	<300	50% >	800	10	3,000	5,000	1.2	1.4	15	60
Women 15-18 yrs.			<30%	<10%	<300	50% >	1200	15	3,000	4,000	1.1	1.3	15	60
Women 19-24 yrs.			<30%	<10%	<300	50% >	1200	15	3,000	4,000	1.1	1.3	15	60
Women 25-50 yrs.			<30%	<10%	<300	50% >	800	15	3,000	4,000	1.1	1.3	15	60
Women 51+ yrs.			<30%	<10%	<300	50% >	800	10	3,000	4,000	1.0	1.2	13	60
Pregnant			<30%	<10%	<300	50% >	1200	30	3,000	4,000	1.5	1.6	17	70
Lactating			<30%	<10%	<300	50% >	1200	15	3,000	6,000	1.6	1.8	20	95

[a]Divide totals by 3 or number of days assessed.
[b]Percentages: Protein and Carbohydrates = multiply average by 4 and divide by average calories,
    Fat and Saturated Fat = multiply average by 9 and divide by average calories.
[c]Use Table 3.1 (Chapter 3) for all categories.
[d]Protein intake should be .8 grams per kilogram of body weight. Pregnant women should consume an additional 15 grams of daily protein, while lactating women should have an extra 20 grams.
[e]Based on recommendations by nutrition experts.
*Adapted from *Recommended Dietary Allowances*, © 1989, by the National Academy of Sciences, National Academy Press, Washington, D.C.

─────── *FIGURE 2A.3* ───

Daily Nutrient Intake Form for Computer Software Use

Date: _____

Name: _____ Age: _____ Weight: _____

Sex: Male-M, Female-F (Pregnant-P, Lactating-L, Neither-N)

Activity Rating: Sedentary (limited physical activity)   = 1
                  Moderate physical activity   = 2
                  Hard labor (strenuous physical activity)   = 3

Number of days to be analyzed: _____   Day: _____

No.	Code*	Food	Amount
1			
2			
3			
4			
5			
6			
7			
8			
9			
10			
11			
12			
13			
14			
15			
16			
17			
18			
19			
20			
21			
22			
23			
24			
25			
26			
27			
28			
29			
30			
31			

*When done, to advance to the next day or end, type 0 (zero).

LAB 2B
ACHIEVING A BALANCED DIET

HOMEWORK ASSIGNMENT

Name:_____ Date:_____ Grade:_____

Instructor:_____ Course:_____ Section:_____

Assignment: This laboratory experience should be carried out as a homework assignment to be completed over the next seven days.

Lab Resources: "New American Eating Guide" chart and list of "Nutritive Value of Selected Foods" (Figure 2.10 in Chapter 2 and Appendix A).

Objective: To meet the minimum daily required servings of the four basic food groups.

Instructions

Keep a seven-day record of your food consumption using the "New American Eating Guide" and the form given in Figure 2B.1. Whenever you have something to eat, record the food code from the "Nutritive Value of Selected Foods" list contained in Appendix A and the "+", "NP" (no points), or "-" characters from the "New American Eating Guide" in the corresponding spaces provided for each day. Individuals on a weight reduction program should also record the caloric content of each food. This information can be obtained from the list of foods, the food container itself, or some of the references given at the end of the list of foods (Appendix A). The information should be recorded immediately after each meal, since it will be easier to keep track of foods and the amount eaten. If twice the amount of a particular serving is eaten, the calories must be doubled and two "+", "-", or "NP" characters should also be recorded. At the end of the day, the diet is evaluated by checking whether the minimum required servings for each food group were consumed, and by adding up the "+" and "-" points accumulated. If you have met the required servings and end up with a positive score, you are well on your way to achieving a well-balanced diet.

FIGURE 2B.1
Daily Diet Record Form

Name: _____   Course: _____   Section: _____   Date: _____

Code[a]	Food	Amount	Score +, −, or NP[b]	Calories[c]	Beans, Grains, & Nuts	Fruits & Vegetables Vit. A	Fruits & Vegetables Vit. C	Fruits & Vegetables Other	Milk Products	Poultry, Meat, Fish, & Eggs
Totals										
Recommended Standard			+ Score	d	4	1	1	2	2	2
Deficiencies										

Number of Servings

[a,c] See list of nutritive value of selected foods in Appendix A.   [b] See Figure 2.10: New American Eating Guide.   [d] Use value obtained from Table 3.1.

LAB 3A
ESTIMATION OF DAILY CALORIC REQUIREMENT

Name:_____ Date:_____ Grade:_____

Instructor:_____ Course:_____ Section:_____

Necessary Lab Equipment: Tables 3.1 and 3.2 from Chapter 3.

Objective: To determine an estimated daily caloric requirement with exercise for weight maintenance and or reduction.

Computation Form for Daily Caloric Requirement

A. Current body weight _____

B. Caloric requirement per pound of body weight (use Table 3.1) _____

C. Typical daily caloric requirement without exercise to maintain body weight (A × B) _____

D. Selected physical activity (e.g., jogging)* _____

E. Number of exercise sessions per week _____

F. Duration of exercise session (in minutes) _____

G. Total weekly exercise time in minutes (E × F) _____

H. Average daily exercise time in minutes (G ÷ 7) _____

I. Caloric expenditure per pound per minute (cal/lb/min) of physical activity (use Table 3.2) _____

J. Total calories burned per minute of physical activity (A × I) _____

K. Average daily calories burned as a result of the exercise program (H × J) _____

L. Total daily caloric requirement with exercise to maintain body weight (C + K) _____

M. Number of calories to subtract from daily requirement to achieve a negative caloric balance** _____

N. Target caloric intake to lose weight (L - M) _____

* If more than one physical activity is selected, you will need to estimate the average daily calories burned as a result of each additional activity (steps D through K) and add all of these figures to L above.
** Subtract 500 calories if the total daily requirement with exercise (L) is below 3,000 calories. As many as 1,000 calories may be subtracted for daily requirements above 3,000 calories.

LAB 3B
BEHAVIORAL OBJECTIVES
FOR EXERCISE, NUTRITION, AND WEIGHT MANAGEMENT

Name:_____ Date:_____ Grade:_____

Instructor:_____ Course:_____ Section:_____

Necessary Lab Equipment: None.

Objective: The participant will prepare a plan to initiate a lifetime exercise, nutrition, and weight management program.

Lab Preparation: Chapters 2 and 3 must be read prior to this lab.

Please Answer All of the Following:

1. State your own feelings regarding your current body weight.

_____

_____

_____

2. If you suffer from eating disorders, indicate what type of professional advice you will seek to help you overcome this condition.

_____

_____

_____

3. Is your present diet adequate according to the nutritional analysis?   _____ Yes   _____ No

   3A. If your answer to the previous question was "no," state what general dietary changes are necessary to achieve a balanced diet and/or lose weight (e.g., increase or decrease caloric intake, decrease fat intake, increase intake of complex carbohydrates, etc.).

_____

_____

_____

   3B. Specifically list foods that will help you to meet the recommended dietary allowances in areas where you may have deficiencies (see Figures 2.1, 2.2, and the "Nutritive Value of Selected Foods" list in Appendix A).

_____

_____

_____

3C. List foods that you should avoid to help you achieve better nutrition and/or a balanced diet.

_____

_____

_____

4. Indicate your feelings about participating in an exercise program.

_____

_____

_____

5. Will you commit to participate in a combined aerobic and strength-training program?*   _____ Yes   _____ No

If your answer is "yes," proceed to the next question.

If you answered "no," please review Chapters 2 and 3 again and read Chapters 4, 5, 7, and 8.

6. List aerobic activities that you enjoy or may enjoy doing.

_____

7. Select one or two aerobic activities in which you will participate regularly.

_____

8. List facilities available to you where you can carry out the aerobic and strength-training program.

_____

_____

_____

9. Indicate days and times that you will set aside for your aerobic and strength-training program (four to six days should be used for aerobic exercise and three nonconsecutive days for strength-training).

Monday: _____

Tuesday: _____

Wednesday: _____

Thursday: _____

Friday: _____

Saturday: _____

Sunday: A complete day of rest once a week is recommended to allow your body to fully recover from exercise.

*Flexibility programs are necessary for the development and maintenance of good health and adequate fitness but are not effective in the achievement of weight loss. Stretching exercises should be conducted regularly either to warm up or cool down in conjunction with your aerobic and strength-training program (*see* Chapters 9 and 10).

LAB 4A
CARDIOVASCULAR ENDURANCE ASSESSMENT

Name: _____   Date: _____   Grade: _____

Instructor: _____   Course: _____   Section: _____

Necessary Lab Equipment:

1.5-Mile Run: School track or premeasured course and a stopwatch.

Step Test: A bench or gymnasium bleachers 16¼ inches high, a metronome, and a stopwatch.

Astrand-Ryhming Test: Weight scale, stopwatch, and a bicycle ergometer that allows for regulation of workloads either in kilopounds per meter or watts and a stopwatch.

University of Houston Non-Exercise Test: Skinfold calipers or weight scale.

Objective: To assess maximal oxygen uptake and the respective cardiovascular endurance classification.

Lab Preparation: Wear exercise clothing, including jogging shoes. Be prepared to take the Step Test, the Astrand-Ryhming Test, and/or the 1.5-Mile Run Test. Avoid vigorous physical activity twenty-four hours prior to this lab.

I. 1.5-Mile Run Test (Conduct this test last if either or both of the other tests are also performed.)

1.5-Mile Run Time: _____ minutes and _____ seconds.

Maximal Oxygen Uptake (*see* Table 4.1, Chapter 4): _____ ml/kg/min.

Cardiovascular Fitness Classification (Table 4.6): _____

II. Step Test

Fifteen-second recovery heart rate: _____ beats.

Maximal Oxygen Uptake (Table 4.2): _____ ml/kg/min.

Cardiovascular Fitness Classification (Table 4.6): _____

III. Astrand-Ryhming Test

A. Weight in pounds   _____ lbs.

B. Weight in kilograms (A ÷ 2.2046)   _____ kg.

C. Workload   ____ kpm.

D. Exercise heart rates	30-Sec. Pulse count	Heart Rate in BPM			30-Sec. Pulse count	Heart Rate in BPM
1. First minute:	_____	_____		4. Fourth minute:	_____	_____
2. Second minute:	_____	_____		5. Fifth minute:	_____	_____
3. Third minute:	_____	_____		6. Sixth minute:	_____	_____

E. Average heart rate for the fifth and sixth minutes ＿＿＿＿＿ bpm

F. Maximal oxygen uptake in liters per minute (Table 4.4) ＿＿＿＿＿ L/min

G. Correction factor (Table 4.5) ＿＿＿＿＿

H. Corrected maximal oxygen uptake in liters per minute (F × G) ＿＿＿＿＿ L/min

I. Maximal oxygen uptake in milliliters per kilogram per minute (H × 1000, divided by B) = ＿＿＿＿
   × 1000 = ＿＿＿＿＿＿ ml/kg/min

J. Cardiovascular Fitness Classification (Table 4.6): ＿＿＿＿＿＿＿＿＿＿

IV. University of Houston Non-Exercise Test

Percent Fat (N−Ex % Fat) Model

Men   Max VO2 = 56.370 − (.289 × A) − (.552 × %Fat) + (1.589 × PAR)
Women   Max VO2 = 50.513 − (.289 × A) − (.552 × %Fat) + (1.589 × PAR)

          Max VO2 = ＿＿＿＿ − (.289 × _) − (.552 × ＿＿) + (1.589 × ＿＿)

Body Mass Index (N-Ex BMI) Model

Weight in kg = weight in pounds ÷ 2.2046 = ＿＿＿＿ ÷ 2.2046 = ＿＿＿＿

Height in meters = height in inches × .0254 = ＿＿＿＿ × .0254 = ＿＿＿＿＿

BMI = Weight in kg ÷ $Height^2$ in meters

BMI = ＿＿＿＿ ÷ (＿＿＿＿)^2 = ＿＿＿＿＿

Men   Max VO2 = 67.350 − (.381 × A) − (.754 × BMI) + (1.951 × PAR)
Women   Max VO2 = 56.363 − (.381 × A) − (.754 × BMI) + (1.951 × PAR)

          Max VO2 = ＿＿＿＿ − (.381 × _) − (.754 × ＿＿) + (1.951 × ＿＿)

          Maximal Oxygen Uptake: ＿＿＿＿＿＿ ml/kg/min

          Cardiovascular Fitness Classification (Table 4.6): ＿＿＿＿＿＿＿＿＿

V. Cardiovascular Endurance Objectives

1. Indicate what cardiovascular endurance classification you would like to achieve by the end of the semester:

   ＿＿＿＿＿＿＿＿＿＿＿＿＿＿＿＿＿＿＿＿＿＿＿＿＿＿＿＿＿＿＿＿＿＿＿＿＿＿

2. Briefly state how you are planning to achieve this objective (also refer to Lab 3B, questions 6, 7, 8, and 9):

   ＿＿＿＿＿＿＿＿＿＿＿＿＿＿＿＿＿＿＿＿＿＿＿＿＿＿＿＿＿＿＿＿＿＿＿＿＿＿

   ＿＿＿＿＿＿＿＿＿＿＿＿＿＿＿＿＿＿＿＿＿＿＿＿＿＿＿＿＿＿＿＿＿＿＿＿＿＿

   ＿＿＿＿＿＿＿＿＿＿＿＿＿＿＿＿＿＿＿＿＿＿＿＿＿＿＿＿＿＿＿＿＿＿＿＿＿＿

   ＿＿＿＿＿＿＿＿＿＿＿＿＿＿＿＿＿＿＿＿＿＿＿＿＿＿＿＿＿＿＿＿＿＿＿＿＿＿

LAB 5A
CARDIOVASCULAR EXERCISE PRESCRIPTION

Name:_____ Date:_____ Grade:_____

Instructor:_____ Course:_____ Section:_____

Necessary Lab Equipment: None.

Objective: To write your own cardiovascular exercise prescription.

Intensity of Exercise

1. Estimate your own maximal heart rate (MHR)

   MHR = 220 minus age (220 − age)

   MHR = 220 − _____ = _____ bpm

2. Resting Heart Rate (RHR) = _____ bpm

3. Heart Rate Reserve (HRR) = MHR − RHR

   HRR = _____ − _____ = _____ beats

4. Training Intensities (TI) = HRR × TI + RHR

   60 Percent TI = _____ × .60 + _____ = _____ bpm

   70 Percent TI = _____ × .70 + _____ = _____ bpm

   85 Percent TI = _____ × .85 + _____ = _____ bpm

5. Cardiovascular Training Zone. The optimum cardiovascular training zone is found between the 70 and 85 percent training intensities. However, individuals who have been physically inactive or are in the poor or fair cardiovascular fitness categories should use a 60 percent training intensity during the first few weeks of the exercise program.

   Cardiovascular Training Zone: _____ (70% TI) to _____ (85% TI)

   Rate of Perceived Exertion (see Figure 5.2, Chapter 5): _____

Mode of Exercise

   Select any activity or combination of activities that you enjoy doing. The activity has to be continuous in nature and must get your heart rate up to the cardiovascular training zone and keep it there for as long as you exercise.

Cardiovascular Exercise Prescription

The following is your weekly program for cardiovascular endurance development. If you are in the average, good, or excellent fitness category, you may start at week five. After completing this twelve-week program, in order for you to maintain your fitness level, you should exercise in the 70 to 85 percent training zone for about twenty to thirty minutes, a minimum of three times per week, on nonconsecutive days. You should also recompute your target zone periodically because you will experience a significant reduction in resting heart rate with aerobic training (approximately ten to twenty beats in about eight to twelve weeks).

Week	Duration (min.)	Frequency	Training Intensity	10-Sec. Pulse Count[a]
1	15	3	Approximately 60%	
2	15	4	Approximately 60%	
3	20	4	Approximately 60%	_____ beats
4	20	5	Approximately 60%	
5	20	4	About 70%	
6	20	5	About 70%	
7	30	4	About 70%	_____ beats
8	30	5	About 70%	
9	30	4	Between 70% and 85%	
10	30	5	Between 70% and 85%	
11	30-40	5	Between 70% and 85%	_____ to _____ beats
12	30-40	5	Between 70% and 85%	

[a]Fill out your own 10-sec. pulse count under this column.

LAB 5B
EXERCISE HEART RATE AND CALORIC COST OF PHYSICAL ACTIVITY

Name:_____ Date:_____ Grade:_____

Instructor:_____ Course:_____ Section:_____

Necessary Lab Equipment: A school track (or premeasured course) and a stopwatch. Each student should also bring a watch with a second hand.

Objective: To monitor exercise heart rate and determine the caloric cost of physical activity based on exercise heart rate.

Lab Preparation: Wear exercise clothing, including jogging shoes. Do not engage in vigorous physical activity prior to this lab. Read the information on "predicting caloric expenditure from exercise heart rates" in Chapter 5.

Procedure

1. **Cardiovascular Training Zone.** Look up your cardiovascular training zone at 70 and 85 percent of heart rate reserve in Lab 5A. Record this information in beats per minute and in ten-second pulse counts in the blank spaces provided below.

Beats/Minute   10-Sec. Count

70 percent intensity = _____   _____

85 percent intensity = _____   _____

2. **Resting Heart Rate and Body Weight.** Determine your resting heart rate prior to exercise and your body weight in kilograms (divide pounds by 2.2046).

Resting heart rate: _____ beats per minute (bpm)

Body weight: _____ lbs. ÷ 2.2046 = _____ kg

3. **Walking Heart Rate, Oxygen Uptake, and Caloric Expenditure.** Walk two laps around a 400-meter (440-yard) track at an average speed of 75 to 100 meters per minute. Try to maintain a constant speed around the track. You can monitor your speed by starting the walk at the beginning of the 100-meter straightway and making sure that you have walked at least 75 meters and no more than 100 meters in one minute. As soon as you complete the two laps (800 meters), notice the time it required to walk this distance and immediately check your exercise heart rate by taking a ten-second pulse count. Record this information in the spaces provided below. Do not record the time until after you have checked your pulse. Exercise heart rates will remain at the same rate for about fifteen seconds following cessation of exercise. Therefore, you need to check your pulse as soon as you finish the walk, after noticing the 800-meter walk time.

10-sec. pulse count = _____ beats or _____ bpm

800-meter time = _____ min. + (_____ sec./60) = _____ min.

Speed in mts/min.* = 800/800-meter time = 800/ _____ = _____ mts/min.

Oxygen uptake (VO_2) at this walking speed (use Table 5.2)

VO_2 = _____ ml/kg/min

VO_2 in L/min = (VO_2** × BW in kg)/1000 = _____ × _____ /1000 = _____ L/min

Caloric expenditure = VO_2 in L/min × 5 × 800-meter time (min.) =

= _____ × 5 × _____ = _____ calories

_____
*mts/min.: meters per minute
**VO_2 in ml/kg/min

4. Slow-Jogging Heart Rate, Oxygen Uptake, and Caloric Expenditure. Slowly jog 800 meters (two laps) around the track. Try to maintain the same slow-jogging pace throughout the two laps. Do NOT jog fast or sprint. This is not a speed test and is intended to be a slow jog only. As soon as you complete the 800 meters, notice the time it required to complete the distance and immediately check your exercise heart rate by taking another ten-second pulse count. Record this information below.

10-sec. pulse count = _____ beats or _____ bpm

800-meter time = _____ min. + (_____ sec./60) = _____ min.

Speed in mts/min. = 800/800-meter time = 800/ _____ = _____ mts/min.

Oxygen uptake (VO_2) at this jogging speed (use Table 5.2)

VO_2 = _____ ml/kg/min

VO_2 in L/min = (VO_2** × BW in kg)/1000 = _____ × _____ /1000 = _____ L/min

Caloric expenditure = VO_2 in L/min × 5 × 800-meter time (min.) =

= _____ × 5 × _____ = _____ calories

5. Fast-Jogging Heart Rate, Oxygen Uptake, Caloric Expenditure and Recovery Heart Rates. Jog another 800 meters at a faster speed around the track. Again, try to maintain the same jogging pace throughout the two laps. Do NOT sprint. Your heart rate should not exceed 180 beats per minute on this test. As soon as you complete the 800 meters, notice your time for the two laps and check your ten-second pulse count. Record this information below. You should also check your two- and five-minute recovery heart rates after this run and record these rates below.

10-sec. pulse count = _____ beats or _____ bpm

800-meter time = _____ min. + (_____ sec./60) = _____ min.

Speed in mts/min. = 800/800-meter time = 800/ _____ = _____ mts/min.

Oxygen uptake (VO_2) at this jogging speed (use Table 5.2)

VO_2 = _____ ml/kg/min

VO_2 in L/min = (VO_2** × BW in kg)/1000 = _____ × _____ /1000 = _____ L/min

Caloric expenditure = VO_2 in L/min × 5 × 800-meter time (min.) =

= _____ × 5 × _____ = _____ calories

Recovery Heart Rates

	10-Sec. Count	Beats/Minute
Two minutes	_____	_____
Five minutes*	_____	_____

*Your five-minute recovery heart rate should be below 120 beats per minute. If it is above 120, you have most likely overexerted yourself and, therefore, need to decrease the intensity of exercise (and/or duration when exercising for long periods of time). If your five-minute recovery heart rate is still above 120 after decreasing the intensity of exercise, you should consult a physician regarding this condition.
**VO_2 in ml/kg/min

LAB 9B
POSTURE EVALUATION

Name:_____ Date:_____ Grade:_____

Instructor:_____ Course:_____ Section:_____

Necessary Lab Equipment: A plumb line, two large mirrors set at about an eighty-five-degree angle, and a Polaroid camera (the mirrors and the camera are optional — *see* "Posture Evaluation" in Chapter 9).

Objective: To determine current body alignment.

Lab Preparation: To conduct the posture analysis, men should wear shorts only and women shorts and a tank top. Shoes should also be removed for this test.

Lab Assignment: The class should be divided in groups of four students each. The group should carefully study the posture form given in this lab and then proceed to fill out the form for each member according to the instructions given under "Posture Evaluation" in Chapter 9. If no mirrors and camera are available, three members of the group are to rate the fourth person's posture while he/she first stands with the side of the body and then with the back to the plumb line. A final score is obtained by totaling the points given for each body segment and looking up the posture rating according to the total score in Table 9.5.

Results

Total Score: _____

Posture Improvement

Indicate which areas of your posture need to be corrected and what steps you can take to make improvements.

_____

_____

_____

_____

FIGURE 9B.1

Posture Analysis Form*

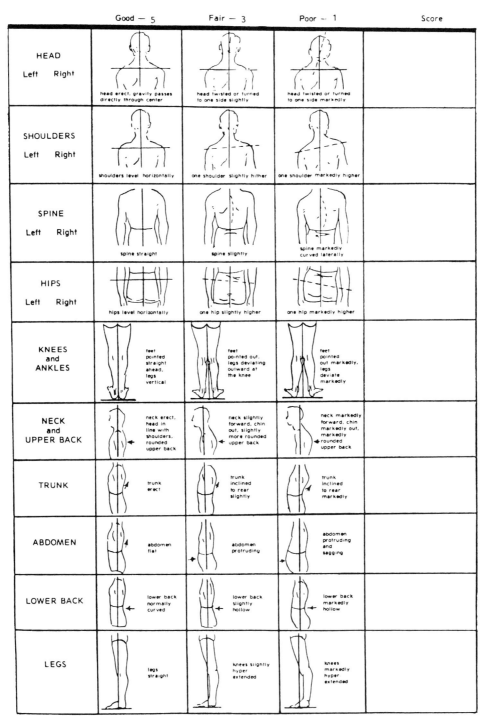

TOTAL SCORE

*Adapted with permission from *The New York Physical Fitness Test: A Manual for Teachers of Physical Education.* New York State Education Department (Division of HPER), 1958.

LAB 10A
SAMPLE FLEXIBILITY DEVELOPMENT PROGRAM

Name:_____ Date:_____ Grade:_____

Instructor:_____ Course:_____ Section:_____

Necessary Lab Equipment: Minor implements such as a chair, a table, an elastic band (surgical tubing or a wood or aluminum stick), and a stool or steps.

Objective: To introduce the participant to a sample stretching exercise program, which may be carried out throughout life.

Lab Preparation: Wear exercise clothing and prepare to participate in a sample stretching exercise session. All of the flexibility exercises are illustrated in Chapter 10.

Introduction

Perform all of the recommended flexibility exercises given in Chaper 10. Use a combination of slow-sustained and proprioceptive neuromuscular facilitation stretching techniques. Indicate the technique(s) used for each exercise, and, where applicable, the number of repetitions performed and the length of time that the final degree of stretch was held.

Stretching Exercises

Exercise	Stretching Technique	Repetitions	Length of Final Stretch
Lateral Head Tilt	_____	_____	NA*
Arm Circles	_____	_____	NA
Side Stretch	_____	_____	_____
Body Rotation	_____	_____	_____
Chest Stretch	_____	_____	_____
Shoulder Hyperextension	_____	_____	_____
Shoulder Rotation	_____	_____	NA
Quad Stretch	_____	_____	_____
Heel Cord Stretch	_____	_____	_____
Adductor Stretch	_____	_____	_____
Sitting Adductor Stretch	_____	_____	_____
Sit-and-Reach Stretch	_____	_____	_____
Triceps Stretch	_____	_____	_____

*Not Applicable

LAB 10B
EXERCISES FOR THE PREVENTION AND REHABILITATION OF LOW BACK PAIN

Name:_____ Date:_____ Grade:_____

Instructor:_____ Course:_____ Section:_____

Necessary Lab Equipment: A chair.

Objective: To introduce the participant to an exercise program for the prevention and rehabilitation of low back pain.

Lab Preparation: Wear exercise clothing and prepare to participate in the lab session. All of the exercises for this lab are illustrated in Chapter 10.

I. Stretching Exercises

Perform all of the recommended exercises for the prevention and rehabilitation of low back pain given in Chapter 10. Indicate the number of repetitions performed for each exercise.

Exercise	Repetitions
Single-Knee to Chest	_____
Double-Knee to Chest	_____
Upper and Lower Back Stretch	_____
Sit-and-Reach Stretch	_____
Gluteal Stretch	_____
Side and Lower Back Stretch	_____
Trunk Rotation and Lower Back Stretch	_____
Pelvic Tilt	_____
Abdominal Curl-Up	_____
Abdominal Crunch	_____

II. Proper Body Mechanics

Perform the following tasks using the proper body mechanics given in Figure 10.3 in Chapter 10 (check each item off as you perform the task):

_____ Standing (Carriage) Position

_____ Sitting Position

_____ Bed Posture

_____ Resting Position for Tired and Painful Back

_____ Lifting an Object

III. "Rules To Live By — From Now On"

Read the eighteen "Rules To Live By — From Now On" given in Figure 10.3, Chapter 10, and indicate below those rules that you need to work on to improve posture and body mechanics and prevent low back pain.

_____

_____

_____

_____

Questionnaire Answer Sheet

Could You Be an Addict?*

1. _____ Yes _____ No
2. _____ Yes _____ No
3. _____ Yes _____ No
4. _____ Yes _____ No
5. _____ Yes _____ No
6. _____ Yes _____ No
7. _____ Yes _____ No
8. _____ Yes _____ No
9. _____ Yes _____ No
10. _____ Yes _____ No
11. _____ Yes _____ No
12. _____ Yes _____ No
13. _____ Yes _____ No
14. _____ Yes _____ No
15. _____ Yes _____ No
16. _____ Yes _____ No
17. _____ Yes _____ No
18. _____ Yes _____ No
19. _____ Yes _____ No
20. _____ Yes _____ No

Alcohol Abuse: Are You
Drinking Too Much?**

1. _____ Yes _____ No
2. _____ Yes _____ No
3. _____ Yes _____ No
4. _____ Yes _____ No
5. _____ Yes _____ No
6. _____ Yes _____ No
7. _____ Yes _____ No
8. _____ Yes _____ No
9. _____ Yes _____ No
10. _____ Yes _____ No
11. _____ Yes _____ No

*More than ten "yes" answers may indicate a problem with addictive disease. You should seek immediate professional help.
**One "yes" answer becomes a warning sign. Two or more "yes" answers suggest that you may already be becoming dependent on alcohol. Three or more "yes" answers indicate that you may have a serious problem, and you should get professional help.

LAB 16C
THE PREVENTION INDEX

Name:_____ Date:_____ Grade:_____

Instructor:_____ Course:_____ Section:_____

Necessary Lab Equipment: None required.

Objective: To determine your personal prevention index based on the 21 most significant health-promoting behaviors.

Preparation: The Prevention Index is an annual measure of the effort Americans are making to prevent disease and accidents and to promote good health and longevity. Prior to completing this questionnaire, read the section on The Prevention Index contained in Chapter 16.

Please carefully check "YES" or "NO" to each of the following questions.

Yes   No

☐   ☐   1. Do you have a blood pressure reading at least once a year?

☐   ☐   2. Do you go to the dentist at least once a year for treatment or a checkup?

☐   ☐   3. Avoid eating too much salt or sodium?

☐   ☐   4. Avoid eating too much fat?

☐   ☐   5. Eat enough fiber from whole grains, cereals, fruits, and vegetables?

☐   ☐   6. Avoid eating too many high cholesterol foods, such as eggs, dairy products, and fatty meats?

☐   ☐   7. Get enough vitamins and minerals in your diet?

☐   ☐   8. Avoid getting too much sugar and sweet food?

☐   ☐   9. Is your body weight within the recommended range for your sex, height, and bone structure?

☐   ☐   10. Do you exercise strenuously (that is, so you breathe heavily and your heart and pulse rate are accelerated for a period lasting at least 20 minutes) three days or more a week?

☐   ☐   11. Do you smoke cigarettes now?

☐   ☐   12. Do you consciously take steps to control or reduce stress in your life?

☐   ☐   13. Do you usually sleep a total of 7 to 8 hours during each 24-hour day? (if you usually sleep either more or less than this, please mark "no".)

☐   ☐   14. Do you socialize with close friends, relatives or neighbors at least once a week?

☐   ☐   15. In general, when you drink alcoholic beverages, do you consume less than 14 drinks per week and less than two on any single day? (Mark "yes" only if the answer to both parts of this question is "yes". If you never drink at all, also mark "yes". A "drink" means a drink with a shot of hard liquor, a can or bottle of beer, or a glass of wine.)

☐   ☐   16. Do you wear a seat belt all the time when you are in the front seat of a car?

☐   ☐   17. Do you drive at or below the speed limit all the time? (If you don't drive, please mark "yes".)

☐   ☐   18. Do you ever drive after drinking? (If you don't drink, please mark "no".)

*The Prevention Index: A Louis Harris & Associates, Inc. survey conducted for Prevention Magazine.

Yes   No

☐   ☐   19. Do you have a smoke detector in your home?

☐   ☐   20. Does anyone in your household smoke in bed?

☐   ☐   21. Do you take any special steps or precautions to avoid accidents in and around your home?

Interpreting The Prevention Index (PI)

The correct answer for questions 11, 18, and 20 is "no." The correct answer for all other questions is "yes." Add up your total number of correct responses. Then, divide that number by 21 to obtain the percentage of the 21 Prevention Index behaviors that you practice.

$$PI = \frac{\text{Number of correct answers}}{21} =$$

RATINGS

Prevention Index	Category
90>	Excellent
70-89	Good
60-69	Average
<59	Poor

LAB 16D
SELF-EVALUATION AND BEHAVIORAL OBJECTIVES FOR THE FUTURE

Name:_____ Date:_____ Grade:_____

Instructor:_____ Course:_____ Section:_____

Necessary Lab Equipment: None required, unless fitness tests are repeated.

Objective: To conduct a self-evaluation of the objectives achieved during this course and write behavioral objectives for the future.

Lab Preparation: Read the section on self-evaluation and behavioral objectives for the future given in Chapter 16. If time allows and technicians are available, repeat the assessments for the health-related components of physical fitness.

Part A: Self-Evaluation

In this first part you will conduct a self-evaluation of the objectives that you accomplished in this course. To carry out this assignment, you will need to review the objectives written in previous laboratories. If you were able to repeat the various assessments, you can objectively indicate if your objectives were met. If you were unable to conduct the reassessments, subjectively determine how well you reached your objectives (only answer the "yes" or "no" questions under number 1 below).

1. Did you accomplish your objectives for:

   Cardiovascular Endurance (see Lab 4A) _____ Yes _____ No

   Pre-assessment Max. VO$_2$: _____ ml/kg/min   Fitness Classification: _____

   Post-assessment Max. VO$_2$: _____ ml/kg/min   Fitness Classification: _____

   Body Composition (see Lab 6A) _____ Yes _____ No

   Pre-assessment Percent Body Fat: _____   Body Composition Classification: _____

   Post-assessment Percent Body Fat: _____   Body Composition Classification: _____

   Muscular Strength and Endurance (see Lab 7A) _____ Yes _____ No

   Pre-assessment Percentile Rank: _____   Fitness Classification: _____

   Post-assessment Percentile Rank: _____   Fitness Classification: _____

   Muscular Flexibility (see Lab 9A) _____ Yes _____ No

   Pre-assessment Percentile Rank: _____   Fitness Classification: _____

   Post-assessment Percentile Rank: _____   Fitness Classification: _____

2. Indicate those nutritional and dietary changes that you were able to implement this semester (refer to Chapters 2 and 3 and Labs 2A, 2B, 3A, and 3B).

   _____

   _____

   _____

3. Did you implement your regular exercise program as outlined in Labs 3B, 5A, and Chapters 5, 8, and 10?

_____

4. Indicate any lifestyle changes that you were able to make that will decrease your personal risk for cardiovascular disease and cancer. (Including stress management and smoking cessation. Refer also to Labs 12A and 13B).

_____

_____

_____

5. Briefly evaluate this course and indicate whether it has had an effect on the quality of your life and your personal well-being.

_____

_____

_____

_____

PART B: Behavioral Objectives for the Future

   Using the Wellness Compass, rate yourself for each component and plan objectives for the future according to the following instructions:

1. Color in red a number from five to one to indicate where you stood on each component at the beginning of the semester (five = poor rating, one = excellent or ideal rating).
2. Color in blue a second number from five to one to indicate where you stand on each component at the present time.
3. Select one or two components that you intend to work on in the next two months. Start with components where you feel you will have a high chance for success. Color in yellow the intended objective (number) to accomplish by the end of the two months. Once you achieve your objective, you may later color another number, also in yellow, to indicate your next objective.

*Wellness Compass**

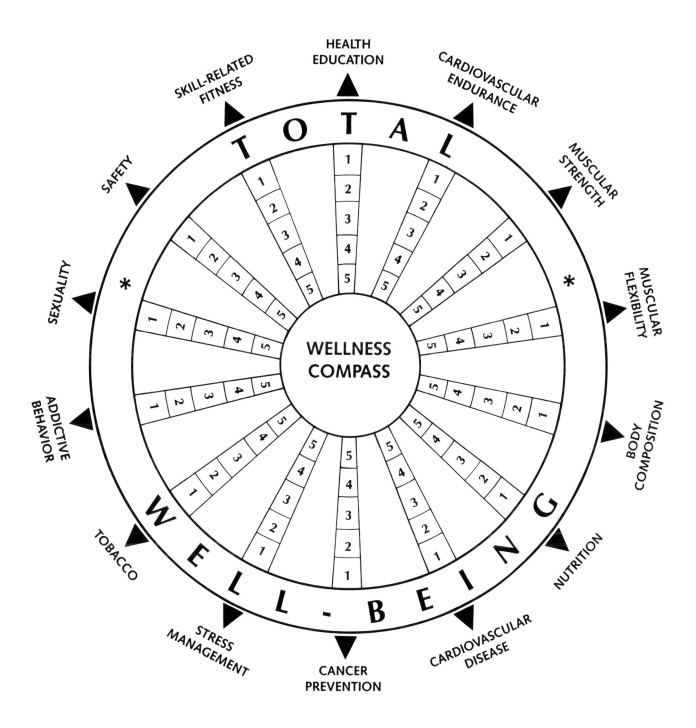

Indicate below one or two general objectives that you will work on in the next couple of months and write specific behavioral objectives that you will use to accomplish each general objective (you may not need eight specific objectives, only write as many as you need).

General Objective: _____

Specific Objectives:

1. _____

2. _____

3. _____

4. _____

5. _____

6. _____

7. _____

8. _____

General Objective: _____

Specific Objectives:

1. _____

2. _____

3. _____

4. _____

5. _____

6. _____

7. _____

8. _____

Appendix A

Nutritive Value of
Selected Foods

— Table A.1 —
Nutritive Value of Selected Foods

Code	Food	Amount	Weight gm	Calories	Protein gm	Fat gm	Sat. Fat gm	Cholesterol mg	Carbohydrate gm	Calcium mg	Iron mg	Sodium mg	Vit A I.U.	Thiamin (Vit B₁) mg	Riboflavin (Vit B₂) mg	Niacin mg	Vit C mg
1.	Almond Joy, candy bar	1.5 oz.	42	227	2.5	12	10.2	0	28	3	1.2	0	0	0.03	0.00	0.0	0
2.	Almonds, shelled	1/4 c	36	213	6.6	19	1.4	0	9	83	1.7	2	0	0.09	0.33	1.3	0
3.	Apple, raw, unpared	1 med	150	80	0.3	1	0.0	0	20	10	0.4	1	120	0.04	0.03	0.1	6
4.	Apple juice, canned or bottled	1/2 c	124	59	0.1	0	0.0	0	15	8	0.7	1	0	0.01	0.03	0.1	1
5.	Applesauce, canned, sweetened	1/2 c	128	116	0.3	0	0.0	0	31	5	0.7	3	50	0.02	0.01	0.0	2
6.	Apricots, canned, heavy syrup	3 halves; 1¾ tbsp liq.	85	73	0.5	0	0.0	0	19	9	0.3	1	1,480	0.02	0.02	0.3	3
7.	Apricots, dried, sulfured, uncooked	10 med halves	35	91	1.8	0	0.0	0	23	23	1.9	9	3,820	0.00	0.06	1.2	4
8.	Apricots, raw	3 (12 per lb)	114	55	1.1	0	0.0	0	14	18	0.5	1	2,890	0.06	0.04	0.6	11
9.	Asparagus, cooked green spears	4 med	60	12	1.3	0	0.0	0	2	13	0.4	1	540	0.10	0.11	0.8	16
10.	Avocado, raw	1/2 med	120	185	2.4	19	3.2	0	7	11	0.6	4	310	0.12	0.22	1.7	15
11.	Bacon, cooked, drained	2 slices	15	86	3.8	8	2.7	30	1	2	0.5	153	0	0.08	0.05	0.8	0
12.	Bacon, lettuce, tomato sandwich	1	130	327	11.6	19	4.7	21	31	84	2.5	661	426	0.42	0.28	4.1	12
13.	Bagel	1 3½ in.	68	180	7.0	1	0.2	0	35	20	2.1	124	0	0.26	0.20	2.4	0
14.	Banana, raw	1 sm (7¼")	140	81	1.0	0	0.0	0	21	8	0.7	1	180	0.05	0.06	0.7	10
15.	Banana, nut bread	1 slice	50	169	3.0	8	1.5	33	22	18	0.9	172	49	0.09	0.09	0.8	1
16.	Beans, green snap, cooked	1/2 c	65	16	1.0	0	0.0	0	3	32	0.4	4	340	0.05	0.06	0.3	8
17.	Beans, lentils	1/4 c	50	53	3.9	0	0.0	0	10	12	1.0	0	10	0.03	0.04	0.4	0
18.	Beans, lima (Fordhook), froz., cooked	1/2 c	85	84	6.0	0	0.0	0	17	40	2.1	1	240	0.15	0.08	1.1	15
19.	Beans, red kidney, cooked	1 c	185	218	14.4	1	0.0	0	40	70	4.4	6	10	0.20	0.11	1.3	0
20.	Beans, refried	1/2 c	145	148	9.0	1	0.2	0	25	71	2.6	614	0	0.07	0.08	0.7	9
21.	Bean sprouts, mung, raw	1/2 c	52	18	2.0	0	0.0	0	4	10	0.7	3	10	0.07	0.07	0.4	10
22.	Beef, chuck, cooked	3 oz.	85	212	25.0	12	7.8	80	0	11	3.1	43	20	0.05	0.19	3.8	0
23.	Beef, corned, canned	3 oz.	85	163	21.0	10	8.0	70	0	22	5.0	802	0	0.02	0.27	3.9	0
24.	Beef, ground, lean	3 oz.	85	186	23.3	10	5.0	81	0	10	3.0	57	20	0.08	0.20	5.1	0
25.	Beef, meatloaf	1 piece	111	246	20.0	15	6.1	125	6	37	2.4	434	181	0.08	0.23	4.1	1
26.	Beef, round steak, cooked, trimmed	3 oz.	85	222	24.3	13	6.0	77	0	10	3.0	60	20	0.07	0.20	4.8	0
27.	Beef, rump roast	3 oz.	85	177	24.7	9	4.0	80	0	10	3.1	61	10	0.06	0.19	4.4	0
28.	Beef, sirloin, cooked	3 oz.	85	329	19.6	27	13.0	77	0	9	2.5	48	50	0.05	0.15	4.0	0
29.	Beef, T-bone steak	3 oz.	85	403	16.7	37	15.6	66	0	7	2.2	40	23	0.07	0.14	3.5	0
30.	Beef, thin, sliced	3 oz.	85	105	18.5	3	1.4	36	0	11	1.8	1,409	0	0.07	0.16	4.5	0
31.	Beer	12 fl. oz.	360	151	1.1	0	0.0	0	14	18	0.0	25	0	0.01	0.11	2.2	0
32.	Beer, light	12 fl. oz.	354	96	0.7	0	0.0	0	4	17	0.1	10	0	0.03	0.10	1.3	0
33.	Beets, red, canned, drained	1/2 c	80	32	0.8	0	0.0	0	8	15	0.6	164	15	0.01	0.02	0.1	2
34.	Beet greens, cooked	1/2 c	73	13	1.3	0	0.0	0	2	72	1.4	55	3,700	0.05	0.11	0.2	11
35.	Biscuits, baking powder	1 med	35	114	2.5	6	1.1	0	18	60	0.8	272	0	0.06	0.06	0.7	0
36.	Blueberries, fresh cultivated	1/2 c	73	45	0.5	0	0.0	0	11	10	0.8	1	75	0.02	0.05	0.4	10

#	Food	Measure															
37.	Bologna	1 slice (1 oz.)	28	86	3.4	8	3.0	15	0	2	0.5	369	0	0.05	0.06	0.7	0
38.	Bologna, turkey	2 slices	57	113	7.8	9	3.0	56	1	47	0.9	498	0	0.03	0.09	2.1	0
39.	Bouillon, broth	1 cube	4	5	0.8	0	0.0	0	0	0	0.0	960	0	0.00	0.00	0.0	0
40.	Brandy	1 oz.	28	69	0.0	0	0.0	0	11	0	0.0	1	0	0.00	0.00	0.0	0
41.	Bread, Corn	1 slice	78	161	5.8	6	0.1	0	23	94	0.9	490	120	0.10	0.15	0.5	1
42.	Bread, Cracked wheat	1 slice	25	65	2.3	1	0.2	0	12	16	0.7	106	0	0.10	0.10	0.8	0
43.	Bread, French enriched	1 slice	35	102	3.2	1	0.2	0	19	15	0.8	203	0	0.10	0.08	0.9	0
44.	Bread, Oatmeal	1 slice	25	65	2.1	1	0.2	0	12	15	0.7	124	0	0.12	0.07	0.9	0
45.	Bread, Pita pocket	1 piece	60	165	6.2	1	0.1	0	33	49	1.5	339	0	0.27	0.13	2.3	0
46.	Bread, Pumpernickel	1 slice	32	80	2.9	1	0.2	0	15	23	0.9	277	0	0.11	0.17	1.1	0
47.	Bread, Rye (American)	1 slice	25	61	2.3	1	0.0	0	13	19	0.4	139	0	0.05	0.02	0.4	0
48.	Bread, white enriched	1 slice	25	68	2.2	1	0.2	0	13	21	0.6	127	0	0.06	0.05	0.6	0
49.	Bread, whole wheat	1 slice	25	61	2.6	1	0.6	0	12	25	0.8	132	0	0.06	0.03	0.7	0
50.	Broccoli, cooked drained	1 sm stalk	140	36	4.3	0	0.0	0	6	123	1.1	14	3,500	0.13	0.28	1.1	126
51.	Broccoli, raw	1 sm stalk	114	38	4.1	0	0.0	0	7	117	1.3	17	2,835	0.10	0.23	0.9	125
52.	Brownies, with nuts	1	20	95	1.3	6	2.3	18	11	9	0.4	51	20	0.05	0.05	0.3	0
53.	Brussels sprouts, froz., cooked, drained	1/2 c	78	28	3.2	0	0.0	0	5	25	0.8	8	405	0.06	0.11	0.5	63
54.	Bulgur, wheat	1 c	135	227	8.4	1	0.0	0	47	27	1.8	809	0	0.07	0.04	3.2	0
55.	Burrito, bean	1	166	307	12.5	9.5	3.6	14	45	173	2.4	983	283	0.15	0.22	2.3	5
56.	Burrito, combination, Taco Bell	1	175	404	21.0	16	0.0	0	43	91	3.7	300	1,666	0.34	0.31	4.6	15
57.	Butter	1 tsp	5	36	0.0	4	0.4	12	0	1	0.0	46	160	0.00	0.00	0.0	0
58.	Buttermilk, cultured	1 c	245	88	8.8	0	1.3	5	12	296	0.1	319	10	0.10	0.44	0.2	2
59.	Cabbage, boiled, drained wedge	1/2 c	85	16	0.9	0	0.0	0	3	36	0.3	10	100	0.02	0.02	0.1	21
60.	Cabbage, raw chopped	1/2 c	45	11	0.6	0	0.0	0	3	22	0.2	9	60	0.03	0.03	0.2	21
61.	Cake, Angel food, plain	1 piece	60	161	4.3	0	0.0	0	36	5	0.1	170	0	0.01	0.08	0.1	0
62.	Cake, Carrot	1 piece	96	385	4.2	21	4.1	74	48	44	1.3	279	75	0.11	0.12	0.9	1
63.	Cake, Cheesecake	1 piece (3½")	85	257	4.6	16	9.0	150	24	48	0.4	189	216	0.03	0.11	0.4	4
64.	Cake, Chocolate, w/icing	1 piece	69	235	3.0	8	3.6	37	40	41	1.4	181	100	0.07	0.10	0.6	0
65.	Cake, Coffee	1 piece	72	230	4.5	7	2.5	47	38	44	1.2	310	120	0.14	0.15	1.3	0
66.	Cake, Devil's food, iced	1 piece	99	365	4.5	16	5.0	68	55	69	1.0	233	160	0.02	0.10	0.2	0
67.	Cake, Pound	1 piece	30	120	2.0	5	1.0	32	15	20	0.5	98	200	0.05	0.06	0.5	0
68.	Cake, White, choc. icing	1 piece	71	268	3.5	11	3.7	2	48	35	0.3	162	40	0.19	0.14	1.6	0
69.	Candy, hard	1 oz.	28	109	0.0	0	0.0	0	28	6	0.5	9	0	0.00	0.00	0.0	0
70.	Cantaloupe	1/4 melon 5" diam.	239	35	2.0	0	0.0	0	10	20	0.8	17	4,620	0.06	0.04	0.6	45
71.	Caramel (candy, plain or choc.)	1 oz.	28	113	1.1	3	1.6	0	22	42	0.4	64	0	0.01	0.05	0.1	0
72.	Carrots, cooked, drained	1/2 c	73	23	0.7	0	0.0	0	5	24	0.5	10	7,615	0.04	0.04	0.4	5
73.	Carrots, raw	1 carrot 7½" long	81	30	0.8	0	0.0	0	7	27	0.5	34	7,930	0.04	0.04	0.4	6
74.	Cashew, roasted, unsalted	2 oz.	57	326	9.2	27	5.4	0	16	23	2.3	10	0	0.24	0.10	1.0	0
75.	Cauliflower, cooked, drained	1/2 c	63	14	1.5	0	0.0	0	3	13	0.5	6	40	0.06	0.05	0.4	35
76.	Celery, green, raw, long	1 outer stalk 8"	40	7	0.4	0	0.0	0	2	16	0.1	50	110	0.01	0.01	0.1	4
77.	Cereal, All-Bran	1/4 c	21	53	3.0	0	0.1	0	16	17	3.4	242	947	0.28	0.33	3.8	11
78.	Cereal, Alpha Bits	1 c	28	111	2.2	1	0.0	0	25	8	1.8	219	1,875	0.40	0.40	5.0	0
79.	Cereal, Bran	1/2 c	30	72	3.8	1	0.0	0	22	25	3.0	247	2,000	1.00	0.80	3.0	20
80.	Cereal, Cheerios	1 c	23	89	3.4	1	1.2	1	16	38	3.6	246	949	0.32	0.32	4.0	12
81.	Cereal, Corn Chex	1 c	28	111	2.0	0	0.1	0	25	3	1.8	271	75	0.40	0.07	5.0	15

Table A.1
Nutritive Value of Selected Foods (continued)

Code	Food	Amount	Weight gm	Calories	Protein gm	Fat gm	Sat. Fat gm	Cholesterol mg	Carbohydrate gm	Calcium mg	Iron mg	Sodium mg	Vit A I.U.	Thiamin (Vit B₁) mg	Riboflavin (Vit B₂) mg	Niacin mg	Vit C mg
82.	Cereal, Corn Flakes	1 c	25	97	2.0	0	0.0	0	21	3	0.6	251	180	0.29	0.55	2.9	9
83.	Cereal, Cream of Wheat	1 c	244	140	3.6	1	0.1	0	29	54	10.9	5	0	0.24	0.07	1.5	0
84.	Cereal, Frosted Mini-Wheats	4 biscuits	31	111	3.2	0	0.0	0	26	10	2.0	9	2,050	0.40	0.50	5.5	16
85.	Cereal, Fruit & Fibre w/dates	1 c	56	180	6.0	2	0.3	0	42	20	9.0	340	3,780	0.75	0.85	10.0	0
86.	Cereal, Granola, Nature Valley	1/2 c	57	252	5.8	10	7.0	0	38	36	1.9	116	41	0.20	0.10	0.4	0
87.	Cereal, Grape Nuts	1/2 c	57	202	6.6	0	0.0	0	47	22	2.5	394	3,815	0.80	0.80	10.0	0
88.	Cereal, Life	1 c	44	162	8.1	1	0.1	0	32	154	11.6	229	0	0.95	1.00	11.6	0
89.	Cereal, Nutri-Grain Wheat	1 c	44	158	3.8	1	0.1	0	37	12	1.2	299	2,915	0.60	0.70	7.7	23
90.	Cereal, Oatmeal, quick, cooked	1/2 c	120	66	2.4	1	0.2	0	12	11	0.7	262	0	0.10	0.03	0.1	0
91.	Cereal, Raisin Bran	1 c	49	160	4.0	1	0.2	0	40	25	24.0	293	2,500	0.51	0.57	6.7	0
92.	Cereal, Rice Krispies	3/4 c	22	85	1.4	0	0.0	0	19	3	1.4	255	971	0.30	0.30	3.8	11
93.	Cereal, Shredded Wheat	1 c	19	65	2.1	0	0.0	0	11	8	0.6	1	0	0.06	0.05	0.9	0
94.	Cereal, Special K	1 c	21	83	4.2	0	0.0	0	16	6	3.4	199	1,430	0.30	0.30	3.8	11
95.	Cereal, Sugar Corn Pops	1 c	28	108	1.4	0	0.0	0	26	1	1.8	103	1,875	0.40	0.40	5.0	15
96.	Cereal, Sugar Frosted Flakes	1 c	35	133	1.8	0	0.0	0	32	1	2.2	284	2,315	0.50	0.50	6.2	19
97.	Cereal, Sugar Smacks	1 c	37	141	2.7	1	0.1	0	32	4	2.4	100	2,500	0.49	0.57	6.7	20
98.	Cereal, Total	1 c	33	116	3.3	1	0.1	0	26	56	21.0	409	8,845	1.70	2.00	23.3	70
99.	Cereal, Wheat Chex	1 c	46	169	4.5	1	0.2	0	38	18	7.3	308	0	0.60	0.17	8.1	24
100.	Cereal, whole wheat, cooked	1/2 c	123	55	2.2	0	0.0	0	12	9	0.06	260	0	0.08	0.03	0.8	0
101.	Cereal, whole wheat flakes, ready-to-eat	1 c	30	106	3.1	1	0.0	0	24	12	2.0	310	1,410	0.35	0.42	3.5	11
102.	Cereal, 40% Bran Flakes	1 c	39	125	4.9	1	0.1	0	31	19	11.2	363	2,610	0.51	0.59	6.9	0
103.	Cereal, 100% Bran	1/2 c	33	89	4.2	2	0.3	0	24	23	4.1	229	0	0.80	0.90	10.4	31
104.	Champagne	4 oz.	113	87	0.2	0	0.1	0	2	6	0.4	7	0	0.00	0.01	0.1	0
105.	Cheese, American	1 oz. slice	28	100	6.0	8	5.6	27	0	188	0.1	307	343	0.01	0.10	0.0	0
106.	Cheese, Bleu	1 oz.	28	100	6.0	8	5.3	25	1	89	0.1	510	204	0.01	0.11	0.3	0
107.	Cheese, Cheddar	1 oz.	28	114	7.0	9	6.0	30	0	204	0.2	171	300	0.01	0.11	0.0	0
108.	Cheese, Cottage, 2%	1/2 c	113	103	15.5	2	1.4	10	4	78	0.2	459	79	0.03	0.21	0.2	0
109.	Cheese, Cottage, creamed	1/2 c	105	112	14.0	5	6.4	15	3	99	0.3	241	180	0.03	0.26	0.1	0
110.	Cheese, Creamed	1 oz.	28	99	6.0	8	3.0	31	1	167	0.3	71	320	0.02	0.14	0.0	0
111.	Cheese, Feta	1 oz.	28	75	4.5	6	4.2	25	1	140	0.2	316	180	0.04	0.23	0.3	0
112.	Cheese, Monterey jack	1 oz.	28	106	6.9	9	5.4	26	0	212	0.2	152	405	0.00	0.11	0.0	0
113.	Cheese, Mozzarella, skim	1 oz.	28	80	7.6	5	3.1	15	1	207	0.1	150	216	0.01	0.10	0.0	0
114.	Cheese, Parmesan	1 tbsp	5	23	2.1	2	1.0	4	0	69	0.1	93	45	0.00	0.02	0.0	0
115.	Cheese, Ricotta, part skim	1 oz.	28	39	3.2	2	1.4	9	1	77	0.1	35	160	0.01	0.05	0.0	0
116.	Cheese, Souffle	1 portion	110	240	10.9	19	9.5	189	7	221	1.1	400	880	0.06	0.26	0.2	0
117.	Cheese, Swiss	1 oz.	28	107	8.0	8	5.0	26	1	272	0.1	74	360	0.01	0.10	0.0	0
118.	Cheese puffs, Cheetos	1 oz.	28	158	2.2	10	4.8	5	14	17	0.4	344	130	0.01	0.03	0.3	0
119.	Cheeseburger, McDonald's	1	115	321	15.2	16	6.7	40	29	170	2.9	736	353	0.30	0.24	4.4	2
120.	Cherries	10	75	47	0.9	0	0.0	0	12	15	0.3	8	450	0.20	0.24	1.6	41
121.	Chicken, BK Broiler sandwich, Burger King	1 sandwich	168	379	24.0	18	3.0	53	31	48	2.3	764	350	0.42	0.22	9.2	5

#	Food	Measure														
122.	Chicken breast, roast w/skin	1	98	193	29.2	8	2.1	83	0	14	1.0	69	91	0.07	0.12	12.5	0
123.	Chicken chow mein	1 c	250	255	31.0	11	3.6	75	10	58	2.5	718	250	0.08	0.23	4.3	10
124.	Chicken, drumstick Kentucky Fried	1	54	136	14.0	8	2.2	73	2	20	0.9	320	30	0.04	0.12	2.7	0
125.	Chicken, drumstick, roasted	1	52	112	14.1	6	1.6	48	0	6	0.7	47	52	0.04	0.11	3.1	0
126.	Chicken McNuggets	6	111	329	19.5	21	5.2	64	15	11	1.3	521	92	0.16	0.14	7.7	2
127.	Chicken, patty sandwich	1	157	436	24.8	23	6.1	68	34	44	1.9	2,732	47	0.13	0.26	9.2	4
128.	Chicken, wing, Kentucky Fried	1	45	151	11.0	10	2.9	70	4	0	0.6	300	0	0.03	0.07	0.0	0
129.	Chicken, roast, light meat without skin	3 oz.	85	141	27.0	3	0.4	45	0	10	1.2	54	51	0.03	0.09	9.9	0
130.	Chicken, roast, dark meat without skin	3 oz.	85	149	24.0	5	0.8	50	0	11	1.5	54	127	0.06	0.19	4.7	0
131.	Chili con carne	1 c	255	339	19.1	16	5.8	28	31	82	4.3	1,354	150	0.08	0.18	3.3	8
132.	Chocolate fudge	1 oz.	28	115	0.6	3	2.1	1	21	22	0.3	54	0	0.01	0.03	0.1	0
133.	Chocolate, milk	1 oz.	28	147	2.0	9	3.6	5	16	65	0.3	27	80	0.02	0.10	0.1	0
134.	Chocolate, milk w/almonds	1 oz.	28	150	2.9	10	4.4	5	15	61	0.6	23	30	0.03	0.13	0.3	0
135.	Clam, canned, drained	3 oz.	85	83	13.0	2	0.2	50	2	46	3.5	750	93	0.01	0.09	0.9	9
136.	Cocoa, hot, with whole milk	1 c	250	218	9.1	9	6.1	33	26	298	0.8	123	318	0.10	0.44	0.4	2
137.	Cocoa, plain, dry	1 tbsp	5	14	0.9	1	0.0	0	3	7	0.6	0	0	0.01	0.02	0.1	0
138.	Coconut, shredded, packed	1/2 c	65	225	2.3	23	20.0	0	6	8	1.1	165	0	0.03	0.01	0.3	2
139.	Cod, batter fried	3.5 oz.	100	199	19.6	10	3.9	55	8	80	0.5	100	2	0.02	0.02	1.8	0
140.	Cod, cooked	3 oz.	85	144	24.3	4	1.5	60	0	27	0.9	63	150	0.06	0.09	2.7	0
141.	Cod, poached	3.5 oz.	100	94	20.9	1	0.3	60	0	29	0.5	110	2	0.08	0.08	3.0	0
142.	Coffee	3/4 cup	180	1	0.0	0	0.0	0	0	1	0.2	2	0	0.00	0.00	0.1	0
143.	Coleslaw	1 c	120	173	1.6	17	1.0	5	6	53	0.5	144	190	0.06	0.06	0.4	35
144.	Collards, leaves without stems, cooked, drained	1/2 c	95	32	3.4	1	2.0	0	5	178	0.8	28	7,410	0.01	0.19	1.2	72
145.	Cookies, Chocolate chip homemade	2 2¼" diam.	20	103	1.0	6	1.7	14	12	7	0.4	70	20	0.02	0.02	0.2	0
146.	Cookies, Fig bars	4 bars	56	210	2.0	4	1.0	27	42	40	1.4	180	31	0.08	0.07	0.7	0
147.	Cookies, Oatmeal raisin	2 2" diam.	26	122	1.5	5	1.3	1	18	9	0.6	74	20	0.04	0.04	0.5	0
148.	Cookies, Peanut butter, homemade	2 cookies	24	123	2.0	7	2.0	11	14	10	0.5	71	12	0.03	0.03	0.9	0
149.	Cookies, sandwich, all	4 cookies	40	195	2.0	8	2.0	0	29	12	1.4	189	0	0.90	0.07	0.8	0
150.	Cookies, Shortbread	4 cookies	32	155	2.0	8	2.9	27	20	13	0.8	123	40	0.10	0.09	0.9	0
151.	Cookies, Vanilla	5 1¾" diam.	20	93	1.0	3	0.8	10	15	8	0.1	50	25	0.00	0.01	0.0	0
152	Cookies, Vanilla wafers	10 wafers	40	185	2.0	7	1.8	25	29	16	0.8	150	70	0.07	0.10	1.0	0
153.	Corn, boiled on cob	1 ear 5" long	140	70	2.5	1	0.0	0	16	2	0.5	1	310	0.09	0.08	1.1	7
154.	Corn, canned, drained	1/2 c	83	70	2.2	1	0.0	0	16	4	0.4	195	290	0.03	0.04	0.8	4
155.	Corn chips	1 oz.	28	155	2.0	9	1.8	0	16	35	0.5	233	110	0.04	0.05	0.4	1
156.	Cornmeal, degermed, yellow, enriched, cooked	1/2 c	120	60	1.3	0	0.0	0	13	1	0.5	264	70	0.07	0.05	0.6	0
157.	Crab, canned	1 c	135	135	23.0	3	0.5	135	1	61	1.1	1,350	70	0.11	0.11	2.6	0
158.	Crackers, Cheese	10 crackers	10	50	1.0	3	0.9	6	5	11	0.4	112	25	0.05	0.04	0.4	0
159.	Crackers, Graham	2 squares	14	55	1.1	1	0.3	0	10	6	0.2	95	0	0.01	0.03	0.2	0
160.	Crackers, Ritz	1 cracker	3	15	0.2	1	0.2	0	2	3	0.1	30	0	0.01	0.01	0.1	0
161.	Crackers, Ryewafers, whole grain	2 crackers	14	55	1.0	1	0.3	0	10	7	0.5	115	0	0.06	0.03	0.5	0
162.	Crackers, Saltines	4 squares	11	48	1.0	1	0.3	0	8	2	0.1	123	0	0.00	0.00	0.1	0

Table A.1

Nutritive Value of Selected Foods (continued)

Code	Food	Amount	Weight gm	Calories	Protein gm	Fat gm	Sat. Fat gm	Cholesterol mg	Carbohydrate gm	Calcium mg	Iron mg	Sodium mg	Vit A I.U.	Thiamin (Vit B₁) mg	Riboflavin (Vit B₂) mg	Niacin mg	Vit C mg
163.	Crackers, Soda	1	3	13	0.3	0	0.1	0	2	1	0.1	39	0	0.02	0.01	0.1	0
164.	Crackers, Triscuits	1	5	23	0.4	1	0.3	0	3	0	0.0	0	0	0.00	0.00	0.0	0
165.	Crackers, Wheat Thins	1	2	9	0.2	0	0.1	0	1	1	0.1	17	0	0.01	0.01	0.1	0
166.	Cranberry juice	1 c	253	145	0.1	0	0.0	0	36	8	0.4	5	5	0.02	0.02	0.1	90
167.	Cream, light coffee or table	1 tbsp	15	20	0.5	2	0.5	5	1	16	0.0	7	70	0.00	0.02	0.0	0
168.	Cream, heavy whipping	1 tbsp	15	53	0.3	6	1.3	12	1	11	0.0	5	230	0.00	0.02	0.0	0
169.	Croissant	1	57	235	4.7	12	4.0	13	27	20	2.1	452	50	0.17	0.13	1.3	0
170.	Croissants (Sara Lee)	1 roll	18	59	1.6	2	0.3	0	8	22	0.6	105	0	0.14	0.09	0.8	0
171.	Croissan'wich, egg, cheese Burger King	1 sandwich	110	315	13.0	20	7.0	222	19	112	1.8	607	500	0.22	0.37	1.4	0
172.	Cucumbers, raw pared	9 sm slices	28	4	0.3	0	0.0	0	1	7	0.3	2	70	0.01	0.01	0.1	3
173.	Dates hydrated	5	46	110	0.9	0	0.0	0	29	24	1.2	1	20	0.04	0.04	0.9	0
174.	Doughnut, plain	1	42	164	1.9	8	2.0	19	22	17	0.6	210	30	0.07	0.07	0.5	0
175.	Doughnut, yeast raised	1	27	235	4.0	13	5.2	21	26	17	1.4	222	2	0.28	0.12	1.8	0
176.	Dressing, Bleu cheese	1 tbsp	15	77	0.7	8	1.9	4	1	12	0.0	8	32	0.00	0.02	0.0	0
177.	Dressing, French	1 tbsp	16	83	0.1	9	1.4	0	1	2	0.1	184	0	0.00	0.00	0.0	0
178.	Dressing, French, low cal	1 tbsp.	15	24	0.0	2	0.2	0	2	6	0.1	306	0	0.00	0.00	0.0	0
179.	Dressing, Italian	1 tbsp.	15	69	0.1	9	1.3	0	2	1	0.0	73	29	0.00	0.00	0.0	0
180.	Dressing, Italian, low cal	1 tbsp.	15	10	0.0	1	0.0	0	1	1	0.0	136	1	0.00	0.00	0.0	0
181.	Dressing, Ranch style	1 tbsp.	15	54	0.4	6	0.9	6	1	15	0.0	65	36	0.01	0.02	0.0	0
182.	Dressing, Thousand island	1 tbsp.	15	60	0.2	6	1.0	4	2	2	0.1	110	75	0.00	0.01	0.0	1
183.	Dressing, Thousand island, low cal	1 tbsp.	15	25	0.1	2	0.2	2	3	2	0.1	153	70	0.00	0.00	0.0	0
184.	Eggs, hard cooked	1 large	50	72	6.0	5	1.8	250	1	24	1.0	113	520	0.05	0.13	0.0	0
185.	Egg, fried with butter	1	46	95	5.4	6	2.4	278	1	28	0.9	162	320	0.04	0.13	0.0	0
186.	Egg McMuffin	1	138	327	18.5	15	5.9	259	31	226	2.9	885	591	0.47	0.44	3.8	1
187.	Egg salad sandwich	1	111	325	10.0	19	3.9	215	28	95	2.5	461	242	0.29	0.29	2.1	0
188.	Egg, scrambled, with milk, butter	1 egg	64	95	6.0	7	3.0	282	1	54	0.9	176	510	0.04	0.18	0.0	0
189.	Eggs, white	1 large	33	17	3.6	0	0.0	0	0	3	0.0	48	0	0.00	0.09	0.0	0
190.	Eggs, yolk, raw	1 yolk	17	63	2.8	6	1.7	248	0	26	1.0	8	390	0.04	0.07	0.0	0
191.	Enchilada, beef	1	200	487	21.8	23	8.8	63	26	425	2.9	262	595	0.02	0.27	3.5	5
192.	Enchilada, cheese	1	230	632	25.3	34	17.6	82	31	876	2.6	596	1,672	0.13	0.40	1.2	15
193.	Figs, dried	1 large	21	60	1.0	0	0.0	0	15	26	0.6	1	20	0.16	0.17	3.9	0
194.	Filet of Fish, McDonald's	1	131	402	15.0	23	7.9	43	34	105	1.8	709	152	0.28	0.28	3.9	4
195.	Fish, sticks	2	56	140	12.0	6	1.6	52	8	22	0.6	106	40	0.06	0.10	1.2	0
196.	Flounder	3 oz.	85	171	25.5	7	1.0	60	0	21	1.2	201	0	0.06	0.06	2.1	3
197.	Flour, all purpose enriched	1 c	125	455	13.0	1	0.0	0	95	20	3.6	3	0	0.55	0.33	4.4	0
198.	Flour, whole wheat	1 c	120	400	16.0	2	0.0	0	85	49	4.0	4	0	0.66	0.14	5.2	0
199.	Frankfurter, cooked	1	57	176	7.0	16	5.6	45	1	4	1.1	627	0	0.09	0.11	1.5	0
200.	Frankfurter, turkey, cooked	1	45	102	6.4	8	2.7	39	1	58	0.8	454	60	0.04	0.08	1.7	0
201.	French toast	1 piece	65	123	4.9	4	1.1	73	15	79	1.1	189	285	0.15	0.17	1.1	0
202.	Fruit cocktail	1 c	245	91	1.0	0	0.0	0	24	22	1.0	12	370	0.05	0.02	1.2	5
203.	Fruit cocktail, juice pack	1 c	248	115	1.1	0	0.0	0	29	20	0.5	10	380	0.03	0.04	1.0	7

#	Food	Serving															
204.	Grapefruit, raw white	1/2 med	301	56	1.0	0	0.0	0	15	22	0.5	1	10	0.05	0.03	0.3	52
205.	Grapefruit, juice unsweetened canned	1/2 c	124	50	0.6	0	0.0	0	12	11	0.2	2	10	0.05	0.03	0.3	46
206.	Grapes, seedless, European	10 grapes	50	34	0.3	0	0.0	0	9	6	0.2	2	50	0.03	0.03	0.2	2
207.	Grape juice, unsweetened bottled	1/2 c	127	84	0.3	0	0.0	0	21	14	0.4	3	0	0.05	0.03	0.3	0
208.	Gravy, beef, homemade	1 tbsp	17	19	0.3	2	1.0	1	1	1	0.1	49	0	0.01	0.01	0.2	0
209.	Haddock, fried (dipped in egg, milk, bread crumbs)	3 oz.	85	141	17.0	5	1.0	54	5	33	0.9	150	0	0.03	0.06	2.7	3
210.	Halibut, broiled with butter or margarine	3 oz.	85	144	21.0	6	2.1	55	0	15	0.6	114	570	0.03	0.06	7.2	1
211.	Ham (cured pork)	3 oz.	85	318	20.0	26	9.4	77	0	9	2.6	48	0	0.43	0.20	3.8	0
212.	Ham, lunch meat	1 slice	28	37	5.5	1	0.5	13	.3	2	0.2	405	0	0.26	0.06	1.4	7
213.	Hamburger, Big Mac	1	204	581	25.1	36	12.0	85	40	207	5.0	999	388	0.49	0.39	7.3	3
214.	Hamburger bun	1 bun	40	129	3.7	2	1.0	0	23	61	1.3	271	2	0.22	0.15	1.8	0
215.	Hamburger, McDorald's	1	99	257	13.0	9	3.7	26	30	63	3.0	526	231	0.23	0.23	5.1	2
216.	Hamburger, Quarter pounder	1 burger	160	427	24.6	24	9.1	80	29	98	4.3	718	115	0.35	0.32	7.2	3
217.	Hamburger, Quarter pounder, with cheese	1 burger	186	525	29.6	32	12.8	107	31	255	4.8	1,195	640	0.37	0.41	7.1	3
218.	Honey	1 tbsp	21	64	0.0	0	0.0	0	17	1	0.1	1	0	0.00	0.01	0.1	0
219.	Honeydew melon	1 slice (1/10 melon)	129	45	0.6	0	0.0	0	12	8	0.1	13	25	0.10	0.02	0.8	32
220.	Hotdog bun	1 bun	40	115	3.3	2	1.0	0	20	54	1.2	241	2	0.20	0.13	1.6	0
221.	Ice cream, vanilla	1/2 c	67	135	3.0	7	4.4	27	14	97	0.1	42	295	0.03	0.14	0.1	1
222.	Ice cream core	1 small	115	185	4.3	5	2.2	24	30	183	0.1	109	218	0.06	0.36	0.4	1
223.	Ice cream cone, Dairy Queen	medium	142	230	6.0	7	4.6	15	35	200	0.0	150	300	0.09	0.26	0.0	0
224.	Ice cream, hot fudge sundae	1	164	357	7.0	11	5.4	27	58	215	0.6	170	233	0.07	0.31	1.1	2
225.	Ice milk, vanila	1/2 c	61	100	3.0	3	1.8	13	15	102	0.1	45	140	0.04	0.15	0.1	1
226.	Instant breakfast, whole milk	1 c	281	280	15.0	8	5.1	33	34	301	8.0	286	2,057	0.39	0.46	5.2	29
227.	Instant breakfast, skim milk	1 c	282	216	15.4	0	0.0	4	35	312	8.0	292	1,635	0.39	0.41	5.2	29
228.	Jams or preserves	1 tbsp	7	18	0.0	0	0.0	0	5	1	0.1	1	1	0.00	0.00	0.0	0
229.	Jelly	1 tbsp	18	49	0.0	0	0.0	0	13	4	0.3	3	0	0.01	0.01	0.0	1
230.	Kale, fresh ccooked, drained	1/2 c	55	22	2.5	0	0.0	0	3	103	0.9	24	4,565	0.06	0.10	0.9	51
231.	Kiwi fruit, raw	1 med	76	46	1.0	0	0.0	0	11	20	0.3	4	65	0.02	0.04	0.4	75
232.	Kool Aid, with sugar	1 c	240	100	0.0	0	0.0	0	25	0	0.0	0	0	0.00	0.00	0.0	6
233.	Lamb leg, roast, trimmed	3 oz.	85	237	22.0	16	7.3	60	0	9	1.4	53	0	0.13	0.23	4.7	0
234.	Lamb loin chop, broiled, lean	3 oz.	84	183	25.0	8	3.4	78	0	16	1.7	70	7	0.10	0.23	5.7	0
235.	Lasagna, homemade	1 piece	220	357	23.6	18	8.3	50	27	413	2.8	703	1,008	0.19	0.30	3.3	6
236.	Lemon juice, fresh	1 tbsp	15	4	0.1	0	0.0	0	1	1	0.0	0	7	0.00	0.00	0.0	7
237.	Lemonade (concentrate)	12 oz.	340	137	0.2	0	0.1	0	36	11	0.6	11	73	0.02	0.07	0.1	13
238.	Lentils, cooked	1/2 c	100	106	8.0	0	0.0	0	19	25	2.1	0	20	0.07	0.06	0.6	0
239.	Lettuce, crisp head	1 c sm chunks	75	10	0.7	0	0.0	0	2	15	0.4	7	250	0.05	0.05	0.2	5
240.	Lettuce, cos or romaine	1 c chopped	55	10	0.7	0	0.0	0	2	37	0.8	5	1,050	0.08	0.04	0.2	10
241.	Liver, beef, fried	1 slice 3 oz.	85	195	22.0	9	2.5	345	5	9	7.5	156	45,390	0.22	3.56	14.0	23
242.	Liverwurst, fresh	1 slice 1 oz.	28	87	5.0	7	3.5	50	1	3	1.5	0	1,800	0.06	0.37	1.6	0
243.	Lobster	1 c	145	138	27.0	2	1.0	293	0	94	1.2	305	0	0.15	0.10	0.0	0
244.	M&M's, Chocolate, plain	1 oz.	28	140	1.9	6	3.3	6	19	47	0.5	24	30	0.01	0.07	0.2	0
245.	M&M's, Chocolate, w/peanuts	1 oz.	28	145	3.2	7	3.2	7	17	36	0.4	17	15	0.02	0.05	0.9	0
246.	Macaroni, enriched, cooked	1/2 c	70	78	2.4	0	0.0	0	16	6	0.7	1	0	0.10	0.06	0.8	0
247.	Macaroni and cheese	1/2 c	100	215	8.2	11	4.0	21	20	181	0.9	543	430	0.10	0.20	0.9	0
248.	Margarine	1 tsp	5	34	0.0	4	0.7	2	0	1	0.0	46	160	0.00	0.00	0.0	0

Table A.1
Nutritive Value of Selected Foods (continued)

Code	Food	Amount	Weight gm	Calories	Protein gm	Fat gm	Sat. Fat gm	Cholesterol mg	Carbohydrate gm	Calcium mg	Iron mg	Sodium mg	Vit A I.U.	Thiamin (Vit B$_1$) mg	Riboflavin (Vit B$_2$) mg	Niacin mg	Vit C mg
249.	Mars bar	1 bar	50	240	4.0	11	4.8	0	30	85	0.6	85	1	0.02	0.16	0.5	0
250.	Matzo	1 piece	30	117	3.0	0	0.0	0	25	*	*	0	*	*	*	*	*
251.	Mayonnaise	1 tsp	5	36	0.0	4	0.7	3	0	1	0.0	28	13	0.00	0.00	0.0	0
252.	Milk, chocolate, 2%	1 c	250	180	8.0	5	3.1	17	26	284	0.6	151	143	0.09	0.41	0.3	2
253.	Milk, evaporated whole	1/2 c	126	172	9.0	10	5.8	40	13	329	0.2	149	405	0.05	0.43	0.2	2
254.	Milk, lowfat (2% fat)	1 c	246	145	10.0	5	3.1	5	15	352	0.1	150	200	0.10	0.52	0.2	2
255.	Milk shake, chocolate	1 (10 fluid oz.)	340	433	11.5	13	7.8	45	70	383	1.1	328	312	0.20	0.83	0.5	0
256.	Milk shake, strawberry	1 (10 fluid oz.)	340	383	11.4	10	6.0	37	64	384	0.4	281	418	0.14	0.61	0.5	4
257.	Milk shake, vanilla, McDonald's	1	289	323	10.0	8	5.1	29	52	346	0.2	250	346	0.12	0.66	0.6	3
258.	Milk, skim	1 c	245	88	9.0	0	0.3	5	12	296	0.1	126	10	0.09	0.44	0.2	2
259.	Milk, whole (3.5% fat)	1 c	244	159	9.0	9	5.1	34	12	288	0.1	120	350	0.07	0.40	0.2	2
260.	Milky Way bar	1 bar	60	260	3.2	9	5.4	14	43	86	0.5	140	125	0.03	0.15	0.2	1
261.	Molasses, medium	1 tbsp	20	50	0.0	0	0.0	0	13	33	0.9	3	0	0.01	0.01	0.0	0
262.	Muffin, blueberry	1	45	135	3.0	5	1.5	19	20	54	0.9	198	40	0.10	0.11	0.9	1
263.	Muffin, bran	1	45	125	3.0	6	1.4	24	19	60	1.4	189	230	0.11	0.13	1.3	3
264.	Muffin, cornmeal	1	45	145	3.0	5	1.5	23	21	66	0.9	169	80	0.11	0.11	0.9	0
265.	Muffin, English, plain	1	57	140	4.5	1	0.3	0	26	96	1.7	378	0	0.26	0.18	2.1	0
266.	Muffin, English w/butter	1	63	186	5.0	5	2.3	15	30	117	1.5	310	164	0.28	0.49	2.6	1
267.	Mushrooms, fresh cultivated	1/2 c sliced	35	12	1.0	0	0.0	0	2	4	0.5	4	0	0.04	0.12	2.4	1
268.	Mustard greens, cooked drained	1/2 c	70	16	1.7	0	0.0	0	3	96	1.2	13	4,060	0.05	0.10	0.4	33
269.	Noodles, egg, enriched cooked	1/2 c	80	100	3.3	1	0.0	0	19	8	0.7	2	55	0.11	0.07	1.0	0
270.	Nuts, Brazil	1 oz. (6-8 nuts)	28	185	4.1	19	4.8	0	3	53	1.0	0	0	0.27	0.03	0.5	0
271.	Nuts, Pecans	1 oz.	28	195	2.6	20	1.4	0	4	21	0.7	0	40	0.24	0.04	0.3	1
272.	Nuts, Walnuts	1 oz. (14 halves)	28	185	4.2	18	1.0	0	5	28	0.9	1	10	0.09	0.04	0.3	1
273.	Oil, Corn	1 tbsp.	15	125	0.0	14	1.8	0	0	0	0.0	0	0	0.00	0.00	0.0	0
274.	Oil, Olive	1 tbsp.	15	125	0.0	14	1.9	0	0	0	0.0	0	0	0.00	0.00	0.0	0
275.	Oil, Safflower	1 tbsp.	15	125	0.0	14	1.3	0	0	0	0.0	0	0	0.00	0.00	0.0	0
276.	Oil, Soybean	1 tsp.	5	44	0.0	5	2.0	0	0	0	0.0	0	0	0.00	0.00	0.0	0
277.	Okra, cooked, drained	1/2 c	80	23	1.6	0	0.0	0	5	74	0.4	2	390	0.11	0.15	0.7	16
278.	Olives, black, ripe	10 extra large	55	61	0.5	7	1.0	0	1	40	0.8	385	30	0.00	0.00	0.0	0
279.	Onions, mature, cooked, drained	1/2 c sliced	105	31	1.3	0	0.0	0	7	25	0.4	8	40	0.03	0.03	0.2	8
280.	Onion rings, fried	3	30	122	1.6	8	2.3	0	11	9	0.5	113	68	0.08	0.04	1.1	0
281.	Onion rings (Brazier) Dairy Queen	1 serving	85	360	6.0	17	6.0	15	33	20	0.4	125	0	0.09	0.00	0.4	2
282.	Orange juice, froz. reconstituted	1/2 c	125	61	0.9	0	0.0	0	15	13	0.1	1	270	0.12	0.02	0.5	60
283.	Orange, raw (medium skin)	1 med	180	64	1.3	0	0.0	0	16	54	0.5	1	260	0.13	0.05	0.5	66
284.	Oysters, Eastern, breaded, fried	1 oyster	45	90	5.0	5	1.4	35	5	49	3.0	70	220	0.07	0.10	1.3	4

285.	Oysters, raw, Eastern	1/2 c (6-9 med)	120	79	10.0	2	1.3	60	4	113	6.6	145	370	0.17	0.22	3.0	0
286.	Pancakes	1 6" diam x 1/2" thick	73	169	5.2	5	1.0	36	25	74	0.9	310	90	0.12	0.16	0.9	0
287.	Pancakes, buckwheat	1 4 in. diam.	27	55	2.0	2	0.9	20	6	59	0.4	125	17	0.04	0.05	0.2	0
288.	Pancakes w/butter, syrup	1 large	100	250	4.0	5	1.9	24	47	1	1.1	535	160	0.13	0.18	1.1	2
289.	Papaya, raw	1/2 med	227	60	0.9	0	0.0	0	15	31	0.5	5	2,660	0.06	0.06	0.5	85
290.	Parsnips, cooked	1 large 9" long	160	106	2.4	1	0.0	0	24	72	1.0	13	50	0.11	0.13	0.2	16
291.	Peaches, canned, heavy syrup	1 half 2⅛ tbsp liq.	96	75	0.4	0	0.0	0	19	4	0.3	2	410	0.01	0.02	0.6	3
292.	Peaches, canned, juice pack	1 half	77	34	0.5	0	0.0	0	9	5	0.2	3	147	0.01	0.01	0.5	3
293.	Peaches, raw, peeled	1 2¾" diam.	175	58	0.9	0	0.0	0	15	14	0.8	2	2,030	0.03	0.08	1.5	11
294.	Peanut butter	2 tbsp	32	188	8.0	16	1.0	0	6	18	0.6	194	0	0.04	0.04	4.8	0
295.	Peanut butter, jam sandwich	1	100	340	11.4	14	2.6	0	45	87	2.3	414	1	0.32	0.22	5.3	0
296.	Peanuts, roasted	1 oz.	28	166	7.0	14	1.0	0	5	21	0.6	119	0	0.09	0.04	4.9	0
297.	Pears, canned, heavy syrup	1 half 2¼ tbsp liq.	103	78	0.2	0	0.0	0	20	5	0.2	1	0	0.01	0.02	0.1	1
298.	Pears, canned, juice pack	1 half	77	38	0.3	0	0.0	0	10	7	0.2	3	3	0.01	0.01	0.2	1
299.	Pears, raw	1 pear	180	100	1.1	1	0.0	0	25	13	0.5	2	30	0.03	0.07	0.2	7
300.	Peas, canned, drained	1/2 c	85	75	4.0	0	0.0	0	14	22	1.6	200	585	0.08	0.05	0.7	7
301.	Peas, frozen, cooked drained	1/2 c	80	55	4.1	0	0.0	0	10	15	1.5	92	480	0.22	0.07	1.4	11
302.	Peppers, sweet, raw	1 pepper 3¼" x 3" diam.	200	36	2.0	0	0.0	0	8	15	1.1	21	690	0.13	0.13	0.8	210
303.	Pickles, dill	1 large 4" long	135	15	0.9	0	0.0	0	3	35	1.4	1,928	140	0.00	0.03	0.0	8
304.	Pickles, sweet	1 large 3" long	35	51	0.2	0	0.0	0	13	4	0.4	0	30	0.00	0.01	0.0	2
305.	Pie, Apple	1 piece (3½")	118	302	2.6	13	3.5	120	45	9	0.4	355	40	0.02	0.02	0.5	1
306.	Pie, Apple, fried	1 pie	85	255	2.2	14	5.8	14	32	12	0.9	326	15	0.09	0.06	1.0	1
307.	Pie, Blueberry	1 piece (3½")	158	380	4.0	17	4.0	0	55	26	2.1	423	140	0.17	0.14	1.7	6
308.	Pie, Cherry	1 piece (3½")	118	308	3.1	13	5.0	137	45	17	0.4	355	40	0.02	0.02	0.5	1
309.	Pie, Cherry, fried	1 pie	85	250	2.0	14	5.8	13	32	11	0.7	371	95	0.06	0.06	0.6	1
310.	Pie, Chocolate cream	1 piece (1/6 pie)	175	311	7.4	13	4.5	15	42	160	1.1	427	170	0.15	0.30	1.1	1
311.	Pie, Lemon meringue	1 piece (1/6 pie)	140	355	4.7	14	3.5	137	53	25	1.4	395	330	0.10	0.14	0.8	4
312.	Pie, Pecan	1 piece (1/6 pie)	138	583	6.3	24	3.9	13	92	35	1.9	304	206	0.22	0.17	1.1	0
313.	Pie, Pumpkin	1 (3½")	114	241	4.6	13	3.0	70	28	58	0.6	244	2,810	0.03	0.11	0.6	0
314.	Pineapple, canned, heavy syrup	1/2 c	128	95	0.4	0	0.0	0	25	14	0.4	2	65	0.10	0.03	0.3	9
315.	Pineapple, canned, juice pack	1/2 c	125	75	0.5	0	0.0	0	20	17	0.3	1	24	0.12	0.24	0.3	12
316.	Pineapple, raw	1/2 c diced	78	41	0.3	0	0.0	0	11	13	0.4	1	55	0.07	0.03	0.2	13
317.	Pizza, Cheese, Thin 'n Crispy, Pizza Hut	1/2 10" pie	*	450	25.0	15	7.0	125	54	450	4.5	1,200	750	0.30	0.51	5.0	1
318.	Pizza, Cheese, Thick 'n Chewy, Pizza Hut	1/2 10" pie	*	560	34.0	14	6.0	110	71	500	5.4	1,100	1,000	0.68	0.68	7.0	1
319.	Plums, Japanese and hybrid, raw	1 plum 2⅛" diam.	70	32	0.3	0	0.0	0	8	8	0.3	1	160	0.02	0.02	0.3	4
320.	Popcorn, cooked, oil	1 c	11	55	0.9	3	0.5	0	6	3	0.3	86	20	0.01	0.02	0.1	0
321.	Popcorn, popped, plain, large kernel	1 c	6	12	0.8	0	0.0	0	5	1	0.2	0	0	0.00	0.01	0.1	0
322.	Pork, roast, trimmed	2 slices 3 oz.	85	179	24.0	8	2.2	65	0	11	3.1	863	0	0.55	0.22	4.3	0
323.	Pork, sausage, cooked	1 sm link	17	72	2.8	6	2.1	13	1	0	0.3	221	0	0.00	0.00	0.0	0
324.	Potato, au gratin	1 c	245	228	5.6	10	6.3	12	32	203	0.8	1,076	380	0.05	0.20	2.3	8
325.	Potato, baked in skin	1 potato 2⅓ x 4¼"	202	145	4.0	0	0.0	0	33	14	1.1	6	0	0.15	0.07	2.7	31
326.	Potato chips	10 chips	20	114	1.1	8	2.1	0	10	8	0.4	150	0	0.04	0.01	1.0	3
327.	Potato, French fried long	10 strips 3½-4"	78	214	3.4	10	1.7	0	28	12	1.0	5	0	0.10	0.06	2.4	16

Table A.1

Nutritive Value of Selected Foods (continued)

Code	Food	Amount	Weight gm	Calories	Protein gm	Fat gm	Sat. Fat gm	Cholesterol mg	Carbohydrate gm	Calcium mg	Iron mg	Sodium mg	Vit A I.U.	Thiamin (Vit B$_1$) mg	Riboflavin (Vit B$_2$) mg	Niacin mg	Vit C mg
328.	Potato, Hashbrowns, McDonald's	1 patty	55	144	1.4	9	3.0	4	15	5	0.4	325	6	0.06	0.01	0.8	4
329.	Potato, mashed, milk added	1/2 c	105	69	2.2	1	0.4	8	14	25	0.4	316	20	0.09	0.06	1.1	11
330.	Potato salad w/eggs, mayo	1/2 c	125	179	3.4	10	7.8	85	14	24	0.8	662	262	0.10	0.08	1.1	12
331.	Potato, hash brown	1/2 c	78	170	2.5	9	3.5	0	22	12	1.2	456	27	0.09	0.02	1.9	5
332.	Pretzel, thin, twists	1 oz.	28	113	2.8	1	0.3	0	23	8	0.6	456	0	0.09	0.07	1.2	0
333.	Prunes, dried "softenized" without pits	5 prunes	61	137	1.1	0	0.0	0	36	26	0.1	4	860	0.05	0.09	0.9	2
334.	Prune juice, canned or bottled	1/2 c	128	99	0.5	0	0.0	0	24	18	5.3	3	0	0.02	0.02	0.5	3
335.	Pudding, Chocolate, canned	5 oz.	142	205	3.0	11	9.5	1	30	74	1.2	285	155	0.04	0.17	0.6	0
336.	Pudding, Tapioca, canned	5 oz.	142	160	3.0	5	4.8	1	28	119	0.3	252	5	0.03	0.14	0.4	0
337.	Pudding, Vanilla, canned	5 oz.	142	220	2.0	10	9.5	1	33	79	0.2	305	1	0.03	0.12	0.6	0
338.	Quiche, Lorraine	1 piece	242	825	18.0	66	31.9	392	40	290	1.9	898	2,250	0.15	0.44	1.7	1
339.	Raisins, unbleached, seedless	1 oz.	28	82	0.7	0	0.0	0	22	18	1.0	8	10	0.03	0.02	0.1	0
340.	Raspberries, fresh	1 c	123	60	1.1	1	0.0	0	14	27	0.7	0	80	0.04	0.11	1.1	31
341.	Raspberries, frozen	1 c	250	255	1.7	1	0.0	0	62	38	1.6	3	75	0.05	0.11	1.5	41
342.	Rice, brown, cooked	1/2 c	96	116	2.5	1	0.0	0	25	12	0.5	275	0	0.09	0.02	1.3	0
343.	Rice, white enriched, cooked	1/2 c	103	113	2.1	0	0.0	0	25	11	0.9	384	0	0.12	0.01	1.1	0
344.	Rice, wild, cooked	1/2 c	100	92	3.6	0	0.0	0	19	5	1.1	2	0	0.1	0.16	1.6	0
345.	Roll, hard, white	1 roll	50	155	5.0	2	0.0	0	30	24	1.4	313	0	0.20	0.12	1.7	0
346.	Rueben sandwich	1	237	488	28.7	28	10.4	85	30	364	5.3	1,685	461	0.25	0.44	3.9	12
347.	Salad, Chef, Burger King	1 serving	273	178	17.0	9	4.0	103	7	128	1.6	568	4,750	0.35	0.26	3.6	15
348.	Salad, Chicken, Burger King	1 serving	258	142	20.0	4	1.0	49	8	32	1.3	443	4,600	0.14	0.17	8.5	20
349.	Salad, Chicken w/celery	1/2 c	78	266	10.5	25	4.1	48	1	16	0.7	199	153	0.03	0.08	3.3	1
350.	Salad, Tuna	1 c	205	375	33.0	19	3.3	80	19	31	2.5	877	53	0.06	0.14	13.3	6
351.	Salami, dry	1 oz.	28	128	7.0	11	1.6	24	0	4	1.0	349	0	0.10	0.07	1.5	0
352.	Salmon, broiled with butter or margarine	3 oz.	85	156	23.0	6	2.2	53	0	0	0.9	99	150	0.15	0.06	8.4	0
353.	Salmon, canned Chinook	3 oz.	85	179	16.6	12	0.8	30	0	131	0.7	105	197	0.03	0.01	6.2	0
354.	Sardines, canned drained	1 oz.	28	58	7.0	3	1.0	20	0	124	0.8	233	60	0.0	0.06	1.5	0
355.	Sauerkraut, canned	1/2 c	118	21	1.2	0	0.0	0	5	43	0.6	878	60	0.04	0.05	0.3	17
356.	Scallops, breaded, cooked	6 pieces	90	195	15.0	10	2.5	70	10	39	2.0	298	105	0.1	0.11	1.6	0
357.	Sherbet	1/2 c	97	135	1.1	2	1.3	7	29	52	0.2	44	92	0.02	0.04	0.1	2
358.	Shrimp, boiled	3 oz.	85	99	18.0	1	0.1	128	1	99	2.7	0	60	0.00	0.03	1.5	0
359.	Shrimp, fried	7 medium	85	200	16.0	10	2.5	168	11	61	2.0	384	130	0.06	0.09	2.8	0
360.	Snickers bar	1 bar	61	290	6.6	4	5.4	0	37	70	0.5	170	25	0.03	0.11	1.8	0
361.	Soda pop, cola	12 oz.	369	144	0.0	0	0.0	0	37	27	0.0	30	0	0.00	0.00	0.0	0
362.	Soda pop, diet	12 oz.	340	2	0.1	0	0.0	0	0	13	0.1	31	0	0.00	0.00	0.0	0
363.	Soda pop, Ginger ale	12 oz.	366	113	0.0	0	0.0	0	29	0	0.0	45	0	0.00	0.00	0.0	0
364.	Soda pop, Lemon-lime	12 oz.	340	138	0.0	0	0.0	0	35	8	0.2	38	0	0.00	0.00	0.0	0
365.	Soda pop, Root beer	12 oz.	340	140	0.0	0	0.0	0	36	17	0.2	45	0	0.00	0.00	0.0	0
366.	Soup, Chicken, cream	1 c	248	191	7.5	12	4.6	27	15	180	0.7	1,046	710	0.07	0.26	0.9	1
367.	Soup, Chicken noodle	1 c	241	75	4.0	2	0.7	7	9	17	0.8	900	711	0.05	0.06	1.4	0
368.	Soup, Clam chowder, Manhattan	1 c	244	78	4.2	2	0.4	2	12	34	1.9	1,808	460	0.06	0.05	1.3	3

No.	Food	Serving															
369.	Soup, Clam chowder, north east	1 c	248	163	9.5	7	3.0	22	16	187	1.5	992	160	0.07	0.24	1.0	4
370.	Soup, Cream of mushroom condensed, prepared with equal volume of milk	1 c	245	216	7.0	14	5.4	15	16	191	0.5	955	250	0.05	0.34	0.7	1
371.	Soup, Minestrone	1 c	241	80	4.3	3	0.5	2	11	34	0.9	911	1,170	0.05	0.04	0.9	1
372.	Soup, Split pea, condensed, prepared with equal volume of water	1 c	245	145	9.0	3	1.1	0	21	29	1.5	941	440	0.25	0.15	1.5	1
373.	Soup, Tomato, condensed, prepared with equal volume of water	1 c	245	88	2.0	3	0.5	0	16	15	0.7	970	1,000	0.05	0.05	1.2	12
374.	Soup, Tomato with milk	1 c	248	160	6.0	6	2.9	17	22	159	1.8	932	850	0.13	0.25	1.5	68
375.	Soup, vegetable beef, condensed, prepared with equal volume of water	1 c	245	78	5.0	2	0.0	0	10	12	0.7	1,046	2,700	0.05	0.05	1.0	0
376.	Soup, Vegetarian vegetable	1 c	250	70	2.1	2	0.3	0	12	21	1.1	823	1,505	0.05	0.05	0.9	1
377.	Sour cream	1 tbsp	14	30	0.4	3	1.8	6	1	16	0.0	8	135	0.01	0.02	0.0	0
378.	Sour cream, imitation	1 tbsp.	14	29	0.3	3	2.5	0	1	0	0.0	14	0	0.00	0.00	0.0	0
379.	Spaghetti, in tomato sauce with cheese	1 c	250	260	8.8	9	2.0	10	37	80	2.3	955	1,080	0.25	0.18	2.3	13
380.	Spaghetti, plain, cooked	1 c	140	155	5.0	1	0.1	0	32	11	1.7	1	0	0.20	0.11	1.5	0
381.	Spaghetti, whole wheat, cooked	1 c	125	151	6.6	1	0.1	0	32	19	1.1	16	0	0.21	0.09	1.5	0
382.	Spaghetti, with meatballs and tomato sauce	1 c	248	332	18.6	11.7	3.0	75	39	124	3.7	1,009	1,590	0.25	0.30	4.0	22
383.	Spareribs, cooked	3 oz.	85	377	17.8	33	12.0	73	0	8	2.2	31	0	0.37	0.18	2.9	0
384.	Spinach, canned, drained	1/2 c	103	25	2.3	1	0.0	0	4	121	2.6	242	8,200	0.02	0.12	0.3	15
385.	Spinach, froz., cooked, drained	1/2 c	103	24	3.1	0	0.0	0	4	116	2.2	54	8,100	0.07	0.16	0.4	20
386.	Spinach, raw, chopped	1 c	55	14	1.8	0	0.0	0	2	51	1.7	39	4,460	0.06	0.11	0.3	28
387.	Squash, summer, cooked	1/2 c	90	13	0.8	0	0.0	0	3	23	0.4	1	350	0.05	0.07	0.7	9
388.	Squash, winter, baked mashed	1/2 c	103	70	1.9	0	0.0	0	18	41	1.0	1	6,560	0.05	0.14	0.7	8
389.	Strawberries, frozen, sweetened	1 c	250	245	1.4	0	0.0	0	66	28	1.5	8	31	0.04	0.13	1.0	106
390.	Strawberries, raw	1 c	149	55	1.0	1	0.0	0	13	31	1.5	1	90	0.04	0.10	0.9	88
391.	Stuffing, bread, prepared	1/2 c	70	250	4.6	15	3.1	0	25	46	1.1	627	455	0.09	0.10	1.3	0
392.	Sundae, choc. Dairy Queen	medium	184	300	6.0	7	4.9	79	53	200	1.1	175	300	0.06	0.26	0.0	0
393.	Sugar, brown granulated	1 tsp	5	17	0.0	0	0.0	0	5	4	0.1	0	0	0.00	0.00	0.1	0
394.	Sugar, white granulated	1 tsp	4	15	0.0	0	0.0	0	4	0	0.0	0	0	0.00	0.00	0.0	0
395.	Sweet potato, baked	1 potato 5" long	146	161	2.4	1	0.0	0	37	46	1.0	14	9,230	0.10	0.08	0.8	25
396.	Syrup (maple)	1 tbsp	20	50	0.0	0	0.0	0	13	33	0.2	3	0	0.00	0.00	0.0	0
397.	Taco shell	1 shell	10	60	1.1	3	0.3	0	9	26	0.3	62	36	0.00	0.01	0.3	0
398.	Taco, Taco Bell	1	83	186	15.0	8	0.0	0	14	120	2.4	79	120	0.09	0.16	2.9	0
399.	Tangerine	1 med 2⅛" diam.	116	39	0.7	0	0.0	0	10	34	0.3	2	360	0.05	0.02	0.1	27
400.	Tartar sauce	1 tbsp.	14	74	0.2	8	1.2	4	1	3	0.1	182	54	0.00	0.00	0.0	0
401.	Tea, brewed	1/4 c	180	0	0.0	0	0.0	0	0	0	0.0	0	0	0.00	0.00	0.0	0
402.	Tomato juice, canned	1 c	244	42	1.9	0	0.1	0	10	22	1.4	881	1,357	0.12	0.08	1.6	45
403.	Tomato sauce (catsup)	1 tbsp	15	16	0.3	0	0.0	0	4	3	0.1	156	105	0.01	0.01	0.2	2
404.	Tomato, canned	1/2 c	121	26	1.2	0	0.0	0	5	7	0.6	157	1,085	0.06	0.04	0.9	21
405.	Tomato, raw	1 tomato 3½ oz.	100	20	1.0	0	0.0	0	4	12	0.5	3	820	0.05	0.04	0.6	21
406.	Tortilla chips	1 oz.	28	139	2.2	8	1.1	0	17	82	1.0	140	7	0.01	0.02	0.2	0

— *Table A.1*
Nutritive Value of Selected Foods (continued)

Code	Food	Amount	Weight gm	Calories	Protein gm	Fat gm	Sat. Fat gm	Cholesterol mg	Carbohydrate gm	Calcium mg	Iron mg	Sodium mg	Vit A I.U.	Thiamin (Vit B₁) mg	Riboflavin (Vit B₂) mg	Niacin mg	Vit C mg
407.	Tortilla, corn, lime	1 6" diam.	30	63	1.5	1	0.0	0	14	60	0.9	0	6	0.04	0.02	0.3	0
408.	Tortilla, flour	1	35	105	2.6	3	0.4	0	19	21	0.5	134	0	0.13	0.08	1.2	0
409.	Tostada	1	148	206	9.2	18	3.0	14	25	167	1.8	200	445	0.06	0.13	0.8	6
410.	Trout, broiled w/butter, lemon	3 oz.	85	175	21.0	9	4.1	71	0	26	1.0	122	300	0.07	0.07	2.3	1
411.	Tuna, canned, oil pack, drained	3 oz.	85	167	25.0	7	1.7	60	0	7	1.6	0	70	0.04	0.10	10.1	0
412.	Tuna, canned, water pack, solids and liquid	3½ oz.	99	126	27.7	1	0.0	55	0	16	1.6	161	0	0.0C	0.10	13.2	0
413.	Turkey, roast (light and dark mixed)	3 oz.	85	162	27.0	5	1.5	73	0	7	1.5	111	0	0.04	0.15	6.5	0
414.	Turnip, cooked, drained	1/2 c cubed	78	18	0.6	0	0.0	0	4	27	0.3	27	0	0.03	0.04	0.3	17
415.	Turnip greens, cooked drained	1/2 c	73	19	2.1	0	0.0	0	3	98	1.3	14	5,695	0.04	0.08	0.4	16
416.	Veal, cooked loin	3 oz.	85	199	22.0	11	4.0	90	0	9	2.7	55	0	0.06	0.21	4.6	0
417.	Veal cutlet, braised, broiled	3 oz.	85	185	23.0	9	4.0	109	0	9	0.8	56	5	0.06	0.21	4.6	0
418.	Vegetables, mixed, cooked	1 c	182	116	5.8	0	0.0	0	24	46	2.4	348	4,505	0.02	0.13	2.0	15
419.	Waffles	1 waffle	75	205	6.9	8	2.7	59	27	179	1.2	515	49	0.14	0.23	0.9	0
420.	Watermelon	1 c diced	160	42	0.8	0	0.0	0	10	11	0.8	2	940	0.05	0.05	0.3	11
421.	Wheat germ, plain toasted	1 tbsp	6	23	1.8	1	0.0	0	3	3	0.5	0	10	0.11	0.05	0.3	1
422.	Whiskey, gin, rum, vodka 90 proof	1/2 11 oz (jigger)	42	110	0	0	0.0	0	0	0	0.0	0	0	0.00	0.00	0.0	0
423.	Whopper, Burger King	1 sandwich	270	614	27.0	36	12.0	90	45	64	4.9	865	550	0.34	0.41	6.1	12
424.	Whopper with cheese, Burger King	1 sandwich	294	706	32.0	44	16.0	115	47	176	4.9	1,177	950	0.34	0.48	6.1	12
425.	Whopper, double, Burger King	1 sandwich	351	844	45.0	53	19.0	169	45	72	7.2	933	550	0.35	0.56	9.4	12
426.	Wine, dry table 12% alc.	3½ fl. oz.	102	87	0.1	0	0.0	0	4	9	0.4	5	0	0.00	0.01	0.1	0
427.	Wine, red dry 18.8% alc.	2 fl. oz.	59	81	0.1	0	0.0	0	5	5	0.0	4	0	0.01	0.02	0.2	0
428.	Yeast, brewers	1 tbsp	8	23	3.1	0	0.0	0	3	17	1.4	10	0	1.25	0.34	3.0	0
429.	Yogurt, fruit	1 c	227	231	9.9	2	1.6	10	43	345	0.2	125	104	0.08	0.40	0.2	2
430.	Yogurt, plain low fat	1 8-oz. container	226	113	7.7	4	2.3	15	12	271	0.1	115	150	0.09	0.41	0.2	2

"0" represents both less than 1 and 0

Sources:

Nutritive Value of American Foods in Common Units. *Agriculture Handbook No. 456.* U.S. Dept. of Agriculture. Washington, D.C. 1988.

Young, E. A., E. H. Brennan, and C. L. Irving, Guest Eds. Perspectives on Fast Foods. *Public Health Currents,* 19(1), 1979, Published by Ross Laboratories, Columbus, OH.

Dennison, D. *The Dine System: the Nutrition Plan For Better Health.* C. V. Mosby Company St. Louis, Missouri, 1982.

Pennington, S. A. T. and H. N. Church. *Food Values of Portions Commonly Used.* Harper and Row Publishers, New York, 1985.

Kullman, D. A. *ABC Milligram Cholesterol Diet Guide.* Merit Publications, Inc. North Miami Beach, Florida 1978.

Food Processor nutrient analysis software by Esha Corporation, P.O. Box 13028, Salem, Oregon, 97309. With permission.

Appendix B

The Recommended Quality and Quantity of Exercise for Developing and Maintaining Cardiorespiratory and Muscular Fitness in Healthy Adults*

AMERICAN COLLEGE of SPORTS MEDICINE

POSITION STAND

The Recommended Quantity and Quality of Exercise for Developing and Maintaining Cardiorespiratory and Muscular Fitness in Healthy Adults

This Position Stand replaces the 1978 ACSM position paper, "The Recommended Quantity and Quality of Exercise for Developing and Maintaining Fitness in Healthy Adults."

Increasing numbers of persons are becoming involved in endurance training and other forms of physical activity, and, thus, the need for guidelines for exercise prescription is apparent. Based on the existing evidence concerning exercise prescription for healthy adults and the need for guidelines, the American College of Sports Medicine (ACSM) makes the following recommendations for the quantity and quality of training for developing and maintaining cardiorespiratory fitness, body composition, and muscular strength and endurance in the healthy adult:

1. Frequency of training: 3–5 $d \cdot wk^{-1}$.

2. Intensity of training: 60–90% of maximum heart rate (HR_{max}), or 50–85% of maximum oxygen uptake ($\dot{V}O_{2max}$) or HR_{max} reserve.[1]

3. Duration of training: 20–60 min of continuous aerobic activity. Duration is dependent on the intensity of the activity; thus, lower intensity activity should be conducted over a longer period of time. Because of the importance of "total fitness" and the fact that it is more readily attained in longer duration programs, and because of the potential hazards and compliance problems associated with high intensity activity, lower to moderate intensity activity of longer duration is recommended for the nonathletic adult.

4. Mode of activity: any activity that uses large muscle groups, can be maintained continuously, and is rhythmical and aerobic in nature, e.g., walking-hiking, running-jogging, cycling-bicycling, cross-country skiing, dancing, rope skipping, rowing, stair climbing, swimming, skating, and various endurance game activities.

5. Resistance training: Strength training of a moderate intensity, sufficient to develop and maintain fat-free weight (FFW), should be an integral part of an adult fitness program. One set of 8–12 repetitions of eight to ten exercises that condition the major muscle groups at least 2 $d \cdot wk^{-1}$ is the recommended minimum.

RATIONALE AND RESEARCH BACKGROUND

Introduction

The questions "How much exercise is enough," and "What type of exercise is best for developing and maintaining fitness?" are frequently asked. It is recognized that the term "physical fitness" is composed of a variety of characteristics included in the broad categories of cardiovascular-respiratory fitness, body composition, muscular strength and endurance, and flexibility. In this context fitness is defined as the ability to perform moderate to vigorous levels of physical activity without undue fatigue and the capability of maintaining such ability throughout life (167). It is also recognized that the adaptive response to training is complex and includes peripheral, central, structural, and functional factors (5,172). Although many such variables and their adaptive response to training have been documented, the lack of sufficient in-depth and comparative data relative to frequency, intensity, and duration of training makes them inadequate to use as comparative models. Thus, in respect to the above questions, fitness is limited mainly to changes in $\dot{V}O_{2max}$, muscular strength and endurance, and body composition, which includes total body mass, fat weight (FW), and FFW. Further, the rationale and research background used for this position stand will be divided into programs for cardiorespiratory fitness and weight control and programs for muscular strength and endurance.

Fitness versus health benefits of exercise. Since the original position statement was published in 1978, an important distinction has been made between physical activity as it relates to health versus fitness. It has been pointed out that the quantity and quality of ex-

---

[1] Maximum heart rate reserve is calculated from the difference between resting and maximum heart rate. To estimate training intensity, a percentage of this value is added to the resting heart rate and is expressed as a percentage of HR_{max} reserve (85).

ercise needed to attain health-related benefits may differ from what is recommended for fitness benefits. It is now clear that lower levels of physical activity than recommended by this position statement may reduce the risk for certain chronic degenerative diseases and yet may not be of sufficient quantity or quality to improve $\dot{V}O_{2max}$ (71,72,98,167). ACSM recognizes the potential health benefits of regular exercise performed more frequently and for a longer duration, but at lower intensities than prescribed in this position statement (13A,71,100,120,160). ACSM will address the issue concerning the proper amount of physical activity necessary to derive health benefits in another statement.

Need for standardization of procedures and reporting results. Despite an abundance of information available concerning the training of the human organism, the lack of standardization of testing protocols and procedures, of methodology in relation to training procedures and experimental design, and of a preciseness in the documentation and reporting of the quantity and quality of training prescribed make interpretation difficult (123,133,139,164,167). Interpretation and comparison of results are also dependent on the initial level of fitness (42,43,58,114,148,151,156), length of time of the training experiment (17,45,125,128,139, 145,150), and specificity of the testing and training (5,43,130,139,145A,172). For example, data from training studies using subjects with varied levels of $\dot{V}O_{2max}$, total body mass, and FW have found changes to occur in relation to their initial values (14,33,109, 112,113,148,151); i.e., the lower the initial $\dot{V}O_{2max}$ the larger the percentage of improvement found, and the higher the FW the greater the reduction. Also, data evaluating trainability with age, comparison of the different magnitudes and quantities of effort, and comparison of the trainability of men and women may have been influenced by the initial fitness levels.

In view of the fact that improvement in the fitness variables discussed in this position statement continues over many months of training (27,86,139,145,150), it is reasonable to believe that short-term studies conducted over a few weeks have certain limitations. Middle-aged sedentary and older participants may take several weeks to adapt to the initial rigors of training, and thus need a longer adaptation period to get the full benefit from a program. For example, Seals et al. (150) exercise trained 60–69-yr-olds for 12 months. Their subjects showed a 12% improvement in $\dot{V}O_{2max}$ after 6 months of moderate intensity walking training. A further 18% increase in $\dot{V}O_{2max}$ occurred during the next 6 months of training when jogging was introduced. How long a training experiment should be conducted is difficult to determine, but 15–20 wk may be a good minimum standard. Although it is difficult to control exercise training experiments for more than 1 yr, there is a need to study this effect. As stated earlier, lower

doses of exercise may improve $\dot{V}O_{2max}$ and control or maintain body composition, but at a slower rate.

Although most of the information concerning training described in this position statement has been conducted on men, the available evidence indicates that women tend to adapt to endurance training in the same manner as men (19,38,46,47,49,62,65,68,90,92,122, 166).

Exercise Prescription for Cardiorespiratory Fitness and Weight Control

Exercise prescription is based upon the frequency, intensity, and duration of training, the mode of activity (aerobic in nature, e.g., listed under No. 4 above), and the initial level of fitness. In evaluating these factors, the following observations have been derived from studies conducted for up to 6–12 months with endurance training programs.

Improvement in $\dot{V}O_{2max}$ is directly related to frequency (3,6,50,75–77,125,126,152,154,164), intensity (3,6,26,29,58,61,75–77,80,85,93,118,152,164), and duration (3,29,60,61,70,75–77,101,109,118,152,162, 164,168) of training. Depending upon the quantity and quality of training, improvement in $\dot{V}O_{2max}$ ranges from 5 to 30% (8,29,30,48,59,61,65,67,69,75–77,82,84,96, 99,101,102,111,115,119,123,127,139,141,143,149, 150,152,153,158,164,168,173). These studies show that a minimum increase in $\dot{V}O_{2max}$ of 15% is generally attained in programs that meet the above stated guidelines. Although changes in $\dot{V}O_{2max}$ greater than 30% have been shown, they are usually associated with large total body mass and FW loss, in cardiac patients, or in persons with a very low initial level of fitness. Also, as a result of leg fatigue or a lack of motivation, persons with low initial fitness may have spuriously low initial $\dot{V}O_{2max}$ values. Klissouras (94A) and Bouchard (16A) have shown that human variation in the trainability of $\dot{V}O_{2max}$ is important and related to current phenotype level. That is, there is a genetically determined pretraining status of the trait and capacity to adapt to physical training. Thus, physiological results should be interpreted with respect to both genetic variation and the quality and quantity of training performed.

Intensity-duration. Intensity and duration of training are interrelated, with total amount of work accomplished being an important factor in improvement in fitness (12,20,27,48,90,92,123,127,128,136,149,151,164). Although more comprehensive inquiry is necessary, present evidence suggests that, when exercise is performed above the minimum intensity threshold, the total amount of work accomplished is an important factor in fitness development (19,27,126,127,149,151) and maintenance (134). That is, improvement will be similar for activities performed at a lower intensity-longer duration compared to higher intensity-shorter duration if the total energy costs of the activities are equal. Higher intensity exercise is associated with greater cardiovascular risk (156A), orthopedic injury (124,139) and lower compliance to training than lower intensity exercise (36,105,124,146). Therefore, programs emphasizing low to moderate intensity training with longer duration are recommended for most adults.

The minimal training intensity threshold for improvement in $\dot{V}O_{2max}$ is approximately 60% of the HR_{max} (50% of $\dot{V}O_{2max}$ or HR_{max} reserve) (80,85). The 50% of HR_{max} reserve represents a heart rate of approximately 130–135 beats·min^{-1} for young persons. As a result of the age-related change in maximum heart rate, the absolute heart rate to achieve this threshold is inversely related to age and can be as low as 105–115 beats·min^{-1} for older persons (35,65,150). Patients who are taking beta-adrenergic blocking drugs may have significantly lower heart rate values (171). Initial level of fitness is another important consideration in prescribing exercise (26,90,104,148,151). The person with a low fitness level can achieve a significant training effect with a sustained training heart rate as low as 40–50% of HR_{max} reserve, while persons with higher fitness levels require a higher training stimulus (35,58,152,164).

Classification of exercise intensity. The classification of exercise intensity and its standardization for exercise prescription based on a 20–60 min training session has been confusing, misinterpreted, and often taken out of context. The most quoted exercise classification system is based on the energy expenditure (kcal·min^{-1}·kg^{-1}) of industrial tasks (40,89). The original data for this classification system were published by Christensen (24) in 1953 and were based on the energy expenditure of working in the steel mill for an 8-h day. The classification of industrial and leisure-time tasks by using absolute values of energy expenditure have been valuable for use in the occupational and nutritional setting. Although this classification system has broad application in medicine and, in particular, making recommendations for weight control and job placement, it has little or no meaning for preventive and rehabilitation exercise training programs. To extrapolate absolute values of energy expenditure for completing an industrial task based on an 8-h work day to 20–60 min regimens of exercise training does not make sense. For example, walking and jogging/running can be accomplished at a wide range of speeds; thus, the relative intensity becomes important under these conditions. Because the endurance training regimens recommended by ACSM for nonathletic adults are geared for 60 min or less of physical activity, the system of classification of exercise training intensity shown in Table 1 is recommended (139). The use of a realistic time period for training and an individual's relative exercise intensity makes this system amenable to young,

TABLE 1. Classification of intensity of exercise based on 20–60 min of endurance training.

Relative Intensity (%)		Rating of Perceived Exertion	Classification of Intensity
HR_{max}*	$\dot{V}O_{2max}$* or HR_{max} reserve		
<35%	<30%	<10	Very light
35–59%	30–49%	10–11	Light
60–79%	50–74%	12–13	Moderate (somewhat hard)
80–89%	75–84%	14–16	Heavy
≥90%	≥85%	>16	Very heavy

Table from Pollock, M. L. and J. H. Wilmore. *Exercise in Health and Disease: Evaluation and Prescription for Prevention and Rehabilitation*, 2nd Ed. Philadelphia: W.B. Saunders, 1990. Published with permission.
* HR_{max} = maximum heart rate; $\dot{V}O_{2max}$ = maximum oxygen uptake.

middle-aged, and elderly participants, as well as patients with a limited exercise capacity (3,137,139).

Table 1 also describes the relationship between relative intensity based on percent HR_{max}, percentage of HR_{max} reserve or percentage of $\dot{V}O_{2max}$, and the rating of perceived exertion (RPE) (15,16,137). The use of heart rate as an estimate of intensity of training is the common standard (3,139).

The use of RPE has become a valid tool in the monitoring of intensity in exercise training programs (11,37,137,139). It is generally considered an adjunct to heart rate in monitoring relative exercise intensity, but once the relationship between heart rate and RPE is known, RPE can be used in place of heart rate (23,139). This would not be the case in certain patient populations where a more precise knowledge of heart rate may be critical to the safety of the program.

Frequency. The amount of improvement in $\dot{V}O_{2max}$ tends to plateau when frequency of training is increased above 3 d·wk^{-1} (50,123,139). The value of the added improvement found with training more than 5 d·wk^{-1} is small to not apparent in regard to improvement in $\dot{V}O_{2max}$ (75–77,106,123). Training of less than 2 d·wk^{-1} does not generally show a meaningful change in $\dot{V}O_{2max}$ (29,50,118,123,152,164).

Mode. If frequency, intensity, and duration of training are similar (total kcal expenditure), the training adaptations appear to be independent of the mode of aerobic activity (101A,118,130). Therefore, a variety of endurance activities, e.g., those listed above, may be used to derive the same training effect.

Endurance activities that require running and jumping are considered high impact types of activity and generally cause significantly more debilitating injuries to beginning as well as long-term exercisers than do low impact and non-weight bearing type activities (13,93, 117,124,127,135,140,142). This is particularly evident in the elderly (139). Beginning joggers have increased foot, leg, and knee injuries when training is performed more than 3 d·wk^{-1} and longer than 30 min duration per exercise session (135). High intensity interval training (run-walk) compared to continuous jogging training was also associated with a higher incidence of injury (124,136). Thus, caution should be taken when recommending the type of activity and exercise prescription for the beginning exerciser. Orthopedic injuries as related to overuse increase linearly in runners/joggers when performing these activities (13,140). Thus, there is a need for more inquiry into the effect that different types of activities and the quantity and quality of training has on injuries over short-term and long-term participation.

An activity such as weight training should not be considered as a means of training for developing $\dot{V}O_{2max}$, but it has significant value for increasing muscular strength and endurance and FFW (32,54,107, 110,165). Studies evaluating circuit weight training (weight training conducted almost continuously with moderate weights, using 10–15 repetitions per exercise session with 15–30 s rest between bouts of activity) show an average improvement in $\dot{V}O_{2max}$ of 6% (1,51–54,83,94,108,170). Thus, circuit weight training is not recommended as the only activity used in exercise programs for developing $\dot{V}O_{2max}$.

Age. Age in itself does not appear to be a deterrent to endurance training. Although some earlier studies showed a lower training effect with middle-aged or elderly participants (9,34,79,157,168), more recent studies show the relative change in $\dot{V}O_{2max}$ to be similar to younger age groups (7,8,65,132,150,161,163). Although more investigation is necessary concerning the rate of improvement in $\dot{V}O_{2max}$ with training at various ages, at present it appears that elderly participants need longer periods of time to adapt (34,132,150). Earlier studies showing moderate to no improvement in $\dot{V}O_{2max}$ were conducted over a short time span (9), or exercise was conducted at a moderate to low intensity (34), thus making the interpretation of the results difficult.

Although $\dot{V}O_{2max}$ decreases with age and total body mass and FW increase with age, evidence suggests that this trend can be altered with endurance training (22,27,86–88,139). A 9% reduction in $\dot{V}O_{2max}$ per decade for sedentary adults after age 25 has been shown (31,73), but for active individuals the reduction may be less than 5% per decade (21,31,39,73). Ten or more yr follow-up studies where participants continued training at a similar level showed maintenance of cardiorespiratory fitness (4,87,88,138). A cross-sectional study of older competitive runners showed progressively lower values in $\dot{V}O_{2max}$ from the fourth to seventh decades of life, but also showed less training in the older groups (129). More recent 10-yr follow-up data on these same athletes (50–82 yr of age) showed $\dot{V}O_{2max}$ to be unchanged when training quantity and quality remained unchanged (138). Thus, lifestyle plays a significant role in the maintenance of fitness. More inquiry into the relationship of long-term training (quantity and quality), for both competitors and noncompetitors, and physiological function with increasing age is necessary before more definitive statements can be made.

Maintenance of training effect. In order to maintain the training effect, exercise must be continued on a regular basis (18,25,28,47,97,111,144,147). A significant reduction in cardiorespiratory fitness occurs after 2 wk of detraining (25,144), with participants returning to near pretraining levels of fitness after 10 wk (47) to 8 months of detraining (97). A loss of 50% of their initial improvement in $\dot{V}O_{2max}$ has been shown after 4–12 wk of detraining (47,91,144). Those individuals who have undergone years of continuous training maintain some benefits for longer periods of detraining than subjects from short-term training studies (25). While stopping training shows dramatic reductions in $\dot{V}O_{2max}$, reduced training shows modest to no reductions for periods of 5–15 wk (18,75–77,144). Hickson et al., in a series of experiments where frequency (75), duration (76), or intensity (77) of training were manipulated, found that, if intensity of training remained unchanged, $\dot{V}O_{2max}$ was maintained for up to 15 wk when frequency and duration of training were reduced by as much as $^2/_3$. When frequency and duration of training remained constant and intensity of training was reduced by $^1/_3$ or $^2/_3$, $\dot{V}O_{2max}$ was significantly reduced. Similar findings were found in regards to reduced strength training exercise. When strength training exercise was reduced from 3 or 2 $d \cdot wk^{-1}$ to at least 1 $d \cdot wk^{-1}$, strength was maintained for 12 wk of reduced training (62). Thus, it appears that missing an exercise session periodically or reducing training for up to 15 wk will not adversely effect $\dot{V}O_{2max}$ or muscular strength and endurance as long as training intensity is maintained.

Even though many new studies have given added insight into the proper amount of exercise, investigation is necessary to evaluate the rate of increase and decrease of fitness when varying training loads and reduction in training in relation to level of fitness, age, and length of time in training. Also, more information is needed to better identify the minimal level of exercise necessary to maintain fitness.

Weight control and body composition. Although there is variability in human response to body composition change with exercise, total body mass and FW are generally reduced with endurance training programs (133,139,171A), while FFW remains constant (123,133,139,169) or increases slightly (116,174). For example, Wilmore (171A) reported the results of 32 studies that met the criteria for developing cardiorespiratory fitness that are outlined in this position stand and found an average loss in total body mass of 1.5 kg and percent fat of 2.2%. Weight loss programs using dietary manipulation that result in a more dramatic decrease in total body mass show reductions in both FW and FFW (2,78,174). When these programs are conducted in conjunction with exercise training, FFW loss is more modest than in programs using diet alone (78,121). Programs that are conducted at least 3 d·wk^{-1} (123,125,126,128,169), of at least 20 min duration (109,123,169), and of sufficient intensity to expend approximately 300 kcal per exercise session (75 kg person)[2] are suggested as a threshold level for total body mass and FW loss (27,64,77,123,133,139). An expenditure of 200 kcal per session has also been shown to be useful in weight reduction if the exercise frequency is at least 4 d·wk^{-1} (155). If the primary purpose of the training program is for weight loss, then regimens of greater frequency and duration of training and low to moderate intensity are recommended (2,139). Programs with less participation generally show little or no change in body composition (44,57,93,123,133,159, 162,169). Significant increases in $\dot{V}O_{2max}$ have been shown with 10–15 min of high intensity training (6,79,109,118,123,152,153); thus, if total body mass and FW reduction are not considerations, then shorter duration, higher intensity programs may be recommended for healthy individuals at low risk for cardiovascular disease and orthopedic injury.

Exercise Prescription for Muscular Strength and Endurance

The addition of resistance/strength training to the position statement results from the need for a well-rounded program that exercises all the major muscle groups of the body. Thus, the inclusion of resistance training in adult fitness programs should be effective in the development and maintenance of FFW. The effect of exercise training is specific to the area of the body being trained (5,43,145A,172). For example, training the legs will have little or no effect on the arms, shoulders, and trunk muscles. A 10-yr follow-up of master runners who continued their training regimen, but did no upper body exercise, showed maintenance of $\dot{V}O_{2max}$ and a 2-kg reduction in FFW (138). Their leg circumference remained unchanged, but arm circumference was significantly lower. These data indicate a loss of muscle mass in the untrained areas. Three of the athletes who practiced weight training exercise for the upper body and trunk muscles maintained their FFW. A comprehensive review by Sale (145A) carefully documents available information on specificity of training.

Specificity of training was further addressed by Graves et al. (63). Using a bilateral knee extension exercise, they trained four groups: group A, first ½ of the range of motion; group B, second ½ of the range of motion; group AB, full range of motion; and a control group that did not train. The results clearly showed that

the training result was specific to the range of motion trained, with group AB getting the best full range effect. Thus, resistance training should be performed through a full range of motion for maximum benefit (63,95).

Muscular strength and endurance are developed by the overload principle, i.e., by increasing more than normal the resistance to movement or frequency and duration of activity (32,41,43,74,145). Muscular strength is best developed by using heavy weights (that require maximum or nearly maximum tension development) with few repetitions, and muscular endurance is best developed by using lighter weights with a greater number of repetitions (10,41,43,145). To some extent, both muscular strength and endurance are developed under each condition, but each system favors a more specific type of development (43,145). Thus, to elicit improvement in both muscular strength and endurance, most experts recommend 8–12 repetitions per bout of exercise.

Any magnitude of overload will result in strength development, but higher intensity effort at or near maximal effort will give a significantly greater effect (43,74,101B,103,145,172). The intensity of resistance training can be manipulated by varying the weight load, repetitions, rest interval between exercises, and number of sets completed (43). Caution is advised for training that emphasizes lengthening (eccentric) contractions, compared to shortening (concentric) or isometric contractions, as the potential for skeletal muscle soreness and injury is accentuated (3A,84A).

Muscular strength and endurance can be developed by means of static (isometric) or dynamic (isotonic or isokinetic) exercises. Although each type of training has its favorable and weak points, for healthy adults, dynamic resistance exercises are recommended. Resistance training for the average participant should be rhythmical, performed at a moderate to slow speed, move through a full range of motion, and not impede normal forced breathing. Heavy resistance exercise can cause a dramatic acute increase in both systolic and diastolic blood pressure (100A,101C).

The expected improvement in strength from resistance training is difficult to assess because increases in strength are affected by the participants' initial level of strength and their potential for improvement (43,66,74,114,172). For example, Mueller and Rohmert (114) found increases in strength ranging from 2 to 9% per week depending on initial strength levels. Although the literature reflects a wide range of improvement in strength with resistance training programs, the average improvement for sedentary young and middle-aged men and women for up to 6 months of training is 25–30%. Fleck and Kraemer (43), in a review of 13 studies representing various forms of isotonic training, showed an average improvement in bench press strength of 23.3% when subjects were tested on the

---

[2] Haskell and Haskell et al. (71,72) have suggested the use of 4 kcal·kg^{-1} of body weight of energy expenditure per day for a minimum standard for use in exercise programs.

equipment with which they were trained and 16.5% when tested on special isotonic or isokinetic ergometers (six studies). Fleck and Kraemer (43) also reported an average increase in leg strength of 26.6% when subjects were tested with the equipment that they trained on (six studies) and 21.2% when tested with special isotonic or isokinetic ergometers (five studies). Results of improvement in strength resulting from isometric training have been of the same magnitude as found with isotonic training (17,43,62,63).

In light of the information reported above, the following guidelines for resistance training are recommended for the average healthy adult. A minimum of 8–10 exercises involving the major muscle groups should be performed a minimum of two times per week. A minimum of one set of 8–12 repetitions to near fatigue should be completed. These minimal standards for resistance training are based on two factors. First, the time it takes to complete a comprehensive, well-rounded exercise program is important. Programs lasting more than 60 min per session are associated with higher dropout rates (124). Second, although greater frequencies of training (17,43,56) and additional sets or combinations of sets and repetitions elicit larger strength gains (10,32,43,74,145,172), the magnitude of difference is usually small. For example, Braith et al. (17) compared training 2 d·wk^{-1} with 3 d·wk^{-1} for 18 wk. The subjects performed one set of 7–10 repetitions to fatigue. The 2 d·wk^{-1} group showed a 21% increase in strength compared to 28% in the 3 d·wk^{-1} group. In other words, 75% of what could be attained in a 3 d·wk^{-1} program was attained in 2 d·wk^{-1}. Also, the 21% improvement in strength found by the 2 d·wk^{-1} regimen is 70–80% of the improvement reported by other programs using additional frequencies of training and combinations of sets and repetitions (43). Graves et al. (62,63), Gettman et al. (55), Hurley et al. (83) and Braith et al. (17) found that programs using one set to fatigue showed a greater than 25% increase in strength. Although resistance training equipment may provide a

better graduated and quantitative stimulus for overload than traditional calisthenic exercises, calisthenics and other resistance types of exercise can still be effective in improving and maintaining strength.

SUMMARY

The combination of frequency, intensity, and duration of chronic exercise has been found to be effective for producing a training effect. The interaction of these factors provide the overload stimulus. In general, the lower the stimulus the lower the training effect, and the greater the stimulus the greater the effect. As a result of specificity of training and the need for maintaining muscular strength and endurance, and flexibility of the major muscle groups, a well-rounded training program including resistance training and flexibility exercises is recommended. Although age in itself is not a limiting factor to exercise training, a more gradual approach in applying the prescription at older ages seems prudent. It has also been shown that endurance training of fewer than 2 d·wk^{-1}, at less than 50% of maximum oxygen uptake and for less than 10 min·d^{-1}, is inadequate for developing and maintaining fitness for healthy adults.

In the interpretation of this position statement, it must be recognized that the recommendations should be used in the context of participants' needs, goals, and initial abilities. In this regard, a sliding scale as to the amount of time allotted and intensity of effort should be carefully gauged for both the cardiorespiratory and muscular strength and endurance components of the program. An appropriate warm-up and cool-down, which would include flexibility exercises, is also recommended. The important factor is to design a program for the individual to provide the proper amount of physical activity to attain maximal benefit at the lowest risk. Emphasis should be placed on factors that result in permanent lifestyle change and encourage a lifetime of physical activity.

REFERENCES

1. ALLEN, T. E., R. J. BYRD, and D. P. SMITH. Hemodynamic consequences of circuit weight training. *Res. Q.* 43:299–306, 1976.
2. AMERICAN COLLEGE OF SPORTS MEDICINE. Proper and improper weight loss programs. *Med. Sci. Sports Exerc.* 15:ix–xiii, 1983.
3. AMERICAN COLLEGE OF SPORTS MEDICINE. *Guidelines for Graded Exercise Testing and Exercise Prescription*, 3rd Ed. Philadelphia: Lea and Febiger, 1986.
3A. ARMSTRONG, R. B. Mechanisms of exercise-induced delayed onset muscular soreness: a brief review. *Med. Sci. Sports Exerc.* 16:529–538, 1984.
4. ÅSTRAND, P. O. Exercise physiology of the mature athlete. In: *Sports Medicine for the Mature Athlete*, J. R. Sutton and R. M. Brock (Eds.). Indianapolis, IN: Benchmark Press, Inc., 1986, pp. 3–16.
5. ÅSTRAND, P. O. and K. RODAHL. *Textbook of Work Physiology*,

3rd Ed. New York: McGraw-Hill, 1986, pp. 412–485.
6. ATOMI, Y., K. ITO, H. IWASASKI, and M. MIYASHITA. Effects of intensity and frequency of training on aerobic work capacity of young females. *J. Sports Med.* 18:3–9, 1978.
7. BADENHOP, D. T., P. A. CLEARY, S. F. SCHAAL, E. L. FOX, and R. L. BARTELS. Physiological adjustments to higher- or lower-intensity exercise in elders. *Med. Sci. Sports Exerc.* 15:496–502, 1983.
8. BARRY, A. J., J. W. DALY, E. D. R. PRUETT, et al. The effects of physical conditioning on older individuals. I. Work capacity, circulatory-respiratory function, and work electrocardiogram. *J. Gerontol.* 21:182–191, 1966.
9. BENESTAD, A. M. Trainability of old men. *Acta Med. Scand.* 178:321–327, 1965.
10. BERGER, R. A. Effect of varied weight training programs on strength. *Res. Q.* 33:168–181, 1962.

11. BIRK, T. J. and C. A. BIRK. Use of ratings of perceived exertion for exercise prescription. *Sports Med.* 4:1–8, 1987.

12. BLAIR, S. N., J. V. CHANDLER, D. B. ELLISOR, and J. LANGLEY. Improving physical fitness by exercise training programs. *South. Med. J.* 73:1594–1596, 1980.

13. BLAIR, S. N., H. W. KOHL, and N. N. GOODYEAR. Rates and risks for running and exercise injuries: studies in three populations. *Res. Q. Exerc. Sports* 58:221–228, 1987.

13A. BLAIR, S. N., H. W. KOHL, III, R. S. PAFFENBARGER, D. G. CLARK, K. H. COOPER, and L. H. GIBBONS. Physical fitness and all-cause mortality. A prospective study of healthy men and women. *J.A.M.A.* 262:2395–2401, 1989.

14. BOILEAU, R. A., E. R. BUSKIRK, D. H. HORSTMAN, J. MENDEZ, and W. NICHOLAS. Body composition changes in obese and lean men during physical conditioning. *Med. Sci. Sports* 3:183–189, 1971.

15. BORG, G. A. V. Psychophysical bases of perceived exertion. *Med. Sci. Sports Exerc.* 14:377–381, 1982.

16. BORG, G. and D. OTTOSON (Eds.). *The Perception of Exertion in Physical Work.* London, England: The MacMillan Press, Ltd., 1986, pp. 4–7.

16A. BOUCHARD, C. Gene-environment interaction in human adaptability. In: *The Academy Papers,* R. B. Malina and H. M. Eckert (Eds.). Champaign, IL: Human Kinetics Publishers, 1988, pp. 56–66.

17. BRAITH, R. W., J. E. GRAVES, M. L. POLLOCK, S. L. LEGGETT, D. M. CARPENTER, and A. B. COLVIN. Comparison of two versus three days per week of variable resistance training during 10 and 18 week programs. *Int. J. Sports Med.* 10:450–454, 1989.

18. BRYNTESON, P. and W. E. SINNING. The effects of training frequencies on the retention of cardiovascular fitness. *Med. Sci. Sports* 5:29–33, 1973.

19. BURKE, E. J. Physiological effects of similar training programs in males and females. *Res. Q.* 48:510–517, 1977.

20. BURKE, E. J. and B. D. FRANKS. Changes in $\dot{V}O_{2max}$ resulting from bicycle training at different intensities holding total mechanical work constant. *Res. Q.* 46:31–37, 1975.

21. BUSKIRK, E. R. and J. L. HODGSON. Age and aerobic power: the rate of change in men and women. *Fed. Proc.* 46:1824–1829, 1987.

22. CARTER, J. E. L. and W. H. PHILLIPS. Structural changes in exercising middle-aged males during a 2-year period. *J. Appl. Physiol.* 27:787–794, 1969.

23. CHOW, J. R. and J. H. WILMORE. The regulation of exercise intensity by ratings of perceived exertion. *J. Cardiac Rehabil.* 4:382–387, 1984.

24. CHRISTENSEN, E. H. Physiological evaluation of work in the Nykroppa iron works. In: *Ergonomics Society Symposium on Fatigue,* W. F. Floyd and A. T. Welford (Eds.). London, England: Lewis, 1953, pp. 93–108.

25. COYLE, E. F., W. H. MARTIN, D. R. SINACORE, M. J. JOYNER, J. M. HAGBERG, and J. O. HOLLOSZY. Time course of loss of adaptation after stopping prolonged intense endurance training. *J. Appl. Physiol.* 57:1857–1864, 1984.

26. CREWS, T. R. and J. A. ROBERTS. Effects of interaction of frequency and intensity of training. *Res. Q.* 47:48–55, 1976.

27. CURETON, T. K. *The Physiological Effects of Exercise Programs upon Adults.* Springfield, IL: Charles C. Thomas Co., 1969, pp. 3–6, 33–77.

28. CURETON, T. K. and E. E. PHILLIPS. Physical fitness changes in middle-aged men attributable to equal eight-week periods of training, non-training and retraining. *J. Sports Med. Phys. Fitness* 4:1–7, 1964.

29. DAVIES, C. T. M. and A. V. KNIBBS. The training stimulus, the effects of intensity, duration and frequency of effort on maximum aerobic power output. *Int. Z. Angew. Physiol.* 29:299–305, 1971.

30. DAVIS, J. A., M. H. FRANK, B. J. WHIPP, and K. WASSERMAN. Anaerobic threshold alterations caused by endurance training in middle-aged men. *J. Appl. Physiol.* 46:1039–1049, 1979.

31. DEHN, M. M. and R. A. BRUCE. Longitudinal variations in maximal oxygen intake with age and activity. *J. Appl. Physiol.* 33:805–807, 1972.

32. DELORME, T. L. Restoration of muscle power by heavy resistance exercise. *J. Bone Joint Surg.* 27:645–667, 1945.

33. DEMPSEY, J. A. Anthropometrical observations on obese and nonobese young men undergoing a program of vigorous physical exercise. *Res. Q.* 35:275–287, 1964.

34. DEVRIES, H. A. Physiological effects of an exercise training regimen upon men aged 52 to 88. *J. Gerontol.* 24:325–336, 1970.

35. DEVRIES, H. A. Exercise intensity threshold for improvement of cardiovascular-respiratory function in older men. *Geriatrics* 26:94–101, 1971.

36. DISHMAN, R. K., J. SALLIS, and D. ORENSTEIN. The determinants of physical activity and exercise. *Public Health Rep.* 100:158–180, 1985.

37. DISHMAN, R. K., R. W. PATTON, J. SMITH, R. WEINBERG, and A. JACKSON. Using perceived exertion to prescribe and monitor exercise training heart rate. *Int. J. Sports Med.* 8:208–213, 1987.

38. DRINKWATER, B. L. Physiological responses of women to exercise. In: *Exercise and Sports Sciences Reviews,* Vol. 1, J. H. Wilmore (Ed.). New York: Academic Press, 1973, pp. 126–154.

39. DRINKWATER, B. L., S. M. HORVATH, and C. L. WELLS. Aerobic power of females, ages 10 to 68. *J. Gerontol.* 30:385–394, 1975.

40. DURNIN, J. V. G. A. and R. PASSMORE. *Energy, Work and Leisure.* London, England: Heinemann Educational Books, Ltd., 1967, pp. 47–82.

41. EDSTROM, L. and L. GRIMBY. Effect of exercise on the motor unit. *Muscle Nerve* 9:104–126, 1986.

42. EKBLOM, B., P. O. ASTRAND, B. SALTIN, J. STENBERG, and B. WALLSTROM. Effect of training on circulatory response to exercise. *J. Appl. Physiol.* 24:518–528, 1968.

43. FLECK, S. J. and W. J. KRAEMER. *Designing Resistance Training Programs.* Champaign, IL: Human Kinetics Books, 1987, pp. 15–46, 161–162.

44. FLINT, M. M., B. L. DRINKWATER, and S. M. HORVATH. Effects of training on women's response to submaximal exercise. *Med. Sci. Sports* 6:89–94, 1974.

45. FOX, E. L., R. L. BARTELS, C. E. BILLINGS, R. O'BRIEN, R. BASON, and D. K. MATHEWS. Frequency and duration of interval training programs and changes in aerobic power. *J. Appl. Physiol.* 38:481–484, 1975.

46. FRANKLIN, B., E. BUSKIRK, J. HODGSON, H. GAHAGAN, J. KOLLIAS, and J. MENDEZ. Effects of physical conditioning on cardiorespiratory function, body composition and serum lipids in relatively normal weight and obese middle-age women. *Int. J. Obes.* 3:97–109, 1979.

47. FRINGER, M. N. and A. G. STULL. Changes in cardiorespiratory parameters during periods of training and detraining in young female adults. *Med. Sci. Sports* 6:20–25, 1974.

48. GAESSER, G. A. and R. G. RICH. Effects of high- and low-intensity exercise training on aerobic capacity and blood lipids. *Med. Sci. Sports Exerc.* 16:269–274, 1984.

49. GETCHELL, L. H. and J. C. MOORE. Physical training: comparative responses of middle-aged adults. *Arch. Phys. Med. Rehabil.* 56:250–254, 1975.

50. GETTMAN, L. R., M. L. POLLOCK, J. L. DURSTINE, A. WARD, J. AYRES, and A. C. LINNERUD. Physiological responses of men to 1, 3, and 5 day per week training programs. *Res. Q.* 47:638–646, 1976.

51. GETTMAN, L. R., J. J. AYRES, M. L. POLLOCK, and A. JACKSON. The effect of circuit weight training on strength, cardiorespiratory function, and body composition of adult men. *Med. Sci. Sports* 10:171–176, 1978.

52. GETTMAN, L. R., J. AYRES, M. L. POLLOCK, J. L. DURSTINE, and W. GRANTHAM. Physiological effects of circuit strength training and jogging. *Arch. Phys. Med. Rehabil.* 60:115–120, 1979.

53. GETTMAN, L. R., L. A. CULTER, and T. STRATHMAN. Physiologic changes after 20 weeks of isotonic vs. isokinetic circuit training. *J. Sports Med. Phys. Fitness* 20:265–274, 1980.

54. GETTMAN, L. R. and M. L. POLLOCK. Circuit weight training: a critical review of its physiological benefits. *Phys. Sports Med.* 9:44–60, 1981.

55. GETTMAN, L. R., P. WARD, and R. D. HAGMAN. A comparison of combined running and weight training with circuit weight

training. *Med. Sci. Sports Exerc.* 14:229–234, 1982.

56. GILLAM, G. M. Effects of frequency of weight training on muscle strength enhancement. *J. Sports Med.* 21:432–436, 1981.

57. GIRANDOLA, R. N. Body composition changes in women: effects of high and low exercise intensity. *Arch. Phys. Med. Rehabil.* 57:297–300, 1976.

58. GLEDHILL, N. and R. B. EYNON. The intensity of training. In: *Training Scientific Basis and Application*, A. W. Taylor and M. L. Howell (Eds.). Springfield, IL: Charles C Thomas Co., 1972, pp. 97–102.

59. GOLDING, L. Effects of physical training upon total serum cholesterol levels. *Res. Q.* 32:499–505, 1961.

60. GOODE, R. C., A. VIRGIN, T. T. ROMET, et al. Effects of a short period of physical activity in adolescent boys and girls. *Can. J. Appl. Sports Sci.* 1:241–250, 1976.

61. GOSSARD, D., W. L. HASKELL, B. TAYLOR, et al. Effects of low- and high-intensity home-based exercise training on functional capacity in healthy middle-age men. *Am. J. Cardiol.* 57:446–449, 1986.

62. GRAVES, J. E., M. L. POLLOCK, S. H. LEGGETT, R. W. BRAITH, D. M. CARPENTER, and L. E. BISHOP. Effect of reduced training frequency on muscular strength. *Int. J. Sports Med.* 9:316–319, 1988.

63. GRAVES, J. E., M. L. POLLOCK, A. E. JONES, A. B. COLVIN, and S. H. LEGGETT. Specificity of limited range of motion variable resistance training. *Med. Sci. Sports Exerc.* 21:84–89, 1989.

64. GWINUP, G. Effect of exercise alone on the weight of obese women. *Arch. Int. Med.* 135:676–680, 1975.

65. HAGBERG, J. M., J. E. GRAVES, M. LIMACHER, et al. Cardiovascular responses of 70–79 year old men and women to exercise training. *J. Appl. Physiol.* 66:2589–2594,1989.

66. HAKKINEN, K. Factors influencing trainability of muscular strength during short term and prolonged training. *Natl. Strength Cond. Assoc. J.* 7:32–34, 1985.

67. HANSON, J. S., B. S. TABAKIN, A. M. LEVY, and W. NEDDE. Long-term physical training and cardiovascular dynamics in middle-aged men. *Circulation* 38:783–799, 1968.

68. HANSON, J. S. and W. H. NEDDE. Long-term physical training effect in sedentary females. *J. Appl. Physiol.* 37:112–116, 1974.

69. HARTLEY, L. H., G. GRIMBY, A. KILBOM, et al. Physical training in sedentary middle-aged and older men. *Scand. J. Clin. Lab. Invest.* 24:335–344, 1969.

70. HARTUNG, G. H., M. H. SMOLENSKY, R. B. HARRIST, and R. RUNGE. Effects of varied durations of training on improvement in cardiorespiratory endurance. *J. Hum. Ergol.* 6:61–68, 1977.

71. HASKELL, W. L. Physical activity and health: need to define the required stimulus. *Am. J. Cardiol.* 55:4D–9D, 1985.

72. HASKELL, W. L., H. J. MONTOYE, and D. ORENSTEIN. Physical activity and exercise to achieve health-related physical fitness components. *Public Health Rep.* 100:202–212, 1985.

73. HEATH, G. W., J. M. HAGBERG, A. A. EHSANI, and J. O. HOLLOSZY. A physiological comparison of young and older endurance athletes. *J. Appl. Physiol.* 51:634–640, 1981.

74. HETTINGER, T. *Physiology of Strength.* Springfield, IL: C. C Thomas Publisher, 1961, pp. 18–40.

75. HICKSON, R. C. and M. A. ROSENKOETTER. Reduced training frequencies and maintenance of increased aerobic power. *Med. Sci. Sports Exerc.* 13:13–16, 1981.

76. HICKSON, R. C., C. KANAKIS, J. R. DAVIS, A. M. MOORE, and S. RICH. Reduced training duration effects on aerobic power, endurance, and cardiac growth. *J. Appl. Physiol.* 53:225–229, 1982.

77. HICKSON, R. C., C. FOSTER, M. L. POLLOCK, T. M. GALASSI, and S. RICH. Reduced training intensities and loss of aerobic power, endurance, and cardiac growth. *J. Appl. Physiol.* 58:492–499, 1985.

78. HILL, J. O., P. B. SPARLING, T. W. SHIELDS, and P. A. HELLER. Effects of exercise and food restriction on body composition and metabolic rate in obese women. *Am. J. Clin. Nutr.* 46:622–630, 1987.

79. HOLLMANN, W. *Changes in the Capacity for Maximal and Continuous Effort in Relation to Age. Int. Res. Sports Phys. Ed.*, E. Jokl and E. Simon (Eds.). Springfield, IL: Charles C Thomas Co., 1964, pp. 369–371.

80. HOLLMANN, W. and H. VENRATH. Die Beinflussung von Herzgrösse, maximaler O_2—Aufnahme und Ausdauergranze durch ein Ausdauertraining mittlerer und hoher Intensität. *Der Sportarzt* 9:189–193, 1963.

81. No reference 81 due to renumbering in proof.

82. HUIBREGTSE, W. H., H. H. HARTLEY, L. R. JONES, W. D. DOOLITTLE, and T. L. CRIBLEZ. Improvement of aerobic work capacity following non-strenuous exercise. *Arch. Environ Health* 27:12–15, 1973.

83. HURLEY, B. F., D. R. SEALS, A. A. EHSANI, et al. Effects of high-intensity strength training on cardiovascular function. *Med. Sci. Sports Exerc.* 16:483–488, 1984.

84. ISMAIL, A. H., D. CORRIGAN, and D. F. McLEOD. Effect of an eight-month exercise program on selected physiological, biochemical, and audiological variables in adult men. *Br. J. Sports Med.* 7:230–240, 1973.

84A.JONES, D. A., D. J. NEWMAN, J. M. ROUND, and S. E. L. TOLFREE. Experimental human muscle damage: morphological changes in relation to other indices of damage. *J. Physiol. (Lond.)* 375:435–438, 1986.

85. KARVONEN, M., K. KENTALA, and O. MUSTALA. The effects of training heart rate: a longitudinal study. *Ann. Med. Exp. Biol. Fenn* 35:307–315, 1957.

86. KASCH, F. W., W. H. PHILLIPS, J. E. L. CARTER, and J. L. BOYER. Cardiovascular changes in middle-aged men during two years of training. *J. Appl. Physiol.* 314:53–57, 1972.

87. KASCH, F. W. and J. P. WALLACE. Physiological variables during 10 years of endurance exercise. *Med. Sci. Sports* 8:5–8, 1976.

88. KASCH, F. W., J. P. WALLACE, and S. P. VAN CAMP. Effects of 18 years of endurance exercise on physical work capacity of older men. *J. Cardiopulmonary Rehabil.* 5:308–312, 1985.

89. KATCH, F. I. and W. D. MCARDLE. *Nutrition, Weight Control and Exercise*, 3rd Ed. Philadelphia: Lea and Febiger, 1988, pp. 110–112.

90. KEARNEY, J. T., A. G. STULL, J. L. EWING, and J. W. STREIN. Cardiorespiratory responses of sedentary college women as a function of training intensity. *J. Appl. Physiol.* 41:822–825, 1976.

91. KENDRICK, Z. B., M. L. POLLOCK, T. N. HICKMAN, and H. S. MILLER. Effects of training and detraining on cardiovascular efficiency. *Am. Corr. Ther. J.* 25:79–83, 1971.

92. KILBOM, A. Physical training in women. *Scand. J. Clin. Lab. Invest.* 119 (Suppl.):1–34, 1971.

93. KILBOM, A., L. HARTLEY, B. SALTIN, J. BJURE, G. GRIMBY, and I. ÅSTRAND. Physical training in sedentary middle-aged and older men. *Scand. J. Clin. Lab. Invest.* 24:315–322, 1969.

94. KIMURA, Y., H. ITOW, and S. YAMAZAKIE. The effects of circuit weight training on VO_{2max} and body composition of trained and untrained college men. *J. Physiol. Soc. Jpn.* 43:593–596, 1981.

94A.KLISSOURAS, V., F. PIRNAY, and J. PETIT. Adaptation to maximal effort: genetics and age. *J. Appl. Physiol.* 35:288–293, 1973.

95. KNAPIK, J. J., R. H. MAUDSLEY, and N. V. RAMMOS. Angular specificity and test mode specificity of isometric and isokinetic strength training. *J. Orthop. Sports Phys. Ther.* 5:58–65, 1983.

96. KNEHR, C. A., D. B. DILL, and W. NEUFELD. Training and its effect on man at rest and at work. *Am. J. Physiol.* 136:148–156, 1942.

97. KNUTTGEN, H. G., L. O. NORDESJO, B. OLLANDER, and B. SALTIN. Physical conditioning through interval training with young male adults. *Med. Sci. Sports* 5:220–226, 1973.

98. LAPORTE, R. E., L. L. ADAMS, D. D. SAVAGE, G. BRENES, S. DEARWATER, and T. COOK. The spectrum of physical activity, cardiovascular disease and health: an epidemiologic perspective. *Am. J. Epidemiol.* 120:507–517, 1984.

99. LEON, A. S., J. CONRAD, D. B. HUNNINGHAKE, and R. SERFASS. Effects of a vigorous walking program on body composition, and carbohydrate and lipid metabolism of obese young men. *Am. J. Clin. Nutr.* 32:1776–1787, 1979.

100. LEON, A. S., J. CONNETT, D. R. JACOBS, and R. RAURAMAA. Leisure-time physical activity levels and risk of coronary heart disease and death: the multiple risk of coronary heart disease and death: the multiple risk factor intervention trial. *J.A.M.A.* 258:2388–2395, 1987.

100A.LEWIS, S. F., W. F. TAYLOR, R. M. GRAHAM, W. A. PETTINGER,

J. E. Shutte, and C. G. Blomqvist. Cardiovascular responses to exercise as functions of absolute and relative work load. *J. Appl. Physiol.* 54:1314–1323, 1983.

101. Liang, M. T., J. F. Alexander, H. L. Taylor, R. C. Serfrass, A. S. Leon, and G. A. Stull. Aerobic training threshold, intensity duration, and frequency of exercise. *Scand. J. Sports Sci.* 4:5–8, 1982.

101A.Lieber, D. C., R. L. Lieber, and W. C. Adams. Effects of run-training and swim-training at similar absolute intensities on treadmill $\dot{V}O_{2max}$. *Med. Sci. Sports Exerc.* 21:655–661, 1989.

101B.MacDougall, J. D., G. R. Ward, D. G. Sale, and J. R. Sutton. Biochemical adaptation of human skeletal muscle to heavy resistance training and immobilization. *J. Appl. Physiol.* 43:700–703, 1977.

101C.MacDougall, J. D., D. Tuxen, D. G. Sale, J. R. Moroz, and J. R. Sutton. Arterial blood pressure response to heavy resistance training. *J. Appl. Physiol.* 58:785–790, 1985.

102. Mann, G. V., L. H. Garrett, A. Farhi, et al. Exercise to prevent coronary heart disease. *Am. J. Med.* 46:12–27, 1969.

103. Marcinik, E. J., J. A. Hodgdon, U. Mittleman, and J. J. O'Brien. Aerobic/calisthenic and aerobic/circuit weight training programs for Navy men: a comparative study. *Med. Sci. Sports Exerc.* 17:482–487, 1985.

104. Marigold, E. A. The effect of training at predetermined heart rate levels for sedentary college women. *Med. Sci. Sports* 6:14–19, 1974.

105. Martin, J. E. and P. M. Dubbert. Adherence to exercise. In: *Exercise and Sports Sciences Reviews*, Vol. 13, R. L. Terjung (Ed.). New York: MacMillan Publishing Co., 1985, pp. 137–167.

106. Martin, W. H., J. Montgomery, P. G. Snell, et al. Cardiovascular adaptations to intense swim training in sedentary middle-aged men and women. *Circulation* 75:323–330, 1987.

107. Mayhew, J. L. and P. M. Gross. Body composition changes in young women with high resistance weight training. *Res. Q.* 45:433–439, 1974.

108. Messier, J. P. and M. Dill. Alterations in strength and maximal oxygen uptake consequent to Nautilus circuit weight training. *Res. Q. Exerc. Sport* 56:345–351, 1985.

109. Milesis, C. A., M. L. Pollock, M. D. Bah, J. J. Ayres, A. Ward, and A. C. Linnerud. Effects of different durations of training on cardiorespiratory function, body composition and serum lipids. *Res Q.* 47:716–725, 1976.

110. Misner, J. E., R. A. Boileau, B. H. Massey, and J. H. Mayhew. Alterations in body composition of adult men during selected physical training programs. *J. Am. Geriatr. Soc.* 22:33–38, 1974.

111. Miyashita, M., S. Haga, and T. Mitzuta. Training and detraining effects on aerobic power in middle-aged and older men. *J. Sports Med.* 18:131–137, 1978.

112. Moody, D. L., J. Kollias, and E. R. Buskirk. The effect of a moderate exercise program on body weight and skinfold thickness in overweight college women. *Med. Sci. Sports* 1:75–80, 1969.

113. Moody, D. L., J. H. Wilmore, R. N. Girandola, and J. P. Royce. The effects of a jogging program on the body composition of normal and obese high school girls. *Med. Sci. Sports* 4:210–213, 1972.

114. Mueller, E. A. and W. Rohmert. Die geschwindigkeit der muskelkraft zunahme bein isometrischen training. *Int. Z. Angew. Physiol.* 19:403–419, 1963.

115. Naughton, J. and F. Nagle. Peak oxygen intake during physical fitness program for middle-aged men. *J.A.M.A.* 191:899–901, 1965.

116. O'Hara, W., C. Allen, and R. J. Shephard. Loss of body weight and fat during exercise in a cold chamber. *Eur. J. Appl. Physiol.* 37:205–218, 1977.

117. Oja, P., P. Teraslinna, T. Partanen, and R. Karava. Feasibility of an 18 months' physical training program for middle-aged men and its effect on physical fitness. *Am. J. Public Health* 64:459–465, 1975.

118. Olree, H. D., B. Corbin, J. Penrod, and C. Smith. Methods of achieving and maintaining physical fitness for prolonged space flight. Final Progress Rep. to NASA, Grant No. NGR-04-002-004, 1969.

119. Oscai, L. B., T. Williams, and B. Hertig. Effects of exercise on blood volume. *J. Appl. Physiol.* 24:622–624, 1968.

120. Paffenbarger, R. S., R. T. Hyde, A. L. Wing, and C. Hsieh. Physical activity and all-cause mortality, and longevity of college alumni. *N. Engl. J. Med.* 314:605–613, 1986.

121. Pavlou, K. N., W. P. Steffee, R. H. Learman, and B. A. Burrows. Effects of dieting and exercise on lean body mass, oxygen uptake, and strength. *Med. Sci. Sports Exerc.* 17:466–471, 1985.

122. Pels, A. E., M. L. Pollock, T. E. Dohmeier, K. A. Lemberger, and B. F. Oehrlein. Effects of leg press training on cycling, leg press, and running peak cardiorespiratory measures. *Med. Sci. Sports Exerc.* 19:66–70, 1987.

123. Pollock, M. L. The quantification of endurance training programs. In: *Exercise and Sport Sciences Reviews*, J. H. Wilmore (Ed.). New York: Academic Press, 1973, pp. 155–188.

124. Pollock, M. L. Prescribing exercise for fitness and adherence. In: *Exercise Adherence: Its Impact on Public Health*, R. K. Dishman (Ed.). Champaign, IL: Human Kinetics Books, 1988, pp. 259–277

125. Pollock, M. L., T. K. Cureton, and L. Greninger. Effects of frequency of training on working capacity, cardiovascular function, and body composition of adult men. *Med. Sci. Sports* 1:70–74, 1969.

126. Pollock, M. L., J. Tiffany, L. Gettman, R. Janeway, and H. Lofland. Effects of frequency of training on serum lipids, cardiovascular function, and body composition. In: *Exercise and Fitness*, B. D. Franks (Ed.). Chicago: Athletic Institute, 1969, pp. 161–178.

127. Pollock, M. L., H. Miller, R. Janeway, A. C. Linnerud, B. Robertson, and R. Valentino. Effects of walking on body composition and cardiovascular function of middle-aged men. *J. Appl. Physiol.* 30:126–130, 1971.

128. Pollock, M. L., J. Broida, Z. Kendrick, H. S. Miller, R. Janeway, and A. C. Linnerud. Effects of training two days per week at different intensities on middle-aged men. *Med. Sci. Sports* 4:192–197, 1972.

129. Pollock, M. L., H. S. Miller, Jr., and J. Wilmore. Physiological characteristics of champion American track athletes 40 to 70 years of age. *J. Gerontol.* 29:645–649, 1974.

130. Pollock, M. L., J. Dimmick, H. S. Miller, Z. Kendrick, and A. C. Linnerud. Effects of mode of training on cardiovascular function and body composition of middle-aged men. *Med. Sci. Sports* 7:139–145, 1975.

131. No reference 131 due to renumbering in proof.

132. Pollock, M. L., G. A. Dawson, H. S. Miller, Jr., et al. Physiologic response of men 49 to 65 years of age to endurance training. *J. Am. Geriatr. Soc.* 24:97–104, 1976.

133. Pollock, M. L. and A. Jackson. Body composition: measurement and changes resulting from physical training. Proceedings National College Physical Education Association for Men and Women, January, 1977, pp. 125–137.

134. Pollock, M. L., J. Ayres, and A. Ward. Cardiorespiratory fitness: response to differing intensities and durations of training. *Arch. Phys. Med. Rehabil.* 58:467–473, 1977.

135. Pollock, M. L., R. Gettman, C. A. Milesis, M. D. Bah, J. L. Durstine, and R. B. Johnson. Effects of frequency and duration of training on attrition and incidence of injury. *Med. Sci. Sports* 9:31–36, 1977.

136. Pollock, M. L., L. R. Gettman, P. B. Raven, J. Ayres, M. Bah, and A. Ward. Physiological comparison of the effects of aerobic and anaerobic training. In: *Physical Fitness Programs for Law Enforcement Officers: A Manual for Police Administrators*, C. S. Price, M. L. Pollock, L. R. Gettman, and D. A. Kent (Eds.). Washington, D. C.: U. S. Government Printing Office, No. 027-000-00671-0, 1978, pp. 89–96.

137. Pollock, M. L., A. S. Jackson, and C. Foster. The use of the perception scale for exercise prescription. In: *The Perception of Exertion in Physical Work*, G. Borg and D. Ottoson (Eds.). London, England: The MacMillan Press, Ltd., 1986, pp. 161–176.

138. Pollock, M. L., C. Foster, D. Knapp, J. S. Rod, and D. H. Schmidt. Effect of age and training on aerobic capacity and

body composition of master athletes. *J. Appl. Physiol.* 62:725–731, 1987.

139. POLLOCK, M. L. and J. H. WILMORE. *Exercise in Health and Disease: Evaluation and Prescription for Prevention and Rehabilitation*, 2nd Ed. Philadelphia: W. B. Saunders, Co., 1990.

140. POWELL, K. E., H. W. KOHL, C. J. CASPERSEN, and S. N. BLAIR. An epidemiological perspective of the causes of running injuries. *Phys. Sportsmed.* 14:100–114, 1986.

141. RIBISL, P. M. Effects of training upon the maximal oxygen uptake of middle-aged men. *Int. Z. Angew. Physiol* 26:272–278, 1969.

142. RICHIE, D. H., S. F. KELSO, and P. A. BELLUCCI. Aerobic dance injuries: a retrospective study of instructors and participants. *Phys. Sportsmed.* 13:130–140, 1985.

143. ROBINSON, S. and P. M. HARMON. Lactic acid mechanism and certain properties of blood in relation to training. *Am. J. Physiol.* 132:757–769, 1941.

144. ROSKAMM, H. Optimum patterns of exercise for healthy adults. *Can. Med. Assoc. J.* 96:895–899, 1967.

145. SALE, D. G. Influence of exercise and training on motor unit activation. In: *Exercise and Sport Sciences Reviews*, K. B. Pandolf (Ed.). New York: MacMillan Publishing Co., 1987, pp. 95–152.

145A. SALE, D. G. Neural adaptation to resistance training. *Med. Sci. Sports Exerc.* 20:S135–S145, 1988.

146. SALLIS, J. F., W. L. HASKELL, S. P. FORTMAN, K. M. VRANIZAN, C. B. TAYLOR, and D. S. SOLOMAN. Predictors of adoption and maintenance of physical activity in a community sample. *Prev. Med.* 15:131–141, 1986.

147. SALTIN, B., G. BLOMQVIST, J. MITCHELL, R. L. JOHNSON, K. WILDENTHAL, and C. B. CHAPMAN. Response to exercise after bed rest and after training. *Circulation* 37, 38(Suppl. 7):1–78, 1968.

148. SALTIN, B., L. HARTLEY, A. KILBOM, and I. ÅSTRAND. Physical training in sedentary middle-aged and older men. *Scand. J. Clin. Lab. Invest.* 24:323–334, 1969.

149. SANTIGO, M. C., J. F. ALEXANDER, G. A. STULL, R. C. SERFRASS, A. M. HAYDAY, and A. S. LEON. Physiological responses of sedentary women to a 20-week conditioning program of walking or jogging. *Scand. J. Sports Sci.* 9:33–39, 1987.

150. SEALS, D. R., J. M. HAGBERG, B. F. HURLEY, A. A. EHSANI, and J. O. HOLLOSZY. Endurance training in older men and women. I. Cardiovascular responses to exercise. *J. Appl. Physiol.* 57:1024–1029, 1984.

151. SHARKEY, B. J. Intensity and duration of training and the development of cardiorespiratory endurance. *Med. Sci. Sports* 2:197–202, 1970.

152. SHEPHARD, R. J. Intensity, duration, and frequency of exercise as determinants of the response to a training regime. *Int. Z. Angew. Physiol.* 26:272–278, 1969.

153. SHEPHARD, R. J. Future research on the quantifying of endurance training. *J. Hum. Ergol.* 3:163–181, 1975.

154. SIDNEY, K. H., R. B. EYNON, and D. A. CUNNINGHAM. Effect of frequency of training of exercise upon physical working performance and selected variables representative of cardiorespiratory fitness. In: *Training Scientific Basis and Application*, A. W. Taylor (Ed.). Springfield, IL: Charles C Thomas Co., 1972, pp. 144–188.

155. SIDNEY, K. H., R. J. SHEPHARD, and J. HARRISON. Endurance training and body composition of the elderly. *Am. J. Clin. Nutr.* 30:326–333, 1977.

156. SIEGEL, W., G. BLOMQVIST, and J. H. MITCHELL. Effects of a quantitated physical training program on middle-aged sedentary males. *Circulation* 41:19–29, 1970.

156A. SISCOVICK, D. S., N. S. WEISS, R. H. FLETCHER, and T. LASKY. The incidence of primary cardiac arrest during vigorous exercise. *N. Engl. J. Med.* 311:874–877, 1984.

157. SKINNER, J. The cardiovascular system with aging and exercise. In: *Physical Activity and Aging*, D. Brunner and E. Jokl (Eds.). Baltimore: University Park Press, 1970, pp. 100–108.

158. SKINNER, J., J. HOLLOSZY, and T. CURETON. Effects of a program of endurance exercise on physical work capacity and anthropometric measurements of fifteen middle-aged men. *Am. J. Cardiol.* 14:747–752, 1964.

159. SMITH, D. P. and F. W. STRANSKY. The effect of training and detraining on the body composition and cardiovascular response of young women to exercise. *J. Sports Med.* 16:112–120, 1976.

160. SMITH, E. L., W. REDDAN, and P. E. SMITH. Physical activity and calcium modalities for bone mineral increase in aged women. *Med. Sci. Sports Exerc.* 13:60–64, 1981.

161. SUOMINEN, H., E. HEIKKINEN, and T. TARKATTI. Effect of eight weeks physical training on muscle and connective tissue of the m. vastus lateralis in 69-year-old men and women. *J. Gerontol.* 32:33–37, 1977.

162. TERJUNG, R. L., K. M. BALDWIN, J. COOKSEY, B. SAMSON, and R. A. SUTTER. Cardiovascular adaptation to twelve minutes of mild daily exercise in middle-aged sedentary men. *J. Am. Geriatr. Soc.* 21:164–168, 1973.

163. THOMAS, S. G., D. A. CUNNINGHAM, P. A. RECHNITZER, A. P. DONNER, and J. H. HOWARD. Determinants of the training response in elderly men. *Med. Sci. Sports Exerc.* 17:667–672, 1985.

164. WENGER, H. A. and G. J. BELL. The interactions of intensity, frequency, and duration of exercise training in altering cardiorespiratory fitness. *Sports Med.* 3:346–356, 1986.

165. WILMORE, J. H. Alterations in strength, body composition, and anthropometric measurements consequent to a 10-week weight training program. *Med. Sci. Sports* 6:133–138, 1974.

166. WILMORE, J. H. Inferiority of female athletes: myth or reality. *J. Sports Med.* 3:1–6, 1974.

167. WILMORE, J. H. Design issues and alternatives in assessing physical fitness among apparently healthy adults in a health examination survey of the general population. In: *Assessing Physical Fitness and Activity in General Population Studies*, T. F. Drury (Ed.). Washington, D.C.: U.S. Public Health Service, National Center for Health Statistics, 1988 (in press).

168. WILMORE, J. H., J. ROYCE, R. N. GIRANDOLA, F. I. KATCH, and V. L. KATCH. Physiological alternatives resulting from a 10-week jogging program. *Med. Sci. Sports* 2:7–14, 1970.

169. WILMORE, J. H., J. ROYCE, R. N. GIRANDOLA, F. I. KATCH, and V. L. KATCH. Body composition changes with a 10-week jogging program. *Med. Sci. Sports* 2:113–117, 1970.

170. WILMORE, J., R. B. PARR, P. A. VODAK, et al. Strength, endurance, BMR, and body composition changes with circuit weight training. *Med. Sci. Sports* 8:58–60, 1976.

171. WILMORE, J. H., G. A. EWY, A. R. MORTAN, et al. The effect of beta-adrenergic blockade on submaximal and maximal exercise performance. *J. Cardiac Rehabil.* 3:30–36, 1983.

171A. WILMORE, J. H. Body composition in sport and exercise: directions for future research. *Med. Sci. Sports Exerc.* 15:21–31, 1983.

172. WILMORE, J. H. and D. L. COSTILL. *Training for Sport and Activity. The Physiological Basis of the Conditioning Process*, 3rd Ed. Dubuque, IA: Wm. C. Brown, 1988, pp. 113–212.

173. WOOD, P. D., W. L. HASKELL, S. N. BLAIR, et al. Increased exercise level and plasma lipoprotein concentrations: a one-year, randomized, controlled study in sedentary, middle-aged men. *Metabolism* 32:31–39, 1983.

174. ZUTI, W. B. and L. A. GOLDING. Comparing diet and exercise as weight reduction tools. *Phys. Sports Med.* 4:49–53, 1976.

Index